"THE PRIESTING OF ARILAN"

Young Denis Arilan intended to be a priest—the first Deryni priest in two hundred years!

If he were known to be one of the dread Deryni, whose magical talents made them proscribed, he could never be ordained, of course. As part of the strictures imposed as a result of the Council of Ramos, Deryni were forbidden to enter the priesthood on pain of death.

The Church obviously had some way of enforcing its ban. Arilan had watched his friend Jorian fall in agony at the altar during his first celebration of the Mass as a priest. But there was no evidence of how he had been detected or destroyed.

What was there to prevent the same happening to Denis Arilan?

Nevertheless, he was going to be a priest—or die

By Katherine Kurtz
Published by Ballantine Books:

THE LEGENDS OF CAMBER OF CULDI

Volume I: CAMBER OF CULDI
Volume II: SAINT CAMBER
Volume III: CAMBER THE HERETIC

THE CHRONICLES OF THE DERYNI

Volume I: DERYNI RISING
Volume II: DERYNI CHECKMATE
Volume III: HIGH DERYNI

THE HISTORIES OF KING KELSON

Volume I: THE BISHOP'S HEIR
Volume II: THE KING'S JUSTICE
Volume III: THE QUEST FOR SAINT CAMBER

THE DERYNI ARCHIVES

LAMMAS NIGHT

THE
DERYNI
ARCHIVES

Katherine Kurtz

A Del Rey Book

BALLANTINE BOOKS ● NEW YORK

A Del Rey Book
Published by Ballantine Books

Copyright © 1986 by Katherine Kurtz

Library of Congress Catalog Card Number: 86-90861

ISBN 0-345-32678-4

Manufactured in the United States of America

First Edition: August 1986
Sixth Printing: October 1988

Cover Art by Darrell K. Sweet

Map by Shelley Shapiro

ACKNOWLEDGMENTS

"Catalyst," copyright © 1985 by Katherine Kurtz. First published in *Moonsinger's Friends* (Bluejay Books, 1985).

"Healer's Song," copyright © 1982 by Katherine Kurtz. First published in *Fantasy Book*, August 1982.

"Vocation," copyright © 1983 by Katherine Kurtz. First published in *Nine Visions* (Seabury Press, 1983).

"Bethane," copyright © 1982 by Katherine Kurtz. First published in *Hecate's Cauldron* (DAW Books, 1982).

"Legacy," copyright © 1983 by Katherine Kurtz. First published in *Fantasy Book*, February 1983.

CONTENTS

ARJENIE
ARUSTARKIA
TOLAN
NETTERHAVEN
TORENTH
RHEUJAN MTS
ST. ELSDON
CASSAN
MARBURY
EASTMARCH
CARDOSA
RENGARTH
MERAS
CORWYN MTS
TRE'GED
VALORET
ST. IVES
CAERRORIE
GRECOTHA
COLDRE
ST. JARLATH'S
RHENDALL
ST. MARCS
ST. CULLAN'S
DHASSA
STAVENHAM
CULDI
GWYNEDD
VELDUR
KHELDOUR
ST. NEOT'S
KIERNEY
MEARA
CASSAN
RATHARKIN
DHULFERRN
TALACARA
TRURILL
CULLIECAIRE
CASTLEROO
CLOOME
CROGHAN
DRUMCARRIE
COROTH

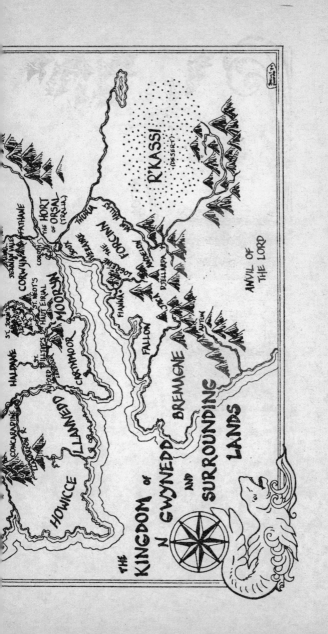

THE KINGDOM of N·GWYNEDD AND SURROUNDING LANDS

R'KASSI
(DESERT)

THE HORT OF ORSAL
(TRALIA)

CORWYN

FATHANE

JENNAN VALE

ST. NEOTS

CORDIN

HUT EIRIAL

THORIN

FORCINN

MER HILLS

HALDANE

ST. PHILIPS

LORD
ORIEL
SEIGNEUR

MOORYN

CARTHMOOR

FIANNA

LOGELINE
THE
RHEMUTH

ARDELYN

DJELLARDA

HOWICCE

COMCARADINE

LLANNEDD

FALLON

BREMAGNE

AUTUN

ANVIL of
THE LORD

INTRODUCTION

Welcome to Gwynedd and the universe of the Deryni. Whether or not you've been here before, you'll likely find it at least somewhat familiar, for Gwynedd and its neighboring kingdoms are roughly parallel to our own tenth, eleventh, and twelfth century England, Wales, and Scotland in terms of culture, level of technology, similarity of social structure, and influence of a powerful medieval Church that extends its machinations into the lives of nearly everyone, highborn or low. The major difference, aside from historical personalities and places, is that magic works; for the Deryni are a race of sorcerers.

In a sense, the term "magic" is almost a misnomer to describe Deryni capabilities, because much of what the Deryni can do falls under the general category of what we would call extrasensory perception or ESP. Telepathy, telekinesis, teleportation, and other "para-

normal" phenomena are functions we are now beginning to suspect may be far more normal than we had
dreamed, as we approach the threshold of the twenty-
first century and science continues to expand our
understanding of human potential. In fact, much of
what we consider science today would have been magic
to the feudal, superstitious, non-technological folk of
the Middle Ages. (They would have scoffed at the notion
that invisible animalcules called "germs" could cause
disease, for *everyone* knew that evil humors made people sick—or, sometimes, the wrath of God.)

Of course, not all "magical" phenomena can be
explained, even by modern science. Complicating matters in Gwynedd is the fact that the Deryni themselves
cannot always distinguish between the various forms
of these phenomena. First there are the *natural* Deryni
abilities, ESP-type functions. Then there is the grey
area of ritual procedures which, when performed with
suitable mental focus, concentrate the operator's own
power to produce certain predictable results. And
finally, there are *super*natural connections that even
the Deryni would regard as magical, which tap into
unknown power sources in unknown ways, at unknown
cost to the well-being of one's immortal soul—the certain existence of which is also unknown. The latter is
a realm that has always been of profound interest to
those engaged in philosophical pursuits, whether those
of science, organized religion, or more esoteric disciplines. (And if we define magic as the art of causing
change in conformity with will, then perhaps *all* Deryni
powers are magical. Denis Arilan will have some
thoughts on supernatural agents in the story bearing
his name.)

The Deryni, then, have abilities and power connections that are not accessible to most people—though Deryni are not omnipotent. At their best, the Deryni might represent the ideal of perfected humankind— what all of us *might* be, if we could learn to rise above our earthbound limitations and fulfill our highest destinies. One would like to think that there is at least a little Deryni in all of us.

With few exceptions, the use of one's Deryni abilities must be learned, like any other skill; and some Deryni are more skilled and stronger than others. Primary proficiencies have to do with balances—physical, psychic, and spiritual—and mastering one's own body and perceptions. Even without formal instruction, most Deryni can learn to banish fatigue, at least for a while, to block physical pain, and to induce sleep— skills that can be applied to oneself or to others, Deryni or not, with or (often) without the conscious cooperation of the subject, especially a human one.

Healing is another highly useful Deryni talent, though rare and requiring very specialized training for optimum use. A properly qualified Healer, provided he has time to engage healing rapport before his patient expires, can deal successfully with almost any physical injury. Treatment of illnesses is necessarily more limited, confined mainly to dealing with symptoms, since medieval medicine has yet to understand disease mechanisms. (Physicians, both human and Deryni, *have* made the connection between cleanliness and decreased likelihood of infection, but lack the technology to discover why this is so.)

Few would take exception to the abilities we have just outlined—other than sleep-induction, perhaps, if it were used to the detriment of a subject unable to resist. What is far more threatening to non-Deryni is the potential use of Deryni powers outside a healing context. For Deryni can read minds, often without the knowledge or consent of a human subject; and they can impose their will on others. Some exceptionally competent Deryni have even been known to take on the shape of another person.

In actual practice, there are definite limitations to the extent of all these abilities, though most non-Deryni have wildly exaggerated notions of what those limitations are, if they even acknowledge their existence. And human fears are not reassured by the fact that some Deryni can tap into energies outside even their own understanding, consorting with powers that may defy God's will. Fear of what is not understood becomes a major theme, then, as the human and Deryni characters interact in the stories.

But humans did not always fear the Deryni as a race, though individual humans may have come to fear certain individual Deryni. For centuries before the Deryni Interregnum, especially under the consolidating rule of a succession of benevolent Haldane kings (some of whom made discreet interaction with a few highly ethical Deryni), Deryni were few enough and circumspect enough in their dealings with humans that the two races lived in relative harmony. The Deryni founded schools and religious institutions and orders, sharing their knowledge and healing talents with anyone in need, their own internal disciplines discouraging any gross abuse of the vast powers at their command. Certainly, there must have been occasional incidents, for the greater powers of the Deryni surely subjected them to greater temptations; but exclusively Deryni outrages must have been rare, for we find no evidence of general hostility toward Deryni before 822. In that year the

Deryni Prince Festil, youngest son of the King of Torenth, invaded from the east and accomplished a sudden coup, massacring all the Haldane royal family except for the two-year-old Prince Aidan, who escaped.

We can blame the ensuing Festillic regime for much of the deterioration of human–Deryni relations after the invasion, for the Deryni followers of Festil I were largely landless younger sons, like himself, and quickly recognized the material gains to be had in the conquered kingdom by exploiting their Deryni advantages. Much was shrugged off or overlooked in the early years of the new dynasty, for any conqueror takes a while to consolidate his power and set up the apparatus for ruling his new kingdom. But Deryni excesses and abuse of power in high places became increasingly blatant, eventually leading, in 904, to the ouster of the last Festillic king by fellow Deryni and the restoration of the old human line in the person of Cinhil Haldane, grandson of the Prince Aidan who had escaped the butchery of the Festillic invaders.

Unfortunately, Deryni magic itself, and not the ill judgment and avarice of a few individuals, came to be blamed for the evils of the Interregnum. Nor, once the Restoration was accomplished, did the new regime waste overmuch time adopting the aims, if not the methods, of their former masters. After the death of the restored King Cinhil, regency councils dominated successive Haldane kings for more than twenty years, for Cinhil's sons were young and died young—within a decade—and the next heir was Cinhil's four-year-old grandson Owain.

Such an enticing opportunity to redistribute the spoils of the Restoration to their own benefit could hardly be overlooked by regents nursing memories of past injustices. With lands, titles, and offices in the offing, the Deryni role in the Restoration soon became eclipsed by more emotion-charged recollections of the Deryni abuses that had triggered the overthrow of Deryni overlords. In the space of only a few years, Deryni remaining in Gwynedd found themselves politically, socially, and religiously disenfranchised, the new masters using any conceivable pretext to seize the wealth and influence of the former rulers.

The religious hierarchy played its part as well. In the hands of a now human-dominated Church, political expedience shifted to philosophical justification in less than a generation, so that the Deryni soon came to be regarded as evil in and of themselves, the Devil's brood, possibly beyond the salvation even of the Church— for surely, no righteous and God-fearing person could do the things the Deryni did; therefore, the Deryni *must* be the agents of Satan. Only total renunciation of one's powers might permit a Deryni to survive, and then only under the most rigid of supervision.

None of this happened overnight, of course. But the Deryni had never been many; and with the great Deryni families gradually fallen from favor or destroyed, most individuals outside the immediate circles of political power, both temporal and spiritual, failed to realize how the balance was shifting until it was too late. The great anti-Deryni persecutions that followed the death of Cinhil Haldane reduced the already small Deryni population of Gwynedd by a full two-thirds. Some fled to the safety of other lands, where being openly Deryni did not carry an automatic death sentence, but many more perished. Only a few managed to go underground, keeping their true identities secret; and many who did go underground simply suppressed what they were, never telling their descendants of their once proud heritage.

This, then, is a very general background of the Deryni, much of which is woven into the stories in this volume; it is told in far greater detail in the novels of the three trilogies set in the Deryni universe. THE LEGENDS OF CAMBER OF CULDI—*Camber of Culdi*, *Saint Camber*, and *Camber the Heretic*—recount the overthrow of the last Festillic king by Camber and his children, and goes on to show what happened immediately after the death of King Cinhil Haldane, thirteen years later. THE CHRONICLES OF THE DERYNI—*Deryni Rising*, *Deryni Checkmate*, and *High Deryni*—take place nearly two hundred years later, when anti-Deryni feeling has begun to abate somewhat among the common folk, but not yet within the hierarchies of the Church. The HISTORIES OF KING KELSON—*The Bishop's Heir*, *The King's Justice*, and *The Quest for Saint Camber*—pick up the story after the CHRONICLES; and future novels will explore the centuries between the reigns of Cinhil's successors and the accession of Kelson Haldane.

The stories in this volume, except for the first one, all fall between the Camber and Deryni Trilogies, and constitute all but one of the shorter works written in the Deryni universe to date. It was felt that the omitted story really needed greater length for proper development—which it will receive in a future novel. Three stories were written specifically for this collection, and have never appeared in print before. At least one of the others has been out of print for some time, and several never got wide distribution. They are all canonical with respect to the novels—that is, what is told here is consistent with what appears in the novels.

Most of them elaborate on incidents or characters that are mentioned in the novels. And some, whatever else they may do, are designed to tantalize with hints of things to come in future novels.

Incidentally, before we move on to the stories, I probably should mention a few points about my approach to Deryni history. I've said that it's a rough parallel to real world history in terms of culture, level of technology, type of government, ecclesiastical involvement, and the like. However, readers have often commented that the stories read like history rather than fantasy. In fact, I've been accused, not entirely tongue-in-cheek, of simply recounting the real history of a world in some other dimension.

Well, I can't answer that. Part of that impression undoubtedly comes from the fact that I was trained as a historian and thus have a historian's eye for detail and a historian's background of real world history from which to draw.

But there are times when I have no idea where the material comes from—I simply know that things happened a particular way. When I'm asked what character A did after event B and I say that I don't know— the characters haven't told me yet—I really am not being facetious. Also, solidly conceived characters tend to do what they are going to do, whether or not that was how the author *thought* they would behave. And sometimes, the only thing I can say is, "I can't tell you why right now; I just know that it happened that way." Sometimes, it even seems to *me* that I'm just tapping into a stream of events that have already taken place, and all I have to do is sit back, observe, and report what I see. Every author does this to some extent, I suspect. But when readers comment on the illusion as much as readers have commented regarding the Deryni, one has to wonder, if only wistfully, whether there isn't at least a mythic truth to the speculation. (I suppose I *could* tell you about some of the times I've sensed Camber peering over my shoulder, agreeing or disagreeing with what I was typing, but that's whimsy—isn't it?)

So, these are tales of the Deryni and those who come into contact with them, as the characters have revealed them to me. I hope you enjoy your sojourn among them.

—Sun Valley, California
June, 1985

CATALYST
FALL, 888

Chronologically, "Catalyst" is the earliest of the Deryni stories written thus far, set some fifteen years before the opening of *Camber of Culdi*. It was written for a *Festschrift* in honor of Andre Norton's fiftieth year of publication. (A *Festschrift* is an anthology in celebration of an author, its stories written by fellow authors who have been influenced by the honoree and who wish to pay him or her tribute.) The major requirement was that the story be of the sort that Andre would enjoy reading.

And so, since I grew up on Andre's books about young people and animals and coming of age (*Starman's Son* was an early favorite), I decided that I ought to respond in kind. Camber's children seemed likely candidates, for at that time, I had not set any Deryni stories earlier than *Camber of Culdi*. A story about Joram, Rhys, and Evaine would also give me an opportunity to play a bit with the character of Cathan, Camber's eldest son, who had been killed off fairly early in the Camber series. In addition, since I had just lost my two elderly cats, Cimber and Gillie, from complications of age, the story could be my memorial to them—for as youngsters, Camber's children surely would have had cats around the castle at Caerrorie. (They would have had dogs, too, but I'm not really a dog person, so I've never gotten into doggy lore. With apologies to dog-lovers, I'm afraid the dogs in this story get rather short shrift.)

From there, it was a simple progression to have Rhys, in the course of discovering that he's going to be a Healer, do for his cat what I hadn't been able to do for my own in the real world. I changed Cimber's name to the soundalike Symber in the story, because Cimber looks too much like Camber on the printed page. The lines ascribed to Lady Jocelyn, describing Symber as "that damned stringbean" while in his gangly adolescence, were words my own mother used to describe my Cimber; but he, like Symber, grew into a magnificent cat. Gillie, who is the unnamed white cat sleeping at Cathan's feet, never did go through that awkward stage. Even as a kitten, she was a perfectly proportioned miniature cat who simply got bigger—and would have twitched her plume-tail in indignation at the mere *thought* that she was ever anything less than grace-ful and beautiful.

So this is for Cimber and Gillie, as well as for Andre. In addition, it is the favorite story of my son Cameron, who was the same age as Rhys and Joram when the story was written and who adores cats at least as much as I do. I think he also liked "Catalyst" because it shows that even Deryni children, with all their advantages, have the same kinds of problems growing up that any other children have.

CATALYST

Biting at his lip in concentration, eleven-year-old Rhys Thuryn stared at the red archer on the board between him and Joram MacRorie and wrapped his mind around it. Smoothly the little painted figure lifted across two squares to menace Joram's blue abbot.

The younger boy had turned to watch rain beginning to spatter against the lights of a tall, grey-glazed window beside them, but at the movement on the board, his blond head jerked back with a start.

"Oh no! Not *my* Michaeline you don't!" he cried, nearly overturning the board as he sprang to his feet to see better. "Rhys, that was a sneaky move! Cathan, what'll I do?"

Cathan, a bored and blasé fifteen-year-old, looked up from his reading with a forebearing sigh, red-nosed and miserable with the cold that had kept him from going hunting with the rest of the household. The white cat napping against his feet did not stir, even when Rhys chortled with delight and knuckled exuberantly at already unruly red hair.

"Hoo! I've got him on the run! Look, Cathan! My archer's going to take his abbot!"

Cathan only blew his nose and huddled a little closer to the fire before burying himself in his scroll again, and Rhys' glee turned to consternation as Joram's warduke floated unerringly across the entire board to take the red archer.

"On the run, eh?" Joram crowed, plopping back onto his stool with triumph in his grey eyes. "What are you going to do about *that*?"

Deflated, Rhys huddled down in his fur-lined tunic to re-evaluate the board. Where had that war-duke come from? What a stupid game!

He had half-expected the outcome, of course. Joram almost always beat him at Cardounet. Even though Rhys was a year older than Joram, and both of them were receiving identical instruction from the Michaelines at Saint Liam's, one of the finest abbey schools in all of Gwynedd, it was a fact that Rhys simply did

not have the gift for military strategy that his foster
brother did. Joram, at ten, had already announced that
he was joining the Michaeline Order when he came of
age, to become a Knight of Saint Michael and eventually a priest as well—to the dismay of his father,
Earl Camber of Culdi.

Nor was it the priesthood Camber objected to—and
Jocelyn, Joram's mother, was clearly pleased that one
of her sons intended to become a priest. Indeed, Camber had often told the boys of the happy years he himself had spent in Holy Orders in his youth, until the
death of his elder brother made him heir to their father's
earldom and he was forced to come home and assume
his family obligations. Barring further unforseen tragedy—for a fever had carried off a brother and sister
only slightly older than Joram earlier in the year—
Joram's brother Cathan would carry on the MacRorie
name in this generation, leaving Joram free to pursue
the religious vocation that had been denied Camber.

No, it was the Michaeline Order itself that gave
Camber cause for concern—the Michaelines, whose
militant warrior-priests were sometimes dangerously
outspoken about the responsibilities they believed went
along with the prerogatives that magic-wielding Deryni
enjoyed. Camber, himself a powerful and highly trained
Deryni, had no quarrel with the Michaelines' ethical
stance in principle; he had always taught his children
the duty that went along with privilege.

In practice, however, the Order's sometimes over-
zealous attempts to enforce that philosophy had led
more than once to disaster—for the Royal House of
Gwynedd was Deryni, and some of its scions among
the worst abusers of Deryni power. Thus far, royal ire
had always been directed against the offending indi-

viduals; but if Joram became a Michaeline, and the
King should one day turn his anger against the entire
Order...

Still, Michaeline schools *did* provide the finest primary training for Deryni children that could be had,
outside the highly specialized instruction given the rare
Healer candidate; and even among the Deryni, a race
blessed—or cursed, according to some—with a wide
assortment of psychic and magical abilities, the Healing gift did not often appear. It was the abuse of power,
sometimes in mere ignorance, that so often led to problems between Deryni and humans—or even Deryni
and Deryni.

That was why Camber had sent Joram and the
orphaned Rhys to attend Saint Liam's—and allowed
them to continue attending, even when Joram began
making starry-eyed plans to join the Michaelines. After
all, the boy could not take even temporary vows until
he turned fourteen. Much might change in four years.
Perhaps Joram would outgrow his infatuation with the
bold and dashing Knights of Saint Michael, with their
distinctive deep blue habits and gleaming white knight's
sashes, and come around to a more moderate choice
of orders, if indeed he felt himself called to be a priest.

Rhys, on the other hand, felt no call to the religious
life, though he was perfectly content taking his training
in the religious atmosphere Saint Liam's provided. Nor
had he any idea yet what he *did* want to do with his
life.

He had no great prospects. His father, though gentle-
born, had been only a second son, so he had inherited
no title or fortune in his own right. Only his mother's
close friendship with Camber's countess, the Lady
Jocelyn, had ensured a place for the infant Rhys when

both parents died in the great plague the year after he was born. He was clever with his hands, worked well with animals, like most Deryni, and had a head for figures—but none of those skills suggested an occupation for a young gentleman.

One thing was certain, Rhys thought, as he continued to survey the game board, considering and discarding a succession of possible but unprofitable moves: he was not cut out to be a soldier. The military strategy and tactics that were Joram's passion were like a foreign language to Rhys. With diligence, and because the subject intrigued Joram, who was his very closest friend, Rhys had mastered enough at least to get by in school and to appreciate that Joram had a natural flair for such things; but he would never be Joram's match, at least in this.

Rarely had he been so dismally aware of that fact as he continued staring at the game board, discarding yet another futile move. The rain hammering now on the window and the roof slates above only added to his depression. Even with the fire and the larger windows here in the solar, it had gotten colder and gloomier as the storm set in, though it was only just past noon.

Perversely, he hoped that Camber and Lady Jocelyn and the rest of the household were getting good and soaked, for having gone off hunting with the king and left them cooped up in the castle with only this dumb game to play! Cathan, who'd been grouchy and irritable all morning with his stupid cold, should be glad they'd made him stay at home, warm and dry and curled up with a fur-lined robe, a cat, and a good book.

As a matter of fact, maybe a book was a good idea. Rhys was bored with trying to beat Joram. He thought he might go find something to read, but before he could decide what, Evaine, the baby of the MacRorie family, came pattering purposefully into the room, flaxen braids coming undone and her black cat, Symber, in her arms. She had the cat just behind the front legs, its body and tail dangling almost to her knees. Oddly, the cat did not seem to mind.

"Cathan, Cathan, there's somebody sneaking around downstairs!" she whispered with six-year-old urgency, scuttling past Rhys and Joram to pause at her older brother's elbow.

Cathan gave a sigh and lowered his manuscript long enough to wipe his nose with a soggy handkerchief.

"I'm sure there is," he croaked hoarsely.

"Cathan, I'm not joking!" she persisted. "I heard them clunking things in the great hall."

"It's probably the dogs."

"The dogs don't make noises like that."

"Then it's the servants."

"It *isn't* the servants!" she replied, stamping a little foot. "Symber came running up the stairs. He was afraid. He doesn't run from the servants."

"He probably got in Cook's way and she booted him with a broom."

"He did *not*!" Evaine insisted, hugging the cat closer. "There's someone down there. Come and see. Cathan, please!"

"Evaine, I'm *not* going downstairs," Cathan snapped. "I don't feel like playing. In case you hadn't noticed, this stupid cold is making me mean and grumpy. Why don't you go pester Joram and Rhys?"

"They're too busy playing their dumb game! Just because I'm little, nobody ever listens to me!"

Rhys, who had been following the exchange with

growing amusement, exchanged a conspiratorial wink with Joram, who had also sat back to grin.

"*We'll* listen to you, won't we, Joram?" he said, delighted at the excuse to leave the hopeless game and do something else.

Apparently Joram had also grown bored with the game, for he joined in without missing a beat.

"Of course we will, little sister," he said, rising and adjusting a dagger thrust through the belt of his blue school tunic. "Why don't you show us where you think you heard them? Can't have prowlers carrying off the silver. Do you think they've tied up the servants?"

"Jor-am!"

"All right, all right!" Joram held up both palms and did his best to assume the more serious mien he thought a future Michaeline Knight should wear. "I said we'd go investigate. Why don't you leave Symber here, where he'll be safe?"

"No!"

"Then, why don't you let *me* carry him?" Rhys reasoned. "That way, you can lead the way and show Joram and me where to look."

"All right, you can carry him," she agreed, handing over the cat. "But I think Joram better go first. He's got a knife."

"Good idea," Joram said, though he had to turn away to keep from grinning. As he stealthily pushed the door to the turnpike stair a little wider, holding a finger to his lips for silence, Rhys hefted the cat's front end onto his left shoulder and supported its weight in the crook of his arm. The cat began purring loudly in his ear as it settled, kneading contentedly with its front paws.

Rhys ignored Cathan's bemused and slightly patronizing smile as he followed Joram and Evaine into the winding stairwell. What did *he* care what Cathan thought? If Evaine had judged Joram best suited to lead a military exercise, she was only acknowledging the obvious—and without any of the hint of ridicule Cathan so often heaped upon Rhys for his lesser military acumen. And it was Rhys to whom she had entrusted her precious Symber—which was a far more important responsibility, in her eyes.

On the other hand, Rhys' military training had not been wholly wasted. Trying to place his slippered feet as quietly as Joram or the cat purring in his arms, he sent a tendril of thought questing into the cat's mind— just in case there *was* something going on below stairs that shouldn't be.

And Symber *had* been frightened by something. The big black cat was too wrapped up in the pleasure and security of perching on Rhys' shoulder, reveling in that special ecstacy that only the feline purr declared, for Rhys to read any details; but he did manage to catch an impression of *something* Symber did not like, that had scared him enough to send him scooting to Evaine for safety. And somehow Rhys did not think it had been Cook with her broom.

He sent that mental impression off to Joram just before they reached the landing, but only the two MacRories had gotten close enough to even touch the curtains across the entry to the great hall before a pair of hairy arms burst through the split in the middle and grabbed each by an arm, jerking them through.

"I told you I'd seen a kid!" a rough voice bellowed.

"Rhys, Rhys!" Evaine shrieked. And a heavy "*Whoof!*" exploded from someone far larger and heavier than Joram as Rhys instinctively ducked and hurled himself through the curtained doorway at the side rather than in the middle, burdened by an armful of suddenly startled cat—and found himself right in the middle of a tangle of struggling bodies, both adult and child.

"Cathan!" Joram screamed, sending up a psychic cry as well, as he squirmed almost out of the grasp of the man who held him and Evaine and somehow managed to get his dagger free of his belt. "Rhys, look out!"

But Rhys was having his own problems as he tried to duck the clutches of another rough-clad man who suddenly loomed right in front of him. He yelped and lost his footing as Evaine's cat launched itself from his shoulder with all its back claws dug in, but the squawk of horrified surprise from his attacker was worth the pain, for Symber landed on the man's bare forearm with all claws out and clung like a limpet, sinking his teeth into the fleshy part of the man's thumb with a ferocious growl.

Cursing and flailing, the man tried to shake the cat off his arm; Symber only dug in with all four sets of claws and held on more tenaciously. Rhys almost managed to tackle one of the man's legs and trip him, but a vicious kick that only narrowly missed his head changed his mind about that. As he rolled clear, trying frantically to see whether there might be more than just the two men and wondering where the dogs were, Evaine wormed out of the grasp of her captor—who was now far more worried about Joram's knife than a child of six—and went for the man molesting her cat, kicking him hard in the shin.

The man howled and whirled around. The reaction cost the cat its grip. As the man grabbed for Evaine and missed, cursing with rage, he made an even more desperate attempt to dislodge the clawing, biting black demon attached to his arm. With a mighty heave, he shook Symber loose and flung him hard against the wall. Evaine wailed as the cat slid to the floor and did not move.

But even worse danger kept Rhys from noticing what happened to cat or girl after that. He was scrambling toward Joram, for Joram was losing the tug of war with his attacker for the knife in his hand, when suddenly a third man towered between them, throwing down a bag of booty with a loud clank and seizing Rhys by a bicep with one hand while the other began to draw a sword.

Rhys tried to remember every trick he'd ever practiced or heard about hand-to-hand fighting in the next few seconds, for he was weaponless, and his opponent was probably three times his age and weight. As he ducked under a blow that would have taken off his head if it had connected, he saw Cathan finally career out of the newel stair doorway with a sword in his hand, shouting urgently for the servants.

He was too busy staying alive to see what happened as the older boy took after the man who was grabbing for Evaine again. As Evaine dove between Cathan's legs for safety, Rhys' concentration was distracted by even more frantic scuffling between Joram and his opponent. Suddenly fire was searing across the back of Rhys' right leg, and it was buckling under him.

The pain was excruciating, the terror worse, as Rhys collapsed and tried to worm out of his assailant's range, clamping a frantic hand to the slash across his calf. His hand came away bloody in the instant he had to look, the thick wool of his grey legging rapidly turning scarlet. He was gasping too hard to utter much physical

sound as the man raised a bloody sword to finish him,
but his desperate psychic cry reverberated in the hall
and beyond as he made a last, determined attempt to
fling himself clear of the descending blade—though he
was sure he was going to die.

He never knew how Cathan managed to intervene;
only that suddenly another sword was flashing upward
to block the blow, shattering the attacker's lesser blade,
driving on to split the man's skull from jaw to crown.
As blood and brains spattered, and before the man even
hit the floor, Cathan was whirling to take on Joram's
opponent. The man who had menaced Evaine was
already moaning on the floor, clutching a belly wound
and trying to crawl out of Cathan's reach.

A handful of male servants finally managed to burst
into the hall at that point, quickly helping Cathan sub-
due and bind the remaining attacker. Only then did
Rhys dare to sit up and take another look at his wound.

Oh, God, it was bad!

His breath hissed between his teeth, and tears welled
in his eyes as he clapped his hand back over the gash
and subsided on the floor again.

The great tendon down the back of his calf was cut
clean through. Despite the depth of the wound, he did
not seem to have bled much after the initial trauma,
but the leg was begining to throb and burn as the first
shock wore off. A Healer might be able to repair the
injury, but if he could not, Rhys would be a cripple for
life.

"I'll send for a Healer!" one of the servants promised, tight-lipped and pale, when he had gotten just a
glimpse of Rhys' leg. "Try to stay calm."

Biting back tears, for he was old enough to know
that crying was not going to help matters any, Rhys

curled into a ball on his left side and closed his eyes, pillowing his head on his left arm and trying to relax while he made himself run through one of the spells he'd been taught to control pain. He was scared, but it was the only thing he knew to do.

It worked, though. When he opened his eyes, the leg was numb, and he was no longer quite so afraid. Joram and a still-sniffing Evaine were kneeling at his side, Evaine cradling a motionless but still-breathing Symber in her arms.

"Is it bad?" Joram asked, craning his neck to see. "*Jesu*, he's hamstrung you! You aren't bleeding very much, though. Father will be back soon. Cathan and I have already Called him."

"I think I Called him, too," Rhys whispered, managing a strained little grin for Evaine's sake as he drew a deep breath to keep the pain and despair from rising again. "Him and any Deryni for two counties. I thought they were going to kill us."

"I think they *may* have killed Symber," Evaine murmured around a little sob of grief, ducking her head over the cat's labored breathing. "That horrid man threw him against the wall! He's still breathing, but he's all limp."

As she lifted plaintive eyes to his, begging him to tell her everything would be all right, he caught Joram's faint head-shake. He had to agree the cat did not look good. Wincing as he shifted his good leg to support the injured one, still holding his wound with his right hand, he tried to think how to make it easier for her.

"I'm sorry, little one," he whispered. "Maybe it isn't as bad as you think. Would you—like to put Symber next to me? Maybe a Healer can fix us both, when one gets here. And if I worry about Symber, maybe I won't worry so much about my leg."

With a brave gulp, Evaine laid the injured cat in the curve of Rhys' left arm, close against his chest and cheek. He could sense how badly the cat was hurt, even though it was unconscious, and he let his fingertips caress one quiet velvet paw as he looked up at Evaine, wishing there were something he could do.

"You—*you're* not going to die, are you, Rhys?" she asked in a very small voice.

He forced himself to give her a reassuring smile. "Don't worry," he said softly. "It's bad, but I'll be all right."

Cathan came and crouched at Rhys' feet to look at the wound, snuffling and wiping futilely at his nose with a blood-stained sleeve, then sat heavily on the floor and let out a forlorn sigh.

"Well, at least Father will be here soon with a Healer. The king's loaning him Dom Sereld. He's one of the best. Damn!" He slammed a bloody fist against the flagstones. "I should have gotten to you sooner! I should have come down when Evaine asked me to! They poisoned the dogs with doctored meat while the servants were busy in the cellar. They must've known most of the household were away."

The steward came with questions about the prisoners after that, and Cathan took Joram with him to see to their handling until Camber should arrive. Evaine stayed with Rhys, though, laying her small hands on his forehead and helping him ease into a floating, twilight state that was even more isolated from his pain. It was something Rhys could have done for himself, as most Deryni with any training could have done, but

the luxury of not *having* to do it released him to drift
off to merciful sleep while he waited for the Healer.

He dreamed about the cat curled in the hollow of
his arm—dreamed that the animal snuggled closer and
buried a cool, damp nose in his side, purring so hard
that the vibration resonated all along his body.

He dreamed of the summer Camber had brought the
kitten home, an endearing scrap of plush black fur with
eyes like peridots and needle-sharp hooks at the tips
of velvet paws. By Christmas, the adorable kitten had
turned, as kittens will, into an awkward, gangling
catling, all huge bat-ears, over-long legs, and a stringy
tail. For months, Lady Jocelyn referred to him as "the
damned stringbean."

By the following summer, however, Symber had
grown into the promise of his kittenhood and become
the sleek, graceful feline Rhys remembered best: friend,
comforter, and counsel-keeping confidant of all the
MacRorie household—though it was Evaine and Rhys
he seemed to prefer. It was that Symber who stayed
in Rhys' dream, his purr rumbling in Rhys' ear and
taking him deeper, deeper...

He started to come up once, but a new presence
pushed him gently down. He thought that perhaps he
should resist, at least until he found out who it was,
but almost immediately he realized that it was a Healer's presence, and that it was all right to let go. He
sensed the anxious brush of Camber's mind against his
own for an instant, and Lady Jocelyn's; but then it
seemed far too much effort to even keep wondering
what would happen. Drowsily, he returned to the dream
of the purring cat.

The next thing he knew, there *was* a cat purring in

his ear. As he opened his eyes, still slightly curled on his left side, a svelte black cat body stretched languidly against his chest and kneaded velvet paws against his arm, butting a moist black nose against his cheek before settling back to sleep with a contented purr. A stranger in a rich tunic of Healer's green was kneeling on his right, wiping just-washed hands on a clean towel.

"Well," the Healer said, giving him a pleased smile, "I'm surprised you didn't finish the job yourself. You did fine work on the cat."

"I what?" Rhys said stupidly, for the man's words made no sense whatever.

The man only chuckled and shook his head, tossing the towel aside. Freckles across his nose and cheeks made him look youthful despite his receding hairline, for there was very little grey frosting his reddish-brown hair, but Rhys guessed him to be approaching fifty. There were little crinkles at the corners of his dark brown eyes, and his neat little beard and mustache were greyer than his hair. He let Rhys roll onto his back, but he restrained him with a hand on his chest when Rhys would have tried to sit up.

"Not yet, son. I want to make sure I've gotten any clots before you move that leg much. Of course, something like a hamstring's a little tricky to manage on oneself," he went on, bending Rhys' restored leg at the knee and stroking his Healer's hands lightly over the area where the wound had been. "I had to have Lord Camber help me with the physical manipulation. Healing's much easier if you can get injured bits back in the general area where they belong, before you start. Hard to heal across a handspan of empty space when you're trying to reattach two cut ends.

"But you'll learn all about that when you get some proper training. Did you really not know? By the way, I'm Sereld, the king's Healer."

"I'm—Rhys Thuryn," Rhys managed to whisper, his head reeling with the implications of what Sereld was saying.

"Yes, I know. And a lot of other people are going to know soon, too. It's cause for celebration when we find a Healer we didn't know about." He finished with Rhys' leg and gently straightened it out again, then cocked his head at Rhys more thoughtfully.

"Were either of your parents Healers, son?"

"No. But they died when I was only a baby."

"Hmmm. Any Healers in the rest of the family?"

"Not that I know of," Rhys whispered. "Did I—did I *really* Heal Symber?"

"The cat? Sure looks that way. Controlled most of your own bleeding, too." Sereld chucked Symber under the chin and grinned as the big cat rubbed its whiskers against his hand and purred even louder. "Well, you needn't thank me, little friend. You've got your own Healer to take care of you from now on."

Still not quite able to believe what he was hearing, Rhys raised up on his elbows.

"But, if I'm—a *Healer*," he spoke the word with awe, "why didn't I know?" he whispered. "Why didn't anyone tell me?"

"I suppose no one thought to check," Sereld said, beginning to take instruments out of a basin of water and drying them with a soft cloth. "Those Michaelines of yours don't know everything, you know. And you're not from a Healer family, after all."

Rhys started as the Healer clinked his clean instruments into a green Healer's satchel.

"On the other hand, you're just about the right age for the gift to show up, if it's going to," Sereld continued. "Naturally, Healing potential can be spotted earlier, if one has cause to look for it; but unless its manifestation is being deliberately guided by Healer training, the first appearance of the actual gift is often triggered by some great need for it to work." He grinned hugely. "I suppose you could say that your furry friend here was a—*catalyst*?"

Rhys groaned at the play on words, but he could not help joining in with Sereld's hearty laughter. He was grinning ear to ear as he let the Healer help him sit up; and Symber's rumbling purr was an echo of Rhys' own joy as he scooped up the cat and gathered it into his lap.

As Camber and the awed Joram and Evaine and all the others came gathering around to offer their congratulations, Rhys knew that there was no longer any question about what he was going to do with his life.

HEALER'S SONG
AUGUST 1, 914

"Healer's Song" is less a story than a recounting of an incident in the lives of some of the Camber characters. The Healer of the title is Rhys, of course; and the song is the *Adsum Domine*, the hymn of the Gabrilite Healers, which embodies much of the ethical code of Healers trained in that tradition. Camber heard parts of it when, as Alister Cullen, he visited Saint Neot's Abbey with Rhys in *Camber the Heretic*, but that was several years after he had heard it in full in "Healer's Song." In the present context, the *Adsum Domine* becomes a framework for the magical dedication of Rhys and Evaine's newborn son, Tieg Joram Thuryn, as a future Healer.

Healer training must have been a fascinating and diverse option for those fortunate Deryni who carried the very rare and specialized Healing gift. The Deryni regarded the vocation of the Healer with the same respect accorded the priestly vocation and counted it just as much a God-spoken call. Hence, it is not surprising that most Healers were trained within the context of a religious order like the Gabrilites.

But besides the school maintained by the Order of Saint Gabriel at Saint Neot's, where Rhys received much of his training, we know of several other options: the rather more secular and pragmatic Varnarite School at Grecotha, attended by Tavis O'Neill (who became Healer to Prince Javan); and at least one Healer school even more elite than Saint Neot's, presumably of religious orientation similar to the Gabrilites, where Dom Emrys received *his* training. (My personal suspicion is that the latter had connections with that mysterious black and white cube-altar that Camber and Joram found beneath Grecotha.) As Morgan and Duncan continue to explore their rediscovered healing potentials in future books, we undoubtedly will be learning more about Healers and their training. (Jebediah's use of a slightly different format for invoking the Quarters suggests that Healers are not the only Deryni whose training and traditions vary.)

As important as the insights into Healer ethics and training, however, is the glimpse that "Healer's Song" gives us of another kind of Deryni ritual than we've usually seen— more a religious observance than a traditional magic-working, far different from the rituals of power assumption we have seen worked on assorted Haldane princes, or the constructions of various magical defenses and the like. It is not even exclusively Christian, though Christian clerics like Joram and Camber/Alister are certainly at home with its form, and Camber administers the Christian sacrament of baptism in the course of the ritual. First and foremost, it is a *Deryni* observance of ancient traditions, perhaps even older than Christianity itself. All of this bespeaks a certain universality in the Deryni way of looking at the universe—*catholicity* in the broad sense, if you will—that has something to say to every person who has ever contemplated his or her relationship with the Creative Force, that entity we usually call God.

Finally, "Healer's Song" is a most intimate portrait of the relationship between Rhys and Evaine, as husband and wife as well as magical partners—revealing glimpses of a rich melding of physical, mental, and spiritual functioning. May we all taste such joy in our own relationships with those we love.

HEALER'S SONG

Evaine's birthing had been much easier this third time, Rhys Thuryn thought, as he stirred an herb posset and turned to glance contentedly across the room where his wife lay with their infant son. Healer though Rhys was, even he had not known for certain what to expect, for they had sensed, almost from the moment of conception, that this child, unlike his brother and sister, would be a Healer, too. Often during Evaine's pregnancy, she had felt the quiver of the child's developing potential ripple at the edge of consciousness. Sometimes she had even had to draw away from Rhys when he was Healing. His patients' pain had disturbed her and the child.

All that had gone dormant in these final weeks before the birth, however, and was slated to remain so for several years. Now, as Rhys crossed to bend protectively over his wife and son, extending the herb-laced wine in gentle offering, Evaine looked up at him and smiled. The babe at her breast suckled lustily, tiny sounds of contentment coming from the little russet-downed head.

"He is definitely your son," Evaine whispered. Her blue eyes danced mischievously as she took the cup from Rhys and sipped. "If the Healer's gift were not sufficient proof, he has your hair, your mouth, your hands..."

Rhys returned her grin roguishly, reading several levels of meaning in her words, then leaned down to kiss the top of the breast not attached to babe, turning his attention next to her lips, still moist with the herbed wine. Enfolding her with mind as well as arms, he kissed her mouth gently but thoroughly, his satisfaction blending with hers in a surge of quiet joy and casual rapport. His Healer's sense caught the answering flutter in her womb, contracting as it should in one so recently delivered of a child, and he let one hand stray lingeringly across the suckling child to rest on her abdomen as he eased onto the bed beside her and lay back against the pillows.

You should rest now, my love, he whispered in her mind.

She settled into the circle of his arms with a contented sigh and slept.

They were still in that position, Evaine and the baby dozing in the shelter of Rhys' arms, when a quiet rap at the door nudged Rhys from his dreamy contemplation. He knew who it should be, and when his lazy mental query confirmed it, he sent a cordial *Welcome!* with his mind.

All three of the smiling men who peered in and then entered were of the militant Order of Saint Michael, with swords at their sides and the white, fringed sashes of Michaeline knighthood tied close about their waists. Two of the men wore cloaks of Michaeline blue, but the third and oldest was garbed in rich episcopal purple. Rhys grinned as the men approached, a detached part of the Healer side of him effortlessly erecting a shield of thought around the sleeping Evaine so she would not be disturbed. He reached out his free hand in welcome as the three surrounded the bed, catching the oldest man's hand and kissing the amethyst on it while his mind greeted, *Camber!* and his lips shaped another name from long habit, for the benefit of the servant who was closing the door.

"How are you, Bishop Alister?" he asked, touching hands with the other two men as the bishop turned his attention to the sleeping woman and child.

Camber MacRorie, whom the world now knew as Bishop Alister Cullen, peered approvingly at his daughter and grandson for a moment, then brushed a feather-touch across the baby's head before accepting the stool which the younger of his Michaeline companions brought up behind him.

"I'm doing very well, for an old man," Camber said with a chuckle, for he neither looked nor felt the nearly sixty years of the man whose identity he wore, much less the sixty-eight years of his own age, and knew that Rhys was aware of that. "I assume that mother and child are doing well?"

"Aye, just resting now. Joram, Jebediah, how are you?"

Joram, but a few years older than the sleeping woman and obviously related, sleeked back a wind-blown strand of pale hair and smiled.

"I don't know about Jeb, but I'm feeling older. This is my fifth time to be an uncle, you know."

Rhys laughed. "Well, you *would* be a Father instead of a father," he quipped. "You priests have no cause to complain. And Jebediah, you didn't *have* to choose the celibate life of an ecclesiastical knight."

"No, but I don't regret it," Jebediah chuckled, folding his arms across his chest. "Each calling has its compensations."

They all chuckled at that, for among the four of them, they likely wielded more power in the running of the Kingdom of Gwynedd than any other six men, including the King. Camber, as Alister Cullen, was Chancellor of Gwynedd, as well as Bishop of the important see of Grecotha, to the north. He once had been Vicar General of the Michaelines. Joram MacRorie, Michaeline priest and knight and Camber's son, functioned as confidential secretary and aide to the chancellor-bishop—a post conveying far more influence than the mere title might have suggested. Jebediah of Alcara, as the Earl Marshal, had the keeping of all Gwynedd's military organization under his command, in addition to remaining Grand Master of the powerful Knights of Saint Michael. Rhys himself was Healer to the Crown of Gwynedd, with responsibility for the health of the three young heirs, as well as that of the King.

But it was the Healer's function which concerned Rhys most at that moment, not any other ramification of temporal or spiritual power. For Rhys' wife, daughter to Camber and sister of Joram, had just given birth to a future Healer—an event of sufficient rarity among the magical race known as the Deryni, to which all of them belonged, that its occurrence had been heralded by special observances since the gift had first been recognized and sought.

That was the reason these three very busy and important men had come to Rhys and Evaine's manor of Sheele, outside the capital—besides their obvious desires to see and greet the newest member of Camber's family and congratulate the parents. This night, Rhys intended to formally dedicate his newborn son to the service of his Healing patrimony, in accordance with Deryni custom. It was fitting that such a rite be witnessed by those closest to the parents and their child.

A few hours later, after dark, when Evaine had awakened and visited with father and brother and friend-like-brother, and all of them had supped, the four men made the necessary preparations while Evaine nursed the babe. It was Lammas night, the first of August, so Jebediah had gotten fresh-baked bread from Saint Neot's that morning for them to share in commemoration. The loaf, in its simple dish of salt-glazed clay, was set on a white-covered table just off center in the chamber—a particularly fitting offering for this dedication, since the finest Healers known were trained at Saint Neot's Abbey. A cup of wine was also produced, though not of so auspicious an origin, and vessels containing water, salt, and chrism—for the child would be baptized by his grandfather during the course of the rite. The bishop draped a white stole around his neck as he joined the others in the center of the room.

"This room has permanent wards built into its walls, so we really need no formal circle, but I'll walk the perimeter once for form's sake anyway," Rhys said, swinging his cloak of Healer's green around his shoulders and clasping it at his throat. "Jebediah, I'll ask you to stand for me in the east. Joram, Father, if you'll take your usual places, south and north..."

They moved where they were bidden and stood facing inward a few yards from the walls, three solidly reassuring forms in royal blue or purple, back-lit by candles set on the floor against the walls. In the west, Evaine sat on a chair with the candlelight behind her and looked like a golden madonna, the baby asleep in her lap.

Stilling his mind in preparation, Rhys walked slowly to Jebediah's side of the circular chamber and moved between him and the candle, then raised both hands to chest-level and turned his palms outward. A moment he paused, letting the energies build in the established Wards and intertwine among his splayed fingers, hard-soft glitter crackling, seen and not quite seen; then he half closed his eyes and began moving to the right along the curve of the wall, though he did not touch it. The others bowed their heads as he passed behind them, all of them aware of the energy extending along the line of his passage like a sheet of verdant fire, the glow all but invisible except in the flicker of peripheral vision.

When he had completed his circuit of the chamber, he stopped behind Jebediah once more and extended his arms slowly to either side, throwing back his head to breathe deeply of the energies he had just raised. The not-light domed above their heads. He dropped his arms and turned back into the circle, touching Jebediah's shoulder in preoccupied comradeship as he passed. Evaine had risen and moved into the center of the circle during his circuit, and now she gave their son into his arms.

She had loosed her hair, and it cascaded around her shoulders like a firefall of molten gold, though the front was caught in slender braids and pulled back from her face. The touch of her hands against his, as they settled the child against his cloak of green, set his nerves to tingling. Atremble, Rhys caught her hand with his free one and clasped it close against his breast, eyes and mind locking with hers in an exchange of such intensity that it started to spill over to the others before he remembered to damp it to more tolerable levels for all their sakes. He caught Camber's flicker of amused indulgence, not quite embarrassed, as he pressed her palm to his lips with the more tender control of his Healer's touch.

God, how I love you! he let the thought extend to her, not caring if the others overheard. *And thank you for our son.*

She did not answer him with words, or even thought of words. Instead, she smiled and leaned a little closer, her hand still clasped in his, to stretch across the babe and touch his lips with hers. He held the balance of their rapport steady, like a flame, as she slowly drew away enough to move around behind him. She did not release his hand until all of them had turned to face the east. Rhys could feel her arms extending behind him to either side, close and cherishing like sheltering wings, though she no longer touched him physically. Her voice was a little lower than usual as she wove the familiar words of the opening invocation.

"We stand outside time, in a place not of earth. As our ancestors before us bade, we join together and are One."

Rhys bowed his head reverently and let himself center into the stillness, his lips brushing against the soft, reddish down of his son's head.

"By Thy Blessed Apostles, Matthew, Mark, Luke, and John; by all Thy Holy Angels; by all Powers of Light and Shadow, we call Thee to guard and defend us from all perils, O Most High," she continued. "Thus it is and has ever been, thus it will be for all times yet to come. *Per omnia saecula saeculorum.*"

"Amen," all of them breathed as one, each signing himself with a cross.

Rhys raised his head as she came around to his right, letting his slight smile mirror her own and those of the others watching as the two of them moved toward Jebediah. The knight bowed slightly as they approached, ushering them to his right as he turned to face the almost-shimmer of the warded walls. He paused, then cocked his head slightly toward Rhys in question.

"Do you mind which invocation I use? I'd like to offer one my father taught me, from a slightly different tradition."

"We would be honored," Rhys murmured with a slight bow, not needing to look at Evaine to know that she agreed.

Jebediah smiled and hitched his thumbs into his white sash, then straightened to address the guardian of the east.

"All honor to Saint Raphael, Physician-Healer, Lord of Wind and Tempest, Prince of Air, thou Eastern Warder! Here stand thy servants Rhys and Evaine, to dedicate their son, a Healer-born!"

Rhys held his infant son aloft for just a moment, balancing the tiny bundle across the palms of his hands, and then the three of them bowed. As they straightened and Rhys and Evaine began moving toward the southern ward, Evaine brushed the knight's shoulder with her fingertips.

"Thank you, Jeb. That was beautiful."

They passed behind Joram, who was sporting a pleased, lopsided grin.

"I'll follow Jebediah's lead, if you don't mind," he murmured. He drew his sword as the two of them moved into place at his right, kissing the cross-hilt in salute before raising the blade to point southward.

"All honor to Saint Michael, the Defender, he who subdues the Serpent, Keeper of the Gates of Eden, Prince of Fire, thou Southern Warder! Here stand thy servants Rhys and Evaine, to dedicate their son, a Healer-born!"

Again Rhys held up the baby and the three of them

bowed, Joram sweeping his blade down in completion of his salute and then sheathing it. He kissed his tiny nephew on the forehead and signed him in blessing before standing back to let them move on. Evaine caught his waist in a fond hug and brushed his lips with hers before moving on with husband and son, and Rhys felt both embrace and kiss as if it had been himself. They stood now in the west, in Evaine's usual place. She bowed her head, stilling all else, then raised her arms in welcome.

"All honor to Saint Gabriel, the Heavenly Herald, Prince of Water and Warder of the West, who didst bring glad tidings to Our Blessed Lady! Here stand thy servants Rhys and Evaine, to dedicate our son, a Healer-born!"

Rhys bowed his head, but he did not yet hold aloft the child.

"In the name of the mother of this child, I would commend him also to the protection of Our Lady," he said softly, turning his head to look Evaine full in the eyes. "For the Healing gift is the gift of mercy and compassion, as well as physical mending, and both are beloved of the Queen of Heaven."

With that, he held the child out for the third time, feeling Evaine's hand extend to touch one tiny arm, the caress of her mind intertwining with his as both of them bowed. Then they were moving on to stand beside Camber.

His face was not the face of Evaine's father, for that had been put aside nearly a decade before, for the sake of a king and a kingdom to be saved; and the risk of detection, even here in sacred circle, was too great to dare unless there were a need. Over the years, they had come to accept that as a necessary caution. It was a small sacrifice when weighed against some others that had been made.

But the love which enfolded the three of them as they stepped into the shelter of Camber's arms was no less tangible for being contained behind a stranger's eyes. Nor, after so long, could Alister Cullen even be counted as stranger any longer. He was a part of Camber now, even though his body lay in a secret vault deep beneath the ground.

"All honor to Saint Uriel, Lord of Death in its season," Camber said softly, his voice carrying a quality which came, perhaps, of being more in years than any other in the room, of having faced the Dark Angel more than once, and having lost all fear.

"Thou who rulest forest tracks and all dry land, the Prince of the Earth, the Warder of the North!" Rhys felt Camber's hand rest on his shoulder, a vital current reverberating through Evaine, as well. "Here stand thy servants Rhys and Evaine, and my dear children—" The beacon of Camber's attention shifted down to the child's face, "—to dedicate their son, a Healer-born!"

Again all bowed, the glow of Camber's uncompromising love following them even when they returned to Jebediah's quarter to complete their circuit of the chamber. Then they were moving back into the center, the other three were coming in, and Camber was taking up the elements of baptism, his white stole gleaming in the glow of their magic.

Rhys laid his son in Joram's arms, then stepped aside, content to let the priests perform this part of the rite. While the greater part of him withdrew in preparation—for the heart of this night's work was yet to come—another part looked on with detached interest. Evaine had settled in her chair to watch, and he laid both hands lightly on her shoulders, all physical passion submerged now as he turned his thoughts inward. Evaine laid her head against his waist, one hand covering one of his, but he knew she felt his gradual retreat into that Healing place where only he could go. He watched her father sign the baby's head with chrism, touch his tongue with salt, pour water as he named him Tieg Joram, "...*in nomine Patris, et Filii, et Spiritus Sancti, Amen.*"

The rite went on, and when it was done, they put the child into his arms again and fell back a few paces, all around. Evaine sat forward expectantly, her face serene and trusting.

The silence settled, ever more profound in the stillness of the warded chamber, and Rhys bowed his head beside his son's. Nudging his conscious mind toward Healing trance, he reached out with his mind to softly intertwine his son's. The rapport came, gently and without much form as the infant stirred in sleep, resounding on an incredible note of harmony as their Healing potentials met and fused for just an instant.

In thought, his mind soared back across the years, to the spellbound days of his Gabrilite apprenticeship and the *Credo* of the Healer-priests who had taught him. His voice could never match those massed choirs at Saint Noet's, but the words at least gave form to his intent. Later, young Tieg must hear the words sung as they should be sung and know the full range of the holy burden which destiny had given him; but for tonight, a solo must suffice.

Rhys held his son against his heart and began to

sing, his rich baritone gaining-strength as the flow of the chant began to soar. *"Adsum, Domine: Me gratiam corpora hominum sanare concessisti..."*

Here am I, Lord:
Thou hast granted me the grace to heal men's
    bodies.
Here am I, Lord:
Thou hast blessed me with the Sight to See men's
    souls.
Here am I, Lord:
Thou hast given me the might to bend the will of
    others.
O Lord, grant strength and wisdom to wield all
    these gifts
only as Thy will wouldst have me serve...

The hymn Rhys raised was the ancient and haunting *Adsum Domine*, heart of the ethical precepts which had governed the conduct of Healers, lay and ecclesiastical alike, for nearly as long as there had been Healers recognized among the Deryni. He could feel the others watching him with wonder as he sang, but he knew that they were experiencing only a pale reflection of the full meaning which permeated the words for a Healer—that even he was losing some of its effect by delivering it alone. When the Healer-monks sang the hymn, their voices wove intricate harmonics that struck at hidden chords within a Healer's mind. Still, the chords were touched in Rhys from memory, and he felt the familiar euphoria fill him as he finished the first section and moved into the versicle. *"Dominus lucis me dixit, Ecce..."*

The Lord of Light said unto me, Behold:
Thou art My chosen child, My gift to man.
Before the daystar, long before thou wast in
    mother-womb,
thy soul was sealed to Me for all time out of mind.
Thou art My Healing hand upon this world,
Mine instrument of life and Healing might.
To thee I give the breath of Healing power,
the awesome, darkling secrets of the wood and
    vale and earth.
I give thee all these gifts that thou mayst know
    my love:
Use all in service of the ease of man and beast.
Be cleansing fire to purify corruption,
a pool of sleep to bring surcease from pain.
Keep close within thy heart all secrets given,
as safe as said in shriving, and as sacred.
Nor shall thy Sight be used for revelation,
unless the other's mind be freely offered.
With consecrated hands, make whole the broken.
With consecrated soul, reach out and give My
    peace...

They were all bound in with Rhys now; and as he
knelt to begin the final antiphon, he felt their longing,
their awe at the power his song conveyed, their near-
bereavement that they would never really know the
length and breadth and height and depth of the universe
that was his to command—or the awful responsibility
that such a universe demanded.

On both his knees, he held his son in outstretched
arms and made his song a prayer. He knew Evaine's
presence close at hand, although she never moved from

where she sat. Her sweet voice blended with his own
even as hearts and minds were intertwined, tentative
at first, then strengthening with every echoed heartbeat. *"Adsum, Domine..."*

> Here am I, Lord:
> All my talents at Thy feet I lay.
> Here am I, Lord:
> Thou art the One Creator of all things.
> Thou art the Omnipartite One Who ruleth Light
>   and Shade,
> Giver of Life and Gift of Life Thyself.
> Here am I, Lord:
> All my being bound unto Thy will.
> Here am I, Lord:
> Sealed unto Thy service, girt with strength to
>   save or slay.
> Guide and guard Thy servant, Lord, from all
>   temptation,
> that honor may be spotless and my Gift
>   unstained...

The silence was profound when he had finished. For
a moment he remained on his knees, humble tears
streaming down his cheeks as he bowed before the
Presence of the All Holy, Which had surely passed Its
countenance over this sacred circle and smiled upon
his son. Then he slowly raised his head and looked
around him, saw them all kneeling, too, each lost in
his own mind and contemplation.

Only Evaine could meet his eyes as he rose and
slowly crossed to lay their son in her arms once more,
her own eyes bright with tears. Only Evaine, he thought,

had understood more than a fraction of what had just transpired.

He eased himself to one knee to slip his arm around her waist, laid his head against her shoulders, and gazed with her in wonder at their son, Tieg Joram, who would one day be a Healer.

VOCATION
DECEMBER 24, 977

"Vocation" takes place on the sixtieth anniversary of the destruction of Saint Neot's, in the ruins of the abbey. The anti-Deryni backlash heralded by that dreadful deed has had sixty years to ferment. No longer are Deryni the masters of Gwynedd. We are near the end of the reign of King Uthyr Haldane, grandson of that Cinhil Haldane restored to the throne by Camber and his kin; Uthyr, whose father, Rhys Michael Haldane, early fell under the influence of an avaricious and rigidly anti-Deryni Council of Regents.

More than half a century of this official stance has gradually eliminated all overt participation by Deryni in the governing of the kingdom, and the stigma of being Deryni has been intensified by religious sanctions imposed by the Council of Ramos—restrictions begun as a reaction against Deryni power in general and magic in particular, but quickly transformed into a moral issue, in which the Deryni are now seen by the Church as evil in and of themselves. Indeed, even the continuation of the Deryni as a race has become questionable, as the harsh anti-Deryni legislations of Ramos extend unto the third and fourth generation. In Gwynedd, bishops' tribunals often burn Deryni; and secular lords holding the right of high justice are free to use or abuse Deryni as they will.

Gilrae d'Eirial is not Deryni, but he has heard stories about them. The days of Deryni power are not so long past that everyone is dead who remembers what it was really like, but men and women of that era are growing fewer and fewer, and stories of the old days become more and more embellished with the exaggerations of legend with each passing year. Gilrae's life thus far has been fairly typical of men of his knightly caste, for he is destined to succeed his dying father as Baron d'Eirial. (The very title suggests that Sir Radulf d'Eirial, Gilrae's father, may have been heir to the breakup of some of the estates formerly held by Deryni or Deryni sympathizers, for Haut Eirial was a holding of the Order of Saint Michael before the Michaelines were ousted from Gwynedd.)

But Gilrae does not want to be Baron d'Eirial—though he has let duty bind him to this course until a more overweening destiny seems to have taken even this option out of his hands. And having failed to choose what he really wanted while he still had the chance, his life now seems reduced to destiny rather than desire. The last thing he expects, as he rides out on this bright December afternoon, is to have his options startlingly renewed.

Incidently, if the name Simonn seems to strike a familiar chord, think back to Camber's visit to Saint Neot's, and a young novice Healer of that name learning how to read his own body processes.

VOCATION

The air was cold and very still as Gilrae, the doomed young heir d'Eirial, reined in his mare at the top of the rise and glanced back the way he had come. He and his mount cast only an odd, truncated shadow on the virgin snow, for the sun was as high overhead as it was like to get on this bright winter day, but crisp, dainty hoofprints stretched back clearly to the point where he had left the main track. Few would dare to follow, for the ruins ahead were believed by most folk to be haunted, but Caprus would have no trouble finding him, if he really wanted to. Caprus had always made it his business to know the whereabouts of his elder half brother, for he had been groomed by his mother from birth to be alert to faults which might turn their father's favor from the son of his first marriage to that of his second. If only Caprus could believe how little his supposed rival sought their father's title—or how little time there was before the title passed again: brother to brother, the next time, instead of father to son.

But Gilrae's last ordeal still lay months in the future. Their father's was in progress, and Gilrae could no longer bear to watch it happening. For the next few hours, Caprus and his mother could keep the death watch without him; they would not miss him anyway, until the old man was dead. And in whatever time remained before Caprus came to fetch him, Gilrae must weight his own soul's yearnings and reach some firm decision. At least the air was clean here at the crest of the Lendours. He did not think he could have borne the closeness of his father's sickroom for another minute.

Gilrae's sigh hung on the frosty air as he touched heels to the mare and urged her up onto the plateau, letting her choose her own footing as he turned his attention to the ruined walls coming into sight. In addition to the initial destruction wreaked on the abbey and its inhabitants, the decay of more than half a century of hard winters and neglect had taken a heavy toll. The scavenging of local crofters had compounded the process, for the smooth blue ashlars from the outer walls made sturdy hearths, cottage walls, and even sheep pens for those bold enough to risk the ghosts and strong enough to cart them away. In some spots, little remained of the outer walls besides foundations.

Gilrae thought about the ghosts as the mare minced her way across a broken, ice-slick courtyard, her ears lacing back at a rabbit that broke from cover. He supposed it was inevitable that the place should have fostered such fears. Even before its fall, Saint Neot's had been rife with forbidden magic. Deryni sorcery had been its mainstay—sorcery which the Church condemned as evil, its practitioners anathema. To be Deryni was to live under sentence of death, if one did not renounce one's hell-born powers and adopt a life of penance and submission. That these particular Deryni were said to have been healers and teachers of healers was immaterial, for the healing had come of their misbegotten powers, and hence from the Devil—or so the priests taught. The abbey's destroyers, crack troops of the young king's regents, had slaughtered the monks to a man, and their students as well, profaning the holy chapel with a sea of blood and desecrating the altar itself with vicious murder.

Nor had that been the extent of the raiders' savagery. When they had finished their brutal, butcher's work and sacked the abbey of its portable wealth, they set upon a systematic destruction of what they could not carry off, smashing the leaded glass and the fine carvings which adorned altar screens, choir stalls, and chapel doorways, scarring the tougher stone with sword and mace blows, and then torching the lot. Rare man-

uscripts of human crafting, as well as heretical Deryni
works, went to feed the flames which licked at the oak-
beamed ceilings, the roof thatching. When, two days
later, the fires at last burned out, men with ropes and
horses pulled down what the flames had spared. More
than half a century later, few walls stood higher than
the withers of Gilrae's mount. In the face of such may-
hem, small wonder that the local folk feared the vengeance of Deryni ghosts.

Gilrae had never met any of those ghosts, of course.
Nor, to his knowledge, had he even met a Deryni, ghost
or otherwise, though the priests warned that the sorcerers were devious, and one could never be too sure.
Even the places formerly inhabited by such men were
to be shunned, the priests said—though Gilrae had not
known that as a young boy; and, as an adult, he had
years of personal experience to tell him that they must
be wrong about this particular place. There was surely
no evil here. And as for ghosts—

Ghosts, indeed! As Gilrae guided his mare through
what remained of gatehouse and porter's lodge, nearing
what once had been the cellar level of a dormitory
block, he remembered the one conversation he and old
Simonn had had about the alleged ghosts—and the
chuckle and look of bemused indulgence he had gotten
for his trouble.

Well, the old man certainly ought to know. He had
been living in these ruins, in defiance of ghosts and
skittish priests, since Gilrae's father was a boy. If there
were ghosts, they had never bothered Simonn—or Gilrae.

But mental debates on the existence of ghosts were
not conducive to watching where one was going. The

mare knew, but Gilrae had not been to the ruins since before his accident, and he had forgotten the depth of the drop as the mare jumped down to the level of the former cellar. The leap was not much farther than the height of the mare's belly, but Gilrae was unprepared, and his right hand gave when he tried to brace himself in old reflex. The jolt threw him against the front of the saddle so hard that he all but lost his seat. The pain that shot up his arm from wrist to shoulder nearly made him faint.

He rode the remaining distance in tight-lipped silence, head bowed in the shadow of his fur-lined cap, useless right hand wedged into the front opening of his leather riding jerkin to keep it from flapping around. When he reached the alcove he often used as a make-shift stable, he dismounted easily enough; but when he tried to loosen the girth, he found he could not do it left-handed. Biting back tears of anger and frustration, he gave the mare an apologetic pat on the neck and turned away, scrambling over the snow-covered rubble toward the open cloister garth. His sword, awkward and unwieldy hanging from his right side rather than his left, kept banging against his boots and tangling between his legs as he climbed up to the cloister level, nearly tripping him several times and bringing the hot tears to his eyes despite his determination to the contrary. The footing was better in the open, though, and he tried to put aside his bitterness as he emerged into sunlight.

The place brought back happier memories. As a boy, he could remember stealing away here for hours at a time, pretending that the ruined church was whole, and he free to choose, never even dreaming that the choices would be taken from him before he could make them.

He had longed to be a priest even then. As a very
young boy, he had dared to pretend he *was* a priest,
and had often played at celebrating Mass with an acorn-
cap chalice and an oak-leaf paten. When he had shyly
confided it to the old priest who was his tutor and
chaplain, and asked whether he might one day become
a priest in fact, the old man had sputtered and ranted
and given him a stiff penance—not only for the sac-
rilege of pretending the sacrifice of the Mass, but for
even thinking of the priesthood when he was the lord's
eldest son. The Church might be for younger sons of
noble families, but not for the heir. Old Father Erdic
had even told his father, in blatant defiance of the seal
of the confessional.

His father's response had been predictable and harsh:
a birch rod applied liberally to Gilrae's bare buttocks
and a week of seclusion in his room, with only bread
and water. Months had passed before Gilrae could slip
away alone again, and he had never again trusted the
forsworn priest. Nor had he given up his acorn and
leaf Masses, at least for a while, though in time the
futility of it all relegated the practice to only a child-
hood memory.

He caught himself smiling as he remembered those
days of youthful innocence, wondering that he ever
could have been so naive. He was twenty now. He was
still the heir d'Eirial, and could become baron at any
moment. The previous Easter, he had been knighted
by King Uthyr himself, who had addressed him as
Right Trusty and Well-Beloved, in anticipation of his
imminent inheritance. Any ordinary man should have
been well content; but all Gilrae d'Eirial had ever really
wanted was to be a priest.

No longer smiling, he turned slow, reluctant steps

across the open space of the cloister garth and headed
toward what remained of the chapel, avoiding the
rougher going of the peripheral walks, with their litter
of charred beams and fallen stones. Fresh sheep drop-
pings confirmed the identity of the last living things to
pass this way, but of other humans there was no trace.
Balancing precariously with only one good hand to
steady him, Gilrae made his way up broken, snow-
slick steps to pause in the shelter of a once-grand
processional doorway, blowing on his gloved fist to
warm it as he surveyed the south transept and crossing
and eastern nave. Only the expected sheep were
browsing in the ruins, nibbling at lichens and tufts of
frost-seared grass.

Removing his cap, for he liked to think of the place
as holy still, he moved on through the transept in the
direction of the choir, musing again on the place's past.
Saint Neot's had fallen, they said, in the same year
good King Cinhil died—the year the bishops had condemned the Deryni as a race and declared them anathema, to be shunned, persecuted, and often even
slaughtered by righteous men because of what they
were. It had been on a Christmas Eve a full three-score
years ago—sixty years ago *today*, Gilrae realized, as
he did the necessary arithmetic in his head.

The sun chose that moment to go behind a cloud,
plunging Gilrae and the ruined choir aisle into shadow,
and he shivered. In the heavy atmosphere of his father's
sickroom, he had nearly forgotten that it was Christmas
Eve. Many people believed that the anniversaries of
terrible events held powerful potential for supernatural
visitations—and what place was more likely than an
altar profaned by murder?

Still chilled by more than cold, he cast a nervous glance in the direction of the desecrated altar. The previous night's snowfall had given it new altar coverings, disguising the vast cracks across the once-hallowed slab, but as the sun re-emerged, the illusion became apparent. The battered edges spoke all too clearly of the violence and the hate of the altar's destroyers, and suddenly Gilrae felt an almost irresistable urge to sign himself in protection—an inclination immediately thwarted by his useless right hand.

Angry both at his helplessness and the superstition which had brought it to mind again, he dashed recklessly up the choir, sword flailing at his side as he plunged and stumbled through the snow. His bravado deserted him as he reached the foot of the altar steps, however. Sobbing for breath, he dropped to both knees on the lowest step and buried his face in his good hand.

Everything was denied him now. Once there had been choices, had he but had the nerve to make them; now, either path he once might have traveled was barred to him. Even were it not for the malignant growth paralyzing his arm, even if there had only been the accident—if he could not wield a sword with a useless right hand, neither could he function as a priest. The Church kept strict standards for the fitness of priestly candidates, and a man who could not properly handle the Mass vessels at the time he sought ordination certainly would not be accepted.

With vision blurred by tears which would no longer be denied, Gilrae yanked at the ties of his fur-lined cloak until he could pull it off and spread it leather-side down on a relatively dry patch of unbroken flags just at the foot of the altar steps. He hardly noticed

the warmth of the sun on his back as he prostrated
himself on the thick, wolfskin pelt, too numb with grief
and loss to do more than lie there weeping bitterly for
several minutes, forehead cradled in his good arm.
Despair shifted to resentment after a while—an angry,
defiant argument with God, protesting the gross unfair-
ness of it all, pleading for reprieve—and then contrition for his presumption.

Very well. If he was meant to die with neither life
fulfilled, then at least let *that* be to the glory of the
One he would far rather have served in other ways.
Setting himself to formal prayer, he admitted his terror
of what lay ahead and offered it up, pleading for the
strength to accept what was ordained. When even that
brought no comfort, he let himself drift in numb dejec-
tion and tried not to think at all, the sun on his back
gradually lulling the last of his terror to resignation.

For a while, only the swirling colors played behind
his closed eyelids; but then, with a bright clarity that
he had only occasionally experienced before, images
began to form behind his eyes.

In his altered vision, it seemed that the abbey walls
rose around him once more, the high, mosaic-lined
vaulting of the choir dome arching protectively over
his vantage point. The sanctuary shone with candlelight, the pale, carved wood of the choir stalls restored,
the ruby glow of a Presence lamp above the high altar
lending the snow-white walls a pinkish tint.

The abbey was peopled once more as well, by silent,
white-robed men with single braids emerging from under
the cowls that fell back upon their shoulders. He sensed
them approaching from the processional door, their
double file splitting around him to enter the choir stalls
to either side. Turning toward the altar as one man,

they made their obeisance in perfect unison, raising their voices in the most beautiful harmony Gilrae had ever heard. Only the first few words were distinct, but they brought back all the poignance of the life to which Gilrae now would never dare aspire.

"Adsum Domine . . ." Here am I, Lord . . .

It was also the response of the candidate for priesthood as he presented himself before his ordaining bishop—words that Gilrae now would never speak.

The anguish that welled up anew in his chest blotted out the vision, and, muffling a sob, he rolled onto his side and then to a sitting position to cradle his throbbing arm. Only then did he become aware that he was not alone; he whirled around on the seat of his leather britches, good hand going for the dagger at his belt.

But even as he turned, he realized that if the intruder had wished him harm, he could have been dead several times over. In any case, the old man sitting on a stone block a few feet away posed no threat. With an uneasy grin, Gilrae let the dagger slip back into its sheath and sat up straighter, surreptitiously dragging his left sleeve across his face, though he pretended only to brush a lock of hair out of his eyes. He should have expected the visit, after seeing the sheep. He hoped the old man had not noticed he had been crying.

"Simonn. You startled me. I thought I was alone."

"I shall leave, if you wish," the man replied.

"No. Don't go."

"Very well."

No one knew who old Simonn was, or where he had come from. He had been old when Gilrae's father had played here as a boy. He tended his sheep, sometimes trading their wool for necessities in the spring; occasionally, he came down to the village church to hear Mass. Simonn the shepherd, Simonn the hermit, Simonn the holy man, some said. Gilrae had discovered quite by accident that the old man could read and write—a skill not easily or often gained by peasants, especially here in the Lendour highlands. Gilrae himself had had to fight for the privilege, and he the lord's son. He had never presumed on their friendship by inquiring too insistently, but he sometimes wondered how much more Simonn was than he appeared. Whoever he was, he had always been a friend to Gilrae.

The old man smiled and nodded, almost as if he had been aware of Gilrae's inner dialogue, but the blue eyes were kindly and unthreatening as they gazed across the short distance between them. When Gilrae did not speak, Simonn raised a white eyebrow and made gentle clucking noises with his tongue.

"So, young Master Gilrae, I've not seen you in many months. What brings you to the hills on this bright Christmas Eve? I should have thought you would be feasting in your father's hall, preparing to welcome the Christ Child."

Gilrae hung his head. It was obvious the old man had not heard, either of his father's illness or his own misfortune. He could feel the wild pulse throbbing through the growth on his inner forearm as he cradled it closer to his midriff. The thought of the two coming deaths, his father's and his own, made his stomach queasy.

"There will be no feasting in Haut Eirial this night, Simonn," he whispered. "My father is dying. I—had to get away for a few hours."

"Ah, I see," the old man said, after a slight pause. "And you are feeling the weight of your coming responsibility."

Gilrae said nothing. If only it were that simple. With two good hands, he supposed he could have resigned himself to the life of a secular lord, governing the d'Eirial lands and keeping the king's peace, as his father wanted. With two good hands, he might even have had the courage to give it all up in favor of his brother and make the choice he had longed to make for years. But the accident, and the resultant—*thing* growing in his arm, had put an end to choices.

He shivered as he inadvertently clutched it closer, instinctively protective of what he feared the most, but despite old Simonn's watchful eyes, he was unable to suppress a grimace as pain shot up his arm. As he looked up defensively, daring the old man to mention it, Simonn casually turned his face toward the ruined altar, going very quiet.

"It is not an easy thing to lose what one loves," Simonn murmured after a moment, apparently testing. "Nor is it ever an easy thing to shoulder responsibilities, even if one welcomes them. And if one finds oneself forced into responsibilities by circumstances, rather than by a choice based on love, the task becomes even more difficult."

"Are you saying that I don't love my father?" Gilrae asked, after a stunned pause.

Simonn shook his head. "Of course not. I think you love him very much, as a son should love his father. If you did not, you would not now be agonizing over the choices you must make. We rarely *ask* for the choices that are placed before us, but they must always be made, nonetheless."

Swallowing with difficulty, Gilrae turned his gaze to the wolfskin lining of the cloak he sat on, unconsciously rubbing his numb right arm to warm it.

"What—makes you think I'm faced with any particular choices, old man?" he said a little belligerently. "My father is dying, and I'm to be Baron d'Eirial. That involves no choices. It is a role I was born to."

"By blood—yes," Simonn replied. "But by spirit—well, I think you did not come to this ruined abbey while your father lay dying and prostrate yourself before its altar because you are overjoyed to be coming into your temporal inheritance. And I do not mean to imply that your grief at your father's passing is not genuine," he added, as Gilrae looked up in astonishment. "I wonder if you even know what drove you to present yourself this way—in this ruined church, before an altar drenched by the blood of scores of holy men."

Gilrae gave a sigh and lowered his eyes again, subdued. Simonn knew part of it, at least. It could not have been hard to guess. They had talked before, if only hypothetically, about the practical considerations of a religious life. Simonn had never quite said, but it was clear that, at least as a boy, he himself had received some kind of instruction in a religious community. Perhaps that was where he had learned to read and write.

"It doesn't matter anyway," Gilrae finally murmured. "The question is academic. There are no choices for me anymore—only duties and responsibilities that I'll be increasingly ill-equipped to handle. God, I almost wish I were dead already!"

Even as the bitter words left his lips, the shocked Simonn was on his feet and darting across the few feet which separated them, grabbing his wrist to shake him. It was the bad wrist, and Gilrae gasped aloud with the pain. Instantly, Simonn was kneeling beside him and shoving back his sleeve, pulling off the glove, running gentle fingers over the swollen flesh.

"How did this happen?" Simonn murmured, turning the forearm and drawing in breath as he spied the blackness spread along the inner side. "Why didn't you tell me you were ill?"

Gilrae swallowed and tried to pull away, feeling like an animal caught in a trap.

"Leave me alone. Please. What difference can it make?"

"It can mean your life!" the old man snapped, holding him with his eyes. "How did this start?"

"A—a fall from a horse, several months ago," Gilrae found himself saying. "I—thought it was only a bad sprain at first, but then the—swelling started."

"Have you much pain?"

Gilrae wrenched his gaze free with a gasp and nodded, staring unseeing at the ground.

"I—can't close my hand anymore, either," he managed to whisper. "I can't hold a sword, and I can't—"

Though he struggled to prevent it, the old dream flashed into memory again: himself, garbed in the vestments of a priest and raising the chalice at the celebration of Mass. Choking back a sob, he shook his head to clear the image from his mind.

There *were* no choices now. That dream would never be; nor would he even be able to be a proper lord to his people. All the doors were closing. Until now, he had never even thought about ending his life before the blackness could, but perhaps he *would* be better off.

"What else can't you do?" old Simonn urged softly, the voice boring into his brain. "What is it you *really* want most?"

"I want another chance, I suppose," Gilrae whispered after a moment, dropping his head to rest his forehead on his knees, no longer minding that his arm still lay in Simonn's hands. "I want it to be last spring, when I was still a whole man, and the decisions were still mine to make. All the choices have been made for me, now. I'll die from this. No one else knows about that part of it except my father's battle surgeon, but it's going to happen." He lifted his head to glance at the useless arm with tear-blurred eyes. "I lacked the courage to follow my own heart when I still had the chance—and now I can't even follow my father's heart and be a worthy leader for his people, once he's gone."

He found himself staring stupidly into space for a while, but then Simonn's soft sigh was bringing him back.

"I can't help you with your decisions, Gilrae, but I might be able to help you with your arm," the old man said. "It would be rather painful, but the growth could be removed."

Gilrae swallowed noisily, afraid to let himself dare to hope.

"I'd like to believe you, but I don't think so," he managed to murmur. "Gilbert said it would only come back, worse than before, and that it would spread. The arm could be cut off—that *might* stop it, *if* I survived the amputation—but what good would that do? It wouldn't allow either of the lives I'd choose, if the choices still were mine."

"We always have choices, son," Simonn replied, in a voice so soft and yet so compelling that Gilrae turned to look at him again. "If you choose to let me try to help you, I may be able to make it possible for you to reopen those other choices. What do you have to lose?"

And what, indeed, *did* he have to lose? Gilrae reasoned, as he stared into the old man's eyes and found himself swaying dizzily. As if some force outside himself compelled his movement, he felt his left hand going to the knife at his belt and unsheathing it, handing the blade across to Simonn hilt-first, rising at the old man's beckoning gesture to pull his cloak around himself and mount the altar steps behind him.

"Sit here," the old man whispered, pulling him toward the left-hand corner and setting his back against the cold marble.

Gilrae felt his knees buckle under him, and his back slid slowly down the stone facade until he was sitting, surrounded by the folds of the fur-lined cloak, his sword lying close along his right thigh. Snow still lay in drifts in the north shadow of the altar, and he could not seem to resist as Simonn pushed back the sleeve of his leather tunic and buried the right forearm in the snow to numb it further. The sun was more than halfway down the western sky—how *had* it gotten so late already?—but its light still dazzled Gilrae's eyes as he laid his head against the marble behind him, golden fire also flashing from the blade Simonn polished on a surprisingly clean hem of pale grey undertunic.

When the cold of the snow against his bare arm began to ache more than the original pain, Simonn turned the forearm upward in its bed of melting snow and ran a hand over the area to be excised.

"You needn't watch this," he said, touching ice-cold fingers to the side of Gilrae's face to turn his head away. "Look out at the sunset and think about other things.

Watch the clouds, if you like. Perhaps the shapes will suggest answers to your questions."

The old man's fingers seemed somehow to numb Gilrae's brain as well as the flesh they touched, and he found himself becoming very detached from his still body. As Simonn bent over the upturned forearm and positioned his blade, Gilrae summoned just enough will to glance down and see the steel trace a crimson path along one side of the blackness he had come to hate and fear. The blood welled up scarlet against the snow, steaming in the frigid air, and Gilrae rolled his eyes upward again to gaze at the sky. After a few seconds more, his eyes closed, and he dreamed.

He was in a church again, but it was smaller than the one he had seen before—no more than a chapel, really—and this time, he was a participant rather than an observer, one of four solemn yet joyful young men in white, processing down the narrow nave. Like the others, he carried a lighted candle in his right hand; his left was pressed reverently to the deacon's stole crossing his chest and secured at his right hip. The men in the single row of stalls to either side wore grey habits rather than the white of the previous dream, but a few of them sported the single braid Gilrae had noticed before. Ahead, at the foot of a far more humble altar, waited two men in copes and mitres.

He knelt with his brethren at their feet—a bishop and a mitered abbot, he somehow knew—and though he could not quite make out the words the senior of them spoke, he knew the response. He and his brethren sang it together as they held their candles aloft, the notes floating pure and clear in that holy place.

"*Adsum, Domine* . . ." Here am I, Lord . . .

The scene wavered and dissolved at that, much to

his regret, and for an indeterminable while he simply floated a little sadly in a state of disconnection, only dimly aware of the sunlight on his face, beating on his closed eyelids, and the cold penetrating his cloak and riding leathers from the stone step, the altar at his back, the snow still numbing his right arm past all feeling.

He had no inclination to open his eyes, to move, or even to think. He drifted some more—and then he was back in the dream, humbly kneeling with joined hands before the bishop, swaying a little on his knees as the consecrated hands came to rest on his head.

"Accipe Spiritum Sanctum..."

He imagined he could feel the holy Power surging through every nerve and sinew, the divine Energy filling him to overflowing and then opening him to fill even more. The ecstasy grew so intense that he began to tremble.

Then, suddenly, he was aware of cold hands on either side of his face, and old Simonn's voice gently bidding him open his eyes. He managed to make his dry throat contract and swallow, but he was still disoriented for a moment and could not quite seem to bring Simonn into focus.

"I—you—"

"You're all right. I think you must have fallen asleep on me," the old man murmured, smiling. "Did you dream?"

"I did. How did you know? Simonn, it was wonderful! I—"

Confused, Gilrae raised both hands to rub his temples before he realized that the right hand had obeyed just like the left one, and that there was no longer any pain. A strip of grey cloth bound his right arm from wrist halfway to elbow, but no unnatural bulge disturbed the clean line. Blood stained the snow where his arm had lain, but far less than he might have expected. Simonn was retrieving his dagger even as Gilrae started to speak, burnishing the melted snow from blade and grip and extending it to him hilt-first.

"I believe your father's battle surgeon may have frightened you unduly," the old man said. "It shouldn't come back. You may still have some weakness for a few days, but I think you'll find that you can grip a sword—or anything else you may wish."

"But—"

Simonn shook his head and held up a hand to stop his question, then stood and shaded his eyes against the sun, gazing west beyond the ruins. As Gilrae, too, scrambled to his feet, steadying himself on the corner of the altar, Simonn began kicking fresh snow over the bloodstains at their feet, erasing the visible evidence of what had just occurred.

"Your brother is coming, and an escort with him," Simonn said, glancing up at him as he finished the job. "I fear he brings news which will sadden you—but at least you may now make your decisions based on what you really want, not what your physical condition seemed to dictate. If you value what I have done, say nothing of my part in this, I beg you."

"You have my word," Gilrae promised.

But the old man was already gliding into the ruins, melting into the shadows, and so carefully had he chosen his escape route that even Gilrae, who had watched him go, could detect no sign of his passage.

His brother's voice called out his name then, and Gilrae knew it was only a matter of a few minutes before he was found. Scuttling around the ruined altar

in a panic, hardly daring to believe, he crouched in its
eastern shadow and tore at the bandage on his arm
with trembling fingers, safe for a few more minutes
from even Caprus's prying eyes. Beneath the bandage,
only a yellowed shadow of former bruising showed
where once the fatal blackness had spread—that and
a faint pink line where he thought his blade had gone.
Of the growth there was no trace.

Amazed, he flexed his fingers and made a fist,
watching the tendons ripple under the skin, feeling the
muscles obey. A growing suspicion nagged at the edges
of his mind about old Simonn, but the healing spoke
for itself. He would worry later about its source—and
the promise of the dream. For now, it was sufficient
that a miracle had occurred, and that he had been given
back his choices.

"Lord Gilrae?"

The voice of Sir Lorcan, his father's seneschal,
brought him back to earth with a jolt, and almost guil-
tily he tugged his sleeve back into place and dropped
the bandage onto the snow. No time for contemplating
miracles just now. As he struggled to pull fur-lined
gloves onto damp hands, he could hear the hollow clip-
clop of iron-shod hooves treading on the flagstones
far back in the ruined nave, and the sound infuriated
him.

Fools! Could they not sense that the ground was
holy still? How dared they bring horses into this place?

Indignant at the manner of their intrusion, he hooked
his right hand around the hilt of his sword and stood.
He did not intend to tell them what had happened just
yet. They spotted him as he moved around to the front
of the altar to wait for them, Caprus pointing in his
direction and urging the rest of them to follow faster.

The horses plunged through the snow and slipped and scrambled on the uneven flags, scattering the sheep, their riders watching the footing now, instead of Gilrae.

They were ten in all, Caprus and Lorcan in the lead. Caprus wore a stormy look, for all the pale handsomeness of his bright yellow curls, and Lorcan's lined face was as grave as Gilrae had ever seen it. Father Arnulf and Master Gilbert, the surgeon, rode at their backs, and behind them half a dozen men-at-arms in his father's livery—*his* livery now, he suddenly realized. The men's short lances were reversed in the stirrup-rests, the silver circlet of his father's coronet clutched in the priest's gloved fist. Despite the fact that he had been expecting it, Gilrae suddenly felt very cold.

"Take the horses out of the church," he said quietly, when they reined in at the transept and started to dismount. "Don't argue, Lorcan, just do it."

He could sense Caprus's beginning indignation, but Lorcan murmured something sharply under his breath and turned his chestnut hard into the chest of Caprus' grey, shouldering it into a turn even as the surprised Caprus bit back whatever he had been about to say. Wordlessly the lot of them withdrew halfway along the length of the nave, where Lorcan, Caprus, and the priest and surgeon dismounted and gave their reins to the remaining men. As the horses were led out of the church, the four made their way back toward the altar on foot, muttering among themselves. Lorcan drew slightly ahead and bowed as he reached the foot of the altar steps. He was wearing mail and leathers beneath his fur-lined cloak, as were Caprus and the surgeon.

"I'm sorry, Lord Gilrae. Your father is dead," he

said, his breath hanging on the chill air. "He bade us bring you this."

As he gestured slightly behind him, the middle-aged Father Arnulf stepped forward and extended the coronet in unsteady hands.

"You are confirmed as the heir, my lord," Arnulf said, a shadow of pity flickering behind his eyes as Gilrae reached out to touch the gleaming metal with his left hand only. "Since the king has already acknowledged it, in anticipation of this moment, there can be no question. May God bless you in your endeavors, my lord."

Gilrae could sense the effort it took them not to look at his motionless right hand, but he still was not ready to reveal himself. With a nod to acknowledge all of them, he came slowly down the altar steps. Caprus was watching him with an expression of sorrow mixed with envy, Lorcan looking very uncomfortable. Only the staid Master Gilbert seemed unmoved by it all, though the brown eyes held compassion.

"I thank you, Father," Gilrae murmured, dropping to one knee before the priest. "Would you do me the favor of blessing my father's coronet before you place it on my head? I shall have many difficult decisions ahead of me from this time forward and I shall surely need God's help to persevere."

Not even Caprus could dispute that. As the others knelt around him, warriors' harness clinking softly beneath riding leathers and furs, Gilrae bowed his head and let the priest's blessing roll over him like a wavelet on the lake at Dhassa, trying to think. The coronet across his forehead was cold and heavy, its weight far more than mere metal, pressing into his very soul as he stood and turned away from them, averting his eyes.

The time was come to make his decision. He was baron, but he now had the means to change that, if he dared. Retreating slowly to the altar, he spread his gloved left hand flat on the snow-covered mensa as if in oath, lifting the fingers of his right to brush the edge, shielded behind his body where the others could not see. As the fingers moved and he stared at them, he knew he had not been spared to wear a coronet.

"Sir Lorcan," he said softly, over his shoulder, "were you my father's liegeman?"

"My lord, you know I was."

"And are you now my liegeman?"

"I am your man, my lord," came the crisp reply.

"Thank you. Call the rest of the men here, if you please."

He continued to face the altar, but he could hear uneasy stirrings from Caprus' direction and the low whisper of an exchange between Gilbert and the priest as Lorcan moved off a few paces to signal the men-at-arms to join them. When he sensed the arrival of the others, he drew deep breath and turned, very much aware of the weight of the circlet on his head. The men knelt in a semicircle at the foot of the steps, faces fiercely proud beneath their helmets. Caprus remained with the surgeon and the priest, looking vaguely uneasy as Lorcan moved halfway up the steps to bow.

"As you requested, my lord."

"Yes. Thank you." Gilrae turned his eyes on the men gazing up at him. "Gentlemen, Sir Lorcan has confirmed his continued fealty to me as Baron d'Eirial. Have I your loyalty, as well?"

To murmurs of affirmation, the men drew their

swords and held them toward him with the hilts upper-most, gauntleted hands grasping the naked blades just below the quillons. Gilrae nodded.

"Thank you. I take your actions as oaths sworn. You may stand, but remain where you are, please. Lorcan?"

"My lord."

"Lorcan, I have need of your counsel. Caprus, please come forward."

As the men-at-arms rose and sheathed their weapons, and Lorcan moved silently to Gilrae's left elbow, Caprus came hesitantly to face his brother. He had blanched at the sound of his name, and his glove was tight across his knuckles where his left hand gripped the hilt of his sword as he walked. Wordlessly Gilrae came down the three steps from the altar, pausing where a snowbank stood knee high between them and motioning Caprus to join him. After a slight hesitation, Caprus obeyed, dropping uncertainly to one knee when Gilrae did not speak. Gilrae could sense Lorcan standing slightly behind him, but he did not take his eyes from his brother's. He did not know whether he would like the answer to the question he must now ask Caprus, but if he ever was to dare what his heart desired, an answer was demanded. He prayed God it would be the one he wanted to hear.

"How may I counsel you, my lord?" Lorcan asked quietly.

"A point of jurisdiction. Have I the right, as Baron d'Eirial and a knight of this realm, to mete High and Low Justice in my lands, to all my vassals, great and small?"

"You do, my lord."

High Justice: the power of life and death. He had known it was so, but he had wanted to be sure. Before Caprus could do more than open his mouth to start to protest, Gilrae reached to his sword with his left hand and drew it hilt-first, thrusting it into the snow between them like a javelin.

"Hold your peace, Caprus!" he snapped. "Keep silence and consider well what I am about to ask you. I have my reasons, and I swear I bear you no ill will."

Caprus was trembling with outrage, fists clenched rigidly at his sides, but he said nothing as his brother hooked his other hand in his sword belt and looked down at him. Despite Caprus' repeated mutterings of resentment all their lives about the succession, especially when his mother was around, Gilrae seriously doubted that Caprus had ever been actively disloyal, but he had to be certain—and, more important, his men must be certain. Though he once more had choices open to him, those choices also carried responsibilities.

"Caprus d'Eirial," he said clearly, "I require your solemn oath, before God and these assembled knights, that you have never, in word or in deed, acted against either me or our father to the detriment of our people."

Caprus's lower lip was trembling, but he met Gilrae's gaze squarely. Pride and anger played behind the pale blue eyes.

"How dare you ask such an oath?" he demanded. "And why, after speaking of the High Justice? When have I ever given you cause to doubt my loyalty?"

"Place your hands on the sword and swear it, before God," Gilrae answered. "I am not required to tell you why. Only do it."

For one heart-stopping moment, Gilrae feared Caprus would refuse. The gravity of the question was apparent. But stiff-necked and arrogant as his younger brother sometimes was, Gilrae had never known him to be dishonest or forsworn. Could he not swallow his pride and give his oath?

"Swear it, Caprus," he repeated. "Please."

His faith was rewarded for the second time that afternoon, for all at once Caprus broke their defiant eye contact and yanked off both his gloves, laying bare hands firmly on the quillons, his thumbs resting on the center boss which concealed the sword's holy relics. The face he raised to Gilrae over the sword's cross hilt was tight-jawed, but otherwise expressionless.

"I swear before Almighty God and these assembled knights that I have always been loyal to our father and to you," Caprus said, the words clipped and precise. His gaze hardened, the jaw setting even more stubbornly, but then he seized the sword by its blade and jerked it from the snow, holding it aloft like a talisman between them as he went on.

"I do further swear, of my own free will and desire, that I am today become your liegeman of life and limb and of earthly worship. Faith and truth will I bear unto you, to live and to die, against all manner of folk, so help me God!" He paused to wet his lips uncertainly. "And if you think I ever would have played you false, you're wrong, Gilrae—regardless of what my mother might have had you believe. I was born your lawful brother, and you are now my lawful lord!"

He brought the blade to his lips and kissed the reliquary boss boldly enough, but when he held it out to Gilrae for the oath to be acknowledged, his gaze faltered a little—not with duplicity, but an honest fear that Gilrae might not believe he was sincere. Hardly able to contain his relief, Gilrae took back the sword in his left hand, just under the quillons, and glanced aside at the puzzled Lorcan.

"Sir Lorcan, one further question. Among my other prerogatives as baron, have I the right to create a knight?"

"*A knight?* Aye, my lord, you do, but—"

As Lorcan moved a startled step closer, no less confused than the others murmuring among themselves, Gilrae shook his head and seized the hilt of his sword with his restored right hand, raising it blade-upward in salute to kiss the relics in the hilt. A gasp rippled among them all, for Gilrae had not been able to do that since his fall. The stunned Caprus could only gape at him in astonishment, springing to his feet to grab at Gilrae's sword arm and push back the sleeve to stare.

"Gilrae, your arm—!" he began, genuine joy lighting the blue eyes.

Echoing Caprus's grin, Gilrae pressed his younger brother back to his knees with his free hand and glanced out at all of them, still holding the sword before him.

"Gentlemen, while I prayed this afternoon, something happened that I can't explain," he said quietly. "I was near despair because I thought all my choices had been taken from me. God saw fit to give me all my choices back." He smiled down at his brother. "I hope you will not think ill of me as I give over part of the burden to you, Caprus. I believe it is something you have long wanted, despite your love, and I know now that you will prove worthy of the test."

Before Caprus or any of the rest of them could even begin to question, Gilrae drew himself up formally and raised the sword, bringing the flat of the blade down smartly on Caprus's right shoulder.

"In the name of God and Saint Michael, I dub thee knight, Caprus d'Eirial," he said. The blade lifted to touch the left shoulder. "I give thee the right to bear arms and the duty to protect the weak and helpless."

He brought the blade to rest on Caprus's yellow curls, sighting down the gleaming blade to his brother's tear-bright eyes.

"I give thee also the charge of our father's lands and the meting of justice, high and low," he added, for an instant shifting his glance out over the awed men watching. "Be thou a good knight and gentle lord to these, thy people."

He drew the scabbard from his belt and sheathed the sword, then laid both across the astonished Caprus's hastily raised palms before taking the coronet from his head. He held it high in both his hands, so that there could be no mistaking his fitness for the honor he passed—and no mistaking his intent—then set it firmly on Caprus's head.

"Before God and these assembled witnesses, I renounce all claim to the lands and titles of Eirial, vesting them forever in this Caprus d'Eirial, my brother, true-born son of the late Radulf d'Eirial, and his lawful descendants. This is my irrevocable intent, which I hope will be confirmed without question by our lord the King."

Helping Caprus to his feet, right hand to right, he turned him to face the others. He wondered if his own contentment was as evident as Caprus's incredulous pleasure, and marveled that the choice could have seemed so difficult before.

"My lords, I here present your new Baron d'Eirial.

I command you to give him the same loyalty you gave our father, and which you earlier pledged to me. Do it. I haven't got all night."

Lorcan swore. The men swore. Master Gilbert swore, and even the priest swore. But as Caprus and the others moved off toward the horses, whispering excitedly among themselves and glancing back in awe, Lorcan lingered.

"But, what will you do now?" the old knight whispered, staring as Gilrae watched Caprus and the others disappear against the sunset glare. "You've given up everything, my lord."

"I'm not your lord any longer, Lorcan—and I haven't given up anything that really mattered." Gilrae cocked his head at the other man. "Don't you understand? Before today, I had nothing. And then I was given everything, so that I might choose what I really wanted." He pulled off his right glove and laid his restored hand on the ruined altar.

"Don't you see? This is where I belong. Oh, not here, at this poor, ruined altar. I'm as stunned as you are, that a miracle could have taken place where magic once held sway. But maybe that means that the magic wasn't evil to begin with—I don't know. I do know that I'm not the same man I was when I came here earlier today."

Closing his hand as if to cup something precious, he gazed beyond the altar to where a Presence lamp had burned in his dream.

"I think I've been given a sign, Lorcan—one that I can finally comprehend. It's what I was always looking for—you know that. I don't intend to throw away my second chance."

The old knight shook his head. "You're right. I don't understand." He snorted, then stuck out his hand, which Gilrae took. "If you've found your vocation, though, I pray God will prosper you, my lord."

"Not 'my lord' anymore, Lorcan. Just Gilrae—and maybe *Father* Gilrae someday, if what I pray is true."

"And if it isn't?"

"I think it is," he said with a smile. A slight movement had caught his eye off in the north transept, and he gave Lorcan's hand a final squeeze.

"You'd better go now, old friend. Your new lord is waiting, as is mine. Serve Caprus faithfully, as you would have served me. I have no doubt you'll find him worthy."

The old knight did not speak, but as he bowed over his former master's hand in farewell, he pressed his lips against its back in final homage, battle-scarred fingers briefly caressing the smooth flesh of the once swollen wrist. Then he was turning on his heel and striding down the steps, head ducked down in the collar of his cloak, stumbling a little as he receded down the nave.

Gilrae stared after him, sun-dazzled, then drew on his glove again and turned to lay his hands on the ruined altar once more, bowing his head in blind and wordless thanksgiving. He felt the sun die behind him, and the deepening shadows of the evening, and after a while longer, the touch of a hand on his right shoulder.

"Gilrae?"

"*Adsum*," Gilrae whispered.

Old Simonn's gentle chuckle floated on the air like music as the night's first snowflakes began to drift to earth. Out on the eastern horizon, Gilrae realized that the evening's first star was heralding a personal advent, as well as the coming of the Christmas King.

"Come, young friend," came Simonn's invitation. "But you must save that word for another than myself. Come and I'll take you to an unstained altar."

BETHANE
SUMMER, 1100

With "Bethane," we shift more than a hundred years to the timeframe of Morgan, Kelson, and the rest of the familiar characters of the CHRONICLES OF THE DERYNI. This particular story sprang from two sources: a brief reference in *Deryni Checkmate* to the summer when Alaric Morgan fell out of a tree and broke his arm; and a request to do a story about witches for an antholoy called *Hecate's Cauldron*. I'd never actually referred to old Bethane as a witch, but she certainly fulfills the usual stereotypes about crones and cauldrons and the like. Besides, I'd always been curious about her. Her brief appearance in *Deryni Checkmate* sketched just enough information to be enticing, and asked far more questions than it answered.

Who was Bethane? Who was Darrell, her husband? What happened to him? What happened to her, to make her the way she was? She wasn't always an old hag, living in the hills and eking out a miserable existence from sheep and the offerings of the locals for concocting the odd love potion or practicing folk medicine. She'd obviously had some contact with Deryni, but was she Deryni herself, though ill-trained, or was she something else, like Warin de Grey?

So I melded the two ideas—Alaric's tumble from the tree and the mysterious old woman in the hills, twenty years younger than when we saw her in *Deryni Checkmate*, though already an eccentric old hag—and turned the characters loose. I found out more than I'd bargained for about Bethane, her husband and his associations, and another Deryni I hadn't expected to see in this context; and got yet another glimpse of those dark times of anti-Deryni persecution that had only just begun to ebb to a livable level by the time Alaric Morgan reached young manhood.

BETHANE

Old Bethane shaded her eyes with a gnarled hand and peered out across the meadow with a frown. She had seen the approaching children before. Two of them were sons of the Duke of Cassan; she didn't know about the other two. This time, the four were racing their shaggy mountain ponies across her meadow at a mad gallop, beginning to scatter the scraggly sheep she had spent all morning collecting.

A low growl rose in her throat as she saw one of the boys lean down and whoop at a grazing ewe and her lamb. The ewe bolted in terror and lumbered out of the pony's way, the lamb scampering after, and Bethane lurched to her feet, brandishing her shepherd's crook at the girl child, who was almost upon her.

"Here, now! You stop that!"

The girl's pony stopped stock still, but the girl continued on over the animal's head, legs all akimbo and skirts flying, to land in the grass with a thump as the pony whirled and retreated, bucking and squealing. Bethane grabbed the child's upper arm and hauled her to her feet, giving her a none-too-gentle shake.

"Got you now!" Bethane crowed. "What's the matter with you, riding through here like you owned the free air and frightening an honest woman's sheep? Well, speak up, girl! What do you have to say for yourself?"

As the girl raised wide blue eyes in astonishment, more stunned than hurt, the three boys came galloping toward her. The oldest looked to be twelve or so, though he carried himself like a soldier already. The other two were several years younger, one of them pale blond like the little girl.

"You let my sister alone!" the blond boy shouted, yanking his pony to a halt and glaring at Bethane quite fiercely.

"You'd better not hurt her!" the older boy chimed in. "She didn't mean any harm."

Bethane laughed, almost a cackle, and shook her head. "Not so fast, young masters. I'm owed an apology first." She glared at her captive. "What's your name, girl? What's the idea of chasing my sheep?"

The girl, perhaps five or six, swallowed visibly, not even glancing at her brother and the other two boys, though the hand of the eldest rested on the hilt of his dagger.

"I'm sorry, grand-dame," the girl said in a small voice. "We didn't know the sheep belonged to anyone. I mean, we knew they weren't Duke Jared's, but we didn't think they'd been herded. We thought they were just grazing free."

Bethane did not allow her expression to soften, but

she did relax just a little inside. Perhaps the children had not come to torment her, after all.

"Oh, you did, did you?" she muttered. "Who are you, anyway?"

The eldest boy drew himself up a little haughtily in the saddle and gazed down at her from his advantage of height. "I am Kevin, Earl of Kierney." He nodded toward the other brown-haired boy. "This is my brother, Lord Duncan, and that's Lord Alaric Morgan, Bronwyn's brother. You'd better let her go," he added, a trifle less belligerently.

"Oh, I'd better, eh? Well, I'll tell you one thing, young Earl of Kierney. You'd better learn some manners, if you expect anyone to respect you for more than that high-sounding title you bear. What's your excuse for chasing my poor little ewes?"

As the young earl's mouth gaped—she could tell he was not often spoken to in that manner—his brother moved his pony a little closer and swept off his leather hunt cap in a polite bow.

"Please pardon us, grand-dame. We are all to blame. It was thoughtless on our part. How can we make amends?"

Slowly Bethane released the little girl's arm, studying her and the three boys a little suspiciously. What was there about these children that raised her hackles so? Something fey, something she had not sensed in a long time . . .

But, no matter. Hitching up her greyed and tattered skirts, she leaned against her shepherd's crook and continued to eye them sternly, determined not to speak until all four had backed down from her gaze. She did not have long to wait.

"Very well. Apology accepted. And to balance

accounts, you can help gather up my sheep now, since you helped scatter them."

The blond boy nodded, no trace of resentment in his look. "A fair recompense, grand-dame. We'll see to it at once."

For the next little while, the children applied themselves diligently to the task at hand, eventually rounding up all the sheep they had scattered and even a few Bethane had missed. When they had finished, they spread their noon meal under a large tree across the meadow and settled down to eat. The little girl invited Bethane to join them, but the old woman shook her head wordlessly and retreated to her cave, overlooking the meadow. She wanted no such exalted company. Besides, the oldest boy, Kevin, obviously did not like her much. Only the little girl seemed genuinely concerned about an old widow woman's feelings, even bringing up a napkin full of fresh-baked bread and savory cheese when she and her companions were finished eating. She laid it on a smooth rock and made a graceful little curtsey before heading back down the hill without a word.

Bethane could hardly ignore such a gesture. Besides, she could smell the food. She found the bread soft and pale, so kind to old, jagged teeth and aching gums— bread such as she had not tasted since her youth, when she and Darrell first were wed. And the cheese—how he would have loved that!

With sweet memory for companion, she settled on a sunny ledge just outside the cave to enjoy the last morsels, basking in the summer warmth. The faint murmur of the children still playing in the meadow, the coolish breeze, and the glow of a full stomach soon lulled her to drowsiness, and the old eyes closed. With her wedding ring cradled close beside her cheek, she drifted. She could almost imagine she was young again, her Darrell lying at her side.

He had been a handsome man, perhaps the more so for being of the magical Deryni race, though she had been afraid of him at first. He had risked his life to save her from a life she still chose to forget. The love which had grown between them became a beacon for her soul, a positive focus for the knowledge which before had threatened to destroy her.

He had taught her things, too—a magic beyond the ancient lore of midwifery and conjuring and divination handed down to her by her mother and mother's mother. Though many of their methods had been similar, his powers had come from an elsewhere that she had never tapped; and she, in turn, had taught him how to bid the elemental forces—more homespun magic than the exalted theory and ceremony of the mysterious and much-feared Deryni, but it had worked as well, if in different ways. Together, they had dreamed of shaping a better world, where differences would not give others leave to kill. Perhaps their children would not need to live in fear, as they had done.

But there were to be no children; none that lived, at any rate. Too soon had come a renewed wave of madness in their village, condoned and even encouraged by the local lord. Darrell, unknown to be Deryni by most of their acquaintances, had been a teacher of mathematics in nearby Grecotha. With several of his Deryni colleagues, he also had been tutoring young children of his race in secret, though it was a capital offense against the law of Ramos if they were caught.

They had been betrayed. Agents of the local lord, all armored and ahorse, had raided the small farmhouse where the Deryni *schola* met and slain the teacher schooling them that day. More than twenty children were captured and driven like sheep into a brush-filled pen in the village square, for the lord's man and the village priest meant to burn them as the heretics they surely were.

She remembered the smell of the oil-soaked wood in the pen, as she and Darrell huddled in the crowd which gathered to see sentence carried out. She saw again the looks of dull terror on the faces of the children, most of them no older than the girl Bronwyn and her brother now playing across the meadow. Her stomach churned in revulsion as it had so many years ago, as a line of guards bearing torches marched out of a courtyard behind the square and took up stations around the captive children. The guard captain and the village priest followed, the captain bearing a scroll with pendant seals and cords. The crowd murmured like a wild animal aroused, but the cry was not of horror but anticipation. In all their number, there was no one to plead the cause of these terrified little ones.

"Darrell, we have to do something!" she whispered in her husband's ear. "We can't just let them burn. What if our child were among them?"

She was just seventeen, carrying their first child. Her husband's voice was tinged with despair as he shook his head.

"We are two. We can do nothing. They say the priest betrayed us. Even the confessional is not sacred where Deryni are concerned, it seems."

She bowed her head against his shoulder and covered one ear with a hand, trying to blot out the pious mouthings of priest and captain as holy words were spoken and writs of condemnation read. All pretense of legality and justice was but excuse for murder. The child she carried beneath her heart kicked, hard, and she cradled her arms across her adbomen as she began to sob, clinging to Darrell's arm.

Hoofbeats intruded then, and a disturbance behind them. She looked up to see a band of armed men forcing their horses through the crowd, more of them blocking the exits from the square—stern-looking horse-archers with little recurve bows, each with an arrow knocked to bowstring and more in quivers on their backs. At their head rode a fair-haired young man in emerald green, surely no older than herself. His eyes were like a forest in sunlight as he swept the crowd and urged his white stallion closer to the captain.

"It's Barrett! The young fool!" Darrell whispered, almost to himself. "Oh, my God, Barrett, don't do it!"

Barrett? she thought to herself. *Is the man Deryni?*

"Let the children go, Tarleton," the man named Barrett said. "Your master will not take kindly to children being slain in his name. Let them go."

Tarleton gazed back at him agog, his writ all but forgotten in one slack hand. "You have no authority here, Lord Barrett. These are *my* lord's vassals—Deryni brats! The land will be well rid of them."

"I said, let them go," Barrett repeated. "They can harm no one. How can these infants be heretics?"

"All Deryni are heretics!" the priest shouted. "How dare you interfere with the work of the Holy Mother Church?"

"Enough, priest," Tarleton muttered. At his hand signal, the men holding the torches moved closer to the pen where the children huddled in terror, fire poised nearer the oil-soaked brush.

"I warn you, Barrett, do not interfere," Tarleton

continued. "The law says that those who defy the law of Ramos must die. Whether it happens to these now or later makes no difference to me, but if they die now, *you* doom them to die without blessing, their Deryni souls unshriven. You cannot stop their deaths. You can only make it worse for them."

No one moved for several seconds, the two men measuring one another across the short distance which separated them. Bethane could feel her husband's tension knotting and unknotting the muscles of his arm, and knew with a dull certainty which ached and grew that Barrett was not going to back down. The young lord glanced behind him at his men stationed all around, then dropped the reins on his horse's neck.

"I never *have* liked the law of Ramos," he said in a clear voice, casually raising both hands to head-level as though in supplication.

Instantly he was surrounded by a vivid emerald fire which was visible even in the sunlit square. The gasp of reaction swept through the crowd like a winter wind, chill and fearsome. Tarleton reddened, and the village priest shrank back behind him, crossing himself furtively.

"By my own powers, which are everything those children have not realized, you shall not have those lives," Barrett stated. "This I swear. I can stop you with my powers, if I must, and save at least a few, but many others are likely to die who do not deserve such fate."

The crowd was beginning to look around uneasily for an escape, but Barrett's men had closed the perimeter even more tightly, guarding all exits from the square. There was no place to go.

"I give you this choice, however," Barrett continued, raising his voice above the rising murmur of dismay. "Release the children, allow my men to take them away to safety, and I will give myself into your hands as their ransom. Which will please your lord more? A handful of untrained children, who can do no harm to anyone? Or someone like myself, fully trained and able to wreak havoc any time I choose?—though I would not do so willingly, despite what I know you are thinking."

In the rising panic around them, no one heard Darrell's choked, "No!" except Bethane. Tarleton let the crowd seethe and mutter for several seconds, then held up a hand for silence. He was obviously unnerved by Barrett's implication that he was reading minds, but he put up a brave front, nonetheless. Gradually the crowd noises died down.

"So, the aristocratic Lord Barrett de Laney is a Deryni heretic himself," the captain said. "My lord was right not to trust you."

"Your lord must wrestle with his own conscience in the dark, early morning hours and answer for his own actions at the day of reckoning," Barrett replied.

"A prize, indeed," Tarleton continued, as though he had not heard. "But, how do I know that you would keep your part of the bargain? What good is the word of a Deryni?"

"What good is any man's word?" Barrett returned. "Mine has been my bond for a long as anyone has known me. I give you my word that if you allow my men to take these children out of here, I will surrender myself into your hands and I will not use my powers to resist you. My word on that. My life for the lives of those children. I am able to face my God on those terms."

"You must be mad!" Tarleton replied, a menacing grin beginning to crease his face. "But I accept your terms. Guards, allow His Lordship's men to take the children. Archers, train your arrows on my Lord Barrett and see that he keeps his Deryni word. I have never heard that magic could stop a flight of arrows."

A half-dozen archers stepped from their vantage points on the roof to either side of Tarleton and covered the new hostage. The other guards murmured among themselves, but they obeyed, moving away from the pen to surround Barrett, though they would not approach too closely with the green fire of his magic still flaring close about him. Methodically, Barrett's men rode in one at a time and took the children up in front of them, one to each man, until the pen was empty and the last double-mounted horse had disappeared at a gallop down the main street. Four men remained, arrows still knocked to their little recurve bows. One of them saluted Barrett smartly.

"Sir, your orders will be carried out."

Barrett gave a quiet nod. "I thank you for your service and release you from all other orders. Go now."

The four bowed over their saddlebows, then wheeled as one and galloped off the way the others had gone. When the clatter of steel-shod hooves had died away, Barrett swung down from his horse and began walking slowly toward Tarleton. The crowd parted before him, even Tarleton and the priest backing off a few steps. When he had approached to within a few feet of them, he stopped and bowed his head. The fire died around him, and with his left hand he drew his sword hilt-first and extended it to Tarleton.

"I keep my word, Captain," he said, eyes blazing at the other man.

Tarleton gingerly took the weapon and moved back a pace, and instantly half a dozen of his men were moving in to grasp Bennett's arms and bind him.

"His eyes!" the priest hissed. "Evil! Evil! Beware his eyes, my lord!"

As the crowd took up the cry, Tarleton gestured curtly to his men and turned to lead them back into the yard. Barrett held his head high, but he stumbled as the guards manhandled him away from the crowd.

Old Bethane shook her head in her quasi-dream, resisting the continued memory; but it continued to play itself out before her closed eyes, and she could not seem to open them and stop it.

In the yard beyond the square lay a blacksmith's shop, and just outside the shop, clearly visible from where she and Darrell watched in horror, a brazier held various implements of red-hot iron. To this place the guards of Tarleton led their captive, one of them pausing to pluck a glowing bar of iron carefully from the fire. Then the captive was hidden behind the ring of soldiers which closed in for his torture.

She did not see them blind him, though she knew that it was done. His scream echoed through the square, making her stomach cramp and the child move in her womb. Even as she was squeezing her eyes shut and trying to stop her ears against ever more agonized screams, Darrell was leaning close and pulling a hand away, speaking in a stern, urgent voice.

"*I* gave no word! I'm going after him. If I can get him out, I'll take him to Saint Luke's. Meet me there. God keep you, dearest."

And then, before she could hold him, he was gone, slipping through the crowd and vaulting onto Barrett's horse, the golden fire of his glorious shields blazing up around him as he and the snow-white stallion surged through the crowd and into the yard beyond.

Magic flared, shouts and screams choked off in mid-breath, and the crowd began to panic, pushing away through every exit from the square in mindless stampede. Bethane felt herself carried on their tide whether she willed or no, away from the yard, away from Darrell, and she wept, she raged.

She caught just a glimpse of his horse in the entry to the yard, rearing and screaming and lashing out with battle-trained hooves—and a limp, bloodied form slung across the saddle in front of her husband.

Then the rest of Tarleton's men were pressing close around him, he was breaking away, and the archers were firing at him as he spurred the stallion toward a street on the other side of the square, people falling beneath the hooves and the archers' arrows.

The screams of those around her sent bolts of terror shafting through her mind like the arrows of the soldiers, and she was running with them and screaming and—

Other screams broke through her consciousness, and she sat up groggily to see the child Bronwyn running toward her across the meadow, shrieking at the top of her voice.

"Grand-dame! Grand-dame! Come quickly. My brother's hurt! Oh, come quickly!"

As Bethane struggled to her feet with the aid of her staff, she could see two of the boys bent over the third, far across the meadow. The child was coming far too fast to stop, and nearly knocked her down as she flung her arms around the old woman's waist.

"Oh, come quickly, please, grand-dame. He's hurt! I think his arm is broken!"

She did not want to go. These children were nothing to her but nuisance. But something in the little girl's frantic entreaty reminded her of those other little faces in that long-ago village square, so she fetched her satchel of bandages and healing herbs and hobbled down the rocky hillside, the child tugging at her free hand all the while and urging her to hurry faster, faster.

The others looked up as she approached, the young McLain boy standing almost protectively. It was the blond one who lay on the ground struggling to breathe. The split branch dangling from a high limb overhead told most of the story. A glance at the odd angle of the boy's right arm told the rest. Kevin, the young earl, had had the foresight to slit the boy's sleeve from wrist to shoulder, but the arm thus exposed was already purpling along the bulge of the broken angle. The boy himself was conscious, but breathing raggedly. The fall must have knocked the wind out of him, as well as breaking his arm. At least she could see no blood. That was usually a good sign.

"Well, let's have a look," she said gruffly, heaving herself to her knees at the boy's right and laying aside her satchel. "Can you feel this?"

As she touched the arm above and below the angle of the break, he winced and nodded, but he did not cry out. She tried not to hurt him more, but his face went dead-white several times as she went about the business of assessing the damage.

"Both bones are snapped clean through," she said, when she had finished her appraisal. "It won't be easy to set, or pleasant." She looked across at Kevin. "I can tend it, but you'd best get back to your father's and bring men with a litter. Once it's been set, it mustn't be allowed to shift before it's had time to knit a little."

The young earl's face was pale, but a touch of the old arrogance still lingered in the clear blue eyes. "It's his sword arm, grand-dame," he said pointedly. "Are you sure you can set it properly? Shouldn't I fetch my father's battle-surgeon?"

"Not if you want it to heal straight," she replied with a contemptuous toss of her head. "Most battle-surgeons would just as soon as cut it off. It's a bad break. The wrong manipulation, and the bone could pierce the skin—and then he *would* have to lose the arm. I know what I'm doing. Now go!"

The arrogance was gone. With a sincere and now thoroughly chastened nod of agreement, Kevin scrambled onto his pony and headed off at a gallop. Bethane sent the other two children to find wood for splints, then settled down cross-legged to resume her examination of the broken arm. The boy's breathing had eased, but he still sucked in breath between clenched teeth when her fingers came anywhere near the area of the break. He would need a painkiller before she could do much more.

She pulled her satchel closer and began rummaging inside for the appropriate drugs and herbs, glancing at the boy from time to time through slitted eyes. She left her selection to intuition and was astonished to see that one of the pouches she had withdrawn contained a deadly poison.

Now why? she thought, staring at the pouch and trying to ken a reason. *'Tis but a boy, no enemy, no—*

Sweet gods and elemental lords! The boy was Deryni!

All in a rush, the old bitterness came flooding back: Darrell dying in her arms with the archers' arrows in his back; dying because he had felt compelled to try to save his Deryni comrade; dying because of those Deryni children.

And their own child, stillborn in the awful after-anguish following Darrell's death; and then, a long, long time that she lay sick and despondent at Saint Luke's, not caring if *she* lived or died, and something had snapped inside, never to be mended...

Darrell...

A choked sob welled in her throat, the tears spilling down her weathered cheeks as she pressed the pouch to her withered breasts.

Deryni children had cost Darrell his life. For Deryni children, he had taken the archers' arrows and died. Now another Deryni child lay in her power, helpless to defend himself from her just vengeance. Could she not have just this one life in exchange for her love's?

She reached behind her for one of the cups the children had left after their meal. The first was empty, but the second still contained two fingers' worth—enough to serve her purpose. The boy's eyes were closed, so he did not see her pour the measured dose from pouch to cup, or stir the greyish powder with a handy twig. She might have administered the killing draught without a qualm, had not the boy opened his eyes as she raised his head.

"What's that?" he asked, the grey eyes wide and trusting, though he winced as his arm shifted from having his head raised.

"Something for the pain," she lied, unnerved by his eyes. "Drink. You will feel nothing, after this."

Obediently, he laid his good hand on hers which held the cup, pale lashes veiling the fog-grey eyes. The cup was almost to his lips when he froze, the eyes darting to hers in sudden, shocked comprehension.

"It's poison!" he gasped, pushing the cup aside and staring in disbelief. "You want to kill me!"

She could feel the tentacles of his thought brushing at the edges of her mind and she drew back in fear, letting his head fall to the grass. He moaned, his face going white as he clasped his injured arm to his body and rolled on his side away from her, trying to sit up. She touched his shoulder and murmured one of the old charms to drain him of his strength, knowing he could not concentrate to resist it, with the pain—could only just stay conscious now, even if his training *were* sufficient to resist her spelling, though she doubted that. As she twined her fingers in his hair and yanked his head up-turned, the pain-bright eyes tried to focus on her other hand, as if his gaze might stave off the cup she brought toward him again.

"But, why?" he whispered, tears runnelling narrow tracks from the corners of his eyes. "I never harmed you. I never wished you ill. It can't be for the *sheep*!"

She steeled herself against his pleas, shifting her hand to pinch at the hinges of his jaws and force the mouth to open.

Darrell, my only love, I do it to avenge you! she thought, as the boy groaned and tried to turn his head aside.

But as she set her teeth and moved the cup closer, ignoring his groans and weakening struggles, the sunlight caught the wedding band on her hand, flashing bright gold in her eyes. She blinked and froze.

Darrell—oh, my gods, what am I doing?

All at once she realized how very young the boy

was: no more than eight or nine, for all his earlier posturings of manhood. He was Deryni, but was that his fault, any more than it had been the fault of those other children, or Darrell, or even the self-sacrificing Barrett? Was *this* what Darrell had tried to teach her? Was she mad, even to consider killing a Deryni, like *him*?

With a muted little cry, she flung the cup aside and let him go, burying her face in her hands.

"I'm sorry, Darrell," she sobbed, crushing her lover's ring against her lips. "I'm sorry. Oh, forgive me, my love. Please forgive me, my love, my life..."

When she finally looked up, drying her tears on a tattered edge of her skirt, the boy was on his back again, the grey eyes studying her quite analytically. The fair face was still pinched with pain, the injured arm still cradled in his good one, but he made no move to escape.

"You know what I am, don't you?" he asked, his voice hardly more than a whisper.

At her nod, the grey eyes shuttered for an instant, then turned back on her again.

"This Darrell—was he killed by a Deryni?"

She shook her head, stifling a sob. "No," she whispered. "*He* was Deryni, and died to save another of his kind."

"I think I understand," the boy replied, with a preternaturally wise nod. He drew a deep, steadying breath, then continued. "Listen, you don't have to help me if you don't want to. Kevin will bring the battle-surgeon, even though you said not to. I'll be all right."

"Without a sword arm, young Deryni?" She drew herself up with returning dignity. "Nay, I can't let you chance that. Darrell would never approve. How can you carry on his work without a proper sword arm?"

As his brows knit in question, she replaced the lethal pouch in her satchel and began withdrawing rolls of yellowish bandages.

"I won't offer you another painkiller," she said with a wry smile. "I wouldn't trust either of our judgements in light of what has already passed between us. I *will* set the arm, though. And I give you my word that it will heal as straight as ever, if you follow my instructions."

"Your word? Yes," the boy repeated, glancing aside as Duncan and Bronwyn returned with an assortment of straight pieces of wood.

As she sorted through them, picking four which suited her, she remembered that other Deryni's reply to such a question—*My word is my bond!*—and she knew that she, too, had meant what she said. When she had put the other boy to work whittling knots and twigs from the splints she had chosen, showing him how to carve them flat along one side, she glanced at the injured one with rough affection.

Something in her face must have reassured him— or perhaps he read it in the way Darrell once had known her innermost feelings. Whatever the cause, he relaxed visibly after that, letting his sister cradle his head in her lap and even appearing to doze a little as Bethane made a final inspection of the splints and bandages and prepared to do what must be done.

All three of the children were Deryni, she realized now; and as she bade the other boy kneel down to hold young Alaric's good arm, she sensed that *he* knew she was aware—though how she knew, he would understand no better than Darrell had. She had *tried* to tell Darrell that it was the ancient wisdom...

"Girl, you try to ease him now," she said gruffly, probing above the break and sliding one hand down to his wrist. "A pretty girl can take a man's mind from the pain. My Darrell taught me that."

He had stiffened at her first words, perhaps fearing that she would betray her knowledge to the others; but now he closed his eyes and drew a deep breath, tension draining away as he let it out. Bethane waited several heartbeats, sensing a rudimentary form of one of Darrell's old spells being brought into play, then gave his wrist a squeeze of warning and began pulling the arm straight, at the same time rotating it slightly and guiding with her other hand as the ends of bone eased into place. The boy's breath hissed in between clenched teeth, and his back arched off the ground with the pain; but he did not cry out, and the injured arm did not tense or move except as she manipulated it. When she had adjusted all to her satisfaction, she bound the arm to the splints Duncan held, immobilizing it straight from bicep to fingertips. As the final bandages were tied in place and the bound arm eased to his side, Alaric finally passed out.

Across the meadow, horsemen were approaching at a gallop. Bethane stood as they drew rein, her work completed. A man with a satchel much like her own dismounted immediately and knelt at the boy's side. Two more got down and began unrolling a litter. The fourth man, Lord Kevin mounted pillion behind him, gave the young earl a hand down and then himself dismounted. He was young and fair, in appearance much like her Darrell when first they met.

"I'm Deveril, Duke Jared's seneschal," the man said,

watching as the first man inspected her handiwork. "His Grace and the boy's father are away. What happened here?"

She inclined her head slightly, supporting herself on her shepherd's staff. "Boys will be boys, sir," she answered cautiously. "The young lord fell out of the tree." She gestured with her staff and watched all eyes lift to the broken branch. "I but lent my poor skills to right the lad's hurt. He will mend well enough."

"Macon?" the seneschal asked.

The battle-surgeon nodded approvingly as his patient moaned and regained consciousness. "An expert job, m'lord. If nothing shifts, he should heal as good as new." He glanced at Bethane. "You didn't give him any of your hill remedies, did you, Mother?"

Containing a wry smile, Bethane shook her head. "No, sir. He is a brave lad and would have nothing for his pain. A fine soldier, that one. He will fight many a battle in his manhood."

"Aye, he likely will, at that," Deveril replied, looking at her so strangely that she wondered for a moment whether he had caught her double meaning.

The boy had, though. For when they had laid him on the litter and were preparing to move out, he raised his good hand and beckoned her closer. The battle-surgeon had given him one of *his* remedies for pain, and the grey eyes were almost all pupil, the pale lashes drooping as he fought the compulsion to sleep. Still his grip was strong as he pulled her closer to whisper in her ear.

"Thank you, grand-dame—for several things. I will—try to carry on *his* work."

Bethane allowed herself an indulgent nod, for by the look of his eyes, he would remember nothing when he woke from the battle-surgeon's potion. But just as the litter started to move, he drew her hand closer and touched his lips to her ring—Darrell's ring!—in the same way *he* had always done, so many years ago.

Then the fingers went slack as sleep claimed him, and all the noble party were mounting to leave, the litter bearers gently carrying him out into the golden sunlight. The girl Bronwyn dropped her a grave curtsey—could *she* know what had happened?—and then all of them were heading off across the meadow, toward the castle.

Wondering, she brought her hand to her face and rubbed the smooth gold of the ring against her cheek, her eyes not leaving the departing riders and especially the bobbing litter. But by the time they had disappeared into the afternoon haze, the day's events were hardly more than dimly harkened memories, as her mind flew back across the years.

"Well, Darrell, at least we saved one of them, didn't we?" she whispered, kissing the ring and smiling at it.

Then she picked up her satchel and started up the hill, humming a little tune under her breath.

THE PRIESTING OF ARILAN
AUGUST 1, 1104 — FEBRUARY 2, 1105

The Deryni Bishop Arilan has been a subject of fascination for me ever since he showed up on Kelson's
Regency Council in *Deryni Rising*. I knew, from the beginning, that Arilan was secretly Deryni (though, at that time,
I had no idea the Camberian Council even existed), but
he wasn't revealed as such until *High Deryni*, and I doubt
Brion ever knew. Still, Brion's appointment of a very junior
auxiliary bishop to his privy council must have reflected a
close personal trust and friendship. (In fact, Denis Arilan
was Brion's Confessor at the time of his death—and how
he came to be so will be told in a future novel.)

Arilan's fellow bishops obviously didn't know he was
Deryni either, or he could not have been elected to the
episcopate. Indeed, had the Synod of Bishops known what
Arilan was, he could not even have been ordained a priest—
for, as part of the strictures placed on Deryni as a result
of the Council of Ramos, Deryni were forbidden to enter
the priesthood, on pain of death.

The Church obviously had some way of enforcing its
ban over the years—though Arilan apparently found a way

99

to get around it. The Deryni bishop states in *High Deryni* that, so far as he knows, he and Duncan are the only Deryni to have been ordained in several centuries. (One suspects that Arilan might have had a hand in getting Duncan through safely, though Duncan obviously never knew, or he would have known Arilan was Deryni.)

So, how did the Church keep Deryni out of the priesthood? What was there to stop Dernyi from being secretly ordained anyway? How did Arilan circumvent the ecclesiastical barriers to ordination—and what was the price? What justifications did he have to make, in his own mind? Did he have any regrets?

"Tell me," Duncan demands, in *High Deryni*, "did it never bother you to stand by idly while our people suffered and died for lack of your assistance? You were in a position to help them, Arilan, yet you did nothing."

Arilan counters, "I did what I dared, Duncan. I would it had been more. But . . . I dared not jeopardize what greater good I might achieve by acting prematurely." We can surmise by those words that the price was high.

Incidentally, two acquaintances from the Camberian Council of Kelson's day show up in this story, though they're introduced to the twenty-year-old Denis Arilan by first name only, and he knows nothing of that connection or even of the Council's existence at this time. Unknown to Denis, his brother Jamyl is also a member of the Council—but Denis knows only that Jamyl has powerful friends in high places of some sort, including but not limited to King Brion. We'll be seeing more of the Arilan brothers and their association with the Haldane Royal House in the CHILDE MORGAN TRILOGY.

THE PRIESTING OF ARILAN

I

The twenty-year-old Denis Arilan, vested for choir in black cassock and white surplice, did not know whether God really would strike down any Deryni presuming to seek ordination to the priesthood, but he was about to find out—or rather, his friend Jorian de Courcy was about to find out.

"Embue me with the garment of innocence and the vesture of light, O Lord," Jorian recited softly, from inside the new white alb Denis was pulling over his head. "May I worthily receive Thy gifts and worthily dispense them."

The linen smelled of sunshine and summer breezes, and fell in soft folds over Jorian's cassock as Denis helped him with the ties at the throat.

You don't have to go through with this, you know, Denis whispered mind-to-mind, as only Deryni could, the link enhanced by the contact of their hands.

Three other candidates were also vesting in the library of *Arx Fidei* Seminary on this balmy August morning, each of them also assisted by a senior seminarian, for the usual vesting area in the church sacristy had been taken over by the visiting archbishop and his entourage, as was always the case for ordinations.

What if it's true? Denis went on. *Jorian, listen to me! If they find you out, they'll kill you!*

Jorian only smiled as he took a white silk cincture from Denis and looped it around his waist, murmuring the accompanying prayer as he tied it.

"Bind me to Thee, O Christ, with the cords of love and the girdle of purity, that Thy power may dwell in me."

Jorian, what if it's true? Denis insisted.

Maybe it ISN'T true, Jorian responded mentally, in far more intimate exchange than mere speech would have allowed, especially with others nearby, who must never find out that the two were Deryni. *But we'll never know if someone doesn't take the chance. I'm the logical someone. I'm not highly trained like you are—nor ever wanted to be—so I'll be far less of a loss to our people if I AM caught. Being a priest is what I was born to do, Denis—and if I can't do that, I might just as well be dead.*

That's crazy talk!

Maybe. I'm not turning back now, though, when I'm so close. If I'm supposed to be ordained, God will look after me.

Jorian paused to recite another prayer aloud as he laid the white deacon's stole over his left shoulder and let Denis bend to secure it at the right hip.

"Oh Thou who hast said, 'My yoke is easy and my burden is light,' grant that I may bear Thy blessing to all the world."

And if I DON'T make it, Jorian went on mentally, *maybe you'll make it for me.*

Denis was too well schooled to let himself change expression, as Jorian slipped the maniple over his left forearm and secured it, whispering another prayer, but he knew Jorian was right. Though they had been careful to play down their friendship all through seminary, so that Jorian's fall, if it came, would not drag down Denis as well, neither of them had ever harbored illusions that things could end in other than this ultimate testing. *Someone* must be the forerunner, and Jorian was it. The Church had taught for nearly two centuries that Deryni must not seek priestly ordination, on pain of death, and that God would strike down any Deryni presumptuous enough to try. Tradition had it that He had done so, many times, in the years immediately after the onset of the great anti-Deryni persecutions, early in the tenth century. And every seminary had its horror stories, impressed on every entering seminarian, of what had happened to those who had tried since.

As a result, there had been no Deryni priests or bishops in Gwynedd for nearly two hundred years. None that Denis' teachers knew of, in any event—and they were in a position to know, if anyone was. But if Deryni were ever to reverse the persecution of their people and regain a place of dignity and shared authority in the kingdom, part of the impetus must come from within the Church, by gradually reversing the teaching that Deryni were evil because of the powers they could wield. That meant not only reinfiltrating the Church, but eventually assuming positions of high authority again. Denis Arilan's teachers hoped for nothing less than a bishopric for their prize student and had been relieved, if saddened, when the older and less talented Jorian de Courcy elected to clear the way for Denis by going first.

"Your attention please, reverend sirs," came a low voiced warning from Father Loyall, the abbot's chaplain, as he stuck his tonsured head through the library doorway and then stood aside.

As Father Calbert, the energetic young Abbot of *Arx Fidei*, came into the library with several members of his faculty and a few visiting priests, all eyes turned toward him, the four candidates making hurried last-minute adjustments to their vestments. Denis retreated with the other seniors who had been assisting, and all of them bowed dutifully as Calbert raised both hands in blessing and gave them ritual greeting.

"*Pax vobiscum, filii mei.*"

"*Deo gratias, Reverendissimus Pater,*" they replied in unison.

"Ah, such fine priests you will all make," Calbert

murmured, beaming with approval as he inspected his charges. "Choir, you may go and take your places while I have a few final words with your brethren."

Denis fell into line obediently with the other three, eyes averted, as was seemly, but as he passed closest to Jorian, he sent his mental farewell winging to the other's mind in a final act of defiance—not of Calbert, for he was a most learned and holy man, but of the outrage of a law that made this a day of dread for Jorian when it should have been a day of joy. Without physical contact to facilitate the mental link, and with Jorian not actively seeking it himself, the brief rapport took a great deal of energy, but Jorian's weaker but no less fervent thank-you made it all worthwhile in that instant just before the door closed between them.

Then Denis was out in the cloister garth and falling into line behind the thurifers and processional cross with his classmates, his voice joining with theirs in the entrance hymn as his heart lifted in a final prayer that Jorian might be granted his priesthood—and that God would not smite either of them for their presumption.

"*Jubilate Deo, omnis terra*," he sang with his brethren. "*Servite Domino in laetitia. Introite in conspectu euis in exsultatione...*" Make a joyful noise unto the Lord, all ye lands. Serve the Lord with gladness. Come before His presence with singing...

The Abbey Church of the Paraclete was packed, both because of the archbishop's presence for the ordination and because several of today's priestly candidates were of highborn families in the area—as was Jorian, though most of his blood relatives were dead. That had been yet another factor in allowing Jorain to risk exposure as he did today, for no ecclesiastical or civil reprisals realistically could be visited on the dead—

even Deryni dead. Numb foreboding accompanied Denis Arilan as he moved with the choir procession into the crowded church.

The altar blazed with candles. The candlesticks and altar plate gleamed. The familiar scents of beeswax and incense made Denis' senses soar with an old joy as he followed into his place in the right-hand section of choir stalls ranged to either side of the High Altar, hands joined piously before him.

"Bendicte, anima mea, Domino," the choir sang on, shifting to another psalm. *"Et omnia quae intra me sunt nomini sancto eius . . ."* Bless the Lord, O my soul, and all that is within me, bless His holy name . . .

The archbishop's procession seemed to go on forever; nor did its composition bode well for any Deryni discovered today in deception. The archbishop was bad enough—the fire-breathing Oliver de Nore, Archbishop of Valoret and Primate of All Gwynedd, who was known to have burned Deryni in the south during his days as an itinerant bishop—and two of the priests accompanying him were also gaining a reputation for anti-Deryni zeal. The worst was a Father Gorony, the archbishop's chaplain, already responsible for the ferreting-out and eventual execution of several Deryni. Another was a priest of rising prominence named Darby, newly appointed pastor of nearby Saint Mark's parish, traditionally a stepping stone to a bishopric for favored sons of the Church. Every cleric in Gwynedd had heard of Alexander Darby, whose treatise on Deryni, written during his own seminary days at Grecotha, had become required reading for all aspiring clergy.

But this was no time for Denis to dwell on the foibles of the visitors of *Arx Fidei*. Today was Jorian's, walking third in the line of candle-bearing deacons following at the trail end of the procession led by Abbot Calbert. Despite whatever fears the young Dernyi might have had about his impending fate, his plain, earnest face was suffused with guarded joy as he approached the sacrament for which he had spent his life preparing. Denis prayed again, as he had never prayed before, that Jorian might be spared; and for a time, it appeared his prayer would be answered.

No lightning smote Jorian de Courcy when he answered, *"Adsum"* at the calling of his name and came forward to kneel and hand over his candle to the archbishop with a reverent bow. His tongue did not cleave to his palate as he answered the ritual questions demanded of each candidate. Nor was he struck dead as hands were laid on his head in consecration and blessing, first by the archbishop and then by every other priest present, or when the sacred chrism was spread on his upraised palms.

When, vested in the white chasuble and stole of a priest at last, Jorian and the three other new priests gathered at the altar to concelebrate their first Mass with the archbishop, Denis began to believe they just might make it through without incident. But as Jorian, after receiving Communion from Archbishop de Nore, came forward with a ciborium to assist in administering to the school and congregation, the look of rapture on his face suddenly turned to one of surprise and then fear, and he stumbled.

"O sweet *Jesu*, help me!" Denis heard Jorian murmur, as the new-made priest blanched and staggered to his knees, catching his weight against the altar rail with one hand and nearly spilling the contents of the ciborium in his other.

Father Oriolt, one of the others ordained with Jor-

"My dear sons in Christ, it is my most painful duty to inform you concerning Jorian de Courcy," he said, his tone and the omission of Jorian's new title conveying chill dread to the listening Denis. "I have not been unaware of your concern. I wish I could tell you that Jorian is well—or even that he is dead. Unfortunately, I can do neither. For Jorian de Courcy, unknown to us before today, has been found to be a Deryni spy in our midst."

The disclosure was made dispassionately, with little inflection, but every man and boy in the church gasped. Denis, fighting down a panic that, unchecked, could have triggered a mindless and fatal bolt for escape, used his Deryni talents to force outward calm upon his body so that his reaction seemed no more than any of the others around him, but the clasped hands he raised to his lips in hurried prayer for Jorian were white-knuckled. As whispered reaction among the students shifted to louder speculation, Calbert held up a hand for silence, which was given immediately.

"No, none of us suspected before today. The Deryni are skilled in the arts of deception—but even Deryni magic could not deceive the Lord of Hosts! God has struck down Jorian de Courcy for his pride and disobedience, and God's servants will see that justice is done. Tomorrow, de Courcy will be taken to Valoret for trial before the archbishop's tribunal. Some of you may be asked to make deposition concerning his record here at *Arx Fidei*, for it is unthinkable that a Deryni should have penetrated this close to the Sacred Mysteries."

They were all but forbidden to speak of it further among themselves, but after Compline later that night, when everyone was supposed to be abed, Denis joined several other seniors just outside the dorter to question the newly ordained Father Oriolt, who alone, besides the archbishop's staff and the abbot himself, had seen what transpired in the sacristy after Jorian was spirited away.

"I don't *know* what happened," Oriolt was saying, as Denis eased closer to hear his whispered account more clearly. "I thought he'd just gotten lightheaded from the excitement, and from fasting since yesterday. I know *I* felt a little giddy. That wine the archbishop uses is potent on an empty stomach."

"But, why did he call out for help?" asked Benjamin, one of the seniors who had been serving at the altar and who, like Denis and most of the rest of those gathered, was due to be ordained in the spring, with the next crop of new priests.

Denis cautiously extended his Truth-Reading ability as young Oriolt shook his head and answered.

"I don't know. He was feeling dizzy. He could hardly walk. He almost vomited after we got him into the sacristy. I got his vestments off as fast as I could, figuring the heat might have gotten to him; but he was trembling like a leaf, and his pupils were huge.

"De Nore said we should try to give him some more wine, but that didn't seem to help. I was afraid he was going into convulsions, except that he passed out then. That's when de Nore told me to come back into the sanctuary with him, and that Father Darby would stay with Jorian while we finished the Mass. Apparently Darby's had training as a physician."

Some of the others asked Oriolt a few more brief questions, but the priest had already told everything he saw, and Denis knew it was the truth as Oriolt had perceived it. All of them soon dispersed to go back to their beds, for it technically was forbidden to speak during the Great Silence of the night Offices, but Denis lay staring at the ceiling for well over an hour, a growing suspicion gnawing at the edge of his mind as he considered what he had learned. The symptoms Oriolt had described sounded almost like poisoning, or—

Merasha! It was a Deryni substance, and not generally known to non-Deryni, but *merasha* could have produced Jorian's distress. *Merasha* was a powerful mind-muddling drug that the Deryni themselves had developed to control their own, centuries before. It acted only as a mild sedative in humans, but for Deryni, in even minute doses, it produced dizziness, nausea, and loss of physical coordination and it totally disrupted the ability to concentrate or to use the psychic powers ordinarily accessible to one of their race. Denis had been given the drug several times in the course of his advanced training, so he might recognize its effects and learn how to minimize them if ever it were used against him by an enemy; but even a trained response could not totally cancel out the resultant symptoms— and Jorian had not been well trained. Denis doubted his friend had ever even experienced *merasha* disruption before.

But if Jorian *had* been dosed with *merasha*, how had it been done? Could the Church hierarchy somehow have learned of Deryni susceptability to the drug and used it as their screening device for the priesthood, knowing it would be harmless to human candidates— and fatally revealing of Deryni who so presumed? Was "God's will" actually the Church's will that Deryni not serve as priests, thereby continuing to extend the restrictions laid upon the race in fearful backlash after the Haldane Restoration?

Suddenly he suspected how it had been done, too: the sacramental wine! Oriolt had commented that the wine the archbishop used was very potent. The implication was that the archbishop had brought his own— which, on the surface, was not at all illogical, since a bishop, traveling from parish to parish in the course of his duties, was apt to encounter any number of inferior vintages.

But if, by supplying his own, slightly adulterated vintage, a bishop might indulge a discriminating palate and also ensure that no Deryni slipped past God's will and got ordained—or, if a Deryni *were* ordained, he would not leave the altar without being revealed...

It *had* to be the wine. And de Nore had given it to Jorian twice—no, three times: twice from his own chalice and once in the sacristy, though at least the latter had not been consecrated. It was a scandalous, if not sacrilegious, misuse of the Sacrament the wine conferred, but it certainly would serve the aims of a human ecclesiastical hierarchy irrational with fear of Deryni and smug with the power that their exclusive access to the priesthood and episcopate ensured.

Denis shivered over the implications of his theory for several minutes, huddling miserably under the thin blanket on his bed, not wanting to believe it. If it was true, though, he had to know—and then figure out a way to circumvent it—for his own ordination was only six months away. He tried not to think about what would happen to Jorian, who had not been so fortunate.

Racking his brain to remember who had been

responsible for setup in the sacristy that morning, Denis conjured the faces of two of the younger subdeacons. One of them slept in another dormitory, but the other was a friend of his, one Elgin de Torres, snoring softly only a few beds down from Denis.

Scanning the long room carefully to make sure no one else was awake besides himself, Denis rose stealthily, slipped a church cape over his night robe, and glided silently to Elgin's bed. He knelt slowly at its head, grimacing as one of his knees popped, and cautiously touched one forefinger lightly to the sleeping Elgin's forehead just between the eyes, extending subtle control across the link thus formed.

Elgin, did Archbishop de Nore bring his own wine for Mass today? he asked, demanding the answer only as a thought—not words.

Immediately the memory of Elgin's time in the sacristy surfaced—images of de Nore's chaplain unpacking sumptuous vestments, a jewelled chalice and paten, and a common enough looking flask from which he filled the wine cruet that would go on the altar.

So! De Nore *had* brought his own wine! That didn't necessarily mean that it had been drugged with *merasha*, but it could have been. And all four of the newly ordained priests had drunk from the archbishop's chalice at communion.

But had the *merasha* actually been in the wine already, when Gorony decanted it into the cruet, or was it added later? Or it *could* have been added to the water cruet—in emotional terms, not as serious a profaning of the sacrament as tainting the wine, but the effect would be the same. Denis wondered whether, when Jorian had been given to drink wine a third time

in the sacristy, they had used school wine or wine from
de Nore's personal supply—for that would answer the
question regarding the water—but only Oriolt could
tell him that, of those he might safely ask, and Oriolt
had already gone to bed and was inaccessible, and
would be leaving early in the morning to take up his
new assignment as a priest.

Still, wine or water made little difference. *Merasha*
in the sacrificial cup was diabolical: ultimate betrayal
in the very sacrament the newly ordained priest had
just been empowered to celebrate. It was akin to the
horror story of poisoned baptismal salt used by a rogue
priest to murder an infant Haldane prince, around the
time of Restoration. Denis would never forget his shock,
the first time he'd heard of *that*.

Only, this was even more monstrous, to Denis' way
of thinking, for it put the principal sacrament of the
Church into question, if only for would-be Deryni clergy.
Only priests and bishops received both the bread and
the wine at communion—thank God for that, else no
Deryni would ever dare to approach the altar rail for
the solace and grace the sacrament conferred.

But with *merasha* in the cup, no Deryni priest could
slip through that first, concelebrated Mass with his
ordaining bishop without being betrayed. No wonder
there were no Deryni priests, and had been none for
all these years. How could a priestly candidate avoid—
or know to avoid—the very sacrament for which he
had sought to be ordained?

Denis shuddered as he withdrew from Elgin's mind,
erasing all trace of his tampering as he deepened the
younger man's sleep. He needed confirmation of his
suspicion. If he could sneak into the sacristy without

interference, perhaps he could find some clue to what had happened there—in the cruets, perhaps, if they had not gotten washed properly or at all, in the confusion and disruption of usual procedures following Jorian's apprehension.

It had to be tonight, though, or tomorrow's students assigned to sacristy duty would obliterate whatever faint hints their fellows might have left today. Denis was safe enough as far as the sanctuary, for seminarians of deacon and subdeacon rank had the privilege of going into the church to pray at any time, even during the Great Silence of the early morning hours. But if he were caught in the sacristy, he would have some quick explaining to do—especially with Jorian having just been found out that day.

But he had to take that chance. For if drugged wine *was* the key to the hierarchy's screening process to keep Deryni out of the priesthood, rather than direct divine intervention, then Denis or his mentors might be able to figure out a way around it. And if they couldn't, then Denis' only choices were either to risk the same fate as Jorian, or else to drop out of *Arx Fidei* and disappear altogether, his public usefulness as a secret Deryni forever compromised.

His mission to the sacristy appeared to be doomed from the start, however—at least for tonight. For when he slipped quietly down the night stairs and into the south transept, pausing in shadow to scan the front of the church, two of his classmates were already kneeling in the dim-lit choir stalls. And Father Riordan, the Master of Novices, was just coming down from the altar steps to approach them.

Damn! All Denis needed was for Riordan to tell him

to go back to bed, as he apparently was telling the other two in the choir, through silent signal. Denis would not be *obliged* to go, even if Riordan told him to, but refusal would only create suspicion where none yet existed. He wondered whether the novice master at least might be persuaded to break Silence and tell him something about Jorian—through purely conventional means of encouragement, of course—but he knew he would not dare to press the question if Riordan was not feeling talkative. Even now, Riordan was shooing his two truant students back toward the night stair in the transept—and toward Denis.

Fortunately, however, Riordan's mood seemed at least a little indulgent tonight, judging by the faces of Denis' two classmates who bowed as they passed, on the way back to their dormitory as instructed. And Riordan himself nodded sympathetically to Denis as he saw him and came closer, though he was already raising a hand to signal him to leave.

Denis put on what he hoped was one of his most sorrowful and troubled expressions as he bowed to the novice master, hands tucked modestly in the sleeves of his robe, hoping to make the most of his reputation as one of the school's brighter and more devout students.

"Forgive me for breaking silence, Father, but I couldn't sleep," he whispered. "I've been praying for Jorian de Courcy's soul. Can—can you tell me what will happen to him?"

Riordan stopped and crossed his arms on his chest, breathing out perplexedly.

"You know that breaking silence is forbidden, Denis."

"I'll accept whatever penance you require, Father,"

Denis murmured dutifully, averting his eyes briefly as
he clasped his hands at chest level. "But I—helped
him vest this morning, before . . ." He swallowed. "I've
been thinking about his soul. I thought perhaps my
humble prayers might help bring him to contrition for
what he has done."

Sighing wearily, Riordan turned to glance back
toward the altar, at the great, life-sized crucifix suspended above it, the pale figure of the Crowned King
on the Tree lit red by the Presence lamp that burned
before the tabernacle.

"I know, son. I've been praying for him, too," Riordan murmured. "I don't see how I could have been so
wrong about him. He seemed to have such a strong
vocation, to be so—"

Riordan shook his head bewilderedly and sighed
again. "In any case, they're already taken him to
Valoret. If it—goes as it usually does, they'll—bring
him back here for execution in a month or two."

Execution . . . the stake . . .

Denis shivered and bowed his head over his clasped
hands, closing his eyes against the thought, but the
image sprang up stronger still in his imagination. He
had seen a man burn once, when he was only a young
boy.

"I know," he heard Riordan murmur—and flinched
as the priest's hand came to rest heavily on his shoulder. "It's a terrible way to die. You mustn't dwell on
it. There can be only one consolation: that the flames
will cleanse him of his sins. And perhaps the prayers
of those who knew only his nobler side will help to
engage Our Lord's mercy when Jorian comes before
the Throne of Judgement."

Denis knew Riordan meant well, but it was all he

could do not to despise the man for his pious repetition of the same platitudes humans had been mouthing about Deryni for two centuries. He stumbled back to his bed almost blind with tears of rage that he prayed Riordan would attribute to his sensitive nature. He sobbed into his pillow for a long time before he finally drifted into uneasy sleep for the few hours remaining before Lauds.

More than a week passed before Denis finally found legitimate cause to be in the sacristy alone, washing cruets and sorting linens after a weekday Mass. By then, of course, no trace remained of the mischief of the ordination Mass. Nor had he expected any.

A week after that, however, Denis was able to convey his suspicions to his older brother Jamyl, come to visit him one balmy Sunday afternoon. Sir Jamyl Arilan was a rising luminary at court: friend and confidant of young King Brion Haldane, a newly appointed member of Brion's council of state, and, unbeknownst even to Brion, a Deryni of extremely thorough training. Jamyl had other powerful friends besides those at court, too— very highly placed Deryni connections who commanded even the men who had taught the two Arilan brothers in secret. Denis hoped Jamyl might enlist *their* aid in his behalf.

"Sweet *Jesu*. Den, if this were coming from anyone but you, I wouldn't believe it," Jamyl muttered under his breath, when Denis had imparted all he knew about Jorian's betrayal through words and psychic recall. "What you've described is incredible—and, if true, nearly impossible to counter without subverting the staff of every bishop in Gwynedd. Maybe you should just give it up."

The heavy weight that had grown in Denis' stomach

as he started his recounting rose to his throat. He had
been afraid his brother would say that.

"Jamyl, I can't do that. What reason could I give?
I'm to be ordained in February. I've done *too* well here.
If I left so soon after Jorian, they might suspect why—
and that could endanger all of us. Besides, I have to
do it for Jorian."

Jamyl bowed his head, flicking the end of a riding
crop against his boot as he stared at the ground between
his feet.

"It isn't going well for Jorian, you know," he said
quietly. "I've been keeping tabs on the progress of his
trial, but I can't do anything more direct. De Nore's
had his inquisitors at him ever since the night he was
brought in. The boy doesn't know enough to really
incriminate anyone besides himself—yourself
excepted, of course, and maybe me—"

"Jorian won't betray us—" Denis began hotly.

"Easy! I never said he would! They're running out
of patience with him, though. And when they finally
do—"

Denis swallowed hard. "I know," he whispered.
"Father Riordan says they'll burn him."

"Father Riordan is a perceptive man," Jamyl said
neutrally.

Denis fought down the lump in his throat and looked
away, blinking back tears.

"What about the king?" he ventured, after a moment.
"Couldn't *he* do something? He doesn't hate Deryni."

Sadly, Jamyl shook his head. "Sheltering the odd
Deryni at his court is one thing, Den; trying to pardon
one who's broken canon law is quite another. Brion
doesn't know about me—and young Alaric Morgan is

only half Deryni and son of a man who was close to
Brion's father. Besides, he's only thirteen.

"But Jorian de Courcy not only defied canon law,
he tried to undermine the Church's hierarchy. The bishops can't let that go by—and Brion can't meddle in
the affairs of the Church without endangering his own
status. The bishops traditionally have turned a blind
eye to the Haldane powers in the past—but they
mightn't, if a Haldane king tried to push too hard."

"What about your Deryni friends, then?" Denis
demanded. "They had us trained; they set up Jorian
and me to infiltrate the priesthood. They may not be
able to help *him*—and I'm sure he understands that;
we both knew all along that a risk was involved—but
now that I've found out what we're up against, why
can't they help figure out a way to counter it?"

"I'll see if they can," Jamyl said.

"You will?" Denis stared up at his brother in amazement. "Do you think they really could?"

"I can't promise anything, but I'll certainly look into
it. Can you get away for a few days?"

"Probably not until Christmas. Something important is supposed to happen around Martinmas—at least
that's what student gossip says. In any event, all home
visits are canceled."

"You don't know?" Jamyl said, an odd, strained
look on his face.

"Know what?"

"Martinmas is when they'll burn him, Den."

II

In the nearly three months until Martinmas, Denis
Arilan received but one brief letter from his brother.

To all outward appearance, the letter contained only family news. The seal on the letter gave Denis additional information, however—keyed by Deryni magic to be accessible only to a Deryni, and then only the specific Deryni for whom the message was intended.

The news was not good, though—not concerning Jorian de Courcy, in any case. According to Jamyl, the archbishop's tribunal had, indeed, condemned Jorian and set his execution for Martinmas at *Arx Fidei*, to make an example of him. But Jamyl's Deryni contacts, though unable to do anything for Jorian, had at least come up with a possible plan to help Denis.

They'll need to discuss details with you in person, however, Jamyl had informed him in the seal. *What we have in mind will be risky, both for you and for those who are minded to help you, but they are willing to take the risk if you are. Shortly after Martinmas, do not be surprised to hear that I am deathly ill and may be dying. That will be your ruse to come home for a few days.*

But before the journey home must come another, more terrible journey—this one Jorian's, not Denis'. True to Jamyl's prediction, the ecclesiastical authorities brought Jorian de Courcy back to *Arx Fidei*, that his fellow seminarians might see firsthand what happened to Deryni who attempted to circumvent the Law of God. No one, from the lowliest junior cleric of fourteen to the abbot himself, would be excused from attending.

Martinmas dawned clear and glorious, bright with the promise of a day rare in November, hardly a hint of coming winter in the early morning breeze. Father Riordan stood in for the abbot at morning prayer, for Calbert was already closeted with the archbishop and his staff, who had arrived with the condemned Jorian the night before. Afterward, Riordan led the school to the square outside the abbey church, where scores of students from neighboring schools and a handful of curious outsiders already had gathered to see a Deryni burn.

Denis hardly recognized his friend as the gaunt and stumbling Jorian was led in chains to the stake erected in the center of the yard. No bruises or stripes of the lash or other sign of physical torture marked his body, but Denis could almost count every rib, even from across the yard. By his slack expression and general air of disorientation, Denis guessed he also was under the influence of *merasha* again, and wondered whether they had kept him drugged all the months of his imprisonment.

One thing Denis knew they *had* done almost immediately was to suspend Jorian's priestly function, cruelly separating him from exercise of the only privileges that might have brought him some measure of comfort as his doom drew nearer. They were equally ruthless in ensuring that he did not even *look* like a priest. A breechclout of rough homespun was Jorian's only garment this morning—nothing that might be construed as robe or gown or any other item of clerical attire. As additional insult, he had not been allowed to shave or maintain his tonsure during his imprisonment, either. In a yard full of clean-shaven men and downy-cheeked boys, Jorian's was the only beard; and someone had raggedly hacked off the hair around his grown-out tonsure so that no hint now remained of where the tonsure had been—even that symbol of his former clergy status denied him.

Jorian de Courcy would die excommunicate and

without benefit of the Sacraments as well. Riordan had
read the instrument of anathema to the school before
morning prayers, in a voice so shaky with emotion that
it was almost unintelligible—for the novice master had
been fond of Jorian. Then Riordan had preached a brief
homily on conscience and compassion, never men-
tioning Jorian specifically, but making clear that com-
passionate men of conscience were free to pray for
whom they wished during the silent prayer that would
follow.

That small act of kindness and courage could have
cost Riordan a severe reprimand or even his position,
had anyone from the archbishop's staff overheard, for
official policy permitted no softness where Deryni were
concerned. But only students were present; and all of
them were far too shaken by what was about to happen
to think Riordan's comments at all amiss as they bowed
in silent prayer. During the next few minutes, Denis
had used his powers to spot-check the feelings of those
around him—ordinarily an unthinkable invasion of
others' privacy—and was comforted to confirm that
nearly everyone there truly grieved for Jorian's plight.
That give him hope that the long-held hatred of Deryni
might be abating where it mattered most, for these
young men and boys around him were the future lead-
ership of the Church; and where the Church led, the
people eventually would follow. Meanwhile, if Denis
could succeed where Jorian had failed, perhaps he himself could help turn the Church back to a course of
moderation and tolerance of Deryni.

That hope was little personal consolation to Denis
just now, however—watching the archbishop's exe-
cutioners chain Jorian to the stake. As they drew the
chains snug across Jorian's bare chest, leaving his arms

free, Archbishop de Nore came out on the steps of the abbey church with his chaplain and Abbot Calbert, the latter looking nigh to fainting already, for the world of academia did not prepare even abbots for what must be witnessed today. De Nore's appearance elicited a murmur of anticipation from the watching crowd, and Jorian shuddered visibly, though he did not look in the archbishop's direction. Denis tried to reach out to him in psychic comfort, stretching his powers almost to the limit, but the hazy contact with Jorian's *merasha*-fogged mind was unbearable, and he had to withdraw.

Almost weeping at the injustice of it all, Denis pulled back into his own mind in despair and hugged his arms across his chest, wishing there were something, anything, he could do to ease what lay ahead for his friend— but there was nothing. Jorian must face this final trial with only God for comfort; Denis was powerless to help him.

Fighting down the anger that could destroy him if he let it get out of hand, Denis forced his mind to the discipline of set prayers as de Nore stepped forward, crozier in hand, to preach a lengthy sermon on the evils of the Deryni, and how justice was about to be done to this particular specimen of the race. Jorian merely stood there numbly, hands unbound but dangling listlessly at his sides, as if he simply did not care any more—until de Nore finished, and calmly set a torch to the kindling piled around the condemned priest's feet.

A gasp, half of approbation and half of horror, whispered through the spectators as the flames caught, steadied, and leaped higher, fanned by an errant autumn breeze. Jorian stirred at that, the expressive hands lifting in a pathetic little warding-off gesture that elicited

derisive shouts and catcalls from some of the spectators, seeing it as but one more presumption from this
heretic Deryni who would be priest.

But then Jorian raised his eyes above the heads of
his tormentors and seemed to be searching for something along the roofline of the abbey buildings beyond.
Most of those watching undoubtedly thought he looked
for some hope of rescue or salvation, but Denis fath-
omed his intent almost immediately. Jorian de Courcy,
true to his faith even to the end, was searching for a
cross, and de Nore had had him bound so he could not
even see one.

If Denis had known how to turn his powers to
destruction at that moment, he cheerfully could have
blasted the archbishop into Hell for that—but he had
not yet been taught how, and would be grateful after-
wards that the temptation had not been a real one. The
noble Jorian meanwhile managed quite bravely despite
de Nore, tipping his head back against the stake, eyes
closed, and calmly crossing his hands on his breasts
as the flames licked closer to singe his legs and breechclout, apparently oblivious to the pain the flames must
have caused him as the heat intensified.

Denis could hardly bear to watch, but he made himself do it for Jorian's sake, determined to engrave this
event upon his memory for all time to come, that Jorian's example and the cause for which he died might
never be far from conscious awareness. Jorian de
Courcy was not the first or the last Deryni martyr to
human hatred and fear, but Denis thought he surely
must have been among the bravest. Even at the end,
Jorian never even cried out. Denis was sure he sensed
the precise moment Jorian's soul left his tortured body,
and he sent his silent farewell winging to his friend

even as the soul soared free and into the hands of God. And as the fire blackened and contorted Jorian's earthly remains, and the spectators murmured uncomfortably among themselves, a boyish voice from across the square shouted, "*Sacerdos in aeternum!*"

Sacerdos in aeternum . . . a priest forever. Even the Church dared not dispute the truth of that statement. Ecclesiastical writ might have suspended Jorian from his priestly function, but the holy imprint set upon the soul of a priest at ordination was no more capable of being erased than the anointing of a king. In fact, the very act of sacring a king dated from the time when kings were priests as well as rulers for their people, the rites of coronation gradually evolving from the priestly ordination. What God had conferred through the sacraments of His Church, no mere mortal could reverse, be the recipient Deryni or not.

The shouted phrase, *Sacerdos in aeternum,* then, was pointed reminder of that truth and produced a shocked silence in the watching crowd. Denis had no idea who had said it—though a reckless part of him almost wished *he* had—and no one afterward would admit to having said it, or come forward to betray who *had*. It was as if, in hearing that phrase, everyone present had been poignantly reminded that Jorian de Courcy *was* a priest forever, no matter what else he might have been; and only God could judge him now.

But though the jeering had stopped with the shout, and an almost reverent stillness descended on the square as a column of greasy smoke rose higher and flames enveloped the stake, nothing could cancel out the stark physical horror of what was occurring: the fiery immo- lation of a living being. All reason, both Deryni and merely human intellect, told Denis that Jorian de Courcy no longer inhabited the shiveled husk now writhing in the fire, blackened limbs contorting in the heat—that the movement came of the effect of fire on physical matter and not any desperate last stirrings of a living entity in agony.

But the sight and the stench of burning flesh stirred emotional responses not necessarily governed by reason or intellect, especially in the young. Nor could reason postpone more physical reactions indefinitely. Denis was not the first or the last to crouch with his head between his knees to keep from fainting, or to stagger retching from the square when they were finally allowed to leave, the pyre at last but a mound of smoldering ashes.

And the reek hung about *Arx Fidei* for days, even after Jorian's ashes were cast unceremoniously into the river nearby. When, a week later, in response to the expected news of his brother's ill health, Denis drew rein in the courtyard of his family's manor house of Tre-Arilan, outside Rhemuth, he imagined he could still smell the smoke clinging to his riding cassock.

"Well, I don't suppose there's anything I can say," Jamyl said quietly, when brief greetings had been exchanged with family and retainers and the two were alone at last in Jamyl's private study. "I won't ask you for an account of what happened, because you'd only have to tell it again in a little while. I'm taking you to meet some very important men tonight, Den. I hope you realize what a risk we'll all be taking—and what we've already risked for you."

Denis lowered his eyes, blinking back the tears he had fought to suppress all the way from *Arx Fidei*.

"How much did *he* risk, Jamyl?" he managed to whisper huskily. "It seems to me that he paid the ultimate price. I *won*'t let it be for nothing, even if I have to die trying to handle things alone!"

"I'd hoped you'd say that," Jamyl said, rising to come lay a comforting hand on Denis' shoulder. "And hopefully, there's been enough of dying. Come with me. The others will be waiting."

Denis knew about the secret passageway Jamyl opened beside the fireplace and followed his brother without question as the elder Arilan led boldly into the darkness, each of them conjuring silvery handfire to light their way. He had not known about the Transfer Portal in the little ritual chamber at the other end, however; and he was not expecting Jamyl's next request.

"I've been instructed to bring you through blind," his brother said. "I really have no business whatever taking you where we're going, but it's too difficult to transport one of the items we'll need. You must give me your solemn oath never to speak of what you see and hear. Nor will I be able to answer any of your inevitable questions, once we've come back—not about the place and not about the people. Is that under-stood?"

Denis swallowed uneasily, wondering what he was getting into.

"I understand," he said.

"I need your formal oath, then," Jamyl insisted, his deep blue-violet eyes never leaving Denis' as he held out his hands, palm up. "I need it very specific, fully open to my Reading, and I need it sworn by whatever you hold most sacred."

Awe sent a shiver down Denis' spine as the seri-ousness of Jamyl's demand hit home. He could feel the tingle of the Portal under his feet, the magic of his race all around him, and he opened wide his shields as he laid his hands on his brother's, inviting Jamyl's witness through the powers they both held.

"I swear by my vocation as a priest," Denis said softly, "and by the memory of Jorian de Courcy, whose priesthood I also vow to uphold, that I will never reveal any detail of what I shall witness tonight. This knowledge shall be as inviolate as that of the confessional. And if I break this oath, may I fail in all I endeavor and perish in the gaining of the priesthood that I seek. All this I swear, in the name of the Father, and of the Son, and of the Holy Spirit. Amen."

Only when the oath was completed did he lift his hands from Jamyl's to cross himself in blessing and kiss his thumbnail to seal it. He did not think he had ever sworn a more important or more solemn oath.

"Thank you," Jamyl whispered, lifting his hands to rest on Denis' shoulders. "I had no doubts, but there are others who must be absolutely sure. I'll take you to them now. You'll need to give me complete control for a few minutes."

With a blink, a slowly drawn breath, and a nod of agreement, Denis let familiar rapport form with his brother, relaxing all his shields as he exhaled. As his vision tunneled down to only Jamyl's eyes, nearly all pupil in the dim light of waning handfire, he could feel Jamyl's controls slipping into place, almost welcome after having to keep himself in tight check for so many months. His eyes fluttered closed even before Jamyl's right hand lifted to brush his brow; and the next thing he knew, he was aware that they had gone through the Portal, he had no idea where.

"Keep your eyes closed until I tell you it's all right to open them," Jamyl murmured, taking his right elbow and guiding him forward.

The psychic controls kept him from sensing anything about the space they crossed with their few dozen steps, and a part of him knew that even if he had been physically able to disobey and open his eyes, he would see nothing. He was blind and helpless until Jamyl should choose to release him—though that awareness caused him no concern in his deeply centered state. When, after what seemed like a very long time, Jamyl silently guided him to sit in a high-backed chair, a heavy table surface close in front of it, he had no idea what to expect. Thus he was not surprised when Jamyl had him place both his hands on what felt like a head-sized chunk of polished rock in front of him, and shifted one of his own hands to lightly clasp the back of Denis' neck.

"I'm going to bring two more minds into our link, Den. As soon as we're stable, I want you to let your memory of Jorian's ordination run—everything you yourself witnessed, and everything you learned or heard about afterward. We'll do it now."

Denis' assent had not been asked for and was superfluous in any case, given the depth of Jamyl's controls; but he gave it anyway, trying to actively bridge as the new contacts eased deftly into place, sensing the raw strength of the newcomers beyond even his brother's, though Jamyl was a powerful and highly trained Deryni. The surge of memories began almost at once, shaking him nearly as much as the actual events had done, bittersweet even in the recollection of the earlier parts, before disaster struck—but he would not have blunted them even if that had been within his control, which it was not.

He thought he had weathered it well when the run ebbed to a close, his controllers also having demanded his recall of Jorian's execution; but then they took him deeper still, until he lost all consciousness of any function whatsoever. When he came to his senses again, it was no gradual easing back to awareness; he simply was there, sitting in a chair opposite two men he had never seen before. The table he had sensed before was at his right now, ancient ivory banded with gold, and Jamyl sat perched on the chair arm at his left, gently kneading the tight muscles across the back of his neck, smiling.

Any discomfort besides the one I'm working on? his brother whispered in his mind.

Intrigued by the two strangers and what they had done to him—far beyond Jamyl's ability, he knew—Denis only answered, *No.* The younger of the other two men looked hardly older than Jamyl; he, too, was smiling, pale eyes lit with wry amusement, absently raking the fingers of one hand through a forelock of shortish, white-blond hair that kept slipping over one eye. His tunic was the same vibrant blue as the background of the shield above his head on the back of his chair—something with chevrons and arrowheads, vaguely familiar, though Denis could not quite place it.

The other man appeared to be in his forties, reddish-brown hair winged with grey at the temples, dark eyes very serious in his lean, angular face. He wore scholar's robes over an expensive-looking undertunic and had ink smudges on the first and second fingers of his right hand. He was leaning close to the table to drape a veil of purple silk over the biggest *shiral* crystal Denis had ever seen.

"It's a lovely one, isn't it?" the younger man said, his pleasant baritone catching Denis' attention instantly. "*Shiral*, of course. Don't even think about what it cost. Incidentally, I'm Stefan." He grinned at Denis' blink of confusion. "That's Laran, our physician; and the fellow sitting beside you is Jamyl. I think you know him already. And there's certainly no doubt that you're an Arilan, is there?" He shifted his gaze to Jamyl with a roguish chuckle. "Jamyl, your brother may go even farther than you, someday—if we can get him through his ordination, that is."

Denis swallowed a little uneasily at the light banter. He was not accustomed to hearing anyone besides family address his brother in quite so casual a tone. These men must be close, indeed. As he glanced at Jamyl for reassurance, the man identified as Laran sat in the empty chair beside Stefan's and pulled a stoppered flask from inside his robes, reaching across to set it in Denis' hand.

"That's all that's stopping you right now, young Denis Arilan," Laran said. "Incidentally, you were absolutely right about *merasha* in the wine."

Denis nearly dropped the flask as he realized he must be actually holding some of the *merasha*-laced wine.

"We've been wondering for nearly two hundred years how the bishops kept blocking us from getting some priests ordained," Laran went on. "We don't have to wonder anymore. Unfortunately, *merasha* is the almost ideal substance for screening out Deryni. There's no known antidote, before or after the fact—though we *can* minimize some of the nastier physical effects. In humans, right up to fatal dosages, it only acts as a sedative, the depth varying with the dose and the individual—in that sample, a little drowsiness, perhaps." He waved a hand toward the flask Denis held. "Nothing that can't be explained by simple reaction to strong wine on an empty stomach, in a system already keyed up by the emotional tension of the priestly initiation— and nothing to attract attention to a one-time use of a bishop's private stock of wine for a priest's first communion.

"For Deryni, however—and unfortunately for your young friend Jorian..." He sighed. "But I don't have to tell *you* what happened to him."

Shaking his head, Denis set the flask carefully on the table, then wiped his palms against his thighs distastefully.

"Is that from de Nore's private stock?" he asked.

"No, it isn't," Stefan said. "We haven't even tried to penetrate his staff yet. It will be risky enough when we *do* have to infiltrate, to do whatever we decide to do to help you. That's from another bishop's sacristy, though. And we've spot-checked two others." He grimaced. "They all have a special supply of wine that comes from the archbishop-primate's office on a regular basis and that's used only for ordinations. Needless to say, they're all adulterated with *merasha*. So we can't even consider trying to get you ordained in another diocese."

"I couldn't anyway, having trained at *Arx Fidei*," Denis murmured. "Not without having to answer a lot of very dangerous questions, especially after Jorian. What about switching the wine?"

Laran nodded. "We're working on that. We've even located some untainted wine of the proper vintage. Unfortunately, that isn't the entire solution."

"Why not?"

Laran shrugged. "Well, aside from the obvious logistical problem of actually making the switch without getting caught, there's the question of whether anyone who shouldn't will be able to notice a difference in taste. *Merasha* doesn't have any taste *per se*, but it does have a distinctive aftertaste, as we all know— not as noticeable to humans, I'm told, but nonetheless it's there."

"And you're afraid de Nore will notice, if it *isn't* there," Jamyl guessed.

"Well, he *is* known for his discriminating palate," Laran pointed out. "Not only is that a convenient excuse for bringing along his own wine when he travels and for sending special shipments to the other bishops as a sign of episcopal favor, but he celebrates enough Masses at enough ordinations to know quite precisely what his private stock should taste like. To keep a switch from being detected, I must find something that will give an aftertaste similar to *merasha*, that acts like a light sedative, but that also has no other side effects, for humans or Deryni—probably some combination of substances."

He sighed heavily, then went on. "Or maybe we'll have to go with pure wine and take our chances that de Nore won't notice something's missing. It's better than the alternative. We *know* what *merasha* will do."

"Maybe the pure wine isn't as risky as you think," Denis ventured. "I'll bet that's what he uses for daily Masses. He wouldn't dare use the special vintage every day, if only because of the sedative effect."

"Hmmm, he might have built up a tolerance to that,"
Laran argued, "but your point is well taken. Knowing
how de Nore feels about Deryni, and assuming that
even *he* knows just *what* makes the ordination wine
different—"

Startled, Stefan turned to look at Laran, his intensity cutting off the physician's speculation in mid-
phrase.

"Are you implying that he doesn't *know* there's *merasha* in the wine, or that someone else may be responsible for adding it?" he asked softly.

Laran fluttered ink-stained fingers in a gesture of
impatience.

"Either could be true, Stefan, or neither. That doesn't
really matter. It's been going on for many years, after
all, and individual archbishops come and go. Think
back to how it must have started, though!"

In the blink of an eye, Laran the physician gave way
to Laran the professor, academic intensity displacing
medical dispassion, his sharp features lighting with zeal
as he slipped into the role of lecturer.

"The religious question of good and evil aside, barring Deryni from the clergy served the inheritors of the
Council of Ramos very well," he said. "It concentrated
all spiritual authority in human hands, and a great deal
of temporal authority as well—an action totally jus-
tified in human minds, since everyone knew that Deryni
abuses of power had triggered the Haldane Restoration
and its aftermath. However *we* may deplore it, using
merasha thereafter to screen candidates for the priesthood was only a logical extension of what had already
begun. It was the perfect vehicle for ensuring that our
people would never regain power, for the effects of
merasha on Deryni, to those who did not know better,

would appear to be the wrath of God striking down evil Deryni who would dare aspire to the holy office of priest. All that was wanted was to ensure that it was used consistently."

"A charge that was given to the bishops," Jamyl supplied.

"Probably—at least in part. But since, in the greater picture, no individual bishop lives forever, I think it's worth considering that the Ramos Fathers might have set up some separate, secret, on-going body to be their deputies, to see that only humans rose through the ranks of clergy. Perhaps a small, elite religious order. Perhaps one that makes wine. Sheerest speculation, I suppose, but it bears further thought."

Stefan snorted and folded his arms across his chest.

"I refuse to believe that de Nore doesn't know what he's doing."

"Oh, he may know *exactly* what he's doing," Laran agreed. "That doesn't necessarily rule out a group to back him, however. Perhaps the secret is imparted to each new archbishop by some designated representative, whose job it is to ensure that his bishops use 'specially blessed' wine at ordinations and that they know what to look for. However it's done, it works. We certainly have no Deryni priests or bishops."

Even Denis could find no quarrel with that conclusion, though it almost seemed to anger Stefan. After what seemed like an eternity, Stefan slammed the heel of one hand against the arm of his chair and let out an explosive sigh. Laran only sat back in his chair, once again the cool and analytical physician, and glanced back at the flask of wine on the table beside them.

"Well, then," Laran said amiably. "Whatever we

may or may not have resolved while I played the professor at you—for which I apologize to all—young Arilan is probably right about de Nore declining to use his special wine on a regular basis. Even if it had no Deryni associations, the sedative effect could cause problems over a period of time. So perhaps his experience with *merasha* is limited enough that he would *not* notice a substitution of pure wine for tainted."

"*Perhaps* isn't good enough," Jamyl muttered, getting up from his perch on Denis' chair arm to begin pacing restlessly. "We're talking about my brother's life." He paced a few more steps, thumbs hooked in the back of his belt, then paused to glance back at them.

"I don't suppose we dare just interfere directly with de Nore?" he asked. "It should be possible to induce him to switch the wine himself and then bury the memory."

"Not wise at all," Stefan said. "Any tampering with de Nore could conceivably invalidate Denis' ordination, if it were ever found out what we'd done."

"What about someone on de Nore's staff, then?" Denis asked. "You already said you'd infiltrated other bishops' staffs to get samples of their wine. Doesn't that constitute tampering?"

"Of course," Laran conceded. "But they're not ordaining you."

"Well, here's another thought, then," Denis went on, seizing on sudden inspiration. "De Nore only has a sip of the wine before bringing it down for the new priests to communicate. It's his chaplain who finishes it off and performs the ablutions. Maybe you could tamper with *him*. *He* doesn't have anything to do with ordaining me."

Laran looked dubious, but Stefan slowly began nodding.

"The lad may have a point. What's the name of de Nore's chaplain? Gorony? It's *Gorony*'s taste we have to fool, Laran—not de Nore's. And it's Gorony who's in the ideal position to make a switch. What would it take to keep him from noticing a slight difference in the wine?"

"For me, or for you?" Laran replied, giving Stefan an odd look.

Stefan snorted, a sly smile flashing across his face so quickly that Denis was never sure he really saw it.

"We'll work on it," Stefan said enigmatically. "Meanwhile, it's getting late, and we should be finishing up. I do think Denis should know what he's getting into if we don't succeed, however." He picked up the flask of drugged wine. "Have you got a cup and some water, Laran?"

As Denis stared in horror, Stefan began working the stopper loose from the neck of the flask, Laran rising to leave the room briefly. Denis hardly saw him go.

Surely they didn't really expect him to take *merasha* without a fight, after what had happened to Jorian? He'd had the drug before, of course, in training, but this was different. This was the wine that had betrayed Jorian to his death!

"You may *have* to take it this way, if something goes wrong," Stefan said, answering Denis' unasked questions as he took the empty goblet Laran brought and slowly poured wine into it. "At least if you know what to expect, you may have some chance of hiding your reaction. We'll give you something to counteract what we can, before you leave tonight. Is that about right?"

He held out the goblet, a quarter-filled with dark,

potent-looking wine, and Denis tried to imagine it as de Nore's chalice, his heart hammering in his chest.

"You need to add water now," he managed to whisper.

Coolly Stefan took a second goblet from Laran, filled with water, and held it over the drugged wine, preparing to pour—then thought better of it and offered the water to Denis.

"You'd better do this. You know how much it should be."

Hands shaking, Denis took the goblet and poured—too much.

"You're going to have to add some more wine," he heard himself saying, as Laran took the water from him and began rummaging in his physician's satchel for a drug packet. "I added a little more than I meant to."

"How much would de Nore add?" Stefan asked, slowly pouring more wine until Denis signalled him to stop.

"I don't know," Denis admitted. "I've never served Mass for him—or for any bishop. I—think he'd deliberately go light on the water at an ordination, though, since—so much depends on the wine..."

His voice had trailed off as Stefan set the flask aside, and he had to clasp his hands tightly in his lap to keep them from shaking.

"I'm afraid I have to agree with your logic," Stefan said quietly, moving a little closer with the drugged cup. "Think before you drink this, now. How big a swallow would you normally take, and how small a swallow can you get away with, without arousing suspicion?"

Denis closed his eyes briefly, remembering de Nore's

huge, jewelled chalice. It would have to be a noticeable swallow.

"Here it comes now," he heard Stefan say softly, far closer now, as the rim of the goblet touched his lips. "Remember what I asked you."

Almost without volition, Denis lifted his hands to steady the cup as Stefan tipped it for him to drink. He had never received communion by Cup as well as by Host, for that was reserved for priests and bishops. The wine was rich and fruity, and he was not sure whether he could detect any of the expected *merasha* aftertaste at all as Stefan took the cup away and he carefully swallowed. Laran had come around behind him while he drank and monitored his reaction with a cool hand laid along the side of his throat.

"Well," Stefan murmured, handing off the goblet to an anxious Jamyl, "I'll confess I've never made a study of the size swallow priests take when they drink communion wine, but that seemed plausible to me." His manner was casual as he sat back in his chair, but his eyes never left Denis' face. "Try to keep from showing any distress for as long as you can," he said. "I would estimate you'll have an hour or more before you can safely slip away, if you have to do this for real. With any luck at all, though, that won't be necessary. Tell me, could you taste the *merasha*?"

He was tasting it by then, faintly bitter at the back of his tongue. He did his best to describe it, aware that Laran was delving deeper to catch every nuance of memory about it, but he could feel the drug gradually extending its tendrils of disruption into every corner of his mind, insidious and terrifying, even though he knew he was safe here. He lasted a little longer than

Jorian had, but not nearly long enough to have gotten through the rest of the Mass and subsequent celebrations safely. The dose was a little lighter than those he'd had in training exercises, but that only made it ease him into thrall instead of hitting him like a mountain falling on his head. He tried not to imagine what it had been like for Jorian, who had been given to drink from the chalice a second time—and then given more wine in the sacristy, almost certainly from de Nore's private stock.

His head was throbbing and he could hardly see by the time Laran took pity on him and gave him the second cup, to counteract some of the effect of the first. He never knew how Jamyl got him back through the Portal and into bed. He woke briefly at noon the next day, his head still pounding, but rose only long enough to relieve himself and take another dose of the sedative Laran had sent with Jamyl. He was mostly recovered by the second morning and had time for only a brief visit with Stefan and Laran before he must head back for *Arx Fidei*, his leave now exhausted. This time, the two came to Tre-Arilan, gathering conspiratorially in Jamyl's little ritual chamber.

"I wish I could offer you more encouragement," Stefan said, as Laran rummaged in his medical satchel and Denis watched apprehensively. "We have a plan that we *think* will work, but it's safer for everyone concerned if you don't know what it is."

He took an empty cup and a flagon of water from Jamyl and held the cup toward Laran, who half filled it with wine.

"What's that?" Denis whispered. "I have to go back to school in an hour or so."

"This is Laran's answer to Archbishop de Nore's nasty wine," Stefan said, passing the cup to Denis. "We need you to check it for taste, because with any luck, you'll be drinking this at your ordination instead of de Nore's. Do you want to add the water, or shall I?"

"I'll do it," Denis murmured, nervously adding the necessary amount. "What's in it?"

"Oh, this and that," Laran said with a grin—the first time Denis could ever remember seeing him smile. "I think the effect is a fair approximation of what a human experiences after taking *merasha*, though. You shouldn't feel much."

Denis *hoped* he wouldn't feel much, as Laran slipped into rapport to monitor again and he raised the cup to drink. It tasted about the same to him, even to a faint, bitter after-tang a few seconds after it went down— but then, his palate was not yet as well trained as he would like. At twenty, he was not yet a connoisseur of wines.

"Suppose Gorony *can* taste a difference, though?" he asked, as he waited for whatever effect was going to manifest. "Or suppose you simply can't make the switch?"

"Do you want to bow out?" Stefan countered. "There's still time for that, you know—though it may mean that Jamyl and his family will have to leave Gwynedd, if anyone ever suspects that the reason you left is because you're Deryni."

Denis swallowed hard, knowing what Jamyl's loss in the king's council could cost the slim gains their people had made in the last decade.

"If I'm caught," he whispered, "that will happen anyway. Jamyl, are you going to be there?"

Jamyl laughed uproariously. "Oh, yes, little brother. I'd hardly dare miss it, would I?"

"You're part of the plan, then."

"Part of the problem, part of the solution, I'm afraid."

"We'll do the best we can for you, Denis," Stefan went on softly. "God knows, no one wants a repeat of Jorian's fate. But if you're determined to become a priest—and we *do* need you so badly in that function—I'm afraid this is your only option."

"Why can't I know what you're planning?" Denis asked. "It's my life. Don't I have a right to know?"

"It isn't a matter of 'right to know.' It's a matter of the danger to the rest of us, if it doesn't work and you're taken. So far as we know, Jorian didn't break—and no one is saying that you would—but do you want to have to worry about that, in addition to everything else? If everything goes as it should, there'll be no reason for you to expect anything odd or different is going on. And if it doesn't—well, you'll know that, too."

That was precisely what worried Denis, but he had to admit that their logic was sound. What he did not know, he could not betray—and Deryni senses fine-tuned to the possibilities of the situation should keep him somewhat apprised of how things were progressing. Jamyl would be there, after all. He hoped his brother had a plan to get away if it didn't work, though.

"All right," he murmured around a yawn. "I'm game if you are. Will I hear from you before Candlemas?"

Laran chuckled and finally dismantled rapport, shaking his head as Denis yawned again. "You may—but don't expect it. Incidentally, how do you like reacting like a human?"

"What do you mean?"

"I told you that what you drank simulated the effect of *merasha* on humans. Feeling a little sleepy?"

Denis laughed and shook his head as he yawned again.

"I'm not going to nod off on my horse, am I?"

"No. It shouldn't get any worse than this. You'll be fine by the time you ride into the abbey yard."

But riding into the abbey yard was the *last* thing Denis Arilan was worried about as he made hasty farewells and set out on the journey back to *Arx Fidei*. He wondered how he was going to survive the nearly three months until Candlemas—and whether three months would be enough time for the others to do what *they* needed to do.

III

On the morning slated for his ordination, Denis Arilan found himself outwardly calm as Elgin de Torres helped him vest in a corner of the library. The calm had a numb edge to it, however, for he had heard nothing from his hoped-for saviors or even from his brother since leaving Tre-Arilan in late November. That visit home had cost him his Christmas leave, ostensibly because of his impending ordination and the gap the absence had left in his studies. Denis hoped those were the only reasons and had tried hard not to think about what his allies' silence might mean.

Suppose something had happened to prevent them from executing their plan—whatever the plan was. What if his fate was to be the same as Jorian's, betrayed unto death even in the midst of the joy he had yearned for all his life, in this culmination of his reach toward the priesthood?

He tried to pray as he settled the deacon's stole over his shoulder and let Elgin secure it at his waist, repeating the appropriate words by rote, but he could not get Jorian out of his mind. Nor, he suspected, could any of the other four priestly candidates vesting with him, each one more silent than the next. Jorian's fate haunted every seminarian at *Arx Fidei*, though no one but Denis knew that it had been men, not God, who had betrayed the unfortunate Deryni priest. In ethics class, Charles FitzMichael, Denis' chief competition for top academic honors, had even been bold enough to ask what would happen to someone who did not know he was Deryni, and sought ordination. Would a just but loving God strike down such an unwitting innocent?

Abbot Calbert could supply no ready answer to that one; and his inability had half the school walking on eggshells for the next week—for it was perfectly possible *not* to know, given the persecutions of the last two hundred years and the fact that many Deryni had simply gone underground, hiding and denying their talents, never telling children or grandchildren who and what they really were. Why, *anyone* could be Deryni and not be aware of it!

That was the theory, in any case. Denis tended to think that anyone of Deryni blood would at least *suspect*, especially if trained in the meditation techniques and mental disciplines that clergy candidates were expected to master—but that did not alter the importance of the original question. *Would* a loving but just God strike down an unwitting transgressor, if man did not?

In whispered consultations snatched between classes, or enroute to chapel, or after everyone was supposed to be abed, most of Denis' classmates eventually agreed, albeit uncomfortably, that God's justice and His love might, indeed, be at odds in such a situation—and who could say which way He would tip the balance? After all, God's Church *had* forbidden Deryni to seek the priesthood; therefore, it would be *just* for Him to punish anyone arrogant enough to defy that ban.

But the opposite argument held equal weight. For if God was infinitely loving as well as infinitely just, would He—*could* He—punish a loving son who disobeyed out of ignorance rather than arrogance?

The logic did not help Denis, who knew full well what he was doing, but it gave some comfort to Charles, Benjamin, and the other two being ordained—Melwas and a heavy-set Llanneddi boy named Argostino. Denis could only pray that his own concept of justice matched God's, and that he and the other Deryni who tried to serve that justice would be able to circumvent the impediments put in their way by human fear and hatred.

A partial answer to that last prayer, at least, came most unexpectedly when Abbot Calbert came into the library for his customary final words with the priestly candidates, accompanied by school faculty and several unfamiliar priests. For one of the priests looked suspiciously like the Deryni Stefan—though he walked with a slight limp, and his hair was peppery brown instead of fair.

Denis tried to steal a closer look at the man as the juniors filed out and Calbert bade them all draw nearer, but he dared not be too obvious. Nor was he sure he dared attempt a psychic contact to test, for some humans could sense such a touch.

Calbert seemed to talk for hours, most of his words running into a senseless blur. Only when he had finished and was motioning the five of them to fall into line, did the stranger-priest finally meet Denis' eyes and confirm that he was Stefan.

There are lots of strange priests here today, came Stefan's clear thought as he brushed Denis' shoulder in passing, as if helping shepherd the line of candidates out of the library to join the entrance procession. *The archbishop thinks I'm one of Calbert's, and Calbert thinks I came with de Nore. Stay calm. The switch WILL be made.*

Stefan was moving off with the other priests almost before Denis could register what had been said.

The switch *will* be made! Then, it had *not yet been made!* What if they could not make it?

He could feel a trembling start in the pit of his stomach as he inched along in the entrance procession, second in line, and he thought his heart must be pounding loud enough to drown out the choir's *"Confitebor tibi, Domine, in toto corde meo"*—I will praise Thee, O Lord, with my whole heart. One of the juniors handed him a lighted candle as he passed through the doors into the church, and he made himself use the warmth and flicker of the flame and the faint, honey-sweet scent of beeswax to help him steady his nerves. He must not let his own fear betray him.

He tried not to notice that the church was even more packed than last time. A bishop's visit to a local parish always brought a large turnout, but he suspected that some of the crowd, at least, had been drawn not by de Nore's presence, but by the stories of what had happened at the last *Arx Fidei* ordination. People were standing in the side aisles. Denis wondered desperately where Jamyl was.

He soon guessed Jamyl's part in the operation, however. For as the procession moved slowly down the aisle, heralded by processional crosses, candles, censers, and the voices of the choir continuing their hymn of praise, Denis noticed Malachi de Bruyn and another junior waiting to move a small, white-draped table into the center aisle after he and the other candidates had passed. On the table, with extra ciboria containing bread to be consecrated during the Mass, were the cruets of wine and water that would be used.

Of course! After the ordination itself, members of the new priests' families traditionally brought forward the gifts of bread and wine for communion. Jamyl undoubtedly would be among them. Denis had no idea how his brother was going to do it, but it must be *Jamyl* who was going to make the switch.

He felt a little relieved at that—and even more relieved when he actually *saw* Jamyl standing near the altar rail, left of the aisle. Jamyl's wife and son were not with him, but Denis had not expected that they would be, given the danger to everyone of Arilan name if Denis were found out. Jamyl was to have sent them to safety at Christmastime, there to remain until all of this was resolved.

But, could that possibly be *King Brion* standing at Jamyl's left? Dear God, surely the *king* was not in on this, too?

It *was* Brion, he quickly realized, as he took his place with the others in a line across the foot of the chancel steps, just outside the altar rail, and knelt with his candle held reverently before him. Jamyl's friendship with the king must be even closer than Denis had dreamed, for it was a singular honor for the king to attend an ordination. *Everyone* seemed aware of the royal presence. Perhaps *that* was the reason for the heavy attendance this morning, and not the ghoulish hope of seeing another Deryni brought to light. Even the archbishop paused to bow in the king's direction before taking his seat to examine the candidates.

Denis went through the next half hour in a daze. He responded to the ritual questions with ritual answers when called upon. He prostrated himself with the others for what seemed like an interminable litany to more saints than he had ever heard of. And then, after the archbishop had set his hands on the head of each kneeling candidate for the first time, he remained bowed with his fellow ordinands while all the other priests present came forward to touch each new priest in additional blessing. He let himself read psychic impressions as each pair of hands rested briefly on his head and then moved on to the next man, both bewildered and heartened by what he sensed.

Nervousness in some . . . uncertainty . . . rote performance of an expected physical action in many . . . preoccupation bordering on outright boredom in a very few . . . but in most, regardless of any other emotions, a genuine intention and desire to transmit the unbroken succession of apostolic authority as it had been passed to each participating priest at his own ordination, through a variety of bishops of varying degrees of integrity and sanctity, over a period spanning more than fifty years. At least *that* magic—of passing on the Divine mandate—was permitted, even by the most conservative of the ecclesiastical hierarchy, just as no

one would dispute the magic of the eucharistic celebration that would follow.

Stefan, too, came forward—not really a priest, of
course, but his lack of true priestly authority in no way
detracted from what the others did, and his message
strengthened Denis' hope as the Deryni adept briefly
laid his hands on Denis' bowed head.

Everything is going fine, Stefan told him. *Be of good
cheer. And may God bless and defend you, young
Deryni priest!*

Denis basked in that appellation all through the rest
of the ordination ceremony, even daring to let himself
get caught up in the very un-Deryni magic as his hands
were anointed with the sacred chrism, the more worthily to handle the eucharistic elements, and he was
invested with the chasuble and other physical accoutrements of a priest. God did not strike him dead on the
spot for his presumption—but then, neither had He
struck Jorian until the new priest tried to exercise his
priesthood.

As the moment approached for Denis to do so, he
knew with a cold and humble sobriety that his own
moment of testing was still to come. The archbishop's
treachery aside, who was to dictate *when* an angry God
might exercise His judgment? For that matter, who was
to say that *merasha* itself was not the instrument of
God's wrath? God usually chose to work through mortal agents. What need had He to work outright miracles, when more usual vehicles were at hand?

The Mass resumed where it had left off before the
ordination began. As the choir sang the Offertory, Denis
stood beside the archbishop with his newly ordained
brethren, facing the congregation, and watched Jamyl
and other representatives of the new priests' families

come forward with the gifts of bread and wine. Jamyl had contrived to carry the wine cruet—the other presenters' deference undoubtedly nudged in the proper direction by subtle Deryni persuasion—but Denis could read no hint on his brother's face as to whether he had been able to make the switch. Nor, when Jamyl gave him the cruet, could he coax any kind of mental confirmation as their hands brushed. Jamyl's shields were rigid.

Denis feared the worst. Why else would Jamyl shut him out? Praying that he did not bear his own death in his hands, he set the cruet on the tray the archbishop had received from Benjamin's elderly mother and tried not to stare as de Nore turned briefly to hand tray and cruets to the waiting Father Gorony, who took them back to the altar. His heart was in his throat as he moved mechanically into the place assigned him for the concelebration and watched de Nore offer up the bread, numbly repeating the accompanying prayer with the others.

"*Suscipe, sancte Pater, omnipotens aeterne Deus, hanc immaculatam hostiam...*" Holy Father, almighty and everlasting God, accept this unblemished sacrificial offering, which I, Thy unworthy servant, make to Thee, my living and true God...

The cup was next. With ponderous care, de Nore let Gorony pour wine from the cruet into his great, jewelled chalice, then blessed the water and added but a few drops.

"*Offerimus tibi, Domine, calicem salutaris...*" We offer Thee, Lord, the chalice of salvation...

Denis feared it might not be *his* chalice of salvation—not in *this* world, at any rate—but there was no turning back now. If the switch had not been made, his only remaining hope was a miracle. Denis believed in miracles, but he did not think he had ever been singled out personally as the subject of one. And a miracle had not saved Jorian, who Denis felt had been far more deserving.

He followed numbly through the censing, the lavabo, and the prayers that followed, reciting all the proper words and making all the proper physical responses, but setting his heart on but one plea.

O Lord my God, in You do I put my trust, he prayed. *Save me from all them that persecute me, and deliver me . . . If I can truly serve You best with my death, then I freely offer it, even as I offer this bread and wine upon Your altar—but can I not serve You even better with my life . . . ?*

The choir sang the *Sanctus,* more sweetly than Denis had ever heard it sung—*Holy, Holy, Holy*—and he tried to let the joy it evoked buoy him as he lifted his hands toward the pale, fragile Host the archbishop raised in mystical adoration, whispering the words of consecration with every iota of his faith.

"Hoc est einem corpus meum." This is my body . . .

The chime of the sacring bell plunged him into profound reverence as he and his fellow priests followed the archbishop's bows and elevation, and he hardly dared to look at the chalice the archbishop raised next, faith and fear tumbling wildly in his heart as he echoed de Nore's words.

"Simili modo postquam coenatum est, accipiens et hunc praeclarum Calicem in sanctas ac venerabiles manus suas." In like manner, when He had supped, He took this goodly cup into His holy and venerable hands . . .

Help, Lord, for the godly man ceaseth; for the faithful fall from among the children of men! Denis prayed.

"*Hic est einem calix sanguinis mei . . .*" This is the chalice of my blood, of the new and everlasting covenant, a mystery of faith. It shall be shed for you and many others so that sins may be forgiven. Whenever you shall do these things, you shall do them in memory of me . . .

In a magic that had nothing to do with being either Deryni or human, Denis *became* the sacrifice in that instant, offering up his own life's blood in unreserved dedication, as the Christ had offered His and Jorian had offered his. A profound peace filled him as he followed the rest of the prayers leading to communion and then knelt with the others to receive first the bread and then the wine. The Host was light as dew on his tongue; and he allowed himself but one thought as de Nore brought the great chalice to his lips and he reached up to lightly steady it.

Into Thy hands, O Lord, I commend my spirit. May it be done according to Thy will . . .

"*Sanguis Domini nostri Jesu Christi custodiat animam tuam in vitam aeternam,*" de Nore murmured. May the blood of Our Lord Jesus Christ preserve thy soul unto everlasting life . . .

Barely mouthing his "Amen," Denis drank from the cup. The wine was sweet and heady, lighter than he remembered, igniting a gentle but growing tingle that spread from his stomach, up his spinal column, and out to the tips of his fingers and toes, to explode at the back of his head in a starburst of warmth and light and love—and it was not *merasha*.

Light seemed to fountain from the vessels still on

the altar, from the tabernacle on the credence shelf behind it, from the chalice de Nore carried back to the altar, and Denis sensed a similar energy pulsing through the bodies of all those assembled to assist. Benjamin and Melwas, kneeling reverently to either side of him, had the same glow; and the ciborium de Nore set solemnly in his hands a few minutes later throbbed gently with a rhythm that was the heartbeat of the universe, silvery radiance spilling from the cup to bathe his hands in light that apparently only he could see.

He felt as if he was floating a handspan off the ground as he rose to go down to the communion rail where his brother waited with the other members of the new priests' families to receive the Sacrament. Indeed, he made certain he was *not* floating, for the way he felt—his Deryni powers not only intact but apparently enhanced—he thought he *could* have, given even a whit more provocation. The intimacy of the moment in which, a priest at last, he gave his brother Holy Communion for the first time, was almost too much joy to contain, the awe and wonder on Jamyl's face a sight he would cherish until the day he died.

And when the king slipped in to kneel beside Jamyl, pointedly turning his face toward Denis when de Nore would have come to claim the privilege, Denis could only marvel silently at the sign of royal favor. To give the Sacrament to his king set yet another seal on this most glorious and blessed day of his life.

His perceptions gradually diminished to more normal levels as he settled into ministering to the other communicants come forward to receive, and he sensed a slight lethargy stealing along his limbs as he neared the end, but that was surely from sheer physical fatigue and Laran's medicines, not *merasha*'s insidious corruption. The sedative effect was stronger than he had expected from the one sample he'd had from Laran, but not uncomfortably so—though he did see Charles stifle a yawn, a little farther along the rail, and sensed Melwas and Argostino fighting drowsiness, too.

Physical after-reaction threatened more insistently as he returned to the altar to surrender his ciborium, but he was able to counteract much of it by running through a brief fatigue-banishing spell as he knelt with his brethren to watch de Nore and Gorony consolidate the contents of all the ciboria into one and place it in the tabernacle. Then de Nore returned to his faldstool to kneel in meditation while Gorony performed the final ablutions—the last opportunity for something to go wrong. For if Gorony detected any difference in the taste of the wine...

Fortunately, the nervous seminarian who came forward to pour the wine and water for Gorony was clumsy, and the wine cruet slipped from his shaking fingers and shattered on the marble floor before he or anyone else could prevent it. Gorony's obvious impatience was distracted by the king choosing that moment to rise and slip quietly back up the aisle with his attendants, to escape before the crowds began to leave, and the archbishop's chaplain simply signalled for more wine to be brought from the sacristy—by Stefan, who sternly escorted the disgraced seminarian back into the sacristy, where Deryni persuasion undoubtedly dealt with whatever memory he might have had of his "accident" having been commanded.

"How did you do it?" Denis was finally able to ask his brother later that night, when an oddly tense Jamyl drew him aside for a few moments during the celebration feast, both of them confirming with Deryni senses that they could not be overheard. "It must have been when you brought the cruet forward at the Offertory."

Solemnly, Jamyl shook his head. "I didn't do it, Denis," he whispered. "I couldn't. They were watching too closely. I don't know what happened, but you drank *merasha* and you weren't affected."

"*What?*"

The king chose that moment to come up to Denis for a blessing, curtailing all further discussion with Jamyl, but Denis pondered the implications of Jamyl's revelation for the rest of the evening and, later that night, knelt in trembling question and thanksgiving in the now deserted church.

Or, no, not deserted. The red lamp burning before the tabernacle reminded him of that—if ever he could have forgotten it after what had happened. And as he lifted his eyes timidly to the Crowned King on the cross above the altar, he knew that he had experienced as much of a miracle as any man could ever hope for— and that he would spend the rest of his life trying to serve the purpose of the One Who had spared him today.

O Lord, I am Deryni, but I am also Your child, he prayed. *And though I never really doubted, now I truly believe You have ordained the time to bring Your other Deryni children back into an equal partnership with the sons of humankind—for You have saved me from the wrath of men who would misuse Your Sacrament to destroy me. For this salvation, I give You thanks.*

He swallowed with difficulty and eased back on his heels, trying to still the trembling of his clasped hands.

I think perhaps we Deryni are not really so different from other men after all, Lord, he went on more boldly, searching the serene Face. *You give us gifts the humans*

*do not understand and therefore fear—and some among
our number have, indeed, abused their gifts in the past,
and doubtless will do so in the future—but so doth
mankind in his frailty abuse many other gifts not unique
to the Deryni. We ask no special favor, Lord—only,
let us be judged by our fellows and by You on our
individual merits and failings, and not on the merits
and failings of our race.*

He bowed his head and closed his eyes.

*Adsum, Domine—here am I, Lord. You called me
in the hour of my begetting, and today I have publicly
answered that call and bound me to Your service. Nor
did You forsake me in my hour of need. Give me wisdom and strength, Lord, to know Your will and to do
it as best I can, that I may always be Your true priest
and servant, ministering to all Your children, both
human and Deryni, with tolerance, compassion, and
love . . . That IS why You saved me—isn't it?*

In days to come, whenever he returned to the memory of that jumbled monologue with God, he would
never be really certain whether his imagination had
gotten the better of him, or whether, as he raised his
head, his eyes swimming with tears, the image of the
Sacred King actually had given a slight nod.

LEGACY
JUNE 21, 1105

One of the pivotal events mentioned in *Deryni Rising* and the succeeding books of THE CHRONICLES OF THE DERYNI—though it takes place some fifteen years before the trilogy begins—is King Brion Haldane's slaying of the Marluk, Charissa's father, in a magical confrontation. From the Haldane point of view, of course, the Marluk only got what he deserved, after daring to challenge the rightful King of Gwynedd for his throne and crown.

Quite naturally, the Marluk's supporters disagreed, even as his heiress prepared to take up his fight when she came of age, for both father and daughter came of the senior branch of the House of Festil, whose rival claim to Gwynedd's crown dated from the days immediately post-Interregnum—never mind that the Festils had usurped the throne from a Haldane king in the first place. For more than two hundred years, the descendants of Mark of Festil, the son gotten by Imre, the last Festillic king, on his sister Ariella, stubbornly chose to argue that Cinhil Haldane and his successors were the usurpers, overlooking—especially after a few generations had passed—the stigma

158

normally attached to the offspring of an incestuous brother-sister union.

"Legacy" tells a part of that early story, but from the Festillic side rather than the Haldane: the eye witness account of the Marluk's death as the eleven-year-old Charissa told it, filtered through the perspectives and ambitions of Wencit of Torenth, her distant cousin—who also happened to be next after her in the Festillic succession. It provides an interesting counter to the Haldane version, I think—because official histories are almost always written by the winners, after all. I would venture to guess that most of history's blackest villains—unless they were actually deranged—generally had what were, for them, quite rational reasons for doing what they did. Few sane individuals are nasty just for the sake of being nasty.

By Festillic lights, then, Charissa was no villainess at all, but her father's loyal daughter, born and bred to the expectation that one day she would have to carry on her father's crusade to reclaim the throne he felt was rightfully Festillic. Though some of her seeming callousness in *Deryni Rising* must certainly come of that early horror of seeing her father killed before her eyes, yet is one left with the impression that, for the most part, she simply did what she felt she had to do to satisfy her family honor. One is tempted to wonder how different things might have been for everyone if she had married her cousin Wencit.

Of even more interest to me than Charissa, however, was the insight I gained into the character of Wencit, by watching him react to Charissa's observations. At thirty-two, it is obvious that Wencit of Torenth already had his own best interests firmly in mind—for though of both Torenthi and Festillic royal blood, he was not *born* heir to the crown of Torenth. He was the king's second son, and his elder brother had a son. Someday, I'll write the story of how he came to be king...

LEGACY

The tower chamber was airy and filled with light—rare enough in any castle, but especially at High Cardosa, where the winds swept down the Rheljan range even in summer and forced the shuttering of most windows year-round. This chamber was not shuttered, however, for the russet-clad man reading in a pool of sunlight had more than a passing competence in the working of weather magic. No breath of breeze disturbed the age-yellowed parchment rolls spread on his work table, though the black hart banners and orange pennons declaring the presence of the court of Torenth fluttered and snapped on the gusts outside, and the wind whined among the crenellated battlements.

Nor was the presence of the royal court a commonplace event this far from the Torenthi capital, as advancing age gradually curtailed the movements of the king. Traveling by slow stages, the aging Nimur II, his two sons, and his grandson had arrived with a small entourage nearly a week before, accompanying the vanguard of the Duke of Tolan's forces. Hogan Gwernach, called the Marluk, was bent on reclaiming his Festillic birthright—and that concerned Nimur acutely, since, after Hogan's daughter Charissa, the Festillic succession passed back to the House of Furstan and gave Nimur and his heirs legal claim to the Crown of Gwynedd.

The Furstan claim was very old, dating from the marriage of Mark, son of the last Festillic king, to a daughter of the first Nimur, and strengthened a generation ago when Hogan's grandmother had married a lesser Furstan prince. It would be further confirmed when young Charissa was officially betrothed to the king's grandson at Michaelmas—an expectation not entirely to the liking of the man in the tower, but it could be endured. With a brother and a nephew ahead of him in the succession, it was not likely that Prince Wencit of Torenth would ever rule the combined lands of Torenth and Gwynedd in his own right, even if Hogan was successful; but on the other hand, the larger the Furstan lands became, the larger would be his own portion as only brother of the future king. The genealogy governing all of this was very complicated and a subject far more fitting for the scrutiny of heralds than of princes, but Wencit had made it his business to learn all the nuances, nonetheless. One could never predict with overmuch accuracy just what role the Fates might call upon one to play.

He thought about Hogan and the Festillic claim as he unrolled another parchment. The dispute over Gwynedd was not a new one. Augarin Haldane had first called himself High King of Gwynedd nearly five centuries ago, after uniting several warring factions and petty princedoms in and around the central Gwynedd plain. He and his line had held the gradually growing kingdom for nearly two hundred years, until the first Festil, youngest brother of the then-king of Torenth, had swept into Gwynedd at the head of a Deryni army and accomplished a sudden coup.

The dynasty founded by Festil I lasted slightly more than eighty years—a time called the Interregnum by Haldane loyalists. Then Imre, the last Festillic king, had been ousted by the treachery of a man claiming to be a lost Haldane, assisted by the traitor Earl of Culdi, later briefly called a saint, and the restored Haldane line had reigned ever since.

With an impatient sigh, Wencit turned his attention to the scroll in his hands. Hogan was asserting his claim even now, and Wencit was hard-pressed to divert himself while he waited for his cousin to return. The sunlight dimmed the faded brown ink on the parchment almost past reading, but he knew the words almost by heart anyway. It was one of the few remaining letters of his ancestress Ariella to her brother-lover Imre. The language was archaic, and couched in the manners and innuendoes of two centuries past, but it held the essence of the Festil and Furstan claims which Hogan at this very moment pursued. The child of incest spoken of in Ariella's letter was to become the same Prince Mark who had married the first King Nimur's daughter.

"And so we must stand resolute, my dearest Liege and Lord and Brother, for there are those who will condemn the fruit of our love—if they do not dismiss it as a wantonness on my part—and refuse to accept that the child is yours and, therefore, your heir. But even if the world holds our son bastard, issue of my own indiscretion, still he is a Festil; and if neither of us contracts other marriage, then he must be our heir and follow us upon the throne. Let others think what they will. We are Deryni; we need no other justification!"

Wencit smiled a little at the arrogance, but he did not wholly disagree as his pale, almost colorless eyes skimmed the rest of the letter. Like Imre and Ariella, he and his family were also Deryni, masters of magical abilities not usually granted to ordinary men—except,

in annoying cases, an occasional Haldane, though this
current one, Brion, had evidenced no particular signs
of power. As Wencit read, the power of Ariella's love
came through, even across two centuries of time. He
felt almost like an eavesdropper as his eyes drank in
her last, private words to her brother, and something
akin to Imre's passion stirred in his loins as he imagined
the fiery Ariella suiting action to her promises. Surely
theirs had been one of the great loves of all time. Of
such a love had he himself dreamed, in the days when
he had considered marrying Charissa himself. Not for
the first time, he wondered what his father would do
if something were to happen to Nephew Aldred. He
did not particularly wish the boy ill, but the dream was
tempting.

He sat staring out the window for a long time,
indulging in a quiet fantasy which vacillated between
the live Charissa and the dead Ariella, then blinked
and came back to normal awareness as a disturbance
at the main gate caught his attention. The banner at
the head of the troop which galloped through was that
of his cousin Hogan, but of Hogan himself there was
no sign. In the midst of the mud-spattered company
rode a slump-shouldered young girl cloaked in blue,
mounted on a mouse-grey palfrey.

She was sobbing in Aldred's arms by the time he
could make his way down to the great hall, her fair
hair touseled around her face, sticking in damp tendrils and falling well past her waist. He felt a sharp
twinge of envy for the callow, sweaty-palmed Aldred,
who dared to hold her and give comfort at a time like
this, but he suppressed it quickly. Charissa of Tolan
was all but betrothed to his father's choice. Any resentment he harbored must be kept carefully shielded when

among other Deryni, especially those of his family, with whom few barriers could be maintained without suspicion.

His brother Carolus was there, and also his father, the king, though the old man had had a bad day and leaned heavily on the arm of a liveried attendant. Hassan, Hogan's tactician and the self-appointed bodyguard both to Hogan and his young daughter, was kneeling at the king's feet, black robes dust- and mud-caked, part of his *keffiyeh* drawn over the lower half of his face so that only the sorrowful eyes showed.

More battle-weary and grimy men-at-arms and a few knights were filing dejectedly into the hall, leaving a trail of armor and helmets and weapons as squires helped them to disarm, and Carolus gave brisk orders for their hosting before taking his father's arm and leading the way into a withdrawing chamber behind the dais. When he had settled the king in a high-backed armchair, Carolus motioned the black-clad Hassan nearer. They were only six now: the royal family, Charissa, and the Moor. Hassan uncovered his face as he knelt once more before king and crown prince.

"Very well, what happened?" Carolus asked.

Hassan lowered his eyes. "The Haldane waxed stronger, O my prince. What more can be said? The infidel overwhelmed my master with stolen magic and then cut off his head. We had no idea he possessed such power. *Al Marluk* should have been able to smash him like an insect!"

"*Al Marluk* was betrayed by a fellow Deryni!" Charissa said bitterly, speaking for the first time through her tears. "The half-breed Alaric Morgan helped the usurper. The taint of his magic surrounded the Haldane princeling like a mantle. My father fell by treachery!"

Wencit exchanged a glance with his brother, then glanced at the king. The old man was stunned by the news, taken anew by a bout of palsy; but his mind had not slipped, even if the aging body insisted upon betraying him.

"Morgan helped him?" the king whispered. "The Haldane's squire? But he's still a boy."

"A boy older than I, Sire," Charissa replied haughtily, gathering the shreds of her eleven-year-old dignity as she drew away from Aldred to stand alone. Wencit said and did nothing, but he could not help but feel pride. She was a Festil; but she was also a Furstan, and might have been his own. Her father would have been proud.

"How do you know Morgan helped the usurper?" the king persisted.

Charissa loosed the clasp of her cloak and let it fall to the floor, moving closer to the table beside the king's chair. There she poured dark red wine into an earthen cup, almost brimming the edge. Wencit stiffened, then moved closer to reinforce her if there was need. He knew what she was about to try, though he could tell that Aldred did not, and Carolus only suspected. The king knew, too, and nodded faintly as she took the cup in both hands and raised it to chest level.

"See my father's death through my eyes, Sire," she said softly, bowing her head over the cup and murmuring words under her breath as she passed a hand over the wine. "If I can hold the power long enough, you shall see for yourself and decide whether Brion Haldane was acting alone."

As she set the cup on the table and drew a stool closer, sitting, the others drifted nearer. The king, Carolus, and even Hassan obviously understood now what she was about to do, and Wencit knew that they could have done the same; but young Aldred had not yet mastered the technique, even though he was four years older than Charissa and a year older than Alaric Morgan. Wencit doubted it would give Morgan a moment's hesitation.

Knowing what she planned, he doused all the torches in the wall sconces with a gesture, leaving only the candles on the table burning. Charissa gave him a taut half bow of thanks before snuffing out all but one of the remaining candles. Stillness spread from her like mist as she began to stare into the wine.

"See the clearing at the end of the Llegoddin Canyon Trace, where we met the Haldane's forces," she murmured, breathing on the surface in an arcane pattern. "See my father's host gathering as we waited for the Haldane. Feel the sunlight on your hands and faces and the breeze stirring your hair. See the banners unfurl, silk and gilt, and hear them snapping overhead. Smell the sweat and the fear and the clean, sharp scent of water and pine and trampled earth..."

Images formed on the surface of the wine as she spoke, hazily at first, but then with greater clarity and focus as the watchers themselves slipped into trance and became receptive to the spell she cast. Wencit let himself become a part of it, truly seeing through her eyes and memory, feeling her fears and joys and all the rest as the recollection unfolded.

Sunlight shimmered on the mail and weapons of the Tolan men as they formed a line across the meadow and waited for the enemy to appear. Hogan, mailed and helmed and clad all in white, sat his sorrel greathorse beside Charissa like an elder god, gazing intently across the meadow to the shadowed defile where his archfoe would shortly emerge. Only when all his men were set did he turn his golden eyes to his daughter.

"Be brave, Cara mia," he whispered, shifting his lance to his shield hand so that he could reach across and brush the line of her jaw with a gloved finger. "This is but a temporary diversion. Whatever happens, you carry my blood, the blood of kings. That shall go on."

She shook her head and seized his hand, cradling it against her cheek. "I don't care about blood. I care about you. Promise me you'll come back."

He smiled. "You must care about blood, my dearest one. One day you shall be a queen. But if it is within my power, you know I shall always come back to you." He laid his gloved hand briefly on her head. "If it is not possible, then I leave you with my father's blessing. God keep and protect you, Cara mia."

"You speak as if you mean to die," she whispered, eyes filling with tears. "You must not die. You must not!"

"We must accept what the Fates have decreed for us, Cara mia," he replied, pulling away to take lance once more. "I do not plan to die, but if God wills it, then you must be strong and carry on, and never forget who and what you are."

A sob caught in her throat, but he turned back toward the meadow anyway. Then he was setting spurs to the big destrier and moving out in front of his men, the lion *jambes* and ermine of Tolan quartered with the Haldane lions floating above him on the banner which followed.

Of a sudden, the enemy was before them, the pretender Brion and his brother emerging from the streambed at the canyon mouth on matching greys.

Morgan, looking astonished and a little scared, rode behind them on a black, with the rest of the Haldane men. Above them, supported by Prince Nigel's hand, flew the lion of Gwynedd, which also gleamed on the pretender's breast. But Charissa had eyes for little further detail, for it was the man in the lion surcoat who must be vanquished. The others were as chaff before the wind.

Only a few of the Haldane's men had cleared the stream and canyon narrows before Hogan lowered his lance and signalled the attack. The weight of the Tolan greathorses shook the earth as they galloped toward the surprised enemy. As the distance closed, someone on the other side shouted, "*A Haldane!*" but even when the cry was taken up by others of the pretender's party, it only beat ineffectually against the wordless roar of the Marluk's charging cavalry.

They met with a clash like thunder and lightning, the brittle, hollow shattering of lances weighed against the ring of steel on steel and the more sullen, sickening butcher-sounds of edged metal cleaving flesh, bone, and even mail. Through it all, the Festil banner floated bright and unassailable above the fray, marking Hogan's place, ermine quartered with red, lion's *jambes* dancing beside golden Haldane lions. The two would-be kings were swept apart repeatedly in the heat of battle. It was the Haldane who finally seized the initiative, wheeling his screaming battle stallion in a tight circle as he raised his sword and shouted her father's name.

"Gwernach!"

She saw the melee part. Her father had lost his helmet, or perhaps tossed it aside, and his pale hair floated around his head like a halo as he pushed back his mail coif. Light seemed to radiate from his head and hands, but perhaps that was only the imagination of an eleven-year-old girl. He jerked his horse to a rear, brandishing his own sword above his head, then laughed as he shouted defiance at the man he had come to slay.

"The Haldane is mine!" he cried, cutting down a Haldane knight as he spurred his way toward the long-awaited enemy. "Stand and fight, usurper! Gwynedd is mine by right!"

As the two clashed, their men parting to watch the battle of contending kings, Charissa's vision wavered. To the child, the details of one battle were rather like another, even with her father as one of the principals fighting for his life. She gasped when the horses were slain, first the sorrel and then the grey, turning her face away with tears welling in her eyes for the faithful, unfortunate beasts; but it was not until both men staggered apart to lean panting on their swords that the image again sharpened to specific detail. The men's voices were too low to be heard, but much could be inferred from their actions.

The two seemed to settle down to almost amiable discussion, Hogan's white teeth flashing several times in sardonic grin as he made some point against the Haldane's liking. Once he gestured toward his daughter with his sword, and Wencit could sense the girl's pride as she drew herself up more regally in the saddle.

First the Haldane and then Hogan traced symbols in the dust with their swordpoints then—ritual challenge being offered and accepted. The Haldane faltered at what Hogan drew, but then he caught himself and angrily erased the offending sigil with his boot. Hogan did not appear at all surprised.

Wencit was surprised, though, and startled almost

out of the spell, for he knew what Hogan had been trying to do. Though any Deryni even partially trained in the formal use of magic would have known the spell, the Haldane should not have; but Morgan would have, and could have taught his master. Charissa was right about the half-breed's treachery!

Wencit watched as Charissa's vision showed the two backing apart, warding circles being raised, crimson and blue—circles of which the Haldane also should have had no knowledge. Then battle was being joined once more, this time with energies arcing from sword to sword like directed lightning.

The battle lasted long, though this one was followed with far more interest and understanding on Charissa's part than the physical battle earlier. Neither man moved, but the power flowing between them, flung and deflected, was enormous.

When even Charissa's vision could not pierce beyond the forces being contained in the dueling circle, Wencit shared her brief, queasy moment of apprehension. A little after that, the haze of the circle's dome cleared to reveal one figure staggering to its knees, sword still half-raised in a desperate but futile warding-off gesture. Heartsick, Wencit knew that it was Hogan.

The Haldane towered above him for a long time, weapon poised overhead to strike, but for a long moment something seemed to stay his hand. Fleetingly Wencit dared to hope that Hogan might yet prevail, might yet call forth extra power from some long-forgotten reservoir of strength to blast this base, pretending Haldane from existence.

But then the energies rippled again, and the weapon fell from Hogan's hands. As he fell forward on hands and knees, utterly spent, the victor's sword descended.

Charissa gasped and turned her head away, breaking the spell, and the image on the surface of the wine vanished. A sob caught in her throat, but when Aldred and even Carolus tried to comfort her, she shrank from their touch and shook her head, blinking back new tears and raising her head like the queen she surely was.

"No," she said steadily. "Now I must learn to stand alone and be strong. He is gone, but I shall not forget the manner of his living and dying. Nor shall I forget who was responsible for the latter. I shall avenge him."

"But Charissa," Aldred whispered, "for generations the Haldanes have held the potential for power like our own. What made your father think this Haldane would be different?"

The king cleared his throat and shook his head, brushing tears from rheumy eyes. "We had hopes," he said. "When Brion Haldane's father died, Brion was young. We believed there was no one left to guide him in the assumption of his powers. And when he evidenced no sign of those powers in the past ten years he has been king, we assumed the powers lost. Who would have thought the boy Morgan could do as he apparently has done?"

Flexing the fingers of one hand against the other, Carolus nodded. "We did misjudge him," he agreed, "but it will not happen again. The Haldane still is a usurper. When Aldred and Charissa are wed, we must ensure that their joint inheritance shall include both these kingdoms. We shall be watching both the Haldane and this upstart Deryni half-breed."

As the others nodded agreement, and the king and Carolus began questioning Hassan more fully, Wencit silently reviewed the battle and the following discussion, marking many points to be considered at more leisure. He had learned more than one important thing today. For one, Aldred was a fool. If he came to the throne after Carolus, he could no more hold it than Hogan had been able to stand against the Haldane. Nor did Carolus himself show much better promise, though Wencit had never thought to look at his brother in this light before. That alone was food for much solitary thought and contemplation.

As for the Haldane and Morgan, they, too, merited further study, especially the latter. Though the half-Deryni youth was still scarcely more than a boy, he clearly was going to be a factor to be reckoned with in the future—and he was surely part of the key to eventually destroying the Haldane. Perhaps, if the Fates willed it so, Wencit himself might even be the instrument of Morgan's eventual downfall. Far less likely things were possible. . . .

THE KNIGHTING OF DERRY
May, 1115

Over the years, one of my most popular non-Deryni characters has always been Sean Lord Derry, Morgan's aide. He's an intriguing fellow: loyal, competent, sensitive—and very human. I've often been asked how Morgan and Derry met and how Derry came to be in Morgan's service. So this is that story.

Interestingly enough, it almost didn't get written. Originally, I started writing it from Morgan's point of view, and was having a terrible time getting it to flow. After spending nearly a week working on genealogical charts and timelines—anything to avoid actually sitting down to write it (though at least I now know how Morgan and Duncan are descended from Rhys and Evaine's children)—I finally spent an entire day grinding out about five pages. That was a Friday. I write on a computer these days; and when I sat down at the machine on Monday to resume work on the story, I could not get the computer to access the file on the disk. I couldn't get into the file; I couldn't copy the disk; I was locked out. Apparently, the disk had gone bad.

173

So I made a lame attempt to reconstruct—which almost never works—then dumped everything and started over from scratch, on another disk, only from Derry's point of view, this time—anything to get the words moving again. And this time Derry came alive, and the story flowed.

I almost wish I could say that a later attempt to get into the original file yielded no impediments, once I'd changed the perspective of the story; but it didn't happen that way. Nor am I bold enough to expect divine intervention of *that* magnitude on a regular basis. Like Denis Arilan, I tend to think God works most often through mortal agents—or perhaps, sometimes, through mechanical devices constructed by mortals. Suffice it to say that the first attempt was lost, and good riddance; and that the process of coping with that loss gave me the impetus to rethink my approach and let the story come out the way it should have done in the first place.

The result, whatever sparked it, certainly fills in some interesting background about Derry and his family. Why, after all, would a young nobleman of apparent promise want to become a duke's aide, rather than remain his own master? Alaric Morgan's by then undeniable personal charisma is certainly a very important factor, but might not another part be the wonder of Brion's court, as seen through the eyes of a relatively unsophisticated minor lord of only eighteen, newly knighted, who has only ever seen his king a few times and never spoken to him face-to-face?

We catch another glimpse of the maturing Denis Arilan, too, ten years after his ordination to the priesthood, and see how his role in royal circles has evolved.

THE KNIGHTING OF DERRY

Sean Lord Derry, eighteen and less than a fortnight from knighthood at the hands of King Brion of Gwynedd, let out his breath in a sigh of longing as he watched the horse handlers parade their charges along the narrow, rail-fenced track that led toward the auction yards of the spring horse fair at Rhelledd. The particular object of his longing had yet to appear in the procession, but that hardly mattered, since even the starting price set on the animal Derry wanted was quite beyond his means. An earl he might be, but his holdings in the eastern Marches were quite modest, as earldoms went, and only recently begun to recover from the death duties due the Crown after the demise of Derry's father nine years before. His Uncle Trevor, hardly better off than he, had offered what was, for him, a generous subsidy, as his own gift on the occasion of his only nephew's knighting; but Derry knew that even the combined sum was not nearly enough.

"The bay isn't bad," Uncle Trevor murmured, pointing out a quiet-mannered animal with broad white stockings on its forelegs. "I don't care for his markings, but he has a good chest and kind eyes. I checked his bloodlines, and they're respectable enough. Or, there was a dark brown earlier. You remember him. We could afford either of those, I think."

Derry shrugged, not taking his eyes from the horses still emerging from the far holding yard.

"They're all right," he conceded. "The chestnut though..."

"Well, I can't blame you for wanting him," Trevor said sympathetically, as the stallion in question appeared at the far end of the track. "He's a horse fit for a king, Sean. I only hope you won't be too disappointed if we can't afford him."

"I know we probably can't," Derry replied. "I'm prepared for that. The bay or the brown will be all right, if we don't get the chestnut, but *God*, how I'd love to have that fellow!"

"You and every other horseman present," Trevor muttered.

Nodding distracted agreement, Derry eased up another rail on the restraining fence and craned in the direction of his intended prize, chewing at his lower lip as the stallion was led very near their vantage point. His blue eyes drank in every ripple of hard muscles playing under satin coat as the animal pranced and curvetted against the restraint of his two handlers and occasionally whinnied defiance at the lesser stallions ahead and behind him.

"Sweet *Jesu*, he's magnificent!" Derry breathed, ducking his head in apology to his uncle's scowl of disapproval at the near blasphemy. "Sorry, Uncle."

The stallion *was* magnificent, though: a deep-chested liver chestnut with not a speck of white on him, the finest R'Kassan bloodlines proclaimed in high crest, powerful jowls, and large, intelligent brown eyes. With a stallion like this standing at stud and a careful breeding program, Derry could change the entire character of Marcher remounts within five years. Nor would stud fees from local tenants and lesser nobility in the area hurt Derry's economic state. Such a mount would also do Derry proud when he rode into Rhemuth town to be knighted. It was hardly a week away...

He was dreaming of that glorious day, himself mounted on the chestnut in full warrior's panoply, bright blue bardings glowing in the sunshine, when disaster erupted. Without warning, a small child with flapping skirts and sleeves ducked under the lowest rail of the restraining fence to dart to the other side—and tripped, nearly under the nose of a nasty-tempered grey fidgeting just behind the chestnut.

The startled grey needed no further excuse to explode. Tossing its head and squealing indignation, it went back on it haunches in a perfect *levade*, yanking its startled handler off his feet, then snaked its long neck around to clamp powerful jaws on the man's shoulder and shake him as a terrier might shake a rat, only letting go as the chestnut also reared up at the commotion and whirled to scream a challenge, shedding his handlers with no more effort than if he had shaken off mice.

Derry was already vaulting over the top rail as he heard the sickening, hollow thud of steel-shod hooves connecting with the chest of one of the handlers, and he only narrowly avoided the same fate as he dashed behind the grey to tackle the cringing child and roll both of them clear. The stallions were fighting in earnest by the time he could pick himself up and hoist the child over the rails and into the waiting arms of another man, and grooms and handlers were swarming everywhere, trying to get the other stallions away before more were drawn into battle. In the clouds of dust being raised by the fray, Derry had a hard time seeing what had happened to the original handlers, but he thought he saw one dust-covered form lying motionless near the railing—and another man curled in a ball almost directly beneath the plunging hooves, arms raised in futile attempt to protect his head.

"Sean, no!" he heard his uncle shout, even as he dashed out to attempt a second rescue, snatching for the trailing lead rein of the chestnut.

He managed to get a hand on it, but the stallion jerked its head and pulled him off balance before he could let go, throwing him squarely in the path of one of the grey's plunging forelegs. It was a knee that slammed into his jaw rather than a hoof, thank God— but it still made him see stars as he recoiled and rolled to his feet again. Another hoof flashed dangerously close to his head and grazed his shoulder, opening a deep gash but deflected from bone-breaking force by two men in black suddenly hauling at the grey's head-stall and tackling its neck.

The diversion provided an opportunity for the man on the ground to roll clear, however; and by the time Derry could make another try for the chestnut, twisting one sweat-lathered brown ear to get the stallion's head down, the two black-clad men had the grey subdued.

"Easy, boy! Whoa! Whoa!" Derry crooned, letting up on the ear as the stallion subsided.

One of the men in black had whipped off his leather tunic and used it to blindfold the grey, the better to lead him away from his rival, and Derry's chestnut likewise quieted as Derry stroked and soothed, turning its head away from the grey. But the movement, as the animal pivoted obediently on the forehand, revealed a serious limp to the rear, and the near hind leg was bleeding. Derry could feel every tortured muscle in his own body protesting as he handed over the lead rein to a couple of grooms who suddenly materialized beside him, now that the danger was over, and automatically moved back to check the injured leg. A sick feeling knotted in the pit of his stomach as he ran trembling hands down the sweaty flank and found the damage.

"A nasty bite," said a low, pleasant voice almost at his ear. "And a bowed tendon, I should think. What a pity."

Derry glanced up only long enough to see that it

was one of the black-clad men who had caught the grey stallion—the one who had given up his tunic as a blindfold. Bright mail glinted on the man's chest—unusual to wear under riding leathers—but Derry dismissed that oddity for the moment as he manipulated the injured leg, one hand gentling the stallion against the pain the movement obviously cost.

"I don't think it's torn all the way through," he murmured, kneeling as he set the hoof back on the ground. "If we can stitch and immobilize it, and keep him from ripping it further, he may be all right."

"He'll never be sound for battle," the man said. "Best to let them put him down."

"No!" Derry said. "I have a blacksmith who can make a special shoe to support the leg until it heals. Uncle Trevor, see if you can find me a medical kit, would you? And somebody make sure he doesn't put any weight on that leg. It's worth a try, isn't it?"

As the mail-clad man signalled to someone Derry could not see, taking the horse's head to stroke and soothe, another man in brown leathers came to peer over Derry's shoulder.

"Bowed tendon, eh? Blast the luck! Thanks for your efforts, son, but my man will take over from here. Maclyn, we're going to have to put him down."

"No! You can't!" Derry cried. "At least let me try to fix him."

"It isn't worth the trouble, son. He's never going to be sound."

"Not for battle, no. He could still be used for breeding though. He doesn't have to be sound for that, as long as he isn't in pain."

"It's no good, son."

"Are you the owner?" Derry demanded.

"Yes."

"Then, I'll buy him for what he'd bring from the butchers! And I—I'll buy another proper horse from you as well. I had my eye on two others."

The man stroked his jaw thoughtfully.

"Which two?"

"Well, there was a dark brown one—very muscular—and a bay with odd white forelegs."

"Ah. The bay is one of mine," the man said. "I'm asking two hundred gold marks for him. Give me three and you can have him and this one."

"Julius!" the man in mail admonished. "That's usurous! Dead, this animal isn't worth twenty, hide and all."

"He is if he can eventually stand at stud, my lord," Julius said.

"But that's a gamble," the mail-clad man pointed out. "And you were ready to put the animal down. Let the boy have both for two-fifty, and you'll have made far more from your bad luck than you deserve."

"Well—"

"Come on, Julius," the man wheedled. "I'll buy that black mare at the ridiculous price you're asking."

"*And* her foal?"

"*And* her foal," the man agreed. "But only for an additional fifty. And that's doing *you* a favor!"

"Oh, very well. You drive a hard bargain, my lord."

As the two men shook hands, Derry could hardly believe his good fortune, for the agreed price was hardly half what the chestnut was worth—*if* Derry could make good his boast to repair the injury.

A groom brought a bucket of water, and Derry began

carefully sponging out the stallion's wound, amazed that the animal did not protest. Indeed, the powerful warhorse had grown as meek and quiet as a lamb under the hands of the stranger lord in mail. Derry's head was beginning to throb from the blow to his jaw, and his own blood ran down his left arm as he worked, mingling with the stallion's, but he paid it no mind— nor to his own growing discomfort. He would be all right until he stood up, at least. His Uncle Trevor came to crouch beside him, unrolling a small medical kit with needles and sutures, and Romare, the blacksmith from Castle Derry, eased closer to inspect the injury.

"I've boasted about your talents, Romare," Derry murmured, "but you've taught me everything I know about horses. *Can* we save him?"

"Since you've bought him, it's certainly worth a try, m'lord," Romare replied. "But why don't you let me take over here? I can throw sutures as well as the next man. And someone ought to see your arm. You're bleeding more than you think."

"He's right, you know," said the man in mail, reaching across to grasp Derry's arm below the laceration as Derry rose wobblingly, steadying himself with a hand against the stallion's side. "From the looks of it, you're going to need a few sutures yourself. That's quite a lump you've got on your jaw, too." Bloodstained fingers lifted to lightly brush the knot, already bruising. "Randolph, would you take a look at this, when you're finished with the groom?"

Derry had time to note only pale grey eyes and a shock of short-cropped yellow hair above the man's mail shirt before his vision went dark, and he fainted.

*　*　*

Derry's next awareness was a resurgence of the throb in his jaw, a stinging pain overlying the ache in his left upper arm, and someone humming tunelessly, close to his head. He opened his eyes to see a pleasant-faced man in black bending over him, drawing a damp length of black silk from the bloody ruin of his left shirt sleeve. The stout blue linen had been slit from elbow to shoulder to bare a laceration as long as a man's hand, and the sharp stinging came from the needle the man was using to close the wound.

"Well, hello," the man said, smiling as he drew his thread snug. "You're among the living again, I see. When you fainted, I feared you might have a concussion, but now I think it was simply from the shock. You ought to be fine when you've had some rest."

"How long was I out?" Derry murmured.

"Oh, not very long. I've only just started sewing you up. Actually, I suppose we could have just cleaned and bandaged it, but this will leave you with less scarring. You young men of the nobility end up with enough scars, as it is. Murderous sharp, those warhorses' shoes—and filthy, too, though I think I've gotten the wound clean enough. If you had to miss the cleaning or the suturing, I think you got the best of the bargain by sleeping through the former—not that this is pleasant, I'll grant you. I'm Master Randolph, by the way, and I'm trained to do this, so you needn't worry. My lord didn't want you turned over to just any local barber-surgeon."

Derry did his best not to gape as the man's monologue wound down, though he did stare a bit. The man who had identified himself as Master Randolph appeared to be in his mid-thirties, and bore a small gryphon's head on the badge embroidered on his left breast—shades of green and gold on black, the shield outlined in gold. Derry blinked, vague recognition of the badge nibbling at the edges of memory, then raised his head for a better look at what the man was doing, grimacing as the needle bit again into the edge of the wound.

"You do neat work," Derry murmured, as he laid his head back down and tried not to flinch. "I'm Sean Derry."

"Yes, I know. The Earl Derry. Your uncle told me," the man replied. "Incidentally, he's gone to settle accounts with Julius. Your smithy's working on the chestnut. And you've either driven a very shrewd bargain or bought yourself some very expensive horsemeat and hide."

"I know," Derry replied, laying his good arm across his eyes. "It's a gamble I probably shouldn't have taken. We've spent so much already, getting me outfitted for my knighting. I probably could've gotten the bay for far less, too, if he'd gone to auction. His confirmation is good, but those white legs would've brought the price down."

"Hmmm, he'll be a serviceable mount for you," Randolph said. "And those white legs will make him—distinctive."

Derry started to chuckle at that, stifling a yelp as one of the stitches pinched, and picked up his head to see what Randolph was doing. The wound was perhaps a third closed. As he murmured apologetically and laid his head back, turning his face away, he was startled to find another man crouching on his other side—the man in the mail shirt. Derry wondered when *he'd* come in.

"Well, young Lord Derry, how are you doing?" the

man asked, smiling. "Is the good Master Randolph just about finished torturing you?"

His grey eyes held a hint of fog and summer rain, but lit with sunlight. And contrary to Derry's earlier impression, he was probably little older than Derry himself—mid-twenties, at the most. Derry found himself liking the man instantly.

"I'm afraid you have me at a disadvantage, sir," he said, smiling tentatively. "You both seem to know who *I* am, but I'm afraid I don't know you."

"Hmmm, that isn't important just now," the man murmured. "What *is* important is getting you patched up. You were quite a hero today, you know. The parents of the child you saved are ready to nominate you for sainthood. How's that lump on your jaw? He didn't hit his head anywhere else, did he, Ran?" he asked the surgeon, probing with both hands in Derry's curly brown hair to feel for swelling.

About to pursue the question, Derry felt an almost uncontrollable urge to yawn—and winced in the middle of it, as Master Randolph's needle continued its annoying work.

"Think about something else," the man in the mail shirt said softly, those incredible silvery eyes gently catching and holding his as the man's hands braced his head from either side. "Close your eyes and imagine yourself somewhere else. Detach yourself from the discomfort."

Yawning hugely, Derry obeyed, and found that the discomfort did diminish. In fact, he even dozed. When he came to his senses again, the man in the mail shirt was gone, and Master Randolph was tucking in the last ends of the bandage on his shoulder. Uncle Trevor was sitting on a stool, looking down at him anxiously.

"How do you feel?" Trevor asked.

"Like I've been kicked by a horse in the shoulder and jaw," Derry replied, stirring gingerly to raise himself on his elbows. "Where did my mysterious benefactor go? I wanted to thank him. And who was he?"

Master Randolph smiled as he tossed the last of his instruments in a medical satchel and closed its flap.

"He's gone to take care of business—and he knows you're grateful, son." Randolph stood and slung the satchel's strap over his shoulder. "As to who he was, I expect he'd have told you if he wanted you to know just now. But you'll figure it out. Good day to you, young Lord Derry, and Baron Varagh."

He was gone before Derry could protest. Mystified, Derry sat up and glanced at his uncle.

"Do *you* know who he was?" he whispered. "Obviously some high-born lord—"

"Among the highest born," Trevor said quietly. "What did he do to you?"

"*Do* to me? What do you mean?"

"Did he touch you? Do you remember anything he said?"

"Well, *yes*, he touched me! He was checking to see if I'd hit my—who *was* he, Uncle?"

Trevor snorted, biting back a bitter grimace. "The Duke of Corwyn, Alaric Morgan."

"Cor—Alaric *Morgan*? The Deryni?" Derry breathed.

"Aye."

"Well, bloody hell!" was all Derry could think to say as he lay back again, laying his forearm across his forehead and trying to remember all that had transpired. "So *that* was the great Morgan."

He knew he probably should be afraid, for the magical Deryni were said to be able to corrupt a man's soul with a glance, much less a touch; but somehow he could not feel anything but admiration for what Morgan had done for him, both in the horse yard and after, while Master Randolph tended his wound. He still liked what he had seen in the pale, silvery eyes— and he was not sure he had ever believed what the priests taught about the Deryni as a race.

As for Morgan's forbidden magic—well, if Derry had tasted it when Morgan told him to put the pain from his mind, that hardly smacked of evil in Derry's book. To be free of pain while a surgeon worked—that *had* to be a blessing, not a curse, for any fighting man. And if Morgan had other, less benign powers?

He decided not to think about that possibility. He refused to judge any man on hearsay—even a Deryni. Fearsome powers Morgan might have, but everything Derry had observed of the man spoke of temperance, compassion, and a *noblesse oblige* that could only be born—never created by mere rank. He wondered whether he would see the Deryni duke at court when he went to Rhemuth to be knighted. Morgan was said to be the king's friend, after all. And now that Derry knew who Morgan was, a proper thank-you for his help at Rhelledd seemed entirely appropriate.

The week that followed would have been frantic enough for Derry, dashing about to complete the final preparations for his journey, but it was made all the more grueling by the aftermath of his injuries—nothing serious, but enough to slow him down considerably, for every bone and muscle in his body ached for several days after the incident, and his head throbbed for nearly a week. Because of the possible head injury, Uncle Trevor insisted that Derry return to Castle Derry in a horse litter, himself making the necessary arrangements to leave the chestnut stallion temporarily in a stall at Rhelledd, with the smithy Romare to care for him. Derry's mother, when she was not scolding her only son for having squandered his meager funds on a potentially useless animal, fussed over him unmercifully until it finally was time to leave for Rhemuth.

And so, accompanied by his mother, his sister and her family, and his Uncle Trevor, who would stand as his sponsor, Derry worried about finances on the leisurely ride to the capital, rather than devoting much time to thinking about the Deryni duke, Alaric Morgan. Trevor's son, the eleven-year-old Padrig, rode at Derry's side as page, thrilled to be visiting the capital for the first time; and the boy's enthusiasm helped to restore some of Derry's good humor for the journey. The white-legged bay proved to be a smooth-gaited and even-tempered mount, worth every penny Derry had paid for him *and* the chestnut; and Romare's last report before they left declared the chestnut to be mending well—so perhaps Derry's financial straits were not as desperate as he had feared at first.

Once Derry arrived at Rhemuth, he had little occasion to consider Morgan either. The duke was not in evidence as Derry and the other knightly candidates went through the final rehearsals for the ceremony, though the young Sieur de Vali declared Morgan to be his sponsor when asked. Derry was attended by his Uncle Trevor at the ritual bathing of the candidates that night, receiving the robes of white, black, and red

from him before making confession and beginning his
all-night vigil over his arms in the basilica within the
walls of the castle, but someone else did that duty for
Morgan's candidate.

Not until the actual morning of the knighting ceremony did Derry even see Morgan, waiting quietly at
the back of the great hall beside de Vali, whose overlord Morgan was. As Derry passed him with Trevor
and Padrig, that mere glimpse set all the unasked and
unanswered questions about the man whirling through
Derry's mind.

Morgan certainly did not look like a powerful and
sinister Deryni sorcerer to Derry—though the ducal
image was there, if more subtle than that of most other
men of equivalent rank. Morgan wore a coronet, but
it was only a simple band of hammered gold circling
his brow. And his attire—

Well, Derry had heard before that Morgan nearly
always affected stark black, as he had at Rhelledd, but
Derry had expected something more—well, *sumptuous*, for as important a court function as a mass
knighting, especially since Morgan apparently was,
indeed, standing sponsor to the Sieur de Vali.

Sable silk with a rich, nubbly texture swathed the
duke from throat to gold-spurred heels, formally high-
collared and severe yet somehow relaxed as well, sub-
tly enhanced by an intricate bordure of double tressure
flory-counter flory worked in gold bullion around collar, sleeves, hem, and down the long slits fore and aft.
The white belt of Morgan's knighthood also relieved
the blackness, but the leather-wrapped hilt of his sword
passed almost unnoticed in the shadow of his left sleeve,
its plain black scabbard all but invisible against the
folds of the long court robe. It was Morgan's only

apparent weapon, but Derry would not even allow himself to consider what other defenses the Deryni lord might have at his disposal. He probably wore mail under his robe, too, as he had under the riding leathers at Rhelledd.

Once Derry's name was called to come forward, though, he did not think about Morgan during his own knighting. He was too busy making the proper responses, kneeling for Uncle Trevor to buckle on his sword and spurs, bowing his head for the royal accolade at King Brion's hands. He shivered as the blade of the king's sacred sword touched his shoulders and head, awed to be kneeling at last before his sovereign, whom he had only even *seen* a few times in his life, and then at a distance. And the ancient vows he recited as he set his hands between those of the king and swore his oath of fealty were the first words he and Brion Haldane had ever exchanged.

"I, Sean Seamus O'Flynn, Earl Derry, do become your liege man of life and limb, and of earthly worship. Faith and truth will I bear unto you, to live and to die, against all manner of folk, so help me, God!"

He kissed the royal hands before the king raised him up, flushing with pride as the court cheered his new estate and Queen Jehana girded him with the white belt of his knightly rank. After she had kissed him on both cheeks in congratulation, he bent over her hand in courtly salute, bowed to the king and to the eight-year-old Prince Kelson, seated at his father's right, then moved to the side with a beaming Uncle Trevor to witness the other knightings. As an earl of however modest means, Derry had been among the first to receive the accolade. Hence, he was able to stare with relative impunity when Duke Alaric finally came for-

ward to sponsor the Sieur de Vali, who was only of
baronial rank.

Morgan did his best to remain unobtrusive as his
young vassal knelt to beg knighthood of the king, himself kneeling with bowed head to affix the golden spurs
to de Vali's heels, but even Derry, relatively unsophisticated as he was, could sense the heightened interest of the court in this particular dubbing—or at least
in the candidate's sponsor. The sword with which Morgan invested his charge at the king's command was
well made but of no particularly lavish embellishment,
but from the court's attention, as the weapon changed
hands, Derry wondered whether they expected it to
burst into flames.

It did not. Nor did Morgan. Like any ordinary man,
the Deryni duke remained kneeling quietly to one side
as de Vali received the accolade, made his vows, and
rose to receive his white belt from the queen. Then
Morgan melted into the crowd as the court cheered the
newmade knight. Derry did not see him again until
much later in the day, well after the feast, when he
found the Deryni duke sitting alone in a window embrasure that opened off the rear of the great hall. The
high collar of the black court robe was unfastened at
the throat, the coronet of earlier in the day set aside
on the cushion beside him, but the sunlight made of
the duke's golden hair its own crown of fire as he
hunched over the stiletto he was using to pare his fin-
gernails.

Derry paused at the entrance to the embrasure,
uncertain whether to intrude—or even why he wanted
to—but Morgan looked up almost immediately and
rose.

"Ah, young Lord Derry," the duke said, the stiletto

disappearing so quickly that for an instant Derry considered whether Morgan might have used magic. "Or, should I say, Sir Sean, since you are so newly knighted?" Morgan went on, making him a courtly little bow with both empty palms extended. "In any case, my heartiest congratulations to you, Sir Knight. You are well deserving of the honor bestowed upon you today."

Derry flushed and returned the bow, thinking he probably should be uneasy at being singled out for a Deryni's attention, but only feeling a little self-conscious to be receiving any duke's notice.

"I wouldn't know about that, Your Grace, but I thank you for the compliment, nonetheless. And you can call me Derry, if you like," he added recklessly. "I was only nine when I became an earl, so the title has become almost like a given name, over the years."

"Ah, that can happen," Morgan agreed. "I remember your father. You carry his name as one of your own, do you not?"

"Aye, m'lord. He was Seamus Michael O'Flynn. I am Sean Seamus."

"So I recall, from your oath." Morgan cocked his head and tendered a hesitant little smile as he continued. "I was the king's squire on the campaign when your father received his wounds. I remember he fought very bravely. I was sorry to hear he had later succumbed to his injuries—for your sake, as well as his own. I, too, was only nine when my father died."

Derry blinked in surprise. He had not realized Morgan knew so much about him.

"Then, we—have something in common, Your Grace—besides a love of fine horses. May—may I sit down?" he blurted.

Morgan raised a fine blond eyebrow and crossed his

arms casually on his chest. "Are you certain you want to risk being seen with me by choice? You know what I am."

"I do, my lord."

Derry managed not to flinch as Morgan's pale, silvery gaze flitted across his face, down to his toes and back up again. When Morgan turned half-away and sat down again, gesturing vaguely toward the opposite bench in the window with one graceful hand, Derry felt almost physically relieved.

"Please join me, then," Morgan murmured, "and tell me how fares the stallion we saved from the knackers."

Derry swallowed his trepidation and obeyed, making himself move farther into the embrasure before sitting gingerly opposite the Deryni duke.

"The stallion fares well, my lord," he said. "I thought you might like to know; that's why I sought you out. I also wanted to thank you for helping me drive the bargain that bought him. My smithy's fitted him with a special shoe to keep the injury immobilized while it heals, and I'm told he flourishes—though he's restive, confined to a stall this past week."

"And will grow more restive yet, before he's mended enough to be turned out," Morgan observed. "Still, it's better than putting him down. A pity, even so. I'd hoped to buy him for the king. His Majesty usually favors greys, but that fellow was a mount almost worthy of my lord."

Derry nodded, remembering his own reaction to the stallion and appreciating Morgan's confirming judgment.

"Aye, he was, Your Grace. But if he recovers, could the king not breed to him still? If all goes well, I hope to have him standing at stud by the spring."

Chuckling pleasantly, Morgan raised a droll eyebrow.

"I would venture to guess that the king would be most interested in that prospect," he said. "You must promise me, however, that you will extract a suitable stud fee from the royal purse."

"Charge the king?" Derry gasped.

"Well, if you're to build yourself a reputation as a judge of fine horseflesh, you must put a fitting value on your expertise," Morgan replied. "Besides, you can't tell me that your estate coffers couldn't use the extra income."

"But, the king—"

"Derry, did the king have anything to do with your getting that stallion?"

"No, sir."

"Well, then." Morgan grinned impishly. "On the other hand, if it were I, and not the king, who wished to engage the services of your stallion, and I were to suggest certain, ah, concessions..."

He shrugged eloquently, adopting an expression of innocence quite at variance with his prosperous if sober appearance, and Derry suddenly realized Morgan was testing him, albeit gently.

"I think I understand, Your Grace," he said carefully. "But might I not also be well advised, if I wish to establish my reputation as a judge of fine horseflesh, not to diminish the value of my expertise, even to a fellow expert?"

Morgan only shrugged again, rather more casually than the first time, but the mirth Derry sensed in the grey eyes was well worth any momentary anxiety he might have experienced.

"Well said, my young friend," Morgan said with a

nod. "We'll teach you yet to drive a hard bargain. Incidentally, how did that white-legged bay turn out? Other than those outlandish legs, he looked quite the goer."

Derry allowed himself to smile, relaxing a little in the easy, horsey banter.

"He's the bargain of the lot, sir: smooth-gaited, even tempered. If I use him for breeding one day, I'll hope to avoid the odd markings, but I have no complaints."

"No, nor have I."

As Morgan turned the pale grey eyes directly on Derry again, Derry suddenly felt himself the subject of intense scrutiny—and more than just visual inspection. He nearly stopped breathing. He was not sure he could have broken away from that compelling gaze, but he felt no particular urge to try. He was not afraid, but he grew more curious by the second. And when Morgan did not speak, Derry decided to be bold.

"Are—you reading my mind, my lord?" he whispered.

Morgan smiled and blinked, but did not break his steady gaze.

"No. Do you want me to?"

Derry managed an audible swallow and tried fleetingly to glance away, just to see whether he could, but found himself only shaking his head slightly.

"Why not?" Morgan asked softly. "Are you afraid?"

"No."

"Good."

With that, Morgan deliberately looked away, breaking the contact, and Derry could breathe again.

Derry was *not* afraid, though. Respectful, yes—as he would have been of any clever man who was the king's friend and a duke—but he didn't think that had anything to do with Morgan's magic. Perhaps Derry was naive, but Morgan seemed to be a man of honor, for all that he was Deryni and supposedly to be suspected and shunned by God-fearing men.

Derry *was* curious as to whether Morgan had used his powers that first day they met, however. He had had little time to think about it before, but it now seemed rather odd that he had managed to drift off to sleep while Master Randolph sewed up his arm.

"Did you read my mind before?" he found himself asking timidly, recoiling a little as Morgan turned to look at him again.

Morgan cocked his head in question.

"When?"

"In Rhelledd, when your Master Randolph was stitching up my arm."

"Ah." Morgan smiled fleetingly. "Not really. I did— ah—help you a little with the pain, however."

"How—*help*?" Derry persisted. "Did you use your powers on me?"

Morgan lowered his eyes briefly, then met Derry's again, though not with the previous compulsion.

"Yes. There seemed no point to making you endure more pain, when I could ease it for you. I—hoped I'd been subtle enough that you didn't notice."

"I wouldn't have, if we'd never talked this afternoon," Derry replied. "Why do the priests say that what you do is evil?"

Morgan intertwined his fingers and stretched his arms out in front of him, turning the palms away until the knuckles cracked, apparently using the movement as an excuse not to look at Derry.

"They speak out of ignorance," the duke said after a moment, glancing out the window as he let his hands drop to his lap. "They are slaves to old prejudices, to old grievances done by misguided individuals. The Church did not always view our talents thus."

Derry thought about that for a moment, then shook his head.

"Well, it makes no sense to me, Your Grace. I don't see why everyone can't just live and let live."

"Would that it were that simple."

"Yes. Well." Derry sighed and glanced back into the hall, knowing he should rejoin his uncle soon, but he really did not want to leave.

"I won't be offended if you go now," Morgan said quietly, again studying him with those incredible grey eyes. "And no, I'm not reading your mind. It's only logical to wonder whether you've been missed, though, and to wonder whether anyone has noticed with whom you've been conversing."

"Well, your logic is correct," Derry conceded, shrugging sheepishly. "Do you do that often?"

"Do what?"

"Simply guess what people are thinking, as any ordinary mortal would do, and then let *them* think you did it with magic?"

As Morgan raised both eyebrows in surprise, Derry sensed he was on to something. Throwing all caution to the winds, he went on.

"You *do* do that, don't you, Your Grace?" he ventured. "I'd heard stories before, but until I saw you today, all in black, deliberately cultivating that faintly sinister air—"

All at once, Morgan burst out laughing, slapping a black-clad thigh with one hand and shaking his head as he looked at Derry with mirth and a little wonder.

"You, sir, are far more perceptive than I dreamed.

Perhaps I *should* have read your mind—though I'll swear, all I ever did was block your pain that other time and Truth-Read you today, which hardly even counts. Where do you come by all this wisdom?"

Derry gaped, not comprehending what he had said to cause such a reaction.

"My lord?" he whispered.

"Never mind," Morgan said with a wave of his hand, still chuckling. "I'll tell you this, though, Sean Lord Derry, new-made knight. I like your style. Honesty such as yours is rare enough in this world, and especially toward men like myself—and I don't refer entirely to my more unusual functionings. I suspect you'll find, now that you've been confirmed in your knightly rank, that earls have the same kinds of problems as dukes, in knowing when people are dealing honestly with them."

"Well, I'm only a very minor earl, Your Grace," Derry protested weakly.

"All the more reason you may be just the man I've been looking for," Morgan replied, almost to himself. "Tell me, would you find it of interest to consider entering my service as an aide?"

"*Y-Your* aide, sir?" Derry managed to murmur.

"Well, unless I've read you totally wrong, and you don't *want* to work for me. Any prestige normally attached to the position of a duke's aide is dubious, in my case, as I'm sure you're smart enough to have figured out; but it's essential that I have someone I can trust. I think you could be that man."

"But, you hardly know me, Your Grace."

Morgan smiled. "What makes you think I didn't check you out thoroughly before we had this little talk?"

"You did?" Derry said in a very small voice.

"I did."

"But—I came to *you*! How could you have known—?"

"Well, I didn't *know*, of course," Morgan replied. "Not that you'd approach me in precisely this way. And I certainly didn't know you'd prove to be so— perceptive was the word I used before, I believe, wasn't it?"

"Yes, sir."

"Well, then. Do you think you might be interested in the post? You don't have to tell me whether you accept or not—just whether you'd like to consider it. The financial benefits are only moderate, and the hours are long; but I think you'd find me a fair and honorable lord. And it would never be dull."

Derry was sure of that—and just as sure, without having to think about it any further, that he wanted the position. Lifting his eyes to Morgan's, he let himself be snared in the pale, silvery gaze, allowing himself the most tentative of smiles as he held out his right hand to the Deryni duke.

"Here's my answer and my hand on it, my lord," he said softly. "I don't need to consider it any further. I am your man, if you'll have me."

Grinning, Morgan clasped the offered hand and held it.

"You're sure? I can be very demanding, you know. And I can't guarantee that I'll always be able to explain my actions to your satisfaction; only that I'll always try to act in honor, and for Light rather than Darkness."

"What man could ask for more, my lord?" Derry breathed.

"How do you feel about the Church?" Morgan asked,

releasing Derry's hand. "They don't much approve of me, you know. That's why I stayed away from the basilica last night, even though young Arnaud would love to have had me present. Fortunately, I have an indulgent bishop and a very flexible confessor, and the king's chaplain looks out for me at court, but there are those who would stop at nothing to find an excuse to excommunicate me. It's very fortunate, for example, that the new Archbishop of Valoret was not present today. Edmund Loris does not like me at all. You could be damned by association."

Derry shrugged. "It seems to me I'd be in good company, my lord."

"That depends upon one's point of view," Morgan muttered. "On the positive side, however, you'd have the king's protection for yourself and your family— after my own protection, of course. And I think it safe to say that His Majesty would look kindly on the Earldom of Derry and its dependents."

"Then, what have I to fear, my lord?"

Morgan sighed happily. "Why, nothing, I suppose. God, I never dreamed it would be this easy to convince you. Shall we go and ask the king's blessing, before you change your mind? Our oaths should be witnessed."

"By the king?" Derry breathed, his eyes going wide.

"Of course, by the king!" Morgan muttered, rising and shooing Derry out of the window embrasure as he snatched up his coronet. "Here, take this for me. By all the saints, I think you're more in awe of him than you are of me!"

"Well, he *is* the king, my lord!" Derry whispered. Morgan's coronet seemed to tingle in his hands. "Before today, I'd only even *seen* him half a dozen times—and *never* had him speak to me."

Morgan only shook his head and chuckled as he guided Derry along the perimeter of the hall toward the royal dais. As at the Sieur de Vali's knighting, the Deryni duke did nothing to call attention to himself or his companion, but his mere passage accomplished that. Derry was very aware of being watched, and of how conversations fell off, then resumed after he and Morgan had passed by. He sensed—not precisely an overt hostility toward Morgan, for no one would dare that to the king's friend, in the king's hall, with the king present, but at least a caution, bordering on suspicion; and it was now directed at himself as well as Morgan. Derry could feel their eyes following him, marking how he carried Morgan's coronet, and he avoided looking at his uncle as he passed close to where Trevor stood chatting with one of the barons who held lands adjoining his—though he saw Trevor's shocked expression out of the corner of his eye.

By the time they reached the royal dais, where Brion and a youngish-looking priest sat listening to Queen Jehana tune a lute, young Prince Kelson sitting cross-legged at their feet, Derry had nearly forgotten how awed he was of the king—though that came flooding back into consciousness as Morgan paused at the foot of the steps to bow, Derry nervously echoing his salute. Brion had set his crown aside during the afternoon's feasting, but even without it, there was no mistaking who was Master of Gwynedd.

"Well, Alaric, I see you've been making the further acquaintance of one of our newest knights," the king said easily, setting aside a cup of ale. "Sir Sean O'Flynn, the Earl Derry, I believe?" As Derry made another nervous bow, King Brion grinned. "And I'll bet you thought I wouldn't remember, didn't you, what with all the other new young knights I made today?"

Derry swallowed hard, unsure how to take the royal bantering.

"Sire, you've made the lad speechless," Morgan said, coming to Derry's rescue with a smile. "You must make a point in future to speak to your young knights at other times besides at oath-givings, before full court. *I* don't seem to intimidate him."

"Oh, and does he not, young Derry?" the king said, turning his grey Haldane gaze full on Derry in mock seriousness. "And what mischief is this afoot, that my Deryni duke and one of my newest knights come before me like this?"

"'Tis no mischief, Sire," Derry managed to blurt out, summoning his courage from God knew where. "His Grace has asked—" He glanced at Morgan for support and got a nod of approval. "His Grace has asked that I enter his service, Sire. With Your Majesty's approval, I would ask that you witness our oaths, for I have accepted his offer with all my heart."

Brion nodded, his faint smile almost lost in the close-clipped black beard, and Queen Jehana set down her lute with a cold composure and rose.

"If you will excuse me, my lord," she murmured, "I have just recalled an errand elsewhere. Good day to you, Father Arilan."

Kelson glanced up at his father anxiously as his mother left, but Brion did not seem at all surprised at his queen's behavior. Nor did the priest.

"You must forgive the queen, young Derry," Arilan said softly. "I fear Her Majesty does not share our lord king's affection for his Deryni duke."

"Now, Denis," the king replied. "We mustn't give the lad the wrong idea."

"Best he knows what he will have to face, Sire, if he intends to serve a Deryni," the priest said. "Few are as tolerant as Your Majesty."

Brion snorted, laying a hand on his son's shoulder, then glanced at Morgan, who had not changed expression throughout the exchange.

"Well, Alaric, it does not seem that *all* my young knights are as tongue-tied as you would have me believe," he said lightly. "Young Derry has spoken very well. Would that I had learned his mettle sooner, for I would have taken him to my own service."

"Ah, but by granting him to me, Sire," Morgan pointed out, "you likewise gain his service, for by serving me, he serves you as well."

Brion chuckled, shaking his head in defeat.

"Enough, both of you. I know when I am bested. Denis, would you please hand me my crown?"

Morgan put on his own coronet as the priest rose to obey, and Brion glanced conspiratorially at Derry as he and Morgan knelt.

"You'll want to make the further acquaintance of Father Arilan, if you spend much time with Morgan," Brion said, as the priest handed him his crown and sat down again. "He's one of the few priests at court who won't lecture you about why you shouldn't consort with a Deryni. He's my confessor, and young Kelson's, and I recommend him highly."

Derry darted a quick glance at Arilan, but the priest only shrugged and smiled, gesturing with his eyes toward the crown Brion now held toward the two about to exchange oaths. Morgan had already laid his right hand upon it, and Derry quickly followed suit, awed to be actually touching the crown of Gwynedd.

"Sean Seamus O'Flynn, Lord Derry," Brion said, "do you, here before myself and God as witnesses, solemnly swear that you will render faithful service to Alaric Anthony Morgan, Duke of Corwyn, in all matters saving your duty to your king and the honor of this realm, so help you, God?"

"I do solemnly swear it, my Liege, so help me, God!" Derry whispered fervently.

Brion shifted his gaze to the smiling Morgan.

"And do you, Alaric Anthony Morgan, Duke of Corwyn, here before myself and God as witnesses, solemnly swear that you will be a true and honest overlord to this knight, Sean Seamus O'Flynn, Earl Derry, in all matters saving your duty to your king and the honor of this realm, so help you, God?"

"By my honor and by all the powers I have to command, I swear it, my Lord and my King, so help me, God," Morgan said steadily. "And if ever I should break this oath, may my powers desert me in my hour of need. So be it."

Brion smiled, raising the crown out of their touch to hand it back to Arilan.

"So be it, then," he repeated. "And I wish you both well of the partnership," he added, gesturing for them to rise. "Now, Alaric, have you spoken to Nigel yet about those archers of his? What *can* he have been thinking when he allowed them to use Bremagni bows?—though you mustn't let Jehana hear me speaking ill of her homeland. Still, everyone knows that the R'Kassans are the finest archers around. And Derry, see whether you can find Lord Rhodri, would you?

Denis will help you. He's somewhere in the hall. I can't imagine what's happened to the musicians he promised for this afternoon's entertainment."

"I'll come, too," said the eight-year-old Kelson, scrambling to his feet as Arilan rose to show Derry the way.

So, with that royal and priestly escort, did Sean Lord Derry begin his service both to the Crown of Gwynedd and to Alaric Morgan.

TRIAL
SPRING, 1118

Writing "Trial" was one of the more challenging projects
I've undertaken in the Deryni world. It didn't come as an
answer to a question I asked myself or my characters
about the Deryni; it came of putting together elements that
I was given, and weaving them into a story. I should explain.

In the winter of 1984, I went to a small, new science
fiction convention in the western United States. As sometimes happens to small, new conventions, this one had
underestimated its costs and had run into financial diffi-
culties. To raise money to get themselves out of their mon-
etary crunch, the Con committee asked each of the pros
present to donate something to be auctioned off: an auto-
graphed copy of a book, a manuscript, a dead ballpoint
pen used by the author—whatever might induce fans to
part with some of their cash in a worthy cause. I thought
about the request, then offered the following: I would write
a one-page scene involving the successful bidder with the
Deryni character of his or her choice, general theme to be
specified by purchaser.

Well, I never dreamed what a stir this would create; no

one did. The committee put the scene as the last item on the auction, and the fans went bonkers. When the bidding reached three figures, and people began forming consortia to pool their resources, I upped the ante to a two-page scene, if two or more people won it, with two Deryni characters of their choice.

I honestly don't recall how much the scene brought, though I believe it would have been a quite respectable payment for the average length short story in a typical science fiction or fantasy magazine, but the irony was that the two gentlemen who bought the scene had never read any of the Deryni books! The first buyer, an intense young man with a blondish mustache and the mythically suggestive last name of Stalker, wanted to be a King's Ranger, and voiced a preference for a pretty Deryni lady as companion in the scene—perhaps a minstrel. The other buyer, who goes by the name of Ferris and affects a Norse personna in the SCA (Society for Creative Anachronism), is a swordsmith who shows up at a lot of conventions selling weapons and armor. He wanted to be a version of his SCA self. But they both agreed that I could use my own discretion and put them with whatever Deryni characters I wanted.

So I took down physical descriptions and addresses and promised to get back to them as soon as I could. And I thought a lot, for several months—until suddenly, a storyline started to develop.

Well. I hadn't intended for the exercise to turn into a whole story, but I got carried away. (In fact, as the story began to materialize, I even entertained the notion that I might use it as my contribution to the Andre Norton anthology—but it soon turned the wrong direction for that.) Before I knew it, Ferris was an itinerant swordsmith from Eistenfalla, off the map north of Torenth, who had come to Kiltuin in Corwyn, Morgan's territory, to peddle weapons. Kiltuin, just downriver from Fathane but on the Corwyn side, is a port town held by Ralf Tolliver, Morgan's bishop; and Tolliver runs a tight ship—no lawlessness in Kiltuin.

But Ferris is a foreigner in town and doesn't speak the language very well; and he gets set up by—

But, read the story and see what happens. Stalker didn't get his Deryni minstrel girl, but he did get to be a King's Ranger; and Ferris got far more than he bargained for.

TRIAL

Pain dragged Ferris back to consciousness—a head-splitting point of fire pulsing behind his right ear, someone kicking him repeatedly in the ribs, and pressure crushing the fingers of his sword hand around something hard and sticky-warm.

"*Jesu*, she bled like a stuck pig!" someone muttered, "Watch out he doesn't get you with that knife!"

"He isn't getting *anybody* now!" a second voice answered, another kick punctuating the words. "Let's take care of the bastard!"

More voices joined in—harsh, urgent, conspiratorial—in a tongue Ferris only barely understood, even fully conscious; but their mood was clear even if the exact meaning was not. Sheer survival instinct made him try to arch and roll away from his tormentors, but he could not get the weapon in his hand to connect with anything but air. Two of them pinned his arms then, while two more continued pummeling and kicking. One particularly vicious blow connected with his solar plexus, eliciting a *Whoof!* of anguish and shoving him perilously near unconsciousness.

Where, in the name of the All-Father, was he? And why were these men trying to kill him? The last thing he remembered, he'd been leaving the Green Man Tavern, happily inebriated after drinking part of the profits of a very good sale. In fact, he'd sold the sword off his own belt.

But when he'd heard screams and the sound of a scuffle, and then the scrabble of running feet—

"Here now! What's going on?" a new voice demanded, the snap of authority causing the kicking to stop and Ferris' tormenters to draw back a little in consternation as light bobbled toward them and hard-shod footsteps approached.

"Damn, it's the watch!" one muttered.

"Get the knife away from him!" another responded, wrenching the hilt out of Ferris' numb fingers. "Ho, the watch! Come get this fellow! He's murdered the girl!"

It was only then, as they jerked him to his feet by both arms, that Ferris saw the crumpled body sprawled where he had just lain—and the dark stain spreading on the cobbles around her, bright crimson even by light of the approaching lantern. It soaked her fine linen gown and pooled where it still seeped from terrible wounds in her chest and a gaping slash across her throat.

"Hold him! Don't let him get away!"

But he was not trying to get away. After the beating he had taken, it was all he could do just to stay conscious. A groggy glance at his own clothing revealed that he, too, was covered with blood, and he feared very little of it was his own. His buff leather jerkin was slick with it, and he could feel it stiffening already in the fine hairs on the backs of his hands, clotting in his hair and beard where it had spattered.

"Please, I have done nothing!" he managed to gasp, as the man with the lantern pushed closer, muttering orders to the liveried men following him—and backed away almost immediately to fend off a second man who was trying to get a better look.

"Oh, God, is it Lillas?"

"You don't want to see this."

"He killed her! The bloody bastard's killed her!"

"I never *saw* her before!"

"Quiet, you!"

A knee to Ferris' groin doubled him up with pain, but he knew he must not let them silence him.

"No! By all the gods, I swear it!" he cried. "These men attacked me. I have killed no one!"

"By all the gods, he swears, eh?" One of the men holding Ferris forced him to his knees with a vicious twist of one of his already aching arms. "Heathen bastard!" He spat contemptuously in Ferris' face. "The hell he didn't!"

"Aye, there's no mistaking that!" another chimed in. "He's carved her up right proper, he has. God, would you just *look* at all this blood?"

The second man paid little attention to the exchange, still intent on getting past the sergeant for a look at the girl's body; but he pulled up short when he had seen her, shock and anguished disbelief quickly giving way to cold loathing as he straightened and turned to stare at Ferris.

"Stalker, no!" the man with the lantern cautioned, seizing a handful of the other's sleeve. "Don't do anything stupid!"

But the man addressed as Stalker only shook off the restraint and drew himself a little taller, staring down at Ferris as if he might slay him with a glance, his face white in the lantern light. Unlike the watch, in their town livery of russet and gold, he wore the ciphered leather doublet and thigh-high boots of a King's Ranger, a cockade of egret feathers jutting from the crown of his green leather hunt cap. He might have been of an age with Ferris—certainly no more than thirty—but his face, in his tight-leashed grief, had taken on an ageless and almost androgynous beauty, like statues of the Old Ones Ferris once had seen in the temple at Eistenfalla. For an instant, the man called Stalker *was* one of those Old Ones—and Ferris greatly feared for his very soul, even though he knew he was innocent.

"He's guilty as sin, Ranger," one of Ferris' captors volunteered, taking advantage of the taut silence. "We caught him with the knife in his hand."

"That's right," another agreed. "She was on the ground by the time we got here. There was nothing we could do."

His captors spoke far too fast for Ferris to catch most of what they said after that, but he did not have to understand every word to know that he was in serious trouble. He tried several times to argue his innocence, but he was not fluent enough to think of what to say until the moment was already past to say it— and his head was still spinning from the combined effect of drink and the blows he had taken.

The situation was a classic setup: the stranger in town framed for the crimes of the locals. And a stranger who was a foreigner as well, and who spoke the language badly, would find it nearly impossible to prove his innocence, especially when he appeared to have been taken literally red-handed.

"Well, I don't think we need to waste any more time arguing in the street," the watch sergeant finally said, stepping closer to the ranger. "It's pretty clear what happened."

"Aye, sir," another man of the watch chimed in. "Fresh fruit for the gallows tree, eh, lads?"

The men laughed; and Ferris stiffened, for he understood *those* words all too well. He had seen the rotting
bodies gibbeted outside the town gates. For an instant
he wondered whether they meant to hang him now,
without a trial.

Not that a trial would necessarily help. Kiltuin town
belonged to the Bishop of Corwyn, who had the meting
of High as well as Low Justice within its bounds—and
Kiltuin, rowdy port town and near to the border with
hostile Torenth, was a place where the High Justice
must often be invoked. The right to impose capital
punishment went with the meting of High Justice, and
murder was second only to treason in the list of crimes
meriting the death penalty.

Nor might murder be the only crime of which Ferris
was accused. Bishop Ralf Tolliver was said to be a fair
and honest judge, but he was also a Christian bishop;
and while Ferris respected the faith practiced in Gwynedd, he embraced another religion. Just *what* religion
might become all too clear during trial before a man
like Tolliver. In times not too far past, even in parts of
Ferris' own homeland, those who followed the path of
the All-Father had suffered nearly the same kinds of
terrible persecutions as the Deryni, whose magic was
said to damn them to the Christians' version of the
Seven Hells Ferris feared. Ferris had heard it rumored
that Corwyn's Duke, Tolliver's temporal overlord, was
half Deryni, but he did not know whether to believe
that or not. He had never personally met a Deryni.

"Sergeant, take him before I do something we may
all regret," the ranger said finally, the temperate words
obviously uttered only with the greatest of difficulty
as he averted his eyes from Ferris and the body
stretched motionless beside them. "Only the bishop

may determine what fruit the gallows tree shall bear. His Excellency will see justice done."

The sergeant of the watch let out a sigh of relief and motioned his men forward with a jut of his chin.

"Right. Let's bind him securely, then, lads. He looks like a scrapper. What's your name, man?" he demanded, as they looped the leather around Ferris' wrists and drew them roughly behind him.

That, at least, Ferris understood perfectly well. It was the first time they had bothered to ask him anything. If only he could get them to listen.

"My name is Ferris." He winced as the thongs tightened on his wrists and another was looped around his neck like a halter. "I make swords. I did not kill the girl."

"Sure you didn't," the sergeant said. "That's what they all say. Take him away, lads. The bishop will try him in the morning."

To Ferris' surprise, he suffered no further physical abuse once the watch had him in their charge and led him away. The dungeons beneath the bishop's hall were clean enough and occupied by only a handful of other wretches awaiting justice the next morning, so Ferris was given a cell of his own—though not an opportunity to wash off the blood of the girl he had not slain.

He spent what was left of the night nursing his bruised ribs and throbbing head, the latter made doubly agonizing by his hangover and a tender knot behind one ear. Lying there on the straw, pain dulling his ability to reason, his hand itched for even one of the many blades he had forged over the years, and a chance to use it—if not to fight his way out of here, then at least to cheat the hangman of his prey and die in a manner of his own choosing, for he had little hope that his word would be taken over that of the four toughs who had framed him. In fact, it was probably they who had killed the girl and had seized on his vulnerability— drunk and a stranger in town—to pin the blame on him. Ah, gods, it was hopeless!

It got worse, too. The guards who came to get him shortly after dawn had been well trained, and he never had a chance to even try to escape. All too efficiently, they cuffed his hands in front of him with fine, key-locked manacles, the workmanship worthy of his own skills, and virtually escape-proof. Then they laced a stout wooden bar through his bent elbows and behind the small of his back.

He had expected the restraints, but he had *not* expected the leather gag they buckled tightly around his head, with its wooden mouthpiece like a horse's bit thrust between his teeth and partway down his throat. He retched and gagged almost uncontrollably as they fitted it on him, and found that any attempt to make a sound produced a similar gagging reflex.

"Keep quiet and it isn't all that bad," one of the guards said, as Ferris caught his breath and straightened cautiously to stare at them in shock. The man was a different guard from any of the night before. "You'll get your chance to speak. The witnesses said you'd a foul mouth on you. His Excellency doesn't like to be interrupted when he's hearing a case."

Well, there was little likelihood of that, Ferris thought bitterly, as they took him, staggering a little, up the steep stone stairs and into the bishop's hall, steering him by the ends of the bar through his arms. Had they troubled to ask, he would have given them his word of his silence, but why should they bother? As far as they were concerned, his guilt was a foregone conclusion. All that remained was the bishop's confirmation. As they led him down the length of the hall toward the dais and Bishop Tolliver's chair of state, Ferris made himself study the man who held his life and death in his hands.

The bishop was younger than Ferris had expected: fortyish and fit—no paunchy churchman, he. The tonsured brown hair was scarcely touched with grey, and his clean-shaven face glowed with the healthy tan of one who enjoyed regular outings in the open air. His waist probably had gained no more than a few finger-widths since adolescence.

Polished riding boots with spurs protruded beneath the hem of his purple cassock, and he wore the purple mantle of his office like the prince he was. The hand adorned with a bishop's amethyst was quick and grace-ful as it made some signal to a clark reading back the transcript of the trial just completed, and Ferris thought it might have wielded a sword or a crozier with equal facility.

The steely-eyed appraisal of the trained warrior was in Tolliver's eyes as he flicked his gaze briefly toward the approaching Ferris, and the swordsmith found him-self automatically measuring the man for one of his finer blades—until the bishop's glance shifted to the four well-dressed men lounging on a bench opposite the prisoner's dock. With a start that almost made him choke on his gag, Ferris realized that the men were the same who had accused him the night before—clearly men of substance and some standing in the town!

The shock of that discovery, and the resulting futil-ity of his own position, kept Ferris from paying very much attention to what happened next. He had enough presence of mind to incline his head in respect as his guards paused to salute the bishop—an act that clearly startled more than one person in the hall, not the least of whom was the ranger seated with the clarks to the bishop's right—but mounting the prisoner's dock was an indignity he had hoped never to face. He might be a foreign devil in their eyes, but, by the gods, he was an honest man!

His guards remained with him once he was in place, each with a hand resting on an end of his controlling bar, as if they expected him to try to bolt for freedom. The three men of the previous night's watch sat on a bench between the dock and the bishop. Other people were in the hall as well, but Ferris had no idea whether they had business with the court or were merely curiosity seekers. Far at the back of the hall, on a black-draped catafalque, lay a coffin covered with a black pall. He guessed, with a sickish feeling in his guts, that it was the girl's. Lillis, the ranger had called her.

Ferris tried to follow what his accusers said, but the language barrier and the frustration and discomfort of his own physical situation served to run most of what was said into a vague blur of mounting evidence against him—circumstantial, to be sure, but weighted by the stature of the men who accused him. Each new testimony embellished on the previous one and damned him further.

An unexpected development came with the statement of one of the two black-habited nuns who had prepared the girl's body for burial. Ferris gathered, from what he could catch of the woman's soft, self-conscious testimony, that the girl had been of good family and reputation, convent-educated, and betrothed to the royal ranger seated with the clarks—admirable traits, but hardly pertinent to whether or not Ferris had killed her, so far as he could tell.

But as the bishop pursued his questioning of the woman, the reason suddenly became all too clear. For suddenly she burst into tears and babbled out a short but impassioned accusation, the most prominent word of which was rape.

"I'll kill him!" the ranger screamed, launching himself across the hall at Ferris as the four accusers leaped to their feet and added their own verbal abuse.

Until the ranger actually had his hands around Ferris' throat, Ferris could not believe what he had heard. His vision was going grey by the time the guards could prise the ranger's hands loose and drag him, cursing and weeping, to the foot of the dock to hold him. Ferris' guards hoisted him back to his feet by the bar across his back, checking his gag to make certain he could breathe again, but Ferris hardly cared as he gasped for air. He had caught the sense of the new accusation, if not the exact terms, and it was even more outrageous than the first—and doubly damning.

But while the bailiffs were restoring order to the court, and before the bishop could admonish those responsible for the outburst, two newcomers appeared in the doorway whose presence produced an instant hush and cessation of activity. People on either side of the center aisle rose as the two came forward, the women bobbing self-conscious curtsies and the men tugging at forelocks in respect.

No one told Ferris who they were, of course. The younger one in the bright blue cloak appeared to be a squire or aide—a fresh-faced lad probably still in his teens, moving with the grace of good training, merry blue eyes peering from beneath a mane of untamed brown curls. But the other—

It was *he* who had brought the proceedings so abruptly to a halt, though he was hardly more than a lad himself. No accoutrement of rank or feature of attire had caused the deference he received as he strode toward the dais with the boy at his side. His travel-stained black riding leathers were quite unremarkable for a man whose appearance has just elicited so dramatic a response, the sword at his belt no more than serviceable, so far as Ferris could tell from his own vantage point, though certainly a constant and accustomed part of his life.

Nor was the man particularly physically imposing or menacing, though there was that about him which spoke of unmistakable power come of authority that is not questioned. He was a bit above average height, with the lean, graceful physique of a man accustomed to rigorous physical activity—he was probably a master of the weapon at his side—but he had none of that hardness one often saw in mercenaries or other professional soldiers. On the contrary, his features declared gentle breeding: grey eyes in a handsome, clean-shaven face; firm jaw; a close-cropped cap of pale gold hair, straight and fine.

What was there about him, then, that elicited the respect and subtle apprehension Ferris was noting in the rest of the observers? It was more than mere command presence or even rank. Even the bishop rose as the man reached the foot of the dais steps and continued right up them, his companion pausing to bow before following after. And the bishop bowed to the man before the man bent to kiss his bishop's ring.

"Your Grace, you are most welcome," the bishop said, gesturing for one of the bailiffs to bring another chair. "Pray, what brings you to Kiltuin? I thought you were in Rhemuth."

The man passed a parchment packet to the bishop as he glanced casually around the hall.

"I was. Business recalled me to Coroth, however, so His Majesty asked me to deliver these deeds into your keeping. But, I'm surprised, Ralf. Do you often permit such outbursts in your court?"

Tolliver proffered a grim and tight-lipped smile as he glanced briefly at the documents and then passed them to a clark as the bailiff placed another chair at his right.

"Now, you know better than that. The case has aroused local anger, however. Would you care to assist me in hearing it?"

"Certainly. But as an observer only." The man declined Tolliver's gesture toward the high chair and took the lesser one instead, leather-gloved hands laying a riding crop across leather-clad knees. "What's the fellow done?"

And as he turned his gaze on Ferris, standing dumbfounded in the prisoner's box, Ferris had the fleeting sensation that the man saw into his very soul. He could not look away so long as the grey eyes held him, but as soon as the man's glance shifted back to the bishop, following the low-voiced summary the bishop gave, Ferris desperately turned his face toward the nearer of his two guards in question.

"That's the duke," the man murmured, obviously aware what he was trying to ask. "Now you're really in for it."

And Ferris, glancing back at the man in black, knew

a moment of even greater apprehension than before—for if the Bishop of Corwyn was known to be a stern judge, then the Duke of Corwyn held that reputation doubly. And Alaric Morgan, Duke of Corwyn, was said to be Deryni, privy to dark powers undreamed by ordinary mortals!

"I see," Morgan murmured, still in converse with the bishop. "And the gag?"

Tolliver shrugged. "The witnesses said he was belligerent, that he would be a disruption in the court," he replied, gesturing toward the four well-dressed accusers sitting in the front row, who looked a little less sure of themselves since Morgan's arrival. "It's a common enough precaution, until it's time for the accused to speak."

"Hmmm. It seems to me that yon ranger was more of a disruption than the prisoner," Morgan replied drolly, with a slight nod in the direction of the now reseated and embarrassed Stalker.

"Aye. But the murdered girl was to be his bride, Your Grace," Tolliver said. "And just before you arrived, the good sisters who prepared the body for burial revealed that her attacker's crime was rape as well as murder."

"Ah."

Morgan's face hardened at that, and Ferris could not help shrinking a little harder against the back rail of the dock as the duke's glance flicked disdainfully over him again—though he was as innocent of the one crime as the other.

Not that innocence had much to do with what was happening here today. Even if Ferris were given a chance to tell his side of the story, he knew no one would believe him. Not over the word of the four men who accused him. He was stunned, then, at Morgan's next question of the bishop.

"Have you heard his testimony yet?"

"No, Your Grace. We had just finished the testimony of the witnesses."

"Very well." Morgan gestured toward the guards still standing at Ferris' sides. "Take that bridle off and bring him here."

"Out of the dock, Your Grace?" one of the bailiffs asked, shocked, as the guards moved to obey.

"Unless you intend to have the dock brought here as well," Morgan replied with a wry quirk of his mouth. "Do you think I can't keep him under control, even without the arm restraints?"

Ferris could not help being amazed at the touch of wry humor, even though he also felt apprehension at the vaguely implied threat of Morgan's words. He decided he might even like the man, under other circumstances—and he could hardly blame Morgan for feeling hostility, given the crimes of which Ferris was accused. Was it possible that he might get a fair hearing after all? Both the bishop and Morgan were said to be fair and incorruptable, but would that hold true where a stranger was concerned?

He worked his jaw nervously several times when the gag had been removed, relieved of the discomfort of the bit and straps, and tried not to let his fear show as the two guards walked him out of the dock and toward the dais steps. He thumped to both knees at the bottom of the steps before the guards could make him kneel, giving Morgan and the bishop a deeply respectful bow of his head.

"Please, my lords, let me speak," he pleaded as he straightened to search their eyes. "I—do not know your language very well, but I—am innocent. I swear it!"

The bishop only sighed patiently at the expected denial, but Morgan became more thoughtful, his eyes narrowing a little as he stared back at Ferris.

"This is not your native tongue?" he asked.

Ferris shook his head. "No, my lord. I come from Eistenfalla. I make swords. I—understand well enough to trade in weapons, but not—too fast."

As the bishop shifted in his chair, apparently about to intervene, Morgan waved him off.

"I see. Well, I don't think anyone here speaks your language, so we'll have to make do. Do you understand why you are here?"

Ferris nodded carefully, amazed and grateful that the duke seemed to be willing to listen to his side.

"They say that I killed a woman, my lord—"

"And raped her," the bishop interjected.

"No, my lord!"

"That *is* what they say, is it not?" Morgan replied.

"They say it, yes. But I did not do it, my lord!"

"The holy sisters say otherwise, Alaric," the bishop murmured exasperatedly, "and he was taken with the bloody dagger in his hand. That's her blood all over his clothes. Four witnesses of excellent reputation say they saw him do it."

"Really?" Morgan murmured, coming to his feet with casual grace. "That's very interesting, because I think he's telling the truth."

And as his words sank in and a whisper of surprise and apprehension rippled through the hall, the bishop looking the most startled of all, Morgan glided down the dais steps to stand directly before the kneeling Ferris.

"No one has told me your name," Morgan said, handing off his riding crop to his aide and briskly stripping off his black leather gloves. "What is it?"

Ferris could not take his eyes from Morgan's.

"F—Ferris, my lord," he managed to whisper.

"Ferris," Morgan repeated. "And do you know who I am?"

"The—the Duke of Corwyn, my lord."

"What else do you know about me?" Morgan persisted.

"That—that you are a man of honor, my lord."

"And?"

"And that justice is done in your courts."

"And?"

Ferris swallowed, not wanting to say it.

"Go ahead. What else?" Morgan demanded.

"That—that you are D-Deryni, my lord," Ferris managed to choke out, unable even then to tear his eyes away from Morgan's.

"That is correct," Morgan said, flicking his gaze for the merest of instants to the four witnesses watching with wide-eyed fascination. "Can you tell me what that means to you, that I am Deryni?" he asked quietly.

"That—that you consort with black magic," Ferris found himself saying, to his horror.

Morgan grimaced and gave a heavy sigh. "Magic, yes. The color is rather open to interpretation. I have some special powers, Ferris, but I try to use them only in the cause of justice."

At Ferris' look of uncertainty—for Morgan's vocabulary had begun to exceed his understanding again—the duke stopped and gave him a patient smile.

"You don't understand but half of what I'm saying, do you?"

Ferris dared to shake his head slightly.

"Do you understand when I say that I can tell when a man is lying?"

"*I* am not lying, my lord!" Ferris whispered desperately. "I did not kill the woman! I did not rape her, either!"

"No, I see that you did not," Morgan replied. And as Ferris gasped in astonishment, tears welling in his eyes that he had finally been believed, Morgan added, "But perhaps you can tell us who did."

"But I—I do not know, my lord!" Ferris started to protest.

"Remember last night," Morgan commanded, taking Ferris' head between his hands, thumbs resting on the temples, his eyes holding Ferris from any attempt to draw away.

Ferris feared he might drown in those eyes. He could see nothing else. And Morgan's touch bought a heady helplessness, a sweet-sickly sense of vertigo that started at the top of his head and swooped down to the pit of his stomach, making his knees go to jelly.

He felt the guards supporting him by the ends of his control bar as he sank back on his haunches, beyond any ability to resist what was happening to him; but as his eyes fluttered closed, he lost all awareness of Morgan, the guards, the hall, or any of the rest of his present situation. Suddenly it was night, and he was stumbling down an alley that he hoped led back to the inn where he was staying, wondering whether he should have drunk so much.

Cries, then—shrill and terrified, in pain. Running to see who called—and the sound of footsteps in the shadows. He caught only a glimpse of a still, slight form clad in light-colored clothing, and dark figures scattering at his approach, before someone struck him solidly from behind, and everything went black.

The next thing he knew, he was being beaten and kicked, his head aswim from drink and the blows, covered with blood, trying to cringe from the booted feet. And then the watch was there, and his captors were saying he had done it, and he had no words to tell them of his innocence.

"Release him," he heard a voice say, as he abruptly became aware of his body again and the hands clamped to his temples were removed. "He didn't do it. I think, however, that I know who did."

He opened his eyes in time to see Morgan turning to survey the four witnesses ranged on the bench behind and to his left. The men rose nervously as Morgan looked at them, no longer as self-confident as they had been only minutes before. Their nervousness increased as the bishop signalled half a dozen guards to move in behind them, though the guards made no attempt to touch them.

It was quickly done, to Ferris' continued surprise and awe. While his guards untied his hands and released him, helping him to his feet, Morgan moved before the four witnesses, one by one, and asked each the same three questions: "Did you kill the girl?" "Did you participate in the rape?" "Did you agree among yourselves to accuse the swordsmith?"

The Deryni lord did not touch them; only fixed each with that cool, irresistible silver gaze and commanded the truth. And though only one answered yes to the first question, all four, without exception, answered yes to the second and third. They appeared to be a little dazed as Morgan returned calmly to the dais and the guards moved in to bind their wrists behind them.

"I trust you don't think I've stepped out of line, Bishop," Ferris heard Morgan murmur to Tolliver as he sat once more in the chair at the bishop's right. "Is there any doubt in your mind that justice has been done?"

Tolliver slowly shook his head. "Thank God you arrived when you did, Alaric," he replied softly. "Otherwise, we should have hanged an innocent man."

"Aye, he is," Morgan replied, glancing out at Ferris again, who was rubbing his wrists absently and staring at the Deryni lord in awe. "You are free to go, sword-smith. The men who accused you falsely shall hang for that, and for their other crimes." He ignored the murmurs of consternation as his words sank in on the four guilty men. "I only wish there were some way to repay you for what you have suffered."

Ferris' jaw dropped in amazement, and he wondered whether he had understood correctly. The duke had already given him his life, when he had thought never to see another day. It was he, not Morgan, who should be offering some token of recompense; and glancing at the blade lying close along Morgan's thigh— too short, by a hand-span, to take full advantage of the man's reach, and probably ill-balanced, to boot— Ferris thought he knew what would please.

"You have already paid any debt to me by giving of your justice, my lord," Ferris said, dropping to one knee and giving salute with right fist to heart in the manner of his people. "But may I—ask one favor of Your Lordship?"

"What is it?" Morgan asked.

"I—I would rather speak with you in private, if I may, my lord."

At Morgan's gesture, Ferris rose and mounted the

dais steps, bowing slightly to the bishop and then asking with a glance whether he and Morgan might withdraw a little further. With a nod, Morgan got up and
led him off the dais to one side, hand resting easily on
the hilt of the sword that had given Ferris' swordsmith's eye offense from the floor of the hall.

"I thank you, my lord," Ferris murmured, controlling a smile as he noticed Morgan's young aide taking
up a position of vigilance at a discreet distance outside
the window embrasure they entered. "I—have not the
words in your tongue to express my gratitude. I do not
understand how you did—what you did. I think, from
the look on your bishop's face, that he almost wishes
you had not done it, for he fears your power, even
though he respects you as a man—but I wanted to tell
you that—that I will no longer be afraid when people
speak of the Deryni."

"No?" Morgan replied with a wry little smile. "Then
you will be but a rare one among the many who are."

"You have a skill that you use for the cause of truth,"
Ferris said stubbornly. "My people value the pursuit
of truth. The All-Fa—"

"You need say no more," Morgan said quietly, a
more wistful smile playing about his lips. "I suspected,
from the start, that you worshipped the All-Father.
Your people and mine have both suffered because of
their differences, I think. Is that what you wanted to
tell me?"

"Not—all, my lord," Ferris breathed. "Would you—
would you draw your sword for me?"

"My sword?"

"Yes, my lord. I am a master swordsmith, as I have
said. I noticed that your blade seems short for the reach
of your arm. Can you show me your stance?"

Raising one blond eyebrow, Morgan stepped back a pace and eased the weapon from its sheath, at the same time telling his aide, by sign, that there was no danger. When, at Ferris' direction, he had swung the sword through several basic exercises, he saluted with a flourish and tossed the hilt into Ferris' waiting fist.

"So, swordsmith, is it a goodly blade or no?"

"The swordsman is goodly, my lord," Ferris muttered, as he hefted the blade in his own hand, "but he could be better still, with the right weapon."

Ignoring the duke's look of surprise, Ferris moved farther into the window and laid the blade across his forearm while he turned it to and fro in the light, sighting along the steel for ripples or other imperfections—of which there were none. When he had flexed it between his hands, he motioned Morgan to step back and ran through his own set of exercises designed to test the balance of a blade. When he was done, he flipped it into the air and caught it just beneath the quillons, then extended it back to Morgan, hilt-first.

"Well?"

"It is, indeed, a goodly blade, my lord, but not for you," Ferris said happily. "Save it for your son. I can make you a better."

"*Can* you?" Morgan replied, the one eyebrow rising in wry if dubious question as he slid the weapon back into its scabbard, to the watching aide's obvious relief. "And what might such a blade cost me, master swordsmith?"

"A place to work," Ferris said promptly. "The steel from which to forge it. Enough of your time to fit the weapon to your own style. You deserve a gallant blade, my lord. It is the least I can do. And if you are pleased with my work, perhaps—perhaps you would take me into your service?" he asked recklessly.

Morgan stared into his eyes for so long that Ferris was sure the Deryni lord must be reading his mind, but he did not care. He *liked* this man. He suspected he would have liked him even if Morgan had *not* saved his life. What was more, he respected him. The Duke of Corwyn was a man he could happily serve.

"You know that Deryni can read men's minds, don't you?" Morgan suddenly said, in a very low voice. "Surely that must frighten you."

"I have nothing to hide from you, my lord," Ferris said slowly, meaning every word. "You would be a fair and honest master and do honor to my work. I could not ask for more."

"Only—" Morgan murmured.

Ferris swallowed, suddenly ashamed of his misgiving.

"Only what, my lord?"

"Only, you *are* just a little afraid," Morgan said gently, "which is certainly understandable." He sighed wearily as he turned to gaze out the window. "You wonder whether I was reading your mind just now, and whether I would in the future. I cannot blame you for that."

"Forgive me, my lord," Ferris whispered, certain that any chance of serving the Deryni duke was now gone.

"No, you have a right to wonder," Morgan said. "And you deserve an answer to your unspoken question. I was not reading your mind just now; and I would not in the future, if you served me, except for a specific reason—and then it would only be with your permission, unless there were dire reasons otherwise." He quirked a strained, lopsided smile in Ferris' direction. "I'd have to touch you, in any case."

"As you did out there?" Ferris breathed, remembering the eerie, helpless sensation as Morgan had ordered him to remember.

"Yes. It would be easier if you were cooperating, if I had to do it again."

"But you didn't touch the other four," Ferris pointed out.

"No, but I wasn't reading their actual thoughts, either. I was Truth-Reading. There's a difference."

"Oh." Ferris swallowed uneasily and tried to assimilate all that Morgan had just said.

"I don't know why I'm telling you all this," Morgan muttered. "A man shouldn't tell a total stranger about his limitations." He gave Ferris a sidelong glance. "Maybe it's because I think I *would* like to have you serve me—and it's only fair that you know what you're getting into, if you do. Maybe it's also that I sensed your basic honesty and integrity, when I did have to read your mind."

"I *would* be loyal to you, my lord!" Ferris said fiercely. "I swear by all the gods, I would!"

Smiling, Morgan glanced down at the hilt of the sword at his waist, then back at Ferris.

"By all the gods, I think you would. But this is not the time for either of us to make that kind of commitment. I've just delivered you from the jaws of a very unjust death. It's only natural that you should be grateful. You've offered to make me a better sword in return. I accept. So why don't you ride back to Coroth with me and my aide this afternoon, and I'll put you to work? When you've delivered the sword, *then* we'll decide about the future."

"Done, my lord!" Ferris said, as he and Morgan began moving out of the window embrasure to rejoin Morgan's aide. "But I know what *my* decision will be."

KEY TO ABBREVIATIONS

C   = Catalyst
HS = Healer's Song
V   = Vocation
B   = Bethane
PA = The Priesting of Arilan
L   = Legacy
KD = The Knighting of Derry
T   = Trial
*   = Character or Place appears
      in one or more of the
      Deryni novels.

INDEX OF CHARACTERS

ALDRED, Prince—grandson of Nimur II of Torenth and nephew of Wencit; Deryni; age 15 in June of 1105. (L)

ALISTER Cullen, Bishop—Deryni Chancellor of Gwynedd and Bishop of Grecotha in 914; alter ego of Camber MacRorie. (HS)*

ARGOSTINO, Father—heavy-set young Llanneddi priest ordained with Denis Arilan in 1105. (PA)

ARIELLA, Princess—sister and lover of Imre, the last Festillic King of Gwynedd; Deryni. (L)*

ARILAN, Father Denis—Deryni ordained priest in spring of 1105 at *Arx Fidei* Seminary, age 21. By 1115, he was Confessor to King Brion. (PA; KD)*

ARILAN, Sir Jamyl—elder brother of Denis; age 25 in 1104–5; close friend and confidant of King Brion; member of the Camberian Council. (PA)

ARNULF, Father—aged household chaplain at Castle d'Eirial in 977. (V)

AUGARIN Haldane, King—first High King of Gwynedd. (L)*

BARRETT de Laney—young Deryni lord who negotiated the freedom of a score of condemned Deryni children by offering himself in their place; blinded before rescued by Darrell; later, a member of the Camberian Council. (B)*

BENJAMIN, Father—seminarian at *Arx Fidei*, ordained with Denis Arilan in 1105. (PA)

BETHANE—old woman who keeps sheep near Culdi; wife of Darrell. (B)*

BRION Haldane, King—King of Gwynedd, 1095–1120; father of Kelson and brother of Nigel. (PA; L; KD)*

CALBERT, Father—energetic young Abbot of *Arx Fidei* Seminary in 1104–5. (PA)

CAMBER MacRorie—Deryni Earl of Culdi; father of Cathan, Joram, Evaine. (C; HS)*

CAPRUS d'Eirial, Lord—seventeen-year-old younger son of Sir Radulf, Baron d'Eirial in 977, and half-brother to the heir, Sir Gilrae d'Eirial. (V)

CAROLUS, Crown Prince—elder son of Nimur II and father of Prince Aldred; Deryni; brother of Wencit; 35 in 1105. (L)

CATHAN MacRorie—eldest son of Camber; Deryni; 15 in 888. (C)*

CHARISSA, Lady—daughter and only child of Hogan Gwernach, The Marluk; Deryni; age 11 in summer of 1105. (L)*

CHARLES FitzMichael, Father—young priest ordained with Denis Arilan in 1105. (PA)

CULLEN, Alister—see ALISTER Cullen.

DARBY, Father Alexander—newly appointed pastor of St. Mark's Church, near *Arx Fidei*, in 1104. His treatise on Deryni, written when he was a seminarian at Grecotha, became required study for all aspiring clergy. Trained as a physician. (PA)

DARRELL—husband of Bethane; a teacher of mathematics in Grecotha and secretly Deryni; killed rescuing Barrett de Laney. (B)*

DE COURCY, Jorian—see JORIAN de Courcy.

DE NORE, Archbishop Oliver—Archbishop of Valoret and Primate of All Gwynedd in 1104–5, who ordained Denis Arilan; known to have burned Deryni in the south as a itinerant bishop. (PA)

DERRY, Lord (Sir Sean Seamus O'Flynn)—Marcher

earl knighted by King Brion in spring, 1115; aide to Alaric Morgan. (KD; T)*

DE VALI, Arnaud, Sieur—young vassal of Morgan, knighted with Derry in 1115. (KD)*

DEVERIL, Lord—Duke Jared's seneschal in 1100. (B)*

ELGIN de Torres—junior seminarian at *Arx Fidei* in 1105. (PA)

ERDIC, Father—chaplain to the d'Eirial family in the 960's. (V)

EVAINE MacRorie—daughter of Camber; Deryni; 6 in 888; later, wife of Rhys Thuryn. (C; HS)*

FERRIS—a swordsmith from Eistenfalla; makes a sword for Morgan in 1118–19. (T)

FESTIL I—a younger son of the Torenthi royal house who, in 822, established the Deryni Interregnum in Gwynedd and founded the Royal House of Festil, which reigned for 82 years. (L)*

GILBERT, Master—d'Eirial battle-surgeon. (V)

GILRAE d'Eirial, Sir—twenty-year-old heir to the Barony d'Eirial, who wants to be a priest; elder half-brother of Caprus d'Eirial. (V)

GORONY, Father Lawrence—chaplain to Archbishop de Nore in 1104–5. (PA)*

HALDANE—see AUGARIN; BRION; KELSON; NIGEL; UTHYR.*

HASSAN—Hogan Gwernach's Moorish Deryni tactician, and bodyguard to him and Charissa. (L)

HOGAN Gwernach—see MARLUK, the.

IMRE of Festil, King—last Festillic King of Gwynedd, during the Deryni Interregnum; fathered a bastard son on his sister Ariella. (L)*

JEBEDIAH of Alcara, Sir—Deryni Earl Marshal of Gwynedd and Grand Master of the Order of Saint Michael in 914. (HS)*

JEHANA, Queen—consort to King Brion and mother of Prince Kelson; Deryni, but unknown until Kelson's coronation. (KD)*

JOCELYN, Lady—Camber's countess; Deryni; mother of Cathan, Joram, and Evaine. (C)*

JORAM MacRorie—son of Camber; Deryni; 10 in 888; later, a priest and Knight of Saint Michael. (C; HS)*

JORIAN de Courcy, Father—young Deryni ordained to the priesthood in 1104, age 21; discovered and executed by archbishop's tribunal. (PA)

JULIUS—a horse dealer at the Rhelled horse fair in 1115. (KD)

KELSON Haldane, Prince—heir of King Brion, 8 in 1115. (KD)*

LARAN ap Pardyce—Deryni physician and scholar, age 46 in 1104; an ally of Jamyl and Denis Arilan and member of the Camberian Council. (PA)*

LILLAS—betrothed of Stalker, a King's Ranger; raped and killed in Kiltuin in 1117. (T)

LORCAN, Sir—d'Eirial seneschal in 977. (V)

LORIS, Archbishop Edmund—newly appointed Archbishop of Valoret in 1115; does not like Morgan. (KD)*

LOYALL, Father—abbot's chaplain at *Arx Fidei* in 1104–5. (PA)

MACLYN—a horse-handler employed by Julius at the Rhelledd horse fair of 1115. (KD)

MACON—Duke Jared's battle-surgeon in 1100. (B)

MARK of Festil, Prince—son of Imre and his sister Ariella, and ancestor of Charissa. (L)*

MARLUK, the—Hogan Gwernach, Deryni; father of Charissa; scion of the Festillic line claiming the throne of Gwynedd; killed by King Brion, June 21, 1105, age 45. (L)*

MacRORIE—see CAMBER; CATHAN; EVAINE; JOCELYN; JORAM.

MALACHI de Bruyn—junior seminarian at *Arx Fidei* in 1105. (PA)

MELWAS, Father—young priest ordained with Denis Arilan in 1105. (PA)

MORGAN, Sir Alaric—Deryni Duke of Corwyn. (B; PA; KD; T)*

NIGEL Haldane, Prince—King Brion's younger brother. (L; KD)*

NIMUR II, King—Deryni King of Torenth, 1080–1106; father of Princes Carolus and Wencit. (L)

O'FLYNN, Sir Seamus Michael—Earl Derry; father of Sean Lord Derry; died 1108 of wounds sustained on Mearan campaign with King Brion in 1107. (KD)

O'FLYNN, Sean Seamus, Earl Derry—see DERRY.

ORIOLT, Father—young priest ordained at *Arx Fidei* with Jorian de Courcy in 1104, age 21. (PA)

PADRIG Udaut—Derry's eleven-year-old cousin; son of Trevor Udaut, Baron Varagh. (KD)

RADULF d'Eirial, Sir—Baron d'Eirial; dying father of Gilrae and Caprus. (V)

RANDOLPH, Master—Morgan's physician/battle-surgeon. (KD)*

RHODRI, Lord—royal chamberlain at Rhemuth in 1115. (KD)*

RHYS Thuryn—Deryni foster son of Camber; 11 in 888; later, husband of Evaine MacRorie, and a Healer. (C; HS)*

ROMARE—Derry's blacksmith. (KD)

RIORDAN, Father—Master of Novices at *Arx Fidei* Seminary in 1104–5. (PA)

SERELD, Dom—the King's Healer in 888, approaching 50. (C)

SIMONN—Healer-hermit at ruined St. Neot's in 977. (V)*

STALKER—a King's Ranger based at Kiltuin, a port town near the Torenthi border, in 1118. (T)

STEFAN Coram—a Deryni ally of Jamyl and Denis Arilan and member of the Camberian Council; in his late 20's in 1104–5. (PA)*

TARLETON—guard captain who negotiated with Barrett de Laney for the release of Deryni children. (B)

THURYN—see RHYS; TIEG Joram.

TIEG Joram Thuryn—infant son of Rhys and Evaine; a future Healer. (HS)*

TOLLIVER, Bishop Ralf—Bishop of Corwyn in 1118; holds Kiltuin town directly of Morgan. (T)*

TREVOR Udaut, Baron Varagh—Derry's uncle (mother's brother) and his sponsor for knighthood in 1115; father of Padrig. (KD)

UDAUT—see PADRIG; TREVOR.

UTHYR Haldane, King—King of Gwynedd, 948–980. (V)*

VARAGH, Baron—see TREVOR Udaut.

WENCIT, Prince—second son of Nimur II, King of Torenth; Deryni and brother of Prince Carolus; 32 in 1105. (L)*

INDEX OF PLACE NAMES

ARX FIDEI SEMINARY—near Valoret, where Jorian de Courcy and Denis Arilan studied for the priesthood and were ordained. (PA)

BREMAGNE—kingdom to the east; homeland of Jehana. (KD)*

CARDOSA—fortress city in the Rheljan Mountains, on the Gwynedd–Torenth border. (L)*

CASTLE DERRY—seat of the O'Flynns of Derry, a small earldom in the eastern marches, between Cardosa and Rengarth. (KD)

CORWYN—Morgan's duchy. (KD; T)*

CULDI—Camber's earldom, in northwest Gwynedd. (HS)*

EIRIAL, Barony d'—holding of Sir Radulf d'Eirial; formerly part of Michaeline holding of Haut Eirial. (V)*

GRECOTHA—site of a famous university and seminary. (B; PA)*

GWYNEDD—central and most powerful of the Eleven Kingdoms, ruled by the House of Haldane.*

KILTUIN—port town near the Corwyn–Torenth border, held by the Bishop of Corwyn from the Duke of Corwyn. (T)

MEARA—client-princedom west of Gwynedd, where Derry's father received the wounds from which he later died. (KD)*

RHELJAN Mountains—along Gwynedd–Torenth border. (KD)*

RHELLEDD—site of a famous spring horse fair in northern Corwyn, near the Torenthi border. (KD)*

RHEMUTH—capital of Gwynedd under the Haldanes. (PA; KD)*

R'KASSI—kingdom to the east, famous for its horses and archers. (KD)*

RUSTAN—town in the Rheljan foothills where Brion was to meet the Marluk. (L)*

SAINT LIAM'S ABBEY—site of a school run by the Order of Saint Michael, near Valoret. (C)*

SAINT MARK'S CHURCH—parish church near Valoret. (PA)*

SAINT NEOT'S ABBEY—mother house of the Gabrilite Order, which trained Healers; in the Lendour Mountains of southern Gwynedd. (HS; V)*

SHEELE—Rhys and Evaine's manor near Valoret. (HS)*

TRE-ARILAN—the Arilan family seat near Rhemuth. (PA)

VALORET—Festillic capital of Gwynedd; seat of the Archbishop-Primate of Gwynedd. (PA)*

PARTIAL TIMELINE FOR THE ELEVEN KINGDOMS

822	Festil, Deryni youngest son of the King of Torenth, successfully invades Gwynedd and accomplishes a sudden coup, massacring all the royal family except the two-year-old Prince Aidan Haldane; establishes his capital at Valoret and reigns 17 years.
839–851	Reign of King Festil II. c. 850: final days of St. Torin of Dhassa.
846	Camber Kyriell MacRorie born: third son of the Earl of Culdi.
851–885	Reign of King Festil III.
860	Prince Cinhil Haldane born.
875	Ariella of Festil born.
881	Imre of Festil born.

885–900   Reign of King Blaine of Festil.

888   Fall: "Catalyst."

900–904   Reign of King Imre of Festil.

903–904   *Camber of Culdi*. Prince Aidan Haldane
           dies in Valoret, but reveals that a grand-
           son survives. Prince Cinhil Haldane found
           in a monastery and brought out by Cam-
           ber's children to spearhead a restoration;
           marries Lady Megan de Cameron.

904   December 1–2: The Restoration. Imre of
           Festil deposed by Cinhil Haldane and
           dies.

           December 25: King Cinhil crowned, age
           44.

905–907   *Saint Camber.* January 31: Mark born to
           Ariella in Torenth.

           June 25: Unsuccessful attempt by Ariella
           to overthrow the Restoration. Alister
           Cullen dies killing Ariella, but his iden-
           tity is taken by Camber, who officially
           "dies" on this date.

906   Spring/Summer: Cinhil receives homage
           of Sighere of Eastmarch and goes north
           to help quell a rebellion in Kheldour.

           November 14: Saint Camber canonized.

917–918   *Camber the Heretic*.

917–921   Reign of King Alroy Haldane.

917   February 2: Cinhil dies and is succeeded
           by his twelve-year-old son Alroy. The
           young king's regents shift the court to
           Rhemuth, the old capital. After the mur-
           der of the Deryni Archbishop Jaffray,
           Camber/Alister chosen to succeed him,
           but election overturned by the regents;

Michaelines dispersed.

December: Rhys killed; Council of Ramos begins sessions, lasting into spring, repudiating Camber's sainthood and limiting rights of Deryni in Gwynedd; Trurill Castle sacked.

918	Jebediah killed; Camber goes into limbo.
921–922	Reign of King Javan Haldane.
922–928	Reign of King Rhys Michael Haldane.
928–948	Reign of King Owain Haldane.
948	Mark, son of Imre and Ariella, attempts to retake his throne.

In this century, Rolf MacPherson, a Deryni lord, rebels against the Camberian Council.

948–980	Reign of King Uthyr Haldane.
977	December 24: "Vocation."
980–983	Reign of King Nygel Haldane.
983–985	Reign of King Jasher Haldane.

Durchad Mor puts his armored infantry against the forces of Jasher Haldane, in behalf of Prince Mark-Imre, great-grandson of Imre of Festil.

985–994	Reign of King Cluim Haldane.
994–1025	Reign of King Urien Haldane.
1025	Massive move against Gwynedd by Imre II (972-1025) results in anihilation of the male Festillic line through four generations.
1025–1074	Reign of King Malcolm Haldane. He marries the Princess Roisian of Meara, elder daughter and sole heiress of Jolyon, the last Prince of Meara, who had sided with Imre II. The marriage was to have

settled the Mearan succession on the House of Haldane, but Jolyon's widow, the Princess Urracca, spirits away her two younger daughters, one of whom (Annalind) is twin to Roisian, and heads a party claiming Annalind is the senior and legitimate heiress.

1027	King Malcolm leads an expedition into Meara to hunt Mearan dissidents.
1045	King Malcolm leads a second Mearan expedition.
1060	King Malcolm leads yet another expedition into Meara to hunt Annalind's son Judhael.
1068–1070	Barrett de Laney blinded saving Deryni children. About this time, Lewys ap Norfal, an infamous Deryni, rejects the authority of the Camberian Council.
1074–1095	Reign of King Donal Blaine Haldane.
1076	King Donal leads an expedition into Meara to hunt Prince Judhael again.
1080	King Donal marries Richeldis of Llannedd.
1081	Prince Brion Haldane born.
1087	Prince Nigel Haldane born.
1089	King Donal leads another Mearan expedition.
1091	September 29: Alaric Morgan born.
1092	February 2: Duncan McLain born.
1100	Summer: "Bethane."
	September 24: Sir Kenneth Morgan dies; shortly, the nine-year-old Morgan is sent to court as a page.
	December: Morgan meets King Brion for

first time at Christmas Court.

1104   January 6: Brion marries Jehana of Bremagne.

August 1: Jorian de Courcy, Deryni,
ordained priest but is discovered. "The
Priesting of Arilan."

November 12: Jorian executed.

1105   February 2: Denis Arilan, Deryni,
ordained priest without being discovered.

Spring/Summer: The Marluk, Festillic
heir, challenges King Brion and is killed.

June 21: "Legacy."

July/February: Jehana winters at St. Giles
Abbey.

1106   November 14: Prince Kelson Haldane
born. His designation as Prince of Meara
triggers a new rebellion there.

1107   Spring: Brion puts down the Mearan
rebellion, but Caitrin of Meara, daughter
of Prince Jolyon, escapes. Her husband
and son killed. Sicard MacArdry marries
Caitrin.

Duncan McLain secretly handfasts with
Maryse, daughter of Sicard's elder
brother Caulay, after her brother is killed
in a brawl with a McLain man. To avoid
bloodfeud, the two families part, but
Maryse has conceived.

1108   January 3: Maryse is delivered of a son,
Dhugal, but dies of birth complications;
her mother, Adreana, raises the boy as
twin to her own daughter, born the same
time.

Spring: Duncan hears that Maryse died of a winter fever and puts thoughts of her aside, pursuing earlier inclinations toward the priesthood.

1110   Alaric Morgan is knighted by King Brion.

1112   Denis Arilan, anticipating Duncan's ordination, has himself transferred to Rhemuth to facilitate it.

1113   Easter: Duncan is ordained priest at Rhemuth Cathedral, thanks to secret intervention of Denis Arilan; assigned to parish at Culdi, near his family.

1114   Duncan is sent to the University at Grecotha for two years' further study.

1114–1115   Winter: Duchess Vera, Duncan's mother, dies, thus ending Duncan and Morgan's only source of Deryni training.

Monsignor Denis Arilan becomes King's Confessor to Brion.

1115   May: Sean Lord Derry is knighted at Rhemuth and becomes Morgan's aide; "The Knighting of Derry."

1116   Spring: Denis Arilan brings Duncan to Rhemuth as his secretary and assistant.

Summer: Duncan becomes tutor to Prince Kelson, nearly ten.

1117   Duncan's success as Kelson's tutor leads to an additional appointment as Prince's Confessor.

1118   Denis Arilan, age 35, becomes Auxiliary Bishop of Rhemuth under Archbishop Corrigan and is also appointed to Brion's privy council.

"Trial"

1120   June: Brion signs a new border treaty
              with Wencit of Torenth.
              September: Morgan goes to Cardosa to
              observe border activities.
              November: *Deryni Rising*.
              November 1: Brion killed by Charissa's
              magic.
              November 4: Brion's funeral.
              November 14: Kelson's birthday; Mor-
              gan returns to Rhemuth.
              November 15: Kelson defeats Charissa
              and is crowned in Rhemuth.

1121   Summer: *Deryni Checkmate* and *High
              Deryni*. Troubles with Loris and the bish-
              ops, and campaign against Wencit of
              Torenth, ending with Wencit's defeat at
              Llyndruth Meadows.

1121–1122   Winter: Consolidation of Kelson's court
              at Rhemuth. Morgan spends most of win-
              ter going back and forth between Rhe-
              muth and Coroth, counseling Kelson and
              reestablishing his hold in Corwyn.
              Duncan travels back and forth between
              Rhemuth and Cassan/Kierney, attending
              to his father's affairs and getting his new
              inheritance in order, privately settling
              back into his priestly vocation. Baron
              Jodrell, a bright young Kierney lord,
              becomes a staunch supporter and returns
              to court with him, where Kelson takes
              an instant liking to him and appoints him
              to the privy council.

1122   January: The Council of Rhemuth offi-
              cially censures Loris (in custody since

the previous summer), relieves him of his rank, and sends him into perpetual exile at St. Iveagh's Abbey in Rhendall. (Corrigan died of a heart attack the previous fall, before action could be taken against him.) Bradene of Grecotha elected Primate and Archbishop of Valoret in Loris' place; Cardiel becomes Archbishop of Rhemuth; Arilan is given Dhassa. Various other reshufflings of bishops and sees.

1122   May 1: Morgan marries Richenda in Marley, with Duncan officiating and Kelson in attendance. Afterward, Morgan takes his bride and new stepson back to Corwyn for the summer.

Summer: From Marley, Kelson heads north to progress through his Kheldish lands and evaluate military readiness, keeping a wary eye on Torenth. Meets his Aunt Meraude's brother, Saer de Traherne, the young Earl of Rhendall, and brings him back to court as another counsellor.

Duncan spends most of the summer touring his lands and setting up feudal mechanisms for governing mostly *in absentia*. By the end of the summer, rumors become more strident that supporters of the old Mearan royal line are agitating for Mearan independence, sparked by dissatisfaction that a Deryni priest-duke now rules part of Old Meara.

1122–1123   Winter: Kelson further consolidates his

authority, making plans to progress through Cassan, Kierney, and Meara the following summer and squelch the separatist rumblings with a show of the royal presence. Courts of justice through the winter. Morgan is back and forth several times because Richenda is expecting their first child.

1123   **January 31:** Richenda is delivered of Morgan's daughter, Briony Bronwyn Morgan.

Spring: Young King Alroy of Torenth, only a few months past his 14th birthday, is killed in a fall from a horse while hunting. Rumors begin almost immediately that Kelson engineered the accident, fearing the power of a Torenthi king who had come of age. The nine-year-old Liam becomes king, with his mother Morag again as Regent and various Torenthi lords vying for her hand in marriage.

Summer: Kelson turns his attention toward the worsening Mearan situation, progressing through Meara, Cassan, and Kierney with Duncan, as planned.

Morgan spends most of the summer in Corwyn, just to make sure there will be no Torenthi threat, but joins Kelson in Culdi after the ailing Bishop Carsten of Meara dies, leaving the important See of Meara vacant.

Late November: The Synod of Bishops meets in Culdi to choose a new Mearan prelate, but first elects several new itinerant bishops, Duncan among them (Auxiliary Bishop of Rhemuth, Cardiel's assistant).

LITERARY ORIGINS OF THE DERYNI

How the Series Began

Over the years, the question most often asked by my readers (other than, "When will the next book be out?") probably has been, "How did you get the idea?" My usual response has been that I had this dream...

It's a complex process by which a dream becomes a universe that many readers regard as real, if tucked away in some other dimension. For those interested in that process, I present the stages of evolution between dream and what we now know as THE CHRONICLES OF THE DERYNI.

Though none of the following material should be considered canonical (in the sense that the novels and the short stories in this volume *are* canonical—that is, the "official" or "established version" of Deryni history), it certainly is proto-matter without which there would have been no Deryni series.

THE DREAM THAT BECAME DERYNI

On October 11, 1964, I had a very vivid dream and wrote the following on two 3 x 5 cards when I woke.

Scene: audience chamber of a castle. The young widowed Empress (25) holds audience with her husband's faithful general (40) and his aide (20). She wears a white flowing robe with a black wimple and a simple emerald tiara. Her small son sleeps in the next room. The general endeavors to unlock the secret to the late Emperor's powers, which were left locked in an intricate emerald and gold brooch—he was unable to give her the key—was assassinated by the Blue Witch, who now rules. General is very wise and powerful man; shows Empress how to gain access to her husband's power—(he was left clues by his late Comm-Chief)—key is to jab pin of clasp through hand—10 sec. later, power transference begins, lasts 5 min. Transfer is successful; Empress tries power—works well. Possibility of love between Empress and General after power is regained and mourning over.

LORDS OF SORANDOR:
THE PROTO-DERYNI RISING

About a year after I had the dream above, I wrote the novelette called "Lords of Sorandor." A great deal changed. The kingdom acquired a name—Sorandor—though that would change to Gwynedd in its next incarnation. The infant in arms had become the fourteen-year-old Prince Kelson. The character that would become Jehana (called Sanil in this version) aged enough to have a teenaged son and became a far lesser character—who definitely had no romantic interest in Morgan. And though the Deryni had yet to make an appearance as such, magic certainly had become a major factor.

The basic form of the universe had been established, however—and recognizable parts of "Lords of Sorandor" survive to this day in *Deryni Rising*.

LORDS OF SORANDOR

—BY KATHERINE KURTZ
OCTOBER, 1965

Sanil of Sorandor stood, smoothing the dark mourning veil over her coppery hair as she had done each day for the past month. Resting pale hands on the dresser before her, she studied the green eyes which peered back at her for a long moment, then placed the simple, jet-studded circlet firmly upon her head.

"Your Majesty?" inquired a servant girl softly. "General Sir Alaric Morgan wishes to see you. Shall I say that Your Majesty is receiving no visitors?"

"Morgan? I—no, I suppose I must see him. Where is he now?"

"In the garden, my lady."

"Very well. I'll receive him on the sun porch."

Sanil stepped into the sun room and seated herself on the small, black-draped chair, spreading the somber velvet of her gown in graceful folds around her feet. Several ladies-in-waiting hovered around her person, and in a corner of the room, a young musician strummed softly on a mellowed lute.

The garden door swung open and a tall, black-leather clad figure strode into the chamber, sword and mail glinting dully in the diffused sunlight. Bowing his golden head in obeisance, he knelt at the feet of the queen in a single, fluid motion, his gloved fist going to his chest in salute. Sanil beckoned him to rise.

"Yes, Sir Alaric?"

"Your pardon, my lady. I would have come sooner, but the men have been restless under this new truce, and they feel Brion's loss deeply. He will be much missed."

"Yes, he will." She waited expectantly.

"My lady, I must speak with you alone; it is of the utmost importance."

"Sir Alaric, I . . . Very well." She dismissed the ladies-in-waiting with a curt nod, then motioned to a chair nearby.

"Sir Alaric, out of the love my husband bore for you, I have done as you requested. Brion spoke of you often, you know—that is, when he spoke of government and such at all." She gazed across the room, not seeing him. "Perhaps if he had told me more of what he was doing, I would have been better prepared for what happened," she said, glancing down bitterly at her folded hands. "As it was, I never knew of the constant danger he always lived in until he was already gone."

Looking up, she continued briskly. "But you didn't make this trip to hear me talk about Brion, did you, General?"

"No," answered Morgan, shaking his head. He rose explosively and began pacing the floor, his gloved hands clasping and unclasping.

"My lady," he began, "before your husband entered that last battle when he fell by the hand of the Blue Witch, he spoke to me at length of his divine power of rule, which has been handed down since his royal line began many years ago. He, no doubt, spoke to you on this subject, at least in passing, but you probably dismissed such talk as idle superstition, passed on through the years as justification for divine-right rule. With most men, you would have been correct—but not with Brion."

He turned slowly toward her. "My lady, had he known of the plot of the Blue Witch in time, Brion could have saved himself—indeed, under the right circumstances, he could have destroyed her. But unfortunately, Brion underestimated the Blue One—and worse, he underestimated the extent of her influence among his own men."

His face convulsed in bitter remembrance as he spat out the words. "He was betrayed by a friend!"

He slammed one fist into the other hand, then recovered, remembering where he was. Turning to the queen with a strained smile, he continued.

"Do you remember Brion's aide, Colin of Fianna? Ah, poor Colin," he mused. "The Blue One bewitched him, you know. She induced the smitten lad to drug the king's wine. It was not enough to kill him, she said. It would only make him sleep.

"Colin did as he was bidden, and next morning, the Blue One slew Brion on the field of honour with a blast of magic which he never anticipated—he was too groggy from the drug to catch her intention in time. And Colin, when he saw what he had done, fell on his sword, too proud to die a traitor's death, but too miserable to live."

Morgan sank wearily into his chair, head in hands. "So now we stand under the Blue One's truce," he smiled grimly, "her last token of respect for a most bitter enemy."

Sanil's low sob finally broke the stillness.

"I'm sorry, my lady. I did not mean to open old

wounds, but I thought you should know." He stared at the floor.

"How is Prince Kelson?" he asked, striving to change the subject.

"He is well," answered Sanil, straining to regain her composure. "Tomorrow is his Coronation, you know." She looked at him beseechingly. "I had hoped that was why you came: to see him crowned."

"It is, my lady," he answered. "But to see him crowned a true king—like his father."

"No!" she whispered, horrified. "Brion's powers died with him, if, indeed, he had them. Kelson must reign as a mortal!" She turned wide, afraid eyes on him.

"Kelson cannot rule as a mortal, my lady. The Blue One would slay him even as she did his father; you know that."

"Brion's power did not save *him*. Besides, she surely would not strike down a defenseless boy!"

"You know better than that, my lady," answered Morgan. "But, God willing, Kelson will not have to face the Blue One powerless to stand against her. I have the key to Brion's power—and it must be Kelson's."

"No!" she hissed, half-rising to her feet. "I will not let you do it. Kelson is but a boy."

"Don't be a fool, my lady," he said, grasping her shoulders and forcing her back to her chair. "Think a moment. Tomorrow Kelson will be fourteen, of legal age as far as the monarchy is concerned, and he will be crowned king as such. Would the Blue Witch, who killed his father," he paused for emphasis, "spare the father's son merely because of his youth? She means to rule, lady. Will she let *any* mere mortal stand in her way?"

"No." She forced the word out in a hoarse whisper, relaxing dully into the cushions of the chair.

Morgan released her and stepped back. "Then, you'll permit me to speak with him?"

"Yes," she whispered dazedly, "within the hour."

But her face clouded with resentment as her eyes followed him through the sunny garden door.

II

"What did you tell my mother?"

Morgan's black silken cloak rustled crisply in the sunlight as he whirled to identify the unexpected voice.

"Kelson." Tension turned to pleasure as he recognized the speaker, and a smile flickered across his face. "How did you know I was here?"

The boy sprang lightly down the few stone steps of the summerhouse and walked briskly to the young general's side.

"I saw you leave my mother's chamber, so I followed you. Did I do wrong?" he asked, his grey eyes clouding with apprehension as he sensed his friend's surprise.

"Of course not, my prince," replied Morgan, clapping the boy on the shoulder. "I really came to see you, not your mother. I must admit, however, that she's not terribly fond of me at the moment," he continued. "I reminded her that you are a king."

Kelson snorted mischievously. "She still thinks of me as her 'little boy'. She just doesn't seem to realize that tomorrow I'll be king." He glanced up wistfully. "I wonder what else she thinks the son of Brion *could* do besides rule? Tell me, Morgan. You knew my father well. Do you think that I shall ever be able to fill his place? Answer truly, now, for I shall know if you're only flattering me."

Morgan, hands clasped behind him, walked thoughtfully around the young man, noting the apparent frailness of the slim, young body, yet recalling the tensile steel strength and catlike grace with which he moved. Looking at Kelson, he saw Brion staring back at him, the wide, grey gaze under a thick shock of glossy black hair, the regal carriage of the proud head, the ease with which he wore the royal blue. It was Brion of the Laughing Eyes, Brion of the Flashing Sword, of the Gentle Moods, teaching a young boy to fence and ride; holding court in all the splendor of the monarchy, the boy spellbound at his feet; Brion, asking a friend dearer than life to swear that the boy would always have a protector, should his father die untimely; Brion, on the eve of his death, entrusting the key to his divine power to the man who stood now before his son.

Morgan snapped out of his reverie and motioned the boy to be seated.

"You are the image of Brion, my prince," said the young general, taking a seat on the stone steps. "And he left you well prepared for the task you will undertake tomorrow. I think he knew full well that you might come to the throne at an early age—in fact, he probably expected it, for he gave you the very finest training he knew how.

"From the time you could sit unaided, he had you on horseback daily. Your fencing masters were the finest to be had on the continent, and when they had taught you what they knew, he supplemented them and soon had you out-fencing your former instructors. You studied the old annals of military history and strategy, languages, mathematics—he even let you touch on astronomy and alchemy.

"There was a practical side to your education, too, though. For there was wisdom in the seeming unorthodoxy of allowing a young and sometimes fidgeting crown-prince to sit at his father's side in the council chambers. From the beginning, though you were doubtless unaware of it at first, you acquired the rudiments of the impeccable rhetoric and logic that were Brion's trademark as much as his swordsmanship or his valor. You learned to counsel, and to receive counsel, wisely and unpretentiously. And through it all, you were made to understand that a wise king does not speak in anger, nor judge until all the facts are before him."

Morgan fell silent for a moment, then continued thoughtfully. "I think that in some ways you will be even more a king than Brion was, my prince. You have a sensitivity, an appreciation of the arts, literature, music, that he never quite grasped, though I don't suppose it made him any *less* a king. Oh, he listened dutifully to the philosopher as well as the warrior, but I was never sure he really *understood* them. You *do* understand."

Kelson turned his face to lock the eyes of the general. "You forget one thing, Morgan," he said quietly. "I do not have my father's power, and without it, I fall." He rose impatiently. "Did he give you no clue as to how I am to remain king? What of his assassin? Am I, a mortal, to stand against the Blue Witch without armor? Morgan," he asked his father's friend beseechingly, "what am I to do?"

"You have come to the crux of the matter, my prince," smiled Morgan. "Come. We have been here too long already. It would never do for your mother to find us here at this stage of the game."

Taking the young prince's arm, he began to guide him through the garden, away from the vicinity of the queen's chambers.

Just then, a plump and very out-of-breath lady-in-waiting came scurrying into the garden.

"Your Highness," she squealed, coming to a rather undignified stop. "We have been searching for you everywhere. Your mother, the queen, was *extremely* worried, and you *know* she doesn't approve of your wandering off alone. It's very dangerous." Her speech slowly ground to a halt as she realized that the prince was, by no means, alone.

"Do you hear that, Morgan?" said Kelson, turning to his friend. "'It's very dangerous.' Lady Bolliston," he continued dryly, "would you please inform my lady mother that I have been quite safe here in the garden with General Morgan?"

Lady Bolliston's eyes grew round as she realized Morgan's identity, and a plump hand flew to her lips to mask the scarcely breathed "Oh." She bobbled a hurried curtsey and stammered, "I did not recognize Your Grace."

"That is understandable, Lady Bolliston," he nodded, "for I have not been here in some time. However, I would hope that in the future you would show a bit more respect for your king." He smiled kindly. "Your entrance was not a model of decorum."

Lady Bolliston smiled in spite of herself, thinking that perhaps the late king's general was not such an ogre as the queen pictured him at all, and she murmured an apology.

"But your lady mother does wish to see you immediately, Your Highness," she added.

"Is it about General Morgan?" Kelson querried. When she did not answer, he continued. "I thought as much. Well, tell my lady mother that I am already in council with Sir Alaric and do not wish to be disturbed. You might add that I will be quite safe," he concluded dryly.

"Yes, Your Highness," she curtsied, and fled across the grass to deliver the message. When she was out of sight, Morgan and the prince dissolved into peals of laughter.

"You know, I don't think she meant to let me see you after all, my prince," said Morgan, clasping a black-gloved hand to the younger's shoulder. "We'd best leave before your 'lady mother' comes looking for us herself."

Kelson nodded in agreement, and the two made a rapid exit.

III

Looking up casually from the stoup he was filling, Father Duncan McLain inspected the two young men making their way across the courtyard. He straightened quickly to shade his eyes against the intense glare of the mid-day sun. The younger would be Prince Kelson, the gold-embroidered edge of his velvet cloak glistening in the sunlight. But the older—the young priest's eyes lit with pleasure and surprise—why, it was Alaric!

Placing the now-empty bottle on the floor, he smoothed his rumpled cassock and walked briskly to the portico.

"Alaric," he cried, clasping the other's hand. "This *is* a pleasant surprise. And Kelson." He flung an arm about the shoulders of the grinning young prince to include him in the greeting.

"I really don't believe this," he said, guiding them into the coolness and quiet of the narthex. "My two favorite people, both in the same day. Ah, but Kelson, I see by the look on Alaric's face that this is not purely a social call, is it?"

"You're too perceptive, Duncan," smiled the young general. "I never could fool you, even when we were children. I wondered, though, whether Kelson and I might borrow you and your study for an hour or so of counsel."

Duncan grinned wryly, but nodded assent. "I might have known it would take business to drag you out here, Alaric," he said, scooping up the empty bottle and leading them down the nave. "You know, perhaps I should be your confessor—at least I'd see you once a year that way. But, on second thought, I don't suppose that would be a good idea at all—I know you too well."

The three paused at the transept to bow before the High Altar.

"Oh, come now, Duncan," said Morgan, chuckling softly as he followed the priest out the side door, Kelson close at his heels. "I see you more than that; and besides, it's fifty miles from my castle to the capital."

"No, Alaric, I shall tolerate no more excuses. Either you promise to come visit me more often, or I shall

h you out of my study, and you can find someplace
 to discuss your business." He closed the door
urely behind him and walked to a small, round table
r the center of the room.

"Very well, Duncan," laughed Morgan, as he
tioned the two to be seated. "You have my word."

Morgan took a small leather pouch from his belt and
gan fumbling absorbedly with the cords.

"Now, have you a cloth I can put down, Duncan?"
asked, opening the bag.

Before the priest could answer, Kelson produced a
soft, white silk handkerchief from his sleeve and spread
it out before the general. "Will this do, Morgan?"

"Very well, my prince," he answered, reaching into
the bag and gingerly extracting a bit of gold and bril-
liance which he laid on the silk. "Do you recognize
this, Kelson?"

Kelson exhaled softly, his grey eyes wide with awe
and wonderment. "It is the Ring of Fire, my father's
seal of power."

"May I see that?" asked Duncan, anxiety written in
his eyes.

Morgan nodded assent.

Gathering the silk carefully around his fingers, the
young priest picked up the ring, turning it in the dim
light. The scarlet stones cast scintillating rays on the
damasked walls, and the burnished metal shone warmly.
Duncan examined it minutely, then replaced it on the
table, smoothing the rumpled silk.

"So far, so good," he breathed, a trace of hopeful-
ness crossing his face. "There is more?"

For answer, Morgan reached once more into the
leather bag and brought forth a heavy enamelled brooch

the size of a man's fist. A rampant golden lion shone on the crimson background, and gold-etched scroll-work traced the deeply carved edges.

"What—?" began Kelson, brows knitting in bewilderment.

"The key, my prince," murmured Morgan, leaning back in his chair. "The key to your father's power."

He passed the brooch to Duncan, who scrutinized it briefly, then handed it on to Kelson.

"Brion told me of it the last time I saw him alive. He must have sensed impending danger, for he made me swear that if he fell, the brooch and ring should somehow get to you, Kelson. There is a verse which accompanies the brooch."

"What verse, Alaric?" questioned the priest, leaning forward expectantly. "You have it?"

"Aye," he answered wearily. "But it makes little sense. Listen."

His face assumed a far-away expression as he began to recite:

> *"The eve of Coronation Day*
> *Must power increased to you convey.*
> *A holy man shall be your guide;*
> *A champion bold kneels by your side.*
> *The sinister hand held bravely so:*
> *The Lion's tooth through flesh must go.*
> *The ringing of the sinister hand*
> *Gives all the power you demand."*

"Well," said Duncan, leaning back in his chair and raising an eyebrow. "He didn't give us much to go on, did he?"

"Now, wait, Father," began Kelson agitatedly. "The first part is clear enough: '*The eve of Coronation Day/ Must power increased to you convey*'—this merely says that whatever happens must happen tonight.

"'*A holy man,*' you, Father, '*shall be your guide,/ A champion bold kneels by your side.*'" He looked to Morgan for advice.

"Correct, my prince," he nodded. "This clearly shows the roles that Duncan and I are to play, but what of yours? Now, I don't understand the third stanza at all yet, but the fourth is evidently a reference to the portion of the Coronation ritual when the archbishop places the ring on the king's—the sinister hand! Why didn't I think of that before?"

"Yes, of course," chimed in Kelson. "Father often spoke of such things in heraldic terms. This would be just like him."

"Picking up the brooch, Kelson extended his left hand. "'*The sinister hand held bravely so:/The Lion's tooth through flesh must go.*'"

He looked at the brooch, then at his friends, a quizzical expression on his face. "Morgan, I don't understand. This lion has no tooth. How can...?"

"Wait." Duncan sprang to his feet, reaching for the enamelled ornament. "Let me see that."

Taking it in his hands, he began to inspect it closely, then turned it over to finger the clasp.

"Yes, of course," he whispered, his eyes focused on something beyond. "There is always the obstacle, the barrier, the need for bravery."

Morgan rose slowly, his full attention on Duncan.

"The clasp," he whispered icily, "is the Lion's tooth?"

Duncan's gaze flickered to the present. "Yes."

Kelson stood and reached across the table to run his finger along the three inches of slim golden clasp. He swallowed.

"The Lion's tooth must pierce my hand?"

Duncan nodded impassively.

"It—it will be very painful, won't it?" Kelson asked, his voice very small in the stillness.

Again, Duncan nodded.

"But there is no other way, is there?"

"None, my prince," replied the priest, his face pale against the dark cassock.

Kelson lowered his eyes. "Then, it must be done. Will you make the proper arrangements, Father?"

"Yes, my prince," he replied. "You and Alaric should be back here no later than the hour after Compline." He bowed low.

Kelson inclined his head in thanks. "I will go, then, Father. Between now and Compline, I must learn to be a true king."

He spun on his heel and went out, Morgan close behind, and the weight of kingship rested already heavy on his shoulders.

"God bless you, my prince," breathed the priest, as he raised his hand in benediction.

IV

Morgan followed his young lord silently across the courtyard, sensing the boy's need to be alone with his thoughts. Not until they had nearly reached the entrance to the royal apartments did Kelson speak.

"Morgan," he asked suddenly, "do you really think we know what we're doing?"

"Well," Morgan countered wistfully, "if we don't, and Brion's magic *is* lost forever, at least we will have tried. That's all men *can* do, is try, isn't it, my prince?"

"You're right, of course, Morgan," he answered. "But suppose I'm not ready?"

"You are better prepared than you know, my prince," replied Morgan, reaching for the door.

But before he could touch it, the heavy oak door swung slowly open to reveal a startled and angry queen and her retinue.

"Where have you been, Kelson?" she demanded.

"With General Morgan, Mother. Didn't you get my message?"

Sanil turned her glare on Morgan. "What did you tell him?"

Morgan regarded her thoughtfully, his hands clasped behind him. "I told him about his father, my lady. Beyond that, you will have to ask him."

"Well, Kelson?" she snapped. "What lies has he been filling your head with?"

"Please don't make a scene, Mother," replied Kelson, moving quietly toward his suite. "I scarcely think I need tell *you* what he said; you know what I must do."

When she did not respond, he turned his attention to the officer in charge of his guard.

"Lieutenant, I am retiring for the day, and I do not wish to be disturbed by anyone until morning. Is that clear? General Morgan will spend the night in my quarters."

"Yes, Your Majesty."

"Very well, then," he said, and turned to his mother. "Good night, Mother. I shall see you before the procession tomorrow. I must get some rest."

Pivoting precisely, he entered the apartment, Morgan close behind him, and the bolt shot home with a note of finality. The queen, after a moment's hesitation, retired resignedly down the corridor.

But in the shadows of the columns, there lurked one who was not at all dismayed to see the prince seek seclusion for the remainder of the day. Smiling grimly at the show of royal discord, he waited until the last footsteps of the queen and her retinue had receded down the long passageway, then slipped out the main door, gathering his squire's cloak around him. Going immediately to the royal stables, where a fast horse lay saddled and waiting, he exchanged royal livery for a somber-hued traveling cloak, pulling the voluminous hood well over his face before he set out.

Soon, he was riding away from the city, and within an hour he reined in and left the main road to follow a winding, little-ridden track into the foothills. As he descended the torturous slopes of a steep gorge, he glanced casually around him, and when he reached the bottom, he was not at all surprised to find himself surrounded by fierce, blue-clad warriors.

"Who goes there?" challenged the commanding officer, hand on sword hilt.

"Lord Ian to see the countess," answered the lone rider, throwing back his hood and dismounting as he spoke.

Bowing unctuously, the officer took the horse's reins from Ian and immediately changed his tone of voice to a more servile one.

"My apologies, m'lord. We did not recognize you."

"That is not at all surprising to me," remarked the young lord dryly, "since I did not *wish* to be recognized. Open the portal."

He gestured imperiously and the men moved to comply with his order. A lieutenant pressed his fingers fleetingly over a series of small depressions in the rock, and a large stone slab withdrew to reveal a passageway into the side of the gorge. Ian stepped inside, followed by the men, and the opening was walled off once more. The men dispersed to their various duties, and the newcomer swung down the hallway.

Boots echoing on the marble flagstones, Ian strode resolutely, reflecting on the strange company one was often obliged to keep in order to further one's goals. The Blue One trusted him almost completely now, and there would be time enough after the young prince was deposed to seize the power of the Blue One for himself.

Silver spurs jangled as he clattered confidently down the granite staircase, and the torches in their wrought-iron holders cast russet highlights on his chestnut hair, reflecting, perhaps, the even more russet thoughts beneath it.

He passed the guardpost and took the precise salute nonchalantly, then approached a pair of golden doors and slipped through. Leaning back against the ornate handles, he fixed his gaze intently upon the woman who sat brushing her long, blued silver hair, all thoughts of malice gone for the present, at least from his face.

"Well, Ian?" she querried, her full red lips curving upward with more than a trace of ire.

"The Son of the Lion is caged for the night, my pet," he said silkily, sauntering toward her with a careless intensity. "And there is discord in the royal house-hold. The son is cool toward the mother who is so protective, and the mother quarrels with the general, who has fired the son with tales of the father's valor."

He unclasped the heavy cloak and flung it across a low bench, then sank onto a wide, satin-draped couch, unbuckling his sword as he did.

"And the young prince?" she inquired. "Does he seem ill-at-ease over his imminent coronation?" Her voice was edged with mockery as she laid the silver-backed brush on the dresser top and stood, gathering the gossamer folds of her gown about her in a soft azure cloud.

"I think he is well discomfited," smiled the young lord, reclining on one elbow. "He retires to rest, and has given orders that he's not to be disturbed until morning. If he leaves, we will be informed immediately." His green eyes followed her every move hungrily.

"It is good, Ian," she whispered, her voice lilting into low, bell-like tones as she glided toward him. "You have done well." She rested delicate fingertips on his shoulder and smiled. "The Blue One is pleased to give the same orders for the night."

V

As the Vesper chimes finished their pealing in the distance, Morgan rose cat-like and stretched. Strolling to the window, he drew the drapery slightly to survey the mounting darkness, then let the drape fall heavily into place. He suppressed a yawn as he crossed to an ornate candelabra and struck a light, then carried it to a place near the royal couch.

Kelson opened his eyes abruptly and looked around.

"I must have fallen asleep," he said, raising to one elbow. "Is it time?"

"Not yet, my prince," replied Morgan, going to the wardrobe and casually surveying the garments. "It is yet a while before Compline is rung."

He selected a deep grey silken tunic, the edges worked in gold and pearls, and tossed it on a nearby chair. "This will be suitable, I think."

Sinking wearily into a chair by the fireplace, he contemplated the flames for a few moments as he ran idle fingers through his burnished hair.

"Nay, on second thought, perhaps you'd best get ready."

"You are a strange man, Morgan," declared Kelson as he cocked his head at the young general. "When you told me that I should rest, I was certain I should not sleep a wink, but with a calm voice and low word you stilled my fears, and sleep came."

Morgan replied absently, "You were very tired, my prince." He resumed his air of contemplation, so Kelson, sensing that he would get no further explanation for the moment, slipped quietly to his dressing rooms.

After sitting motionless for some moments, Morgan snapped abruptly out of his melancholy and rose to his feet. Stripping off leather and mail, he washed perfunctorily at a small basin in the valet's quarters, and was pulling on light chain mail over his silken jerkin when Kelson reentered the room.

"You expect trouble?" he asked, eying the steel mesh with nervous distaste.

Morgan chuckled softly. "No, my prince, but 'tis best to be prepared," he said, lacing up the sides. "And I wish to apologize if I was somewhat boorish earlier. I spoke shortly to you when I should have been reassuring. It was thoughtless of me."

Kelson smiled weakly as Morgan buffeted his shoulder in passing, and he gave a deprecating shrug.

"Not so serious, my lad," said Morgan, as he rummaged in his saddlebags to produce a gilt-edged black velvet doublet, which he tugged on over the mail. "Your father would not have used magic to harm his own son—the veiled threats are meant to discourage usurpers, not the rightful heir."

Buckling on sword and cloak, he moved to the wardrobe and took out a wine velvet cloak and held it toward the young prince. Kelson settled the black fox collar of the garment firmly around his shoulders and turned toward the door.

"Not that way," said Morgan, grasping his arm and guiding him to a spot near the balcony window. "Now watch," he commanded.

Pacing off a distance from the wall, Morgan surveyed his position closely, then stood with feet planted firmly on the flagstone floor. He traced an intricate design in the air before him with an outstretched forefinger, and with a sigh, a portion of the wall recessed to reveal a dark stairwell.

Kelson gaped incredulously at Morgan. "How did that get there?" he asked, pointing unbelievingly.

"I imagine someone built it, my prince," remarked the general as he entered the passageway. "There are many like it in the palace. Come."

He held out a hand to the prince as the distant bells

rang Compline, and Kelson clambered after him. Ten minutes later, the two stood at the edge of the dark courtyard, the massive presence of the church looming dark against the night sky. Muffled in darkness, they made their way to the portico and stood in the narthex unobtrusively.

The deserted church was silent now, and the darkness was broken only by the low blaze of votive candles, which splashed their ruby glow over the stone floors and dark stained glass. In the sanctuary, a lone, black-clad figure bowed before the High Altar, his features obscured in the pale crimson aura of the vigil lamp. He turned at the sound of Morgan and Kelson's footsteps in the side aisle and came to meet them in the transept.

"All is ready," whispered Duncan, drawing them toward his study. They were seated around the small table before he spoke again. The Lion brooch winked ominously from its crimson cushion before them.

"Kelson," began the priest softly, his hands folded before him, "what I am about to say concerns mainly you."

Kelson nodded gravely, his face pale in the candlelight, and Duncan continued.

"The ritual we will use is a very simple one: we will enter the church. You will both kneel at the rail. I will give you my blessing, Kelson; and then you, of your own action and volition, must thrust the Lion's tooth through the palm of your left hand. If God is with us, you will feel the surge of power almost immediately. There will be a spinning sensation. You may lose consciousness. This last, I am not sure of. Only time and the deed will tell."

Kelson exhaled softly, his face ashen. "Is there anything more that I am required to know, Father?"

"No, my son," answered Duncan gently.

"Then," the prince continued in a shaken voice, "if there is time, I should like to be alone for a while before it begins."

"Of course, my prince," replied the priest, rising and catching Morgan's eye. "Alaric will help me to vest."

In the sacristy, Morgan broke the silence.

"What if something goes wrong, Duncan?" he asked, holding out the snowy surplice which the priest took carefully. "Suppose it kills him?"

"This is the chance we must take," Duncan answered. "You and I both know what would happen were he to face the Blue One without power—that is a certainty."

He touched a brocaded stole to his lips and settled it around his shoulders. "At least the boy *has* a chance this way. Brion knew his own son. I do not think we can be far wrong. Come," he said, laying a hand on Morgan's shoulder. "We had best get on with it."

They made their way back to the study where a young prince awaited his destiny.

Kelson sat thoughtfully in the study, his eyes focused through the flame of the single candle. Soon, he would either know his father's power, or he would know nothing, and his heart went out to the two loyal friends who were now so totally involved in the awesome drama: Morgan, his father's comrade, who had been almost a second, though younger, father to him; and Duncan, the young priest who had been his tutor almost since he could remember, even before his ordination.

He chided himself briefly for ever having doubted the wisdom of these loyal two, and was comforted by the knowledge that they would stand by him no matter what happened tonight. He rose, smiling, to his feet as the door swung softly open, and Morgan returned the smile reassuringly as he caught Kelson's note of confidence.

"Are you ready, my prince?" asked Duncan, as he picked up the brooch on its cushion and handed it to Morgan.

"Yes, Father," came the reply, and the three filed into the church.

Prince and champion knelt at the altar rail, ungirding their swords and placing them on the floor before them, as the priest stood at the foot of the altar in prayer. Signing himself, Duncan mounted the steps and kissed the altarstone, then turned to the two, his arms out-stretched.

"Dominus vobiscum."

"Et cum spiritu tuo," came their reply.

"Oremus."

The priest turned back to the altar and bowed again in prayer, ending it with a solemn, *"Per omnia saecula saeculorum."*

Morgan and Kelson responded with a low "Amen."

Descending the steps, Duncan stood before the kneeling Kelson and placed his hands firmly on the head of the young prince.

"May Almighty God, the Father, Son, and Holy Spirit, bless you, Kelson. Amen."

He signed the prince in blessing, then reached down and plucked the Lion brooch from its velvet cushion and placed it firmly in Kelson's hands.

"Courage, my prince," he whispered, and returned to the altar, his hands outstretched.

"Domine, fiat voluntas tua!"

Kelson's hands trembled slightly as he poised the golden clasp over his left palm. Then, steeling himself, he plunged the slender shaft through his hand. A gasp of anguish escaped his lips as the point, darker now, protruded on the other side, and he doubled over, moaning softly, as waves of pain throbbed from the wounded hand.

Morgan half-rose to steady his young lord, but Duncan whispered, "No!" as he whirled to face them. "Wait!"

He stared at the agonized prince intently, and Morgan, not daring to interfere, sank back to his knees.

A heavy silence replaced the prince's moans, and he straightened dazedly, bewilderment and confusion evident in his look.

"Father," he whispered, "everything is spinning." He swayed drunkenly, a look of fear coming upon his face. "Father, the darkness. . . ." He crumpled softly to the floor.

"Kelson!" cried the general, leaping to his aid.

Duncan joined him, and kneeling beside him, gently pried open the boy's left hand, a look of wonderment in his eyes.

"We were right," he said, withdrawing the slim shaft and wrapping the hand in a handkerchief. "He has the power now. There can be no mistaking the signs. Come," he continued, stripping off his vestments, "we must get him back to his room. He should sleep until morning, but I'll come with you to see that he's settled for the rest of the night."

Morgan nodded and picked up the unconscious boy, wrapping the red velvet cloak closer around him against the cold. Duncan gathered up the swords, and the two made their way back to the warmth of the royal apartment with their burdens.

Morgan laid Kelson gently on his couch and cleaned the boy's hand with a few deft wipes of clear, pungent fluid on a silk gauze, then bound up the hand while Duncan unlaced the prince's boots. He was removing the velvet cloak when the boy's eyes fluttered open weakly.

"Father? Morgan?" he questioned weakly.

"We are here, my prince," replied Duncan, moving to the boy's right to clasp his hand and kneel attentively.

"Morgan," the boy continued softly, "I heard my father's voice, and then the strangest sensation came over me. It was like being wrapped in woven sunlight or silk. At first I was frightened, but then. . . ."

"Hush now, my prince," said Morgan gently, placing his hand on the boy's forehead. "You must go to sleep now and rest. Sleep now, my prince. I will not be far away."

As he spoke, Kelson's eyelids fluttered briefly, then closed, and his breathing slowed to that of deep slumber. Morgan smiled and smoothed the touseled hair, then arranged the blanket snugly around his young lord. Dousing the light, he beckoned Duncan to join him on the terrace, and the two slipped outside, their silhouettes dark against the midnight sky.

"He trusts you very much, Alaric," said the young priest admiringly.

Morgan leaned against the railing, trying to discern

Duncan's face in the darkness. "And you, my friend."

"True," he replied, his hands on the railing before him as he looked out over the city. "I only hope that we may always remain worthy of his trust. He is very young for a burden such as we have placed upon him tonight. God knows, our task as his champions will not be easier for his power."

Morgan chuckled softly in the dimness. "Did we accept Brion's charge because we thought it would be easy, or because we loved Brion, love his son, and because it is right?"

"You're right, of course, Alaric," the priest sighed. "You know, I sometimes think you understand me better than I understand myself."

Morgan shoved Duncan playfully. "Not so serious, Father McLain. You've done your job well tonight. It was I who was at a loss. In spite of my penchant toward the lighter occult arts, I had no idea what would happen when Kelson made his move."

"But, of course, if you hadn't gotten the key from Brion, the whole thing would have been for nothing," answered Duncan. "I couldn't have helped at all without the brooch and the verse." He laughed quietly. "We'd better stop complimenting each other so that I can get back to the rectory. If I were missed there, it would not be too pleasant, and it would be rather difficult to explain my presence, were I discovered here in the morning. Besides," he added, going back into the room, "there's nothing more that I can do for Kelson tonight. Barring some unforseen event, he should sleep until dawn. And you need to rest, too, Alaric."

Morgan agreed as the two men clasped hands at the passageway, and then Duncan slipped through the entrance, which whispered shut behind him.

Unclasping his cloak, Morgan pulled an over-stuffed chair near the prince's couch and sank down wearily, pulling the cloak around him blanket-wise. He watched Kelson alertly for some moments, and when he had satisfied himself that the prince still slept soundly, he pulled off his boots and relaxed confidently, knowing that he would awaken in an instant, should any situation in the room change.

VI

As Morgan opened one eye, the morning stillness was broken abruptly by a staccato rapping at the door. Instantly alert, he glided to the door and shot back the bolt. A scarlet and blue liveried valet bowed deferentially before him.

"Pardon, Your Grace," said the man earnestly, "but the dressers wish to know when they may come to robe the King for his Coronation."

"Send them in about a half an hour," he answered, "and please ask the guard to send for Father McLain. His Highness will wish to see him before the procession to the Cathedral."

The valet bowed and hurried away as Morgan closed the door. Padding softly to the balcony, the general drew the satin drapes to let the pale morning sunshine stream in, then added wood to the dying fire to warm the icy room. He had just taken a thick woolen dressing gown from the wardrobe, and was pulling it on, when he realized he was being watched. He turned and smiled at Kelson as he knotted the sash around his slim waist.

"Good morning, my prince," he said cheerfully, crossing to Kelson's couch and sitting on the edge.

"The temperature dropped considerably during the night—it will be a cold Coronation Day."

"What time is it, Morgan?" asked the prince, sitting up in bed.

"Not as late as you think, my prince," laughed Morgan, pushing Kelson back on the couch. "Your clothiers will not be here for half an hour, your valet has already prepared your bath, and it is two hours before the procession is to begin. How is your hand?"

He reached across and unwound the bandage to inspect the wounds. "A little bruised, but no great damage done. We'll dispense with the bandage. How do you feel?"

"I feel fine, Morgan. Can I get up now?"

"Certainly, my prince." He gestured toward the dressing room. "I'll send your dressers in as soon as they arrive."

Kelson wrinkled his nose in distaste as he threw back the blankets and climbed out of bed. "Why do I have to have dressers, Morgan? I can dress myself."

"Because a king must have dressers on his Coronation Day," laughed Morgan, propelling the lad toward the door. "After today, you may fire *all* your personal servants if you so wish, but *today* you will be robed as befits a king—you're not supposed to clutter up your mind with the mechanics of putting on strange robes when you *should* be contemplating the responsibilities of kingship—and this means dressers, six of them." He raised his eyebrows in mock horror.

"Six!" groaned Kelson, but he chuckled gleefully as he scampered through the dressing room door. "Morgan, I sometimes think you do these things deliberately." The rest of his speech was cut off by the closing of the door.

Morgan chuckled as he strolled toward the fire, but stopped still when he caught his reflection across the room. Did he really look like that? He glanced down ruefully at his wrinkled tunic, musing that it had done it little good to sleep in it, and ran a hand across a sand-papery chin. The clothes would have to do, since he had no others with him, but the beard...He set to work with soap and razor and had just succeeded in ridding himself of the night's growth when there was a knock at the door.

"Come in," he called, wiping soap out of his eye.

The door opened a crack, and two blue eyes, topped by a shock of straight brown hair, peered around the edge.

"Aha!" said the voice belonging to the eyes. "The prodigal seeketh to amend his appearance. Here." Duncan tossed a large bundle at his surprised friend.

"What?" began Morgan. "Duncan, where did you get these?"

"Oh," said the young priest, as he strolled nonchalantly to where Morgan burrowed in the clothes, "I thought the King's Champion might need garments suitable for the Coronation."

"The King's Champion? How do you know?"

"Well, Kelson tells me a few things that he doesn't tell you. Besides, who did you think it would be, you crazy war horse? Me?"

Morgan laughed delightedly as he shook his head and stripped off his clothes to begin donning fresh garments.

"How's Kelson's hand this morning?" asked the priest, handing Morgan a long scarlet shirt of silk. "I thought I detected a scent of *merasha* when you dressed his wound last night." He gave Morgan a sidelong look.

"The hand is fine," retorted Morgan sheepishly, as he laced up his shirt, "and I was hoping you hadn't noticed the *merasha*. A certain aged tutor of mine would be very upset were he to learn that a priest knew of his dealing in the occult arts."

"Just stay within your own level, Alaric. I'd hate to see you get mixed up in magic you can't handle." He handed the general black silk hose and breeches, which Morgan quickly donned.

"Where is Kelson now?"

"In the bath. He was somewhat, ah, 'upset' about requiring dressers; wanted to know why he couldn't dress himself. I told him that this was one of the trials of kingship, and that at least for today he would have to put up with them."

Duncan chuckled. "He'll be glad for them when he sees everything he has to wear." He sat down, holding out Morgan's light mail jerkin. "Many's the time I've been grateful for even one assistant to help me vest for a very high Mass. Aie," he mused, "there are always so many little laces and ties."

"Here, give me that," snorted Morgan waggishly, as he snatched the jerkin and slipped it over his head. "You know you love it." He wiggled his feet into the shining black boots which Duncan proffered, and there was a knock at the door.

"Kelson's dressers," announced Morgan, giving the buckles a final tug. "Come in."

Six men in precise scarlet livery marched in and bowed crisply, their arms laden with robes and boxes and bundles.

"We are the royal clothiers, Your Grace," stated the first.

Morgan nodded and directed them toward Kelson's dressing room. When they had gone, he shook his head and smiled.

"I pity the poor boy now. You know how he hates to be fussed over."

Duncan shrugged noncommittally as he handed Morgan a black velvet doublet edged with gold and rubies. "It's good for him to know these things, Alaric."

He helped Morgan adjust the wide, split sleeves to show the scarlet beneath, then wrapped a wide satin sash around the general's slim waist.

"My, my, my," he chided, clipping Morgan's sword to a hidden ring on the crimson sash. "I do believe you'll be the most devilishly handsome Champion we've had in a long time."

Morgan paraded before the mirror, strutting like a small boy with a new plaything. "You know, Duncan?" he bantered gaily, "You're right!"

Duncan nearly dropped the crimson-lined cloak he was holding to punch Morgan playfully in the arm.

"And you will also be the most conceited Champion we've ever had!"

He ducked Morgan's retaliatory punch to wag a finger at him in mock indignation from behind a chair.

"Ah, ah, ah. Remember, I am your spiritual father, and I only tell you this for your own good!"

He and Morgan nearly collapsed on the floor in their merriment.

"Quick," gasped Morgan, out of breath, "put my cloak over all this splendor before I explode of puffed-up pride!"

This merely set them laughing again, but they did manage to clip the cape to Morgan's shoulders before they lost control and slumped weakly into two chairs.

A red-liveried clothier poked his head through the door. "Is anything wrong, Your Grace?" he inquired, his eyes round.

Morgan waved him off, still chortling quite delightedly. "No, no everything is fine," he answered, regaining some measure of composure. "But is Prince Kelson ready yet? Father McLain must leave for the Cathedral."

"I'm ready now, Father," said Kelson, sweeping into the room.

Morgan and Duncan rose in unison, almost unbelieving that this white-and-gold clad king was the same boy who had knelt with them so frightened the night before. All in silk and satin, he stood before them like a young angel, the creamy whiteness of his raiment broken only by the play of gold and rubies encrusting the edges. Over the whole was thrown a magnificent ivory cloak, the satin stiff with gold and jewel-work, and in his hands he held a paid of spotless kid gloves and a pair of gold-chased silver spurs. His raven head was bare, as befits an uncrowned monarch.

"I see that you have been informed of your new office, Morgan," he said impishly. "Here," he held out the spurs, "these are for you."

Morgan sank to one knee, his golden head bowing in obeisance. "My prince, I am at a loss for words."

"Nonsense, Morgan," retorted the prince, grinning wryly. "You'd better not be tongue-tied when I need you most." He motioned him to rise. "Here, take these and let my royal clothiers help you finish dressing while I speak with my confessor."

He motioned Duncan to join him on the balcony and

closed the doors. Through the glass, they could see
the dressers fussing over an annoyed Morgan.

Kelson smiled. "Do you think he will be very angry,
Father?"

"I doubt it, my prince. He was too proud when you
walked into the room to be angry for long."

The young prince smiled fleetingly and looked out
over the city. "Father," he asked in a low voice, "what
makes a man a king?"

"I'm not sure anyone can really say, my son,"
answered Duncan thoughtfully. "It may well be that
kings are not so different from ordinary men after all;
except of course, that they have a graver responsibility." Kelson mulled the answer for a long moment, then
turned and knelt at the feet of the priest.

"Father, give me your blessing," he said, bowing
his head. "I do not feel at all like a king."

VII

Thomas Grayson, Archbishop of Sorandor, surveyed the mounting crowd in the streets below his
archepiscopal palace with awe and not a little apprehension as he awaited the hour of the Coronation. In
spite of the bitter cold of the November morning, there
were more people in the streets then he could ever
remember seeing, even at Brion's Coronation fifteen
years before. And yet, it was not a joyous crowd, as
it would have been, but a quiet and well-mannered one,
each upturned face etched in fearful expectation.

They know what their king must face, he thought
grimly, *and they fear for him, as do I. And must we*

all really stand by and watch him fall, with none to lift a hand to save him? Or have Morgan and Duncan some plan, some unknown factor we have not allowed for? Dare I hope?

Sighing resignedly, he turned from his vantage point to prepare for his vesting. Then, once Duncan had arrived, and the retinue had assembled, they would all go to the door of the Cathedral to await the arrival of their new king, and lead him inside to be presented to his people.

Picking up the Lion brooch, Kelson fingered it absent-mindedly for a moment, then, as an afterthought, pinned it to his tunic.

"The coaches are ready for the procession, my prince," called Morgan from the door. "Shall we go?"

"I'm coming," answered Kelson, casting a final look around the room.

"The room will still be here after the Coronation, you know, my prince."

"Yes," replied Kelson wryly, "but I was just wondering whether or not *I* would still be around."

Morgan marched briskly into the room and took Kelson's arm. "Now, I want to hear no more of that kind of talk," he stated, leading the prince to the corridor where his guard of honour waited. "Three hours from now you will be the legally crowned King of Sorandor, and nothing is going to keep that from happening, including your blue friend."

Kelson smiled grimly as they made their way to the downstairs courtyard where the procession waited. "I'll keep that in mind," he said, "though I fear that our blue friend may have other plans for me."

In the courtyard, the entire royal household was

gathered to see its young master off, and the people parted before the young prince as he and his bodyguard moved toward the queen and her carriage.

Surprise at her son's transformation was evident in Sanil's wide green eyes, and she smiled shyly when Kelson bent to kiss her hand in greeting.

"Kelson, my son," she murmured as he helped her into her carriage, "you are a man today. I did not know..."

Morgan stood contentedly in the background, studying the change in the young queen. He noted with approval that she had set aside her mourning attire in deference to her son's Coronation, in spite of the recency of her bereavement. And except for the black lace veiling her emerald tiara, she was clothed in the customary dark green velvet which set off her copper hair and creamy skin to perfection—the green that Brion had loved so well.

Now, as she conversed with Brion's son, she was nearly as radiant as she had been before her tragedy. And when Kelson at last bade farewell, she gazed fondly after him, wonder and pride for her son apparent in every line of her body.

As the young king climbed into his carriage, he and Morgan exchanged triumphant glances, and Morgan signalled the parade-master to begin the march. Swinging up on his ebony war horse beside the royal coach, the young general saluted his monarch, and the entourage began to move slowly towards Sorandor Cathedral.

"Stop pacing, Ian," snapped the Blue One, adjusting the sapphired coronet on her silvered hair. "You make me nervous."

Ian stopped almost in mid-stride.

"Sorry, my pet," he replied good-naturedly. "But I have anticipated this day for many months now, and I'm anxious to be off. You know how I detest waiting."

"Yes," she smiled enigmatically, "I know. I only hope you will not be too disappointed. Even though this young upstart prince does not have his father's power, we must contend with Morgan." She rose distractedly.

"Ah, yes. Morgan. He is the one to watch for. I fear him, Ian, and I fear the power he might wield over our young prince. You must be sure to cut him down in the first moments of your duel—otherwise he may out-fence you. There are rumours that he dabbles in magic, too, though I take little note of such tales. Nevertheless, he is to be destroyed at all costs. Do you understand?"

Ian bowed unctuously. "Of course, my pet," he intoned as he gathered up her silken cloak and brought it toward her. *And after we have eliminated Morgan and his prince, I shall gladly eliminate you,* he thought to himself.

He reached his arms around her to fasten the cold, jewelled clasp at her ivory throat.

"Horses and escort await us at the portal, my lady."

"Thank you, my Lord Ian," she retorted, giving him a sidelong look. "And now, let us be off."

She gestured expansively, and Ian, with a bow and a flourish, threw open the doors. Flanked by four blue-liveried guardsmen, the Blue One and Ian swept down the marble corridor toward their rendezvous with Prince Kelson.

VIII

Kneeling in the great Cathedral, Kelson quickly reflected on the events of the past hour as the Archbishop's voice droned on and on. After entering the Cathedral in solemn procession accompanied by Archbishop Grayson and a dozen prelates of the Church, he had been presented to the people as their rightful sovereign and had, before them and Almighty God, sworn his oath of kingship. Then he had been anointed on head and hands with the holy chrism as a sign of his divine right to rule and knelt for the Archbishop's blessing.

The Archbishop's prayer ended, and Kelson rose to be invested with the symbols of his office, several priests stripping off the jeweled ivory mantle he had worn as Prince of Sorandor. The golden spurs of knighthood were strapped to his heels, and Morgan, as King's Champion, brought forth the sword of state to be kissed by the young monarch and returned to the altar. Duncan and the other prelates were fastening the glittering crimson robe of state about his shoulders when the silence was broken by the echo of steel-shod hooves ringing cold against the cobbled streets outside. Beyond the heavy doors of the Cathedral, chain mail clanked menacingly against naked metal.

As Kelson, his back to the doors, seated himself upon the coronation chair, he flashed a lightning query at Morgan, who nodded almost imperceptibly and edged closer. As the Archbishop gave over the royal sceptre, the Cathedral doors swung open with a muffled crash, and a gust of icy wind swept down the nave, the only sound save the low admonition of the Archbishop.

Stiffening slightly, Kelson saw Morgan freeze as footsteps began to echo down the narrow nave, and he watched the gloved hand of his Champion creep toward the hilt of the great broadsword as the Archbishop raised the gold and crimson ring of fire.

Breathing a small prayer that he would be able to face the Blue One's power, Kelson extended his hand to receive the ring. And as the cool metal circlet glided into place on his forefinger, he broke into a small but triumphant smile which was only skillfully kept from being mirrored in the faces of his two friends. To the side, he saw his mother's face go pale as the hollow footsteps came to an abrupt and ominous halt at the transept.

The Archbishop, ignoring the interlopers, raised the jewelled and filigreed crown of Sorandor.

"Bless, we beseech Thee, O Lord, this crown, and so sanctify Thy servant, Kelson, upon whose head Thou dost place it today as a sign of royal majesty. Grant that he may, by Thy grace, be filled with all princely virtues. Through the King Eternal, Our Lord."

The people were hushed in fear as the crown was placed on the new king's head, and then the silence was broken by the clatter of steel on the sanctuary steps.

Rising majestically to turn and face his challengers, Kelson swiftly appraised the significance of the mailed gauntlet resting on the lowest of the sanctuary steps, then moved confidently to the edge of the area.

"What would you in the House of the Lord?" he demanded, an aura of quiet power overshadowing his youth.

"Your death, Kelson," replied the Blue One, curt-seying mockingly. "Is that so much to ask? I have killed others to gain your throne."

She smiled sweetly, and Ian and a dozen armed warriors glared defiance at the newly-crowned king.

"I do not find your humour amusing this morning, Countess," answered Kelson coldly. "And your man-ners are distinctly lacking in allowing your men to come armed into this place. Have you no respect at all for the proprieties of the people you hope to rule, not to mention your own truce?"

The Countess shrugged unconcernedly and gestured toward the gauntlet of challenge on the step between them.

"Have you forgotten my challenge, Your Majesty? I was under the impression that your illustrious Cham-pion was very eager to fight mine." She continued coldly, "My challenge still stands, as does my Cham-pion. But is yours man enough to pick it up?"

His face colouring slightly, Morgan moved to pick up the challenge, but was halted by Kelson's out-stretched sceptre across his chest.

"You would dare to raise steel against me in this House?" queried Kelson, addressing the blue-clad champion.

Steel whispered against steel as Ian bowed silkily and drew his sword in answer.

"Aye, and in a thousand like it, Prince Kelson," retorted the unctuous young lord as he gestured with his sword. "And if he will not come down and fight, I shall come up and slay him where he stands."

"Save your words for your victory, traitor," replied Morgan, his sword singing from its leather scabbard as he vaulted down the steps to meet his impetuous challenger and pick up the gauntlet. "I take up your challenge in the name of King Kelson and answer it thus!"

He flung the gauntlet at the feet of Lord Ian.

"Well, Morgan," said Ian thoughtfully, his sword point wandering almost lazily before him as he contemplated his enemy, "at last we meet. Then, let us resolve this petty dispute once and for all."

Lunging savagely, he sought to pierce Morgan's defense at once, but the wily general swiftly threw up a singing steel net about him which easily parried each of Ian's renewed attacks. When Morgan had sounded out Ian's technique, he switched to an offensive tack, and within seconds had pinked the challenger. Ian, furious at being touched, charged headlong into the fray as Morgan had hoped, and even as he parried the general's thrust, Morgan's riposte left him open to be run through the side. As sword clattered from the surprised lord's hand, Morgan withdrew his blade, and Ian sank to the floor, his face drained of colour. Morgan, with a contemptuous toss of his head, wiped his blade on the young lord's blood-stained mantle and strolled calmly toward his comrades.

"Morgan!" yelled Duncan, gesturing frantically.

Morgan whirled instantly, but he was not swift enough to completely avoid the dagger which had been aimed at his back. His sword slipped from numbed fingers as he clutched at his shoulder in disbelief, and Ian laughed brokenly from his position a dozen yards away.

"I am amazed, Morgan," he leered drunkenly as death approached. "I had thought you more cautious than to leave a wounded enemy armed. Ah, well, though," he gasped, sketching a hurried salute, "you may yet join me in death." He slumped to the floor, silent at last, and Morgan gazed dully at his former antagonist.

As Duncan and the priests eased Morgan to a sitting position on the steps, Kelson hovered anxiously, his resplendent cloak gathered over one arm as he stooped beside his friend.

"My apologies, my prince," murmured Morgan, beads of perspiration dotting his upper lip as Duncan probed the wound with gentle fingers. "I was a fool to trust him, even in death." He winced and clenched his teeth as Duncan withdrew the slim blade, but then relaxed, half-fainting, as the young priest bound up the wound. Kelson, with a reassuring touch of his friend's hand, rose and descended several steps toward the Blue One.

"The little game is over now, Countess. You may leave."

The Blue One, backed by her guards and her magic, smiled sardonically. "My, but our young prince speaks bold words. One would almost believe that he had power to back him up."

Her icy gaze swept him from head to toe and back again. "But we all know that his father's legacy of power died with him a month ago, don't we?" She smiled sweetly.

"Do we, Countess?" countered Kelson. "But, perhaps you *are* willing to stake your life and power on such a gamble. I warn you, though. If you force me to a show of strength, I cannot promise you mercy."

"Does the Blue One need your mercy, Kelson? No, I think the son of Brion is bluffing, and I call that bluff."

Stepping back a few paces, she raised her hands and cast a line of pale blue fire in a semi-circle behind her.

"Now, Kelson, will you close the ring and duel with me under the laws of ancient ritual, or must I strike you down with wanton magic? How say you, Kelson?"

Kelson regarded her disdainfully for a moment; then, with a slight bow of acquiescence, he handed his sceptre over to a waiting chamberlain and joined the Blue One in the transept. The wine-dark cloak flowed smoothly from his young shoulders as he raised both arms in a single, fluid motion. A deep crimson semi-circle sprang up behind him, its ends meeting those of the blue arc.

The Blue One nodded patronizingly and began an incantation.

> "By Earth and Water, Fire and Air,
> I conjure powers to leave this ring.
> I clear it now. Let all beware.
> Through here shall pass no living thing."

Morgan tugged hard on Duncan's sleeve. "Duncan! Does he know what she's doing? If he completes the spell and joins the two arcs, the circle cannot be broken until one has lost all power."

"I don't know, Alaric. But if he can complete the spell at all, we'll know that he has Brion's magic. Kelson was never taught these things."

Kelson replied:

> "Inside, all Space and Time suspend.
> From here may nothing outward flee
> Nor inward come. It shall not end
> Till two are one and one is free."

As Kelson finished, violet fire flared where the two arcs had been, and then a cold violet line, inscribing a thirty-foot circle, marked off the area where the two must duel.

"You, as Challenged, have the privilege of first strike, my precocious princeling." Her eyes widened a bit when Kelson declined the privilege, but perhaps she had actually expected such a move after his successful completion of the ring, for she nodded acceptance without a word and stretched her hands out before her, palms together. Murmuring some unintelligible syllables, she drew her hands apart, and a sphere of blue light could be seen hovering in mid-air.

Quickly, the thing grew to man-size and took the form of a warrior in full armour, blue shield over arm and blazing sword in hand. Dripping blue fire and vapours, he cocked his head at the young king and advanced across the circle.

Kelson hesitated but an instant, then put right hand to left and drew forth a glowing crimson sword from his closed fist. When the blue warrior came within reach, lightning forked from Kelson's left hand, pinning the blue sword, while Kelson lopped the thing's head off. It struck the floor with a hollow sound, and then the apparition and Kelson's weapons vanished.

The people rumbled in appreciation at their new king's prowess as the Blue One's nimble fingers moved vexedly in the next spell.

> "Spawn of Dagon, Bael's darling,
>   Heed my call which bids thee here.
>   Son of Darkness, hear my order.
>   Come: I charge thee to appear.

Smite this young, ambitious princeling,
Send him to a death of flames.
Wrest from him the usurped power
Which the Blue One justly claims!"

As she spoke, there was a rumbling in the air before
her, and a dense black vapour condensed into a tall,
shadowy form vaguely man-like in shape, but with scaly
hide and long claws and teeth. It stood blinking in the
center as Kelson began a counterspell.

"Lord of Light, in shining splendor
Aid me now, if thou dost hear
The supplication of thy servant,
Battling for his people here.
Lend me strength to smite this demon,
Send it to the depths of hell.
Cleanse this circle of the evil
Which the Blue One doth compel!"

As the creature began to lope across the circle,
mawing mouth and claws dripping blue flame, Kelson
finished his spell. With a decisive gesture, the king
stabbed a ruby-banded finger toward a spot several
yards in front of the monster.

Just at that moment, the sun burst from behind the
clouds to stream through the high stained-glass windows, casting a brilliant, multi-coloured pattern on the
floor where Kelson pointed. The congregation inhaled
in unison as the creature reached the spot, stepped into
it, and began writhing and exuding blue streamers of
flame and smoke. It shrieked in mortal agony, but could
not seem to step out of the blaze of light which seared

its flesh. As it spun in its final throes to crash to the floor, it cried out terribly and pointed an accusing arm at the Blue Witch, then was still. It vanished, and only wisps of pungent blue smoke and crimson and gold flickerings played on the floor where the thing had been.

Kelson lowered his hand, the Ring of Fire winking ominously, and the sun chose that moment to go back behind the clouds. A low sigh of relief swept through the church like a whisper of spring, and settled to a hush as Kelson faced his opponent, grey eyes bright with confidence.

> "And now, O Witch, this farce must end.
> I will no more my powers lend
> To thwart your might. I must defend
> My people, and your power rend.
> Therefore, I take the right of claim
> To instigate the test of flame.
> I call the trial of fiery wall
> Which, in this case, decideth all."

He stabbed a ringed forefinger at his archenemy, and she gathered her steely composure to answer his challenge. Instantly, the two halves of the circle became misted with blue or red auras, and where the two met, a violet fog played along the surface. The line fluctuated wildly for a moment, as each magician sought out the other's weaknesses, but then the line began moving inexorably toward the Blue One.

As she began to lose ground, she began inching back, but her shoulders soon encountered the glassy slickness of the barrier ring. With a low cry, she glanced behind her, then sank to her knees, head bowed in her hands, as the last vestiges of her power were neutralized by Kelson's crimson aura.

When the entire area glowed red, the circle winked out of existence. And the only things left where it had been were a softly weeping woman, human now, and a young king, dazed at his first victory.

Kelson dropped his hand softly to his side, his face impassive, then addressed himself to the Blue One's soldiers.

"Who among you is in charge now?"

The men shuffled uneasily under his steady gaze, and finally a man wearing the insignia of a lieutenant stepped forward and bowed respectfully.

"I am, my lord." He glanced uncertainly at the huddled shape of his former mistress, then continued. "My name is Brennan de Colforth, and I renounce the oath of fealty I took with the Blue One. I swear I never wished you ill, and I ask forgiveness for myself and my men."

"You treacherous dog!" spat the Blue One, scrambling to her feet. "How dare you?"

"Silence," said Kelson, turning toward his Champion. "Morgan? What say you?"

Morgan climbed to his feet and joined the prince, Duncan supporting him. "'Tis a small but noble family of Lanspar to the North, my prince. Old but proud."

"Father?"

"I have never known a de Colforth to swear falsely, my prince," remarked Duncan.

"Very well, then. De Colforth, I give you this proposition: you, and any of your men who will swear loyalty to me, will be pardoned with one stipulation—that you take the Blue One into exile at Shepara and then disband and return to your lands, never to molest me and my people again."

De Colforth dropped to one knee, mailed fist to chest in salute. "I accept Your Majesty's pardon in full humility, and swear to uphold the stipulations of that pardon to the best of my ability." Behind him, a dozen other men joined in the salute.

There was a long moment of silence as all rose to their feet, and then a voice from the rear of the Cathedral cried out, "Long live King Kelson!" And the shout was picked up and carried by a hundred hundred voices.

First Archbishop and clergy, then Champion and peers of the realm, came to kneel and swear their fealty to the new king. And as Kelson formed his retinue to process out of the Cathedral, the sun shone again through the stained glass and cast a puddle of jeweled light at his feet. The church grew hushed. Looking up casually at the window, Kelson smiled and stepped into the light, which turned his jewels to flame, and then, amidst cheers of joy and wonder, he left to show himself to his people.

PRECIS OF DERYNI RISING

In the process of developing the Deryni concept for submission, I wrote the following one-page synopsis for the first trilogy in the Deryni series.

DERYNI RISING

A NOVEL BY
KATHERINE KURTZ

Deryni Rising is the first of a trilogy dealing with the Deryni—that ancient race of quasi-mortal sorcerers, metaphysicians, and dabblers in human affairs whose existence was at once bane and blessing to the people of the Eleven Kingdoms.

Deryni Rising tells how Kelson Haldane came to acquire his father's magical powers and defeat the evil

Charissa, a Deryni sorceress. More important, it introduces the central character of all three books, Alaric Morgan: friend and prodigy of Kelson's father, Brion. Morgan, the half-Deryni General whose talents are so crucial for a Deryni rising. Morgan's priest-cousin Duncan McLain, also half-Deryni, is also introduced.

Deryni Checkmate, second in the series, will establish the socio-political atmosphere of the Eleven Kingdoms in the months immediately following Kelson's coronation. Flashbacks of Morgan's long association with Brion; the proposed and thwarted marriage of Morgan's sister Bronwyn to Duncan's brother Kevin; the reaction of the Bishops' Curia against Morgan and Duncan; the growing unease as a militant Deryni-hater maraudes Morgan's duchy—all combine to set the stage for a new human-Deryni conflict which will be developed in Book III.

Book III will treat the human-Deryni war which is threatened, and will see most of the conflicts resolved.

Further novels are projected if the Trilogy is successful.

SUBMISSION OUTLINE FOR DERYNI RISING

This is the outline I submitted to sell the first trilogy, projecting the course I anticipated *Deryni Rising* would take. Purists may wish to compare this outline with the actual novel, though the differences are largely additions and embellishments rather than changes.

OUTLINE: *DERYNI RISING*

CHAPTER ONE

In far Gwynedd, near the city of Rhemuth, Brion Haldane, Lord of that land, rides to the hounds with his thirteen year-old son, Kelson, and a number of his retainers. During a lull in the chase, Brion and Kelson withdraw to discuss the absence of Morgan, the King's top general, and to speculate on the most recent harassment of the Shadowed One, Charissa, member of the ancient Deryni race of sorcerers. Brion himself, though not Deryni, has extensive powers of his own, through which he has held his kingdom for more than fifteen years—power which will one day be Kelson's. He asks that Kelson promise to send for Morgan if anything should happen to him, and they rejoin the hunt. Brion unwittingly drinks some drugged wine, and the hunt resumes.

Lord Ian falls behind and enters the forest to the east, where he meets Charissa. The two discuss their plot to assassinate Brion that morning and take over the kingdom from Kelson. It is both a power-play and a plan of revenge for Charissa, for it was Morgan who helped Brion gain his power and slay her father fifteen years before—Morgan, the half-Deryni Lord who, in her eyes, has betrayed his Deryni heritage. Kelson will be spared for the moment, but only as bait to lure Morgan to his death.

Ian rejoins the hunt, and the hounds are made to lose the scent. As Kelson rides ahead to see what has happened, Brion is stricken by what appears to be a heart attack. When Kelson reaches his side, Brion has only enough strength to whisper, "Remember...", before he dies. Kelson sends for General Morgan.

CHAPTER TWO

Morgan returns in haste to Rhemuth, arriving the day before the Coronation. He and his military aide, Lord Derry, are sole survivors of an ambush which delayed their coming.

Morgan's arrival creates an uproar. As Deryni, he was already suspect, and now he has been branded a traitor by the lies and rumors planted by Charissa. His announcement of the slaying of his escort adds fuel to the fire. Worse, the slaying leaves a pro-Morgan seat vacant on the Regency Council.

Prince Nigel, brother of the late King, takes Morgan to meet Kelson in the garden, warning him on the way of Queen Jehana's plot against him. The queen wants Kelson to assume the throne of Gwynedd, but without his father's supernatural powers, which she regards as evil. Her method: to bring Morgan before the Council on charges of heresy and high treason. Nigel agrees to talk with the Queen and stall for time. But Morgan's fate will depend ultimately on Kelson's personal ability to manipulate the voting in the Council.

Morgan reflects on the Deryni background and the beginnings of his feud with Jehana while he waits for Kelson. When the boy appears with Kevin McLain, he and Morgan move deeper into the garden to discuss strategy.

Kevin returns to the hall and talks with Derry about the charges against Morgan. For treason and heresy, the penalty is death.

CHAPTER THREE

In her chambers, Jehana considers her plans for Morgan. Nigel arrives and manages to convince her that Brion's death was not a simple heart attack. But instead of the hoped-for cooperation, Jehana declares she is now even more convinced that Kelson must rule as a mortal, without his father's dark powers. Brion's powers did not save *him*. Jehana sends for Kelson and leaves for the Council meeting.

In the garden, Morgan and Kelson discuss Kelson's training for kingship and his mother's hostility to things Deryni. A Stenrect, a deadly creature of supernatural origin, comes within inches of Kelson's hand. Morgan kills it. But from across the garden, his action is seen as attempted murder. Only Kelson's intervention prevents the guards from arresting Morgan on the spot.

They dare linger in the garden no longer. Too much must be done before Morgan is called to the Council, as he is sure to be. They will be able to find temporary sanctuary at St. Hilary's, the royal basilica, where Morgan's cousin Duncan is waiting.

Nigel's attempts to stall the opening of the Council meeting are thwarted. Jehana calls the meeting to order without Kelson and begins proceedings against Morgan.

CHAPTER FOUR

Morgan and Kelson meet with Duncan, Morgan's half-Deryni priest-cousin. In Duncan's study, Morgan produces his Gryphon Signet, which will open a secret compartment in the main altar. Duncan takes the seal and returns shortly with a flat black box, about six inches square. Inside is a folded slip of parchment written in Brion's hand, and another similar box which cannot be opened. The parchment reads:

When shall the Son deflect the running tide?
A Spokesman of the Infinite must guide

The Dark Protector's hand to shed the blood
Which lights the Eye of Rom at Eventide.

Same blood must swiftly feed the Ring of Fire.
But, careful, lest ye rouse the Demon's ire:
If soon thy hand despoil the virgin band,
Just retribution damns what ye desire!

Now that the Eye of Rom can see the light,
Release the Crimson Lion in the night.
With sinister hand unflinching, Lion's Tooth
Must pierce the flesh and make the Power right.

Thus Eye and Fire and Lion drink their fill.
Ye have assuaged the warring might of Ill.
New morn, ring hand. Defender's Sign shall seal
Thy force. No Power Below shall thwart thy will.

Morgan has the Ring of Fire in his pocket. But the
Eye of Rom, a ruby set in an earring, was buried with
Brion. They must open Brion's tomb to retrieve it.

Outside, Archbishop Loris, a militant persecutor of
Deryni, arrives with a detachment of royal guards to
arrest Morgan. The three agree to go to the crypt that
night. Morgan reassures Kelson, then surrenders to
Loris. Loris seizes Morgan and serves him with a writ
commanding him to appear before the Council and
answer to charges of heresy and high treason.

CHAPTER FIVE

The Council is in turmoil when Kelson and Morgan
arrive. Kelson gestures for silence as he takes his place
at the head of the table. His eyes touch briefly on the

empty Council seat as he orders Morgan's sword placed before him on the table. Jehana wastes no time announcing the Council's vote; six to five against Morgan. Morgan is doomed.

Kelson polls the Council and learns that Derry was not permitted to vote in Morgan's absence. Morgan votes for himself, making the vote six to six. Jehana demands she be allowed to vote, since she is no longer chairman in Kelson's absence. Therefore, the vote is seven to six against Morgan.

Kelson orders the formal charges against Morgan read out. Basilica and Cathedral bells toll three as the clerk finishes the reading. Kelson announces he will fill the empty Council seat before continuing: Lord Derry is appointed. Derry votes to acquit Morgan, Kelson breaks the new tied vote, and Morgan is acquitted, eight to seven.

Jehana challenges Kelson's right to appoint Derry without the approval of the Regents. Kelson retorts that he no longer needs approval since the Council is no longer a Regency Council. Kelson came of age with the tolling of the bells. If everyone will recall, it was his afternoon hour of birth which scheduled the Coronation for tomorrow in the first place. The Council is adjourned.

Kelson cuts Morgan's bonds, returns his sword, and sweeps out of the chamber with Morgan and Derry at his heels, leaving a stunned Council in his wake.

CHAPTER SIX

As soon as the three have cleared the Council chambers, Morgan sends Derry to assure Duncan that all is well. Morgan and Kelson will hole up in Kelson's quarters and rest until evening. Derry will return and guard when he has finished.

As the Council disperses, Ian is concerned by the favorable reaction Kelson's brilliant maneuvering is receiving. He slips away and overpowers a guard in a little-used corridor, then uses the man as a medium to contact Charissa. He tells her of the defeat in Council, and the two plot strategy. Ian kills the guard, then smears some of his blood in the rough outline of a gryphon. When he has some of Morgan's knights discover the body later that night, they will require little persuasion to believe that their liege lord is a murderer as well as a traitor.

Morgan wakes shortly after dark. With a set of black and white cubes, he constructs a Master Ward to guard the sleeping Kelson while he searches Brion's library for information on the ritual verse. The boy awakens while Morgan is setting the wards and asks to go along, but Morgan vetoes the request and puts Kelson to sleep with a touch of Deryni control.

Morgan's search of the library discloses nothing. Wearily, he meditates on the possible meaning of the ritual verse, using his Gryphon Seal as a focus for his concentration. For a fraction of a second, he seems to have a vision. There is the fleeting impression of a man's face surrounded by blackness, a feeling both of urgency and reassurance—and the moment is past.

Morgan glances around quickly, but there is no one there. Again, he goes through Brion's books. This time, one well-thumbed volume falls open to a place marked by a slip of parchment in Brion's hand. But it is the picture opposite the passage which chills Morgan most. For the portrait, that of St. Camber of Culdi, is the face he saw in the vision. St. Camber, an ancient Deryni Lord.

Intently Morgan scans the passage, absently pocketing the parchment as he reads. As he closes the volume, he hears the door opening softly behind him and turns to see Charissa stealthily entering the room. She pretends not to be startled when Morgan addresses her, and the two exchange polite conversation and veiled threats. Charissa finally boasts of having "looked in" on Kelson and laughs as Morgan dashes from the room. Then she picks up the volume Morgan was reading and flips worriedly through its pages.

CHAPTER SEVEN

Morgan wakes shortly after dark. With a set of black and white cubes, he constructs a Master Ward to guard the sleeping Kelson while he searches Brion's library for information on the ritual verse. The boy awakens while Morgan is setting the wards and asks to go along, but Morgan vetoes the request and puts Kelson to sleep with a touch of Deryni control.

Morgan's search of the library discloses nothing. Wearily, he meditates on the possible meaning of the ritual verse, using his Gryphon Seal as a focus for his concentration. For a fraction of a second, he seems to have a vision. There is the fleeting impression of a man's face surrounded by blackness, a feeling both of urgency and reassurance—and the moment is past.

Morgan glances around quickly, but there is no one there. Again, he goes through Brion's books. This time, one well-thumbed volume falls open to a place marked by a slip of parchment in Brion's hand. But it is the

picture opposite the passage which chills Morgan most.
For the portrait, that of St. Camber of Culdi, is the
face he saw in the vision. St. Camber, an ancient Deryni
Lord.

Intently Morgan scans the passage, absently pocketing the parchment as he reads. As he closes the volume, he hears the door opening softly behind him and
turns to see Charissa stealthily entering the room. She
pretends not to be startled when Morgan addresses her,
and the two exchange polite conversation and veiled
threats. Charissa finally boasts of having "looked in"
on Kelson and laughs as Morgan dashes from the room.
Then she picks up the volume Morgan was reading and
flips worriedly through its pages.

CHAPTER EIGHT

Morgan returns immediately to Kelson's quarters,
but the boy is safe. Morgan breaks the wards and wakes
Kelson. They make their way through a secret passage
to St. Hilary's but Morgan does not mention his strange
vision.

Duncan shows them an ancient Deryni Transfer Portal to the Cathedral where Brion's body lies. Going
ahead to be sure the way is clear, he encounters Brother
Jerome, the elderly and half-blind sacristan. Duncan
allays the monk's suspicions and sends him on his way
with a Deryni command to forget what he has seen,
then brings Morgan and Kelson through the Portal.

Morgan and Duncan use their Deryni powers to
silence two guards outside the royal crypt. As Morgan
picks the lock on the gate, Lord Rogier comes to check
on the guards. Duncan overpowers Rogier, and the

three enter the crypt. Kelson points out Brion's tomb and brings a candlelabra closer as Morgan and Duncan slide back the cover. After a slight hesitation, Morgan pulls back the white silk shroud covering the face. It isn't Brion!

CHAPTER NINE

The body in the tomb is totally unfamiliar. After agitated speculation, Duncan hypothesizes that Brion's body is possibly still within the crypt, perhaps swapped with another tenant. They begin the grisly task of opening other sepulchers, only to have Morgan suddenly rush back to the original and call the others to his side. He contends that the strange body *is* Brion's, only under a shape-changing spell. Duncan removes the spell, experiencing Brion's death as he releases the final essence, and the body resumes its normal shape.

Morgan removes the Eye of Rom. Duncan leaves his crucifix in Brion's hands to ward off further spell-binding, and they reseal the sepulcher.

Back in Duncan's study, the three gather the elements for the power transfer: the Eye of Rom, the Ring of Fire, and the box with the Crimson Lion. Morgan pierces Kelson's right earlobe and "feeds" the Eye and Ring with the blood from that piercing. Then Kelson, wearing the Eye of Rom, opens the box and removes a large, crimson-enameled brooch with a golden lion emblazoned upon it. They consult the ritual verse again, but they seem to have reached a stalemate: the Lion has no tooth!

CHAPTER TEN

Duncan re-reads the verse. Of course: there is always
the challenge, the obstacle, the need for bravery. The
Lion's Tooth is the clasp of the brooch—three inches
of gleaming gold. And it is this which must "pierce the
flesh and make the power right."

Morgan and Duncan leave the boy to prepare himself. Morgan is frankly uneasy, especially since Duncan
plans to use the secret chapel adjoining his study: a
chapel sacred to, among others, St. Camber. Morgan
tells Duncan of his vision, how it led him to the passage
in the book—and remembers the parchment. Withdrawing it, they read, "St. Camber defend us!"

Duncan is hesitant, for as priest as well as Deryni,
he is well aware how slender is the balance between
good and evil. And St. Camber's sainthood was recalled
long ago by a fearful church. But they have no choice
but to continue. For without his father's powers, Kelson will surely die.

They return to Kelson and enter the chapel. Morgan
and Kelson doff their swords and kneel, and Duncan
begins the ritual. At the appropriate moment, Kelson
plunges the golden shaft through the palm of his hand.
He reels drunkenly as a pale aura surrounds him, then
hallucinates briefly and passes out. Apparently, the
power transfer has worked, though Kelson will not be
able to use his powers until the sequence is completed
tomorrow at the Coronation.

Morgan and Duncan gather up the unconscious
prince and return to Kelson's quarters. As Duncan
closes the passage, a voice from the shadows roars,

"Traitors! Blasphemers! What have you done to Prince Kelson?" Three armed knights emerge from the darkness and advance on Duncan and Morgan.

CHAPTER ELEVEN

Morgan catches the sword Duncan tosses and lowers the unconscious Kelson to the floor. As guards hammer on the door, he and Duncan battle the three knights. Duncan finally kills his man and overcomes one of Morgan's with a Deryni power touch. Morgan disarms the third and holds him at bay, blocking his memory of Duncan as the priest slips out on the balcony to hide. Kelson staggers to his feet and retrieves Duncan's fallen sword as the guards burst in.

The prisoner, one of Morgan's vassals, tells of the guard he and his companions found slain, of the telltale gryphon smeared in the man's dying blood. The guards are ready to seize Morgan, but Kelson forbids it. Morgan could not have killed the guard, for he was with Kelson. When asked how he found the body, the knight replies they "just happened to go there." Did someone tell them to? Kelson insists, sensing he's getting to the source of the frame-up. But the man panics, seizes a dagger from one of the guards, plunges it into his own chest before anyone can stop him. Kelson orders the bodies removed. Morgan slips outside to discover what happened to the corridor guards. He finds them all dead or dying, with Derry, too, very near death.

Kneeling desperately at Derry's side, Morgan remembers something he once read about Deryni. Placing both hands lightly on Derry's forehead, he concentrates through his Gryphon Seal once more, trying to summon up the healing power which Deryni are reputed to have. For an instant, he has the impression of another pair of hands on top of his. Derry's eyes flicker and he passes into a natural sleep, his wounds and injured arm completely healed.

As Morgan stares at his hands in disbelief, he hears a voice behind him say, "Well done, Morgan!"

CHAPTER TWELVE

Morgan whirls defensively, half expecting to see the face in his vision again. But it is Bran Coris who approaches, accompanied by Ewan, Nigel, Ian, and a thoroughly angry Jehana. "Ah, yes. Well done, indeed!" Bran continues. "You've finally killed him, too, haven't you? Now you're the only one alive who knows what really happened on that long ride to Rhemuth?"

"Sorry to disappoint you, but he isn't dead," Morgan retorts, consigning Derry to the care of the surgeons. Jehana rages at Morgan about the slain guard, but she dares do nothing against him. She subsides only when Kelson appears at the door, haggard and worn, and orders them all to disperse. Ian glances back at Morgan as he disappears down the corridor, then calls a guard to attend him.

As the door closes and Duncan is finally able to emerge from hiding, Kelson collapses under the strain. He regains consciousness briefly as Morgan and Duncan put him to bed, and mumbles about seeing faces during the ritual. When Kelson drifts off to sleep again, Morgan crosses to the fireplace and searches rapidly through Kelson's books, finding at last a picture of St.

Camber. *There*, he maintains, is the face Kelson saw. And it's the same one Morgan saw in his vision. He tells Duncan then of healing Derry, and they explore the possibility of a common factor in all three cases.

Duncan comments that at least Kelson seems to have a few useful talents tucked away: Morgan was very clever to teach Kelson those Deryni questioning techniques he used on the guard. Morgan objects: *he* didn't teach Kelson—he thought *Duncan* did. Implication: can Kelson be Deryni? Unless someone else of Deryni blood taught him, which is highly unlikely, it would be impossible for him to know. But if he *is* Deryni, how? Brion, they know, was full human. And Jehana . . . Khadasa! If Jehana *is* Deryni, and doesn't know it, or only suspects, it could explain much of her hostility.

Projections: Deryni blood *may* give Kelson the edge he needs tomorrow against Charissa, especially if the power sequence should fail in any way. On the other hand, it makes Jehana's opposition that much more unpredictable. On that ominous note, Duncan leaves and Morgan settles down for some much-needed sleep.

In his room, Ian binds his captive guard in another communication with Charissa. "He's been to the crypt," Ian tells her, "and he's wearing the Eye of Rom. No one else noticed." "Good," Charissa replies. "Go back to the Cathedral, then. You know what to do."

Ian erases the guard's memory of the event and sends him on his way, then slips out of the palace to carry out his orders. Later, he arrives in Charissa's chambers, where he will remain until morning.

CHAPTER THIRTEEN

Next morning, the royal wardrobers and dressers take Kelson in hand to prepare him for the Coronation. Derry, fully recovered, arrives to assist Morgan with last minute details. Elsewhere, Ian stops a wardrober and makes a switch in Morgan's chain of office, substituting one which will relay information to Charissa.

Duncan arrives and informs Morgan he has been named King's Champion—a great honor, but one which could prove most arduous if physical as well as occult challenge is made at the Coronation.

Kelson appears in his Coronation regalia to congratulate Morgan on his new title. He and Duncan retire to the privacy of the balcony, where the priest reassures Kelson of his suitability for kingship and hears his confession.

Inside, Morgan dons the accoutrements of King's Champion, unaware that his chain of office is now relaying all he says and does to the Shadowed One.

Nigel arrives in a daze, relating a horrible scene of carnage found in the royal crypt early this morning. During the night, someone has ransacked Brion's tomb and stolen the jewels from the body. The two guards were found with their throats neatly slit, and Rogier is dead with his own hand on the dagger and an awful expression on his face. Clutched tightly in his other hand was a gilded crucifix. It is Duncan's.

CHAPTER FOURTEEN

Before the three can react, Jehana bursts angrily into the chamber, full of fresh outrage at the slaying, for Rogier was a distant relative. She knows of the fatal crucifix and confronts Duncan and Morgan with it. But her anger turns to cold fury when she spots the Eye of Rom glittering in Kelson's ear. For she knows it came from Brion's tomb.

"Monster!" she screams. "You would desecrate your own father's tomb, you would *murder* for this power! Oh, Kelson, see what this foul Deryni curse has brought you to!"

She swears she will not attend the Coronation. Morgan realizes explanation is useless at this point, so he issues an ultimatum: either Jehana will attend, or Morgan will Mind-See to discover whether she *is* Deryni as he believes her to be. Jehana is horrified, but the threat is a powerful one: Jehana *has* suspected her origin, though she is not willing to accept it. She agrees reluctantly to go along, but she will have to be watched. All assemble for the procession to the Cathedral.

Charissa has observed the royal friction with great interest and now she, too, begins her journey to the Cathedral. En route, she alerts Ian to the new potential threat of Jehana. She also considers her plans for Morgan and Kelson—and the treacherous Ian.

Kelson's procession arrives at the Cathedral. The participants take their places, Derry keeps watch from a bell tower, and three Archbishops lead Kelson inside to begin the ceremonies.

Kelson takes the Coronation Oath. During the annointing, Derry slips in with word that Charissa is approaching with a band of armed soldiers. The ranking archbishop invests Kelson with the Ring of Fire and the Sword of State. Morgan comes forward to redeem the sword and has Kelson touch his Gryphon Seal to fulfill the final condition of the tirual verse.

But nothing happens. Morgan's Gryphon is not the Defender's Sign. The Cathedral doors crash open and Charissa stands silhouetted in the doorway.

CHAPTER FIFTEEN

As Morgan and Duncan try desperately to think of some other seal which might fulfill the verse, Charissa sweeps down the aisle with her retainers. She forbids the Coronation to continue, then challenges Kelson to mortal combat for the rule of Gwynedd.

Kelson knows Charissa is trying to goad him into a duel of magic, but he pretends to understand her challenge as a traditional trial by combat. He names Morgan as his Champion, and Charissa names Ian. The two battle until Morgan finally inflicts a mortal wound on Ian. But the dying Ian flings his dagger at Morgan with his last effort. Morgan's rigged chain of office impedes his movement and he's gravely wounded in the shoulder. Morgan gets rid of the chain, but the damage is done.

The duel has decided nothing. Charissa renews her challenge, calling for trial by magic according to ancient tradition. Kelson hesitates and Jehana makes her move.

The unleashed power of a full Deryni lashes out at Charissa, guided by the despair of a mother who must try to protect her child at all costs. But Charissa has been expecting just such a move. And Jehana's power is untrained, without control. Charissa tries to kill, but Morgan and Duncan are able to deflect the killing force. Result: Jehana is imprisoned inside a Deryni force-field—one which can be broken only by Charissa's will, or her death.

Charissa regains her composure and taunts Kelson. Will he come down and meet her in honorable combat, or must she strike out now and slay him where he stands, without a fight? Kelson must now make a reply.

CHAPTER SIXTEEN

Kelson's mind reels. He is half-Deryni! Can he use this advantage to gain the power he desperately needs? As he absently rubs the Ring of Fire and searches for some clue, his eyes light on the inlaid marble floor of the transept where Charissa stands. The signs of myriads of saints appear there, and somewhere—yes! There, to the left, is the sign of St. Camber, he who was long ago called *Defensor Hominum*, the Defender of Man. Can this be the Defender's Sign of the verse?

This is the supreme bluff. For in order to survive, Kelson must now proceed as though he already has Brion's power, trusting that he *will* receive it when he steps on the seal. Outwardly calm, Kelson takes up Charissa's challenge and walks toward her. Duncan and the wounded Morgan, watching from the steps, realize the gamble Kelson is taking. But as the boy stops on the seal, they can see no reaction. Charissa begins the spell which Kelson must complete. And as Kelson raises his arms to answer, the air crackles around him in response. The power transfer is at last complete!

The duel begins, a series of spells and counter-spells,

as each searches for the other's weakness. Morgan, his strength rapidly failing, attempts to rediscover the Deryni healing power he used on Derry the night before.

Kelson has been holding his own to this point. But now Charissa conjures up a creature of the darkness on which Kelson's magic seems to have no effect. As he attempts spell after spell, the creature continues to advance across the floor, mawing and shrieking its defiance as it comes.

CHAPTER SEVENTEEN

In a last effort, Kelson murmurs a spell and points in the direction of the monster. At that moment, sunlight shines through a high stained-glass window, throwing a pool of color on the floor just in front of Kelson. The beast ignores it—and dissolves in a curl of smoke, writhing and screaming in rage.

It is the breakthrough Kelson has been watching for. He now challenges Charissa to the ultimate contest, the binding spell which, once made, cannot be broken by either until one of them is dead. Charissa accepts. Kelson defeats the Shadowed One.

With Charissa's death, Jehana is released from her spell. She watches with awe and a growing pride as Kelson mounts the steps to the altar. Morgan, now healed, rises to meet him, and Duncan brings forward the Crown of Gwynedd. As all kneel, three Archbishops elevate the Crown and recite the formula of Coronation.

But to Deryni eyes within the Cathedral, it is as though a fourth figure supports the Crown—a tall, blond man garbed in the shining golden rainment of the ancient

Deryni lords. And the words he speaks are rather different from those of the Archbishops. Here at last, in Kelson of Haldane, is a King for human and Deryni— the first in three hundred years!

Kelson is crowned, the Deryni-seen apparition vanishes, and Morgan comes forward to kneel in homage to the newly-crowned King. Other lords follow suit. As the procession from the Cathedral forms, the sun shines once more through the stained glass, casting a pool of multi-colored sunlight at Kelson's feet. The spectators are hushed in fearful anticipation, for there was death before in the colored sunlight. But Kelson, with a faint smile, steps calmly into the light.

There is no death there now. The pool of sunlight merely turns Kelson's gems to fire, blazes on his Crown like a hundred sunrises.

And then, amid jubilant cheering, he and his loyal friends exit so that Kelson may show himself to his people.

About the Author

Katherine Kurtz was born in Coral Gables, Florida, during a hurricane and has led a whirlwind existence ever since. She holds a Bachelor of Science degree in chemistry from the University of Miami, Florida, and a Master of Arts degree in English history from UCLA. She studied medicine before deciding that she would rather write, and is an Ericksonian-trained hypnotist. Her scholarly background also includes extensive research in religious history, magical systems, and other esoteric subjects.

Katherine Kurtz' literary works include the well known Deryni and Camber Trilogies of fantasy fiction, an occult thriller set in WWII England, and a number of Deryni-related short stories. The first two books of her third Deryni trilogy were published in 1984 and 1985, with the third book due in 1986. At least three more trilogies are planned in the Deryni universe, and several additional mainstream thrillers are also currently in development.

Miss Kurtz lives in southern California with her husband and son, an orange cat called The Marmalade Bear, and a Bentley motorcar named Basil—British, of course. They hope soon to move to a castle in Ireland.